CRA

CORPUS DELICTI

Eisenmenger's relationship with Helena Flemming has deteriorated to the point that Helena wants it to end, leaving Eisenmenger devastated. In order to cope, he throws himself back into his work as a forensic pathologist and is immediately consumed by a disturbing discovery.

CORPUS DELICTI

Keith McCarthy

Severn House Large Print
London & New York

This first large print edition published 2011
in Great Britain and the USA by
SEVERN HOUSE PUBLISHERS LTD of
9-15 High Street, Sutton, Surrey, SM1 1DF.
First world regular print edition published 2009 by
Severn House Publishers Ltd., London and New York.

British Library Cataloguing in Publication Data

McCarthy, Keith, 1960-
  Corpus delicti.
  1. Eisenmenger, John (Fictitious character)--Fiction.
  2. Flemming, Helena (Fictitious character)--Fiction.
  3. Pathologists--England--Fiction. 4. Detective and
  mystery stories. 5. Large type books.
  I. Title
  823.9'2-dc22

ISBN-13: 978-0-7278-7911-0

Severn House Publishers support The Forest Stewardship Council
[FSC], the leading international forest certification organisation. All
our titles that are printed on Greenpeace-approved FSC-certified paper
carry the FSC logo.

MIX
Paper from
responsible sources
FSC   FSC® C018575
www.fsc.org

Printed and bound in Great Britain by the
MPG Books Group, Bodmin, Cornwall.

To my family and friends

PROLOGUE

'Oh, fantastic.'

She didn't need this. Not now, not tonight. She was running late. The A417 was normally a decent road – at least until it became single-carriageway at Nettleton – and it had no reason to be congested like this.

For the next fifteen minutes she crawled along. *Sam will be wondering what's keeping me.*

She tried phoning but as she expected he didn't answer; he always had the bloody thing on silent. Another ten minutes' crawl before she saw in the distance flashing blue and red lights. 'Of course,' she sighed. 'Police.'

She had often heard it said that whenever there was traffic congestion there would be police, and she knew that it was effect rather than cause, but there was a small part of her that wondered...

At last she arrived at the head of the queue. A road-traffic collision ... looked bad, too. There had been a fire.

Despite the delay and her urgency she could not resist nosing around; the traffic was moving so slowly that a quick peek wouldn't make much difference. She slipped out of the line of crawling traffic and slowed the car, pulling in

7

behind the ambulance and immediately a uniformed figure in a fluorescent jacket began to walk towards her. He had on boots seemingly large enough and heavy enough to have housed not just feet but whole acres of corns and bunions. She got out. 'It's all right, Gaskin,' she called.

He stopped. 'Oh, sorry, Inspector. I thought it was a rubber-necker.'

'What's happened?'

'Motorcyclist doing the ton when some old bloke in a Morris Minor pulled out across the road to turn right. Poor bugger on the bike clipped his front offside wing, slid over to the opposite carriageway where he and the bike went under the wheels of an oncoming HGV. Every single one of them, by the look of him.'

'Ouch.'

'Too bloody right. Smashed to bits; the Irish stew in the canteen's got bigger lumps of gristle in it than we've got over there. Mind you, the stew's less well done, though – somewhere along the line this lot burst into flames.'

They had closed the road in both directions. Inspector Beverley Wharton, who had been on her way back from an interview with a woman who complained that the Chief Constable had assaulted her with the aid of a long length of chorizo sausage and a bag of Liquorice Allsorts, could have done without this.

But then, she reasoned, so could the motorcyclist.

There was a hint of twilight in the atmosphere and it gave a bizarrely romantic tinge to

8

the scene before them. Ahead of her two ambulances were lined up, both of them with their back doors open; in one she could see an old man hunched forward, oxygen mask adherent to his face, blanketed shoulders, with a green-clad paramedic bending over him. The other was empty. Further away were five police cars and then beside two fire tenders was a large articulated lorry, its side blackened; she could see the driver being interviewed, see several others standing around while two of their companions were using a laser measuring device, presumably to assess the length of the rubber marks on the tarmac; two photographers did their business over their shoulders. The tarmac under the centre of the lorry was both wet and scorched; a screen had been set up against its side. No one could see what it hid, but everyone could guess. More paramedics chatted nonchalantly to firemen as if they were at a sort of multidisciplinary works outing. This charming tableau was completed on the far side by a hearse and three gentlemen – two tall, one short – who waited patiently for their turn, like carrion crows.

'How long will it take?'

Gaskin shrugged. He was constitutionally morose, readily adopting the rent-a-copper lugubriousness that so many policemen seemed to fall into. 'At least another hour.'

She looked back at the queue of traffic that was now stretching back as far as she could see towards Cirencester. They were being diverted down a side road towards Birdlip but it would

9

still be a long wait for most of them; there would be similar, perhaps worse, problems on the way out of Gloucester.

Gaskin saw her looking. 'I expect we could arrange something to get you home quickly...'

She smiled her gratitude. 'No, thanks. I'll take my chances.'

She turned away and got back in the car without looking back. What did another road-traffic fatality matter to her?

She was exhausted but she got up early anyway.

By the time Andrew Koplick arrived to relieve her, she had been up for an hour. He found her at the computer console, concentrating on the screen.

'I'm sorry I'm late, Violet,' he said at once.

She hadn't heard him come in and her head jerked up. 'Andy!'

He didn't notice how surprised – guilty, even – she looked. 'There was a bad smash last night near Birdlip. The road's been closed all night. Sent me all around the houses.' He paused, noticing how flustered she was. 'You all right? Bad night?'

She made visible efforts to appear normal, smiled tentatively and said, 'Fairly busy ... you know.'

He did indeed. Life as an on-call haematology technician had once been sedate but was now with little to recommend it. The emergencies seemed to come ever more frequently and ever more urgently.

10

'What are you doing?'

'Nothing.' She switched off the computer at the wall socket and the screen went blank immediately. As she stood up he said, 'You're not supposed to do that. IT go bonkers if you leave a session open.'

But she wasn't listening. She said, 'We had an aneurysm. They needed twelve units.'

'Did it survive?'

'No.' She sounded upset but he knew from his own experience that this was only because of the wasted work.

'Shame,' he muttered.

'I must be going.' She began to walk away from him.

'Anything I need to know?'

'No.' Her attitude was stressed, almost pre-occupied; she didn't look at him as she walked out of the laboratory. He watched her go, a puzzled frown on his face.

He'd noticed that recently Violet Esterly had become most peculiar. Previously she had been a cheerful, middle-aged woman; true, she had had her problems with her two teenage sons, but she hadn't let that show at work other than the odd comment. Now, though, she was morose and secretive, almost fearful. He had heard a rumour that she was having trouble with her husband, but didn't dare to ask her the truth of it.

He sighed. None of his business.

All the same he wondered what she had been up to when he surprised her. It had been clear that she hadn't wanted him to see what she was doing on the computer, which in itself was odd. After all, she had presumably only been looking up some lab results. As a haematology technician she had every right to check results, providing she had a legitimate reason to access them.

He had only glimpsed the name briefly but it had been an unusual one and it stuck in his mind's eye. *Fitzroy-Hughes.*

ONE

It is rare to be able to determine to the exact moment when a life changes completely. In the great majority of such shifts, they start so imperceptibly, grow so quietly, insinuate themselves so subtly that it is not within the gift of human perception to point to a time, to an event, to a place and say, 'There. That is when my life altered, when a new phase began.'

On this occasion, Helena Flemming could, though. She could look back five weeks, to a Tuesday, to the morning, to three minutes to eleven, when the phone in her office rang and she picked it up and her secretary announced that her next appointment had arrived. She closed the file that she had been reading, stood up, went to the door, and opened it. In the foyer was Alan Sheldon, who was consulting her because his son had been accused of criminal damage.

He was looking out of the window when she opened the door but turned at once and smiled at her. He had iron-grey hair and bright blue eyes that merely had to open to seem to be laughing, deep creases on his cheeks. He wore thin-rimmed glasses on the end of his nose that he was looking over. He was neatly dressed, not tall, but compact in stature.

And she fell in love with him.

Now, on this Sunday morning, as she lay in bed next to her partner, John Eisenmenger, she tried to reconcile the feelings, desires, duties that were fighting a ferocious battle within her. She tried, in short, to persuade herself that she still had a life with John Eisenmenger.

TWO

Billy almost fucked Charlene that evening.

That he didn't probably killed him.

Charlene was ready for it, though. Of that he knew, just as he knew when the police came into the pub or when it was safe to break into a place.

He'd had his eye on her for a few days. She was short and had bobbed blonde hair; she wore tight jeans and tight T-shirts with V-necks. He had noticed a tattoo of a dagger at the base of her spine that plunged down into the depths of her thong; he had noticed, too, a gold pendant that plumbed in a similar manner the warm darkness of her cleavage...

He decided that he really wanted to go where the dagger dived, and where the pendant plunged.

The Three Tunnes was busy. A cold and wet Saturday night, the football over (and the

Robins successful for once), it was a cheery, rowdy crowd that surrounded Billy as he sat drinking Guinness at the bar and eyed Charlene, who was sitting at a table by the cigarette machine with an Indian tart he didn't recognize. She was drinking whisky and Coke at a prodigious rate; they were talking animatedly and laughing a lot. Billy guessed a lot of their conversation was centred on Spud, with whom she had recently had a well-publicized and rather large argument.

Spud was many things, but above all others he was the kind of person who made people laugh...

But only when he wasn't there.

Billy had had a dispute with Spud some years ago over a squeeze – Spud seemed to think that Billy had been paying too much attention to his consort – and, on rainy mornings when he awoke after a heavy night's jollities, he sometimes still felt the consequences in his bones. This was not, though, going to stop him moving in on Charlene. Billy turned to the girl behind the bar. He waggled his glass with a knowing smile and a wink. The look that she returned might, by the less optimistic, have been interpreted as contemptuous.

Billy was small and wiry and sported a small and inappropriate moustache that he thought was really rather fetching. On most occasions he was convinced with unshakeable certainty that his entire appearance was such that no woman in her right mind could resist him, but tonight not even the mad ones would resist him

15

either, for he was wearing his new yellow leather jacket.

'Another one, please.'

She took the glass, her face devoid of expression which curiously conveyed an impression of disdain, especially when she said tonelessly, 'Nice jacket.'

That she might be sarcastic completely passed him by and he said proudly, 'Thanks.'

He was back looking over towards Charlene as she shook her head pitifully. Over his shoulder he added, 'And a whisky and Coke.'

When he saw her raised eyebrows he explained with a smirk and a nod in Charlene's direction, 'For her.'

As he paid for the drinks she said, 'I wouldn't if I were you. Spud won't like it.'

Billy smirked and proffered another wink. 'Spud's off the scene. She's fair game.'

He picked up the glasses and made his way over to the table, unaware that behind him the barmaid was once more shaking her head, this time murmuring, 'I'm not sure Spud looks at it like that.'

Billy reckoned he had a good technique. It wasn't always totally successful – there was plenty of brainless crumpet in the world, after all – but over the years it had brought him quite a nice volume of pussy. It depended on confidence; tarts liked a confident man, they respected him, gave him time to prove to them that he was worth an hour of their time, and an hour was all Billy reckoned he needed.

Without being asked he sat down at Charlene's table, putting the drink down in front of her, ignoring her companion.

'What's this?' There was a lot of background noise in the pub, what with the jukebox and the raucous laughter of celebrating football fans.

'I bought you a drink.'

She frowned and nodded to the Indian girl. 'What about Trupti?'

Billy didn't even waste the energy in moving his head or his eyes. 'What about her?' He smiled sweetly.

There was an audible noise from Trupti that conveyed indignation.

Charlene, however, found a smile that refused to be smothered. She eyed the beverage. 'What is it?'

'Your favourite.' A pause. 'Like me.'

She had picked the glass up and it was nearly at her lips as he said this. She laughed; not because it was funny but because it was outrageous. Trupti scowled but she was the only one present who seemed to care.

'Says who?'

He heard the coquettish tone and found warmth in his heart and between his legs. 'The guy who's going to show you the best time you've ever had.'

Trupti made an even more audible noise and pointedly drained her glass of its amber contents. She stood up and for the first time Billy paid her some attention. She wasn't ugly, he decided, and he might even have given her a quick one had he had no other choice.

'I'm going to the Kit-Kat.' This was a night-

17

club on the inner ring road. 'You coming?' She addressed this to Charlene.

Charlene replied, 'Maybe later.' It was said without conviction. Trupti gave Billy one last glare, then taking her bright mauve clutch bag from the table strode out haughtily. Billy's eyes widened and he said to Charlene, 'What did I say?'

And to his delight, Charlene giggled. 'You're horrible, you are.' Her tone belied her words. He winked at her as he put his glass to his lips.

'I don't know how you drink that stuff.' Women always said that about Guinness. To emphasize how much he liked it, and therefore his masculinity, he took a deep draught while Charlene sipped her Coke. He already had the evening planned and that made him a very happy chappy.

'I heard you were in hospital.'

Since Billy was clearly no longer in hospital, he felt fairly confident in disposing of that one. 'Nah, not now. I was, though. Couple of weeks ago.'

'What was the matter?'

'Burst appendix. I nearly died.' Which contained a kernel of truth embellished with a complete lie.

It did the trick with Charlene, though. Her eyes widening she asked, 'Did you?'

He nodded gravely from behind the Guinness glass. Putting it down, 'You can see the scar later, if you like.'

This with a wink.

Charlene giggled again and Billy's cockles

were just a little bit warmer.

For the next thirty minutes, as the alcohol seeped into his flesh and the noise into his head, he made apparently aimless talk of the smallest variety; talk that was in fact as carefully constructed as a keynote address to an international conference, that chipped away at Charlene in order to sculpt a willing participant in his passion play.

And he might well have succeeded – might well therefore have lived – had circumstances not fallen as they did.

Spud came in.

Spud was big. Physically large but, *malheureusement*, mentally small; and, unfortunately, no one had told him. He was the kind of physical large that didn't accept the concept of *larger*, that did what it wanted, when it wanted, to whom it wanted. It was the sort of large that had no need of *bright*, that scorned intelligence as something that women and wimps had. It was the kind of large that hadn't quite got around to thinking of Charlene in the past tense, no matter what she might have thought and what Billy might have wanted.

Charlene saw him first. Billy was telling her about his expertise at water sports, happily allowing his enthusiasm to trounce his accuracy, when he became aware that he and his audience had parted company. He looked around.

'Oh, shit,' he murmured.

Spud was staring at them – was actually, when Billy came to apply the magnifying glass

– staring directly at *him*.

Billy knew Spud. This was not surprising, since *everyone* knew Spud – either by reputation or experience. Those who knew him by the former were scared of him; those by the latter were *terrified*. And Billy had experience of Spud; the hospital had offered to give him the X-rays as a souvenir.

He had known that moving in on Charlene was risky, but Billy was a born risk-taker and the fact that everyone else was treating her as if she were radioactive gave him a clear run at the target. He hadn't expected to spend the rest of his life with her – he would rather have joined the Salvation Army – but he had hoped to spend a few hours making various parts of her as moist as he could.

These hopes vanished.

He didn't get around to offering his apologies, wishing her well, asking her forgiveness; he didn't even utter a single syllable, correctly figuring that his future well-being depended on alacrity.

'Oy! You!'

But Billy was gone, skipping through the crowd and the smoke, through the sweat and the bad breath. He barged into two women and a thin, gangly youth, all of whom took it badly when their drinks were spilt. He was quick but Spud was surprisingly rapid when it came to getting hold of people who had given him cause for grievance and Billy only just made it to the doorway in time. He heard a loud crash of wood on brick behind him as he legged it down the darkness of the street, Spud's imprecations following him into the cold air. Even at a distance there was a battery of menace in the ill-defined words and the stentorian tone.

The final words he heard were engulfed by the wind, almost sucked into a howl, but surprisingly discernible. 'I'm gonna fucking kill you, Billy Whipple!'

The last syllable was stretched until it sounded like an animal's cry.

THREE

Dr Eugenie Lyon had been worrying about the case for several days now and was no nearer resolving her problem. The department of histopathology at Cheltenham General Hospital had long since emptied for the evening, leaving her to try to work out this most peculiar of anomalies; she had already spent several hours on the problem and it looked as if she would have to spend several more.

She had been a consultant pathologist for only six months and she was discovering that there was a lot more to the job than the statutory five years' training as organized by the Royal College of Pathologists had led her to believe. It might have given her the minimum of knowledge required but it had been singularly lacking in the one essential ingredient – confidence. She was now officially the end of the line, where the buck not only stopped, it ticked until it exploded. Before, she had had the comfort of being able to ask for help if she couldn't make a diagnosis on a biopsy; if she was wrong in a report, her superior would correct her. It was all part of the learning process.

Now she *was* the superior.

In truth it wasn't quite true to say that she was in a one-way cul-de-sac. There were stratagems available to her to help her out of diagnostic problems; she could always send it away for an expert opinion, for instance. The downside with that was that she couldn't send away just anything. If she consulted a national expert on some piece of dross, she would soon gain a bad reputation; she couldn't afford that.

Another lifeline was to ask her colleagues about cases but she had thrown that one so many times already it was looking decidedly frayed. She seemed to spend three-quarters of the day popping in and out of their rooms with cases; cases, moreover, which they would look at for three seconds before confidently telling her what it was. She was becoming more and more aware that her regular appearances were becoming trying; John Eisenmenger, her locum colleague, would have been the logical choice, given his experience in forensic pathology, but she was afraid that he would just laugh at her if she confided him; this was not a normal problem.

She would have to try to sort this one out herself.

Hell, it was only an autopsy. It wasn't as though someone's life or health depended on it, or as if someone might be undergoing major surgery on her say-so. Anyway, she had the cause of death. That was all that mattered these days. Gone were the days when autopsies undertaken at the behest of the coroner had a public-health role, were seen as much as a chance to explore health and disease as to identify the disguise worn by the Grim Reaper.

And RTCs were usually easy. There was an occasional problem – had the driver had a heart attack just before the accident? Was he wearing a seatbelt? Occasionally she had even been asked to determine whether the deceased was the driver or the passenger – but usually road-traffic collisions were merely a question of charting the injuries and making sure that there was no natural disease of significance.

This one should have been the easiest of the lot. Motorcyclist clips car, falls under the numerous wheels of forty tons of diesel lorry. Lorry not unnaturally brakes but motorcycle and motorcyclist burst into flame. He had been squelched and broiled; other descriptions might be applied but none would be as apt. Every bone (except his left humerus) had been broken and most of his internal organs had been minced and sautéed.

All of which she was quite happy with; she expected no problems when asked to provide the coroner with a cause of death.

Unfortunately, that still left her with a major problem.

Try as she might, there were too many pieces.

FOUR

Billy only stopped running when he was at least a kilometre and several streets away from Spud, heading into the town centre. He rubbed his neck ruefully, breathing heavily as he felt nausea in his stomach and a wet burning sensation in his throat. There had been no need for Spud to be like that. After all, he hadn't touched her, and he had quite reasonably assumed that she was fair game. Spud had very publicly proclaimed Charlene was an 'open-legged slag' not a week before, after all.

Spud was just a touchy bastard...

He sighed. No pussy tonight, he predicted ruefully. There seemed little else to do except set off for home and accordingly he began to head northwards. He lived about three kilometres away and to get there he would have to walk through a light-industrial estate.

He walked briefly down Christie Street before turning right about halfway along. As he passed the various shops, banks and estate agents his mind turned from the unfairness of people like Spud to the question of making a quick buck. He needed some cash because the rent was due and he was two months behind on the car. It was his custom at such times to supplement the Social Security payments by finding suitable premises to burgle. Not that he was an ambitious criminal. He didn't go for banks or post offices, never used a weapon of any kind, and never risked occupied premises; his ethos minimized the risk of capture but it did tend to limit the rewards.

He thought about having a pop at the tobacconist – he could always sell the fags at the Three Tunnes – when he saw a light go on in the flat above it. When it came to larceny Billy saw no point in making life difficult for himself.

Unfortunately the pickings along the route that led to his home proved to be fairly meagre once he had discarded the occupied, the high-security, the derelict and the demolished; those that were left seemed unlikely to yield untold wealth, and once he was into the industrial estates of Swindon Village his hopes began to wane. Although there was little danger of being disturbed since no one lived nearby, the businesses did not deal in large amounts of cash. There was money to be had in nicking tools, but there were also sophisticated alarm systems, many of which were connected directly to the police station.

He began to ponder other ways to come across easy cash, the main contender being his mother, who was starting to dement and who had the happy knack of forgetting that she had given him money within a space of five minutes. It was then, in the heart of the estate, that he came across Gorlin, Goltz and Son. Their sign proclaimed that they were Funeral Directors and Monumental Masons. He reckoned that they were fairly new to the neighbourhood as he was sure that the last time he had passed that way the building had been empty.

Billy perked up; a smile even appeared across his thin, musteline face, one that stretched his pencil-thin moustache slightly. He had worked briefly for an undertaker – not this one – and he recalled that there was always cash and there were always valuables; he knew this because he had siphoned a little off before he left, just to help with expenses. Maybe, then, this was a chance to be taken. The building was single-storey with a yard at its left surrounded by a high wall. He guessed that the hearses would be in the yard together with stocks of chipboard, plywood and marble. The whole place was dark and partially hidden by trees, sited as it was at the edge of the estate.

It seemed perfect.

He didn't think to wonder why it was so large and surrounded by such a high wall.

He first of all walked straight past, not even looking at the building, continuing for about a hundred metres; he kept his eyes open and looked around covertly, seeing no one. He then turned around and retraced his steps, ending this time a hundred metres past in the other direction. Only then did he approach the building. There were two alarm boxes on the outside, he noted; he suspected that these would not prove a great problem since he doubted that they would be connected to a call centre and nobody would be interested in a wailing alarm on a deserted industrial estate. Anyway, one thing was for sure – there would be no one sleeping on the premises.

He walked around the fence, thought about climbing it, deciding that that would be a last resort, especially as he didn't want to risk damage to his jacket. He continued around the back of the building where it backed against a high brick wall, leaving only a narrow passage a metre wide. As he went he tried each window that he passed, finding them all secured...

Billy's brain wasn't into parallel processing; he worked strictly with one thought at a time, and each of those handled after much consideration but little analysis. Once one had fought its way in there, it generally found all exits to be bolted and barred.

Thus, having decided that he was going to burgle Gorlin, Goltz and Son, there was no escape from it and there was no room for any contending ideas to take a foothold. He looked around, found half a brick. A further, brief reconnoitre, then he retreated to the narrow gap at the rear of the building, and holding the brick in the sleeve of his jacket, smashed one of the windows.

...To his surprise the alarm did not sound and a faint twinge of concern made itself known. Was it out of order, or was it a 'silent' alarm that was at this moment sounding in a call centre somewhere?

He opted for alacrity rather than faint-heart-edness and pushed ahead. He reached inside and turned the window latch to allow it to open. Even so, the gap was small but then so was Billy – small and supple; it would be a tight squeeze but he could manage it.

He found himself in an office, which was just where he wanted to be. He didn't have a torch but since he was at the back of the building and it wasn't overlooked, he felt safe in switching on the light. Speed not stealth was his most important priority.

There were two desks, facing each other, three filing cabinets, a desktop photocopier, a fax machine and numerous shelves around the walls, all fully stocked with box files; there was no safe, which was a relief. He went first for the desk drawers. They were locked but someone had helpfully left a screwdriver on top of one of the filing cabinets. The crack of splintering wood was loud enough to give him pause; the breaking of the silence in an empty building always made him wince, even when he was certain it would not be overheard. He hesitated for a moment, looking around the room, seeing nothing inside it. No one came, nothing stirred and he returned his attention to the drawer, discovering the normal office detritus – pens, pencils, a stapler, paperclips, pads of adhesive notes. One of the pens caught his eye; it was a sleek silver ballpoint, one he thought might be expensive, with the name of the firm on its side, and he pocketed it. Then he saw a key ring on which were three keys. Things were looking up, he decided, grabbing them; he went to the filing cabinets, trying the keys in the first one. He was successful with the second key but a brief glance through the drawers revealed only files. The second cabinet was similarly filled. The third, though, contained gold.

In the bottom drawer there was a cashbox. He lifted it out and his heart filled with joy as he discovered how heavy it was.

'Time to go,' he said to himself. There was no point in hanging around trying to open the cashbox here, and he doubted if there would be anything else worth nicking. Anyway, judging by the weight of the box, this was already a worthwhile detour on his way home. He was just about to close the filing cabinet when his eye was caught by the papers on which the cashbox had been resting.

He reached in and pulled the top sheet out.

His reading skills were poor but he had no difficulty with this document; it was a list of names.

One that included his.

FIVE

'What the hell?' he asked no one in particular.

Names, addresses, dates of birth and, the last column, letters beside which was either a plus sign or a minus sign. What did that mean?

He looked again at the paper, looking for further clues but finding none. There was no heading, no explanatory note. Completely bewildered yet unaccountably frightened, he put the paper on top of the filing cabinet and bent back down to look for something else that might help his puzzlement. The thought that his name was written down in a locked cabinet in an undertaker's was chilling; surely there was a straightforward explanation...?

Which was when the door opened.

Momentarily surprised into immobility, Billy just stared, but in contrast the newcomer kept on coming. He was followed by another and before Billy could move they were upon him. They were not dressed as undertakers, and were not behaving like them either; far from it. One, burly and muscular, was in a black leather jacket and dark shirt, the other was taller and wearing a bright red roll-neck jumper. They both wore expressions not unlike the one that had adorned Spud when he had been chasing

Billy out of the pub.

They lunged at him, slamming him back against the filing cabinet, then grabbing hold of his arms and shoulders.

'Get the fuck off!'

There was a brief struggle but Billy was slightly built and these two were mean and muscular. They slammed him against the filing cabinets again, each one bending an arm backwards. He continued to wriggle, garnishing this with an unending and unregarded series of foul-mouthed commands to let him go. Unending and unregarded, at least until one of them smacked him in the side of the jaw, at which the pain shut him up.

A third figure appeared in the doorway, this one in a suit, dapper and clearly concerned to make a good impression. He was slightly tubby.

He looked like a businessman.

He came into the room, a thoughtful frown embellishing the stare he gave Billy. 'Who are you?'

'Fuck off!'

The one in the leather jacket took over holding him, locking both his arms behind him, while his companion came and stood in front of him. He was tall, his eyes were pale and clear; he seemed to be looking at Billy as if he were a newly arrived specimen from some far-flung corner of the empire, one previously unknown to science.

'Please tell us who you are.'

The third one – the one who was well dressed

enough to be on his wedding day – was shaking his head, eyes closed. Billy had the impression that he was sorry about something.

Billy's vocabulary had never been good and, consequently, he had never enjoyed crosswords much. 'Fuck off,' he repeated.

For which Billy received another, harder smack to the jaw, followed by a punch to his stomach that made him want to throw up.

The tall one came forward, his attitude almost casual. He reached into the inside pockets of Billy's leather jacket, brought out his wallet. Billy was still gasping from the blow to his stomach, his face covered in sweat, as he asked, 'What the fuck's going on?'

The man was looking through contents of the wallet. He said, 'Do you have to use that word so much?'

'Fuck off.'

There was a degree of inevitability about what happened next, about the third blow to the jaw, this one so hard that Billy heard a ringing monotone and the pain in his head ate into his jawbone, burrowed into his ear and skewered his eye.

The man in front of him found his Social Security card. 'William Winston Whipple.' He snorted a laugh, then looked up at his captive. 'Good at networking, Mr Whipple?'

Billy heard this feeble joke through a high-pitched tone that wouldn't fade. He didn't understand and shook his head, which hurt the whole of the left side of his face.

The man suddenly narrowed his eyes. 'Wait a

32

minute,' he said. He looked down at the opened drawer of the filing cabinet, from which his eyes tracked to the piece of paper that Billy had been reading and that had now dropped to the floor. The man bent down to pick it up.

Having perused the list, he looked up at Billy and there was, unaccountably, a smile on his face. 'Well, well, Mr Whipple. It seems that we've been expecting you.'

Billy couldn't speak properly because every time he opened his mouth it hurt so much. His words were mumbled through clamped and rapidly swelling jaws. 'Woss going on here?'

The man was smiling quite broadly now. It was a genuine, delighted smile and despite himself Billy began to wonder if the situation might not be as bad as he thought. The man said, 'We were planning to have a talk to you. See if you might be able to help us.'

The swelling was starting to touch his left eye; his face felt hot. 'I don't undershtand.'

'All we need is some ... indulgence on your part. We have a business deal to put to you.'

'Look, I'm sorry I broke in...'

'Come on.'

A brief gesture over Billy's shoulder to his silent assistant and Billy was suddenly being impelled towards the doorway. Billy's rising hope stopped, turned and did a runner. 'What are you doing?' he demanded. He began to struggle again. 'Where are you taking me?'

The one who had come into the room last said nervously, 'Are you sure this is a good idea?'

He was ignored.

Billy was facing an intersection of two corridors; directly opposite there was darkness until, at the end on the left, light fell out in a distorted rectangle. It came into Billy's head that he didn't want to go through that darkness into that room, that he would never emerge from it.

Billy began first to cry, then to scream.

As if anyone cared.

The corridor was too narrow for them to walk abreast and this gave Billy an unexpected, perhaps ultimate chance. As his captors repositioned themselves so that the tall one went ahead and the fat one behind, the grip on Billy's arms loosened. Billy's grasp of mental arithmetic was poor, his knowledge of the kings and queens of England virtual, his ability to remember anything except the price of Guinness minuscule, but his instincts for self-preservation were immensely well developed, in situations like this he could be lightning-fast. He wrenched his arm free, swung round and connected perfectly with the eye socket of the one in the leather jacket. The extent to which the grip on his other arm relaxed was slight but enough. He was free and with a shoulder-charge at the tubby one he was across the office and heading for the open window.

But there the plan went into fucked-up mode.

The gap was too narrow to slide through without wriggling and that took time.

The seconds he took then were the first

seconds of the last part of his life. Whilst he strained every muscle fibre to get through the gap he heard first one, then another of his pursuers enter the room and run towards him.

The knife went into his belly as his chest was passing over the metal sill and his face felt the cold of the night air. The pain was unique, nothing in his memory to touch it; it was at once everything, turning on nausea, turning off his muscles, taking the breath from his chest, the hope from his head. A hand clamped down on his back, trying to push him into the blade. Instinctively he flailed out his legs and felt his heel connect with something hard. The pressure on his back at once vanished and despite the acidic agony in his stomach he thrust himself forward, knocking the knife out on the windowsill, falling to the grass outside, now damp because of heavily falling rain.

He felt unconsciousness swoop down upon him and it was almost an instinctive, primeval reflex that forced him up through the pain on to his feet. Already someone was trying to get through the window after him, just as he heard someone shout, 'Get him!' and with this there was a sound of furniture moving and running steps.

His legs felt boneless, his belly bursting, his head light. He was having trouble hanging on to the thoughts that still bothered to come into his head. His eyes saw blurring, fleeting visions of grass and wet concrete, streetlights and dark buildings and black, black sky, all jumbled together in fractured snatches. His ears heard nothing but the sound of his gasps.

More swirling, shivering unconsciousness came down upon him. He felt as if he was running ever more slowly, his legs moving like disjointed rubber stilts. The world was still kaleidoscopic but he just about managed to make out that he was running between two warehouses. He knew that he was about to dip for the last time into blackness, that his pursuers were not far behind. He had to find somewhere to hide and it was a miracle that he could not appreciate when his blurring eyes found a slightly opened doorway in the side of one of the warehouses. He staggered towards it, then did nothing more than fall against the door. It moved only stiffly on hinges that seemed to be rusty, but he was quickly through, and pushing it closed behind him. Then he could do no more than sit against the metal of the door in total darkness, cold and shivering and feeling that he was nothing but a container of pain.

He could not see nor, because he was soaked through, could he feel the blood flowing from the hole in his abdomen.

SIX

Helena looked down at John as she sat up in bed. He was sleeping peacefully on his side, turned away from her. She noticed that he was turning grey at the temples but immediately turned away from this thought because it reminded her of Alan. He was breathing silently, his trunk barely moving, giving the impression of absolute peace.

She wanted to cry, because she thought that she still loved him dearly. They had been together now for nearly seven years, been through mysteries and experiences that she thought until recently had cemented their partnership irrevocably; on more than one occasion, he had saved her life; perhaps more importantly, on more than one she had saved his.

She should not be feeling like this!

Yet she was. She could not believe it, but she was. She wanted to stay with him for the rest of her life; she wanted to leave him and live with Alan. She loved John; she loved Alan. She was desperately afraid of splitting up with John; she was desperate to do it.

Last night, they made love...

No! Last night you had sex. But was it love? Do

you really still love him?

She had suddenly discovered how fragile is love; how to examine it is to batter it to death; how to seek to look at it is to find it gone; how to question it is forbidden. She did not like this discovery. She had always been afraid of commitment because she found early that to commit is to be vulnerable, and that to be vulnerable is to be afraid. When her parents were murdered and her stepbrother died, she had no one to turn to other than herself; her inner self, the place where she was alone but safe. John Eisenmenger changed that. He came into her life and knocked on the door of her shell; she had not meant to let him in, but like a con man he had worked his magic.

Magic it had indeed been. He was one of the most infuriating human beings ever to draw oxygen from the air. He spent most of the time in his peculiar universe, intellectualizing, seeing things that were not there for other mortals, drawing patterns from abstractions, seeing truths that ought not to be seen; he only occasionally came back to the usual universe – her universe – and even more rarely did he remember to act normally. He told her that he loved her infrequently but she had always known that this was merely because he did not see the need to state the obvious.

And all this had been enough.

Until now.

Now she has met a man who is not unattractive, who is not unintelligent and yet who shows his emotion; who does not seem to want to leave her in any doubt that he loves her.

She asked herself if she was really that shallow. Did she really have to be told every ten minutes that she was still attractive, that someone still had deep feelings for her?

She was rather afraid that she did.

The tea was cold by the time Jean Whipple drank it, as it always was. She had fallen asleep and even when she had been awoken by the juggernaut thundering past her front-room window it had taken her a long time to remember the cup by the armchair. She didn't mind, though; she was used to it.

Her legs hurt. The district nurse had just been and dressed them, and that always made them hurt. She couldn't understand this. Over the next few days the stinging and deep-boned aching would gradually subside, and then the district nurse would call again and once more she would endure an hour of agony as the yellow-stained bandages were unwound and finally stripped from her moist, tender flesh like Sellotape off the reel, and as a sickly pungent odour would billow around her. As if that weren't bad enough, the nurse would then scour them, the fluid that she used fizzing into a rabid froth that always frightened her, even though she no longer looked, stared instead at the grubby ceiling. There would be some relief when fresh bandages were applied, but then over the following hours the stinging and bone-deep aching would return and become heavier and heavier, only gradually fading into the night.

She spent most of her time these days sitting in front of the television, not paying much attention to the shouting, ranting, raving guests on the chat shows or the quiz shows that she never quite seemed to understand, just enjoying the noise and fact that the silent house was in a small corner alive. Only when Billy was at home was there a sense of life about the place, even though most of that time he was in bed, sleeping away the day.

Now she came to think of it, she was fairly sure that Billy hadn't come home yesterday evening. In fact, she hadn't seen him since the day before. Where was he? Had he come in when she was asleep? Gone straight up to his room?

She looked at the golden carriage clock on the sideboard and saw that it was nearly two o'clock; she had slept through lunch again. With no little difficulty she rose from her chair and walked with a shuffling gait to the small hall. Hanging on to the newel post, she peered up the stairs into the cold gloom of the landing.

'Billy? Are you up there?'

Nothing.

'Billy?'

Still nothing.

She frowned, the first faint hints of worry nagging at her. It wasn't like her Billy not to let her know where he was. True, there had been times in the past when he had stayed away for a few days – times when he had to lie low for a while – but he had always let her know, some-how, that he was disappearing for a while, that he was safe. Even when he was staying away just one night he would make sure that she wasn't worrying. He was a good boy to his mother; she couldn't have asked for better. When he had been in hospital having his appendix out, he had made sure that social services knew that she was alone and that she might need help.

She made her way to the small kitchen at the back of the house. She'd have soup for lunch, she decided, but when she looked in the cupboard the tin of tomato soup she had expected to find there had gone. Had she had it and not remembered? Or had Billy been peckish and not replaced it?

She thought briefly about opening a tin of baked beans but decided against this because they always gave her gripes. She opted instead to walk down to the corner shop and buy another tin of soup. She put on her favourite black overcoat, not noticing that there were bird droppings on the back of it, and opened the door just as another large lorry sped past, swirling dust and paper into the air and into her face. She squinted; why did the council let them use this road? It was just a rat-run now, a cut-through between the new shopping centre and the motorway, one that avoided the traffic jams of the bypass. A couple of months ago a ten-year-old girl had been killed by a speeding motorist.

Mr Raman seemed to sell everything and

even if he didn't have something to hand when asked, he could normally get it by the next day. He was friendly and courteous and Mrs Whipple got on well with him. She saw no reason to go anywhere else for anything and she bought everything she needed from him. He greeted her as he always did, with cheery politeness.

'Good day, Mrs Whipple.'

'Hello, Mr Raman. I've come for some soup.'

'Of course, of course. Can I get it for you? What would you like? Oxtail, perhaps? Or chicken?'

'Don't worry. I'll get it.'

He watched her shuffle up the aisle from his vantage point in front of the cigarettes and behind the hot pies and pakoras. 'Are your legs bad today?'

She called back without turning, 'A little.'

She found the soups and picked out a tin of tomato, then decided to take a second, in case Billy wanted some. She came back with them under her arm, her other hand reaching in her coat pocket for her purse, coming out empty. With some embarrassment and a perplexed frown she put the tins down on the papers that were laid out on the counter and tried the other pocket.

'I'm sorry, Mr Raman, I've forgotten my purse.'

He tapped out the prices on the cash register. 'Don't worry. I know you won't cheat me.'

She smiled gratefully. 'I'll pay you tomorrow.'

As she was picking up the tins he asked, 'Is Billy all right? He hasn't been in for his cigarettes today. It's not like him.'

Billy bought a packet of cigarettes every morning, along with his paper and a packet of strong mints. Mrs Whipple frowned at this reminder of Billy's uncharacteristic absence. 'Oh ... I'd take them for him, if I had the money on me...'

He picked out a packet from the appropriate row behind him and slid them across to her. 'He can pay me when he next comes in.'

She left, grateful to Mr Raman, but becoming ever more deeply perturbed by her son's absence.

SEVEN

Violet could hardly wait for Simon – an uncouth and rather rude young man from Whaddon, who chewed continuously and who kept his mouth open continuously, at the same time – to leave. She had an important task to perform and if she could succeed, maybe she would make enough to end this hell and return to normality. She had practically been promised that the successful completion of this task would end her entanglement with Steven.

How had it happened? How had what had seemed to be mutual attraction turned to what had seemed to be love, then soured to this? How had she been so wrong? Wasn't she old

43

enough to know better? Wasn't she yet experienced enough in love and life to know what was important, what was genuine, what was just plain, bloody *sensible*?

She had spent her whole life priding herself that she was in total control of herself, yet in the past six months she proved conclusively that she had been a deluded idiot. She had been completely taken in by him, had completely failed to see that he had had an ulterior motive. Of course he had never really wanted her for herself. For God's sake! How could she have been so stupid? She was a good ten years older than he was, tubbier and probably twenty years beyond him in looks. She had thought that she was intelligent but he had manipulated her so easily, used her vanity against her, enticed her, beguiled her, then used her. She knew now that he had selected her with care and forethought because of who she was and because of her circumstances. Husband made redundant, debts not so much piling up as exploding like mortar bombs around her, and a degree of gullibility that meant not only would she be lacking in insight enough to believe his blandishments, but sufficiently doe-eyed to fall for his story of humanitarian aid.

Thinking about it now, though, this last part was the hardest to swallow. Had she really thought that there was an organization that did such things as he had suggested? That boosted blood donations to underdeveloped countries by the technically illegal but still potentially life-saving act of paying for donations? He had

44

called himself a *blood merchant*, a trader in life, and when he smiled and stroked her hair, she believed him totally; only when she was away from him did she begin to question if his smile was just a little *too* warming, if his breathy voice was quite as sincere as she remembered it. In theory, and although it might be strictly illegal, she was mostly able to convince herself that what he was doing was fundamentally a good thing. Blood for money; blood that was needed. 'We only take a unit, Vi. Only a unit, and that usually from those who could do with the money, anyway.'

Well, yes, she *had* believed him, at least for quite a few months, at least until she had noticed a small paragraph in the local paper, one that reported the disappearance of one Jasper Fitzroy-Hughes, a name she knew very well. It had set her wondering, doubting, and the doubts had grown strong enough to tell him about them. His demeanour had changed almost immediately and dramatically, yet smoothly; from soft and warm affection, to soft and chilling sorrow. He was sorry that she had decided not to cooperate, but she was in too deep now. Had she not realized what the penalties were for what she had done? Aside from the breaches of patient confidentiality, the Human Tissue Act was quite clear about the consequences of trading in blood and blood products. And then there was her husband to consider. Did she really want him to find out what she had been doing?

And, he had added with a gentle smile, the

hotel she had been doing it in?

And with whom?

While the implications of his words had burrowed into her, sickened her, weakened her, given her a feeling of falling down a chasm that was sucking her into its darkness, he had then gone on – in exactly the same voice, almost as if nothing had changed – 'Now, this is a very important commission, Violet. So important, that we'll pay double money. You'd like that, wouldn't you? Very useful, considering the recent vandalism of your husband's car. You told me that you had fallen behind with the insurance on it. That's going to be expensive.'

The possible implication of what he had said had struck her only some time after this conversation, her immediate reaction swamping any higher-level thinking; was it possible that the apparently mindless slashing of the tyres and scratching of the paintwork of their ageing Ford Mondeo had been decidedly *not* mindless? Was it possible that she was being burdened with debts to keep her working for him? Such an idea she would have condemned as paranoid a week or so before, but not now, not now that she had some idea of the reality of her situation.

Her husband had almost been in tears when the vandalism had happened, close to utmost despair, and now, as was being pointed out to her as she sat in the hotel bed and he nonchalantly dressed by the shower-room door, she had a way to alleviate his growing depression.

46

Poor Brian, who was pathetically grateful to her for the extra money she was bringing into the house, that she had had to tell him she was getting because of overtime; a lie but one that fitted nicely with her increased absences from home...

It was unlikely, though, that she would turn up the result he wanted. Would he, she wondered, still remunerate her if she failed? This had never arisen before, because until now the names she had given him had had fairly common blood types, plenty of candidates to choose from. It wouldn't be her fault if she failed and once she would have been sure that this would not have mattered, but things had changed now. The thought of how he might react sickened her.

She might, though, succeed; it wasn't entirely out of the question. Such cases were rare, but not altogether unknown. In a county the size of Gloucestershire, there ought to be at least ten suitable candidates, and maybe even twenty or twenty-five; she had looked this up in a haematology textbook. It wasn't the rarest blood group, far from it. With a bit more luck, one or more of them would have come into the hospital and all their details would be available to her.

Eventually, Simon walked from the lab in his usual slouch and she was able to get on with the database search. The ancient computer system – not even Windows-based – would take at least an hour to trawl through the hospital records even on a Sunday when few other users would be online, so she passed the time doing routine maintenance chores on the black, hulking Coulter counter. The machine took a drop of blood and within minutes churned out accurate statistics on the numbers and types of white blood cells, red blood cells, platelets; on their size and volume and on how much haemoglobin they contained.

After three hours, just after an emergency cross-match for a leaking abdominal aortic aneurysm – the only real excitement of the morning – she returned to the computer, her stomach churning with apprehension at what she would see, relief washing it away when she saw that there was a single name that fulfilled the criteria she had entered.

She was not a religious woman, but she thanked God none the less as she wrote down the name and address on a small scrap of paper that she then put in her purse. She was considerably more relaxed as she went about the rest of her shift, happy that the name of *Helena Flemming* would gain her some much-needed cash.

EIGHT

As soon as Beverley saw her brother she knew that she had been right, that there was something wrong; seriously wrong. That she had heard his voice at all when she answered the phone had been a warning bell because Jack had barely contacted her in the last ten years, not at all in the past three; she had wondered afterwards if she had thought, somewhere in her head, that she would not hear from him again and they had been parted for ever, but she had decided that this was not the case, that the sibling bond between them had still been there through all the years of separation. From the day of her birth they had been close, although obviously she had no direct recollection of her brother's solicitudes in her early life. Their relationship had only deepened as they went through the teenage years and entered adulthood yet, at the same time, their lives had inevitably begun to separate; they had experienced different schools, different universities and different social circles, seen each other only on anniversaries, family occasions, their father's death...

In many ways, they were alike, in many more complete opposites. Both exhibited great in-

49

telligence and both had charm and attractiveness, yet both, too, were hard beneath, armoured against the fools who thought to get to know them too well; paradoxically, in Jack this was seen as a positive, in Beverley, it was something that frightened most men, annoyed most of the rest. Both of them meted out affection with care, treating it as something that they had stopped making some years ago, in short supply with demand growing; and once again, she was aware that for this she was condemned, whereas he was lauded.

It was unfair, but she had come to realize that unfairness was the colour of the universe or, at least, it was the colour of her universe.

Jack had gone through his life with seemingly unstoppable exuberance, with brio, enjoying every last sensation to the full; somehow, though, and try as she might, her life had failed to lift off, had not fallen to its doom, but had not soared, had not gone as she had thought it would.

Did she resent that? She thought that she should, knew that she did not. It was impossible for her to dislike Jack, the wiring in her head precluded it, like expecting a toaster to wash clothes. On the rare occasions that she had seen him, each time she had fallen once again in love with him, found herself jealous of whichever new girlfriend he had in thrall.

'Hi, sis.' As he greeted her for Sunday lunch in the restaurant he used the same words, the same tired drawl as he had over the phone; superficially easy and laconic but laced, she had thought, with a dark melancholy that she couldn't fathom.

She saw at once that he was thinner than the last time she had seen him – Cousin Maeve's wedding, a shambolic affair in Chelsea – and he looked pale enough to pass for the living dead. That he wore, as always, expensive clothes only made the change starker.

He stood and they kissed cheek to cheek, while she smiled welcome through her anxiety. 'It's been a long time,' she said.

As they sat and he leaned forward, his chin resting on folded hands, he said, 'That ghastly wedding of Maeve's.'

'A ghastly wedding for a ghastly girl.'

He laughed, but even that sounded sad. 'Poor old Maeve. She was ever the gooseberry, even at her own wedding.'

'Ever the gooseberry, ever the fool. She got drunk and fell into the best man, I remember.'

The waiter arrived. He was young and looked welcoming, or at least he did so south of the nose, while northwards he just looked bored and tired. He handed out menus and enquired, 'Would you like a drink?'

She had a white-wine spritzer, he tonic water.

Left with their menus, the conversation lulled until he looked at her over his and asked with a wink, 'How's the love life?'

Had anyone else asked this, it would have been facetious, but Jack knew her better than anyone. Despite her foreboding she smiled. 'The same, of course.' Then, to steer him away from further enquiry, she countered, 'How's yours?'

'Ah.' He sighed. 'Helen's gone.'

Did she know Helen? She couldn't recall. Assuming that she was supposed to, she commiserated. 'Oh, I'm sorry.'

His smile was wicked. 'I'm not.'

And they laughed.

Except that it wasn't quite as funny as it should have been, so that when the laughter had passed through their companionship there was left merely awkwardness.

He said, 'I'm renting near here. A small house in Stroud.'

She was delighted. 'That's great. We can see more of each other. Are you working on something?'

Jack was a writer, of sorts. He had never been successful, had never particularly seemed to *desire* success, and had never let it interfere with life. She sometimes thought he had chosen his profession merely as an excuse to travel and to doss and generally to have a bloody good time. He claimed that he got bored easily but she suspected that the reason was broader than that; Jack had never wanted commitment in any area of his life.

He shook his head. Something about the way he did this struck a discord. 'No.'

She was surprised. Jack was always working on something; didn't often produce anything, mind you...

She found herself compelled by the emptiness that followed to ask, 'Jack, what's wrong?'

At first he said, 'Wrong? Nothing.'

52

When she reached out to touch him and he looked down at her thin fingers and perhaps saw himself reflected in the blackberry nail varnish she was wearing, he seemed to deflate. She waited while he delved deep. His next words were happy and sad.

'You're bloody beautiful, sis. I wish sometimes that you weren't my sister. You know that?' She said nothing, couldn't even locate a smile but he wasn't waiting for responses. 'I thought you'd be married by now; married and settled. There must have been a hundred men who would have given everything for the chance.'

She looked down, shook her head slightly; her face was hidden by her hair and she could not see her expression as she murmured, 'No one, not yet.'

'No one up to your standards?'

Or down to them, either.

She said, 'Nowhere near,' and tried it in a frivolous voice that wasn't quite right and so was completely wrong.

Another pause.

His next words were reluctant, almost as if forced from him by the silence, as if she were interrogating him and he had at last been forced to confess. 'About six months ago, I had the flu. Knocked me sideways for a few days.' She was aware that her eyes were wide because she could feel coldness on them, yet she didn't blink. For a brief moment she wondered if he were about to cry. 'And then I got better.' He frowned. 'I don't understand that. I got better.'

He was full of wonder; so full of it that he just sat there and tried to figure it out.

'And...?' she prompted.

He took a deep breath, came back to her. 'And then I noticed that I was having a bit of trouble at the gym. Couldn't do quite as much on the treadmill, pulled up short on the cycle. I went to the doctor. He did some tests. Didn't find anything, of course. Useless bugger.'

He drank some tonic water. The waiter reappeared and they were suddenly forced to remember their menus. He didn't seem to bother that they were distracted, that Jack's order of a chicken Caesar salad and hers of pan-fried sea bream were perfunctory.

'Any wine?' As if he cared.

She was surprised when Jack said, 'What the hell. Yes. A Sancerre, if you have one.'

The waiter consulted the list, found one. 'Is this OK?'

Jack nodded and the waiter departed with the menus, leaving Beverley even more concerned. It wasn't like her brother to drink in the day.

'What happened then?' she asked.

He finished the tonic water but made a face as if it had turned sour. 'What happened then was I got worse. A lot worse.' He laughed. 'God, I was tired. Helen got really pissed off.'

In a totally mistaken attempt to inject some humour she asked, 'Is that why she left you?'

The memory was later to make her squirm. He laughed politely and without any enthusiasm, literally humouring her. 'No,' he reassured her. Then, more to himself, 'No, that wasn't the reason.'

He seemed to abruptly pull out of the dive and she heard again his wicked sense of humour. 'Helen didn't want a waster like me; she wanted a professional man, one who could afford to keep her in a style to which she was sure she could become accustomed.' It was an attempt to see something lighter than the gloom, but it soon waned, then died.

She prompted, 'You were saying you were tired.'

He nodded. 'Yeah. So I went back to the doctor. This time he sent me on to a specialist. First of all a cardiologist then, when he found nothing, a hepatologist.'

He finished, as if that were the punchline, as if now it were time to relax and get on with their meal, the ice broken.

The waiter reappeared. He was slightly built and had protuberant lips around which was a goatee beard that looked as if he had missed it while shaving that morning. He had mislaid his charm bracelet too. Without a word he brought forth an ice bucket in which was the Sancerre. He opened it quickly and efficiently, then poured a token into Jack's glass, who lifted it to his nose, sniffed deeply and then murmured, 'Fine.'

Having poured Beverley half a glassful, then topped up Jack's, the waiter retreated without a single word being spoken. Beverley could wait no longer. With no little trepidation she asked, 'Hepatologists deal with livers, don't they?'

He nodded. 'Diseases of the liver and biliary

system.' He sounded as if he were quoting.

'What did he find?'

'Cirrhosis.'

He sounded the word slowly, as if savouring its finer qualities; a vintage word that should not be hurried.

Shocked, she didn't reply for a moment, the words lost. Then, 'Cirrhosis? But isn't that...'

She looked at the wine and he laughed. 'Alcohol?' As if to challenge her – perhaps to challenge the gods – he picked up his glass and took a deep drink. 'Sometimes. Often. But not me, not this time.'

'What, then?'

He sighed. 'Hepatitis.'

Every explanation only further confused her and she shook her head. 'I don't understand, Jack.'

'Viral hepatitis. Hepatitis B, to be precise.' He looked down at the cutlery, finding the watermark alluring beyond all else. He observed thoughtfully, 'No imagination, these virologists. They give them letters, not proper names. I don't even have a decently titled disease.'

She'd been around police surgeons and pathologists long enough to have acquired a smattering – a splattering, perhaps – of medical knowledge and it was accordingly with some trepidation that she asked, 'How did you get it?'

He looked directly into her eyes and she saw nothing there, not even as he asked, 'Does that matter?' She dropped her gaze and, saying nothing, she made it perfectly plain that it didn't.

Their food arrived and it was actually good; unfortunate then that their appetites had withered. They ate in perfunctory style by unspoken agreement allowing the subject to rest; their talk was shell-like, a fragile surface on which they skated but which had no foundations.

They had no dessert, only coffee – he an espresso, she a cappuccino – and then she had to ask. 'What's the prognosis?'

He replied at once, matter-of-factly; his voice neither rose nor fell, his expression didn't change, the attitude of his body was fixed.

'End-stage.'

It was so unexpected, so shocking, that she heard it but missed it for a moment. 'What?' Despite herself the word was a shouted hiss.

He shrugged, still refusing to play the game of sickness. 'It's end-stage. I've been taking the drugs for four months now, but they've hardly touched the activity of the virus. That means the cirrhosis is on-going, getting worse.'

'But, surely...'

He shook his head. 'No, sis. There's nothing left to do.'

She stared at him. Then inspiration struck. 'What about a transplant? You're on the waiting list...?'

He smiled. He reached out to take her hand. 'I thought that was a wonderful idea, too, but it seems that I'm not eligible.'

'Why not?'

'The virus, sis. Even with a new liver, I'd still have the virus, which means that sooner or later, the cirrhosis would return.'

'So they could do it again.'

He laughed. 'They're short of livers. So short they only give them to people who aren't going to waste them.'

She refused to accept this. She had battled her whole life – fought people who thought she was nothing more than a two-legged vagina, people who thought that beauty and brains were never found in the same room let alone the same woman – and she was unused to losing. 'But that's preposterous! At least it would give you a few more years – years in which they might find a cure, or the number of donated livers might increase...'

'Or they might not,' he pointed out. 'If demand outstrips supply you have to allocate available resources somehow. If you drink too much, they make you stop; if it's a viral cause, you're nowhere. I understand that.'

But she didn't. 'You can't just have given up,' she said wonderingly.

He shrugged almost apologetically. 'Nothing makes you so indignant as the first time that you're told you're going to die. Once you accept that fact, it's amazing how the torment of other indignations just fade into the background.'

She dropped her gaze to the drying beige froth in her empty cup and discovered that she was weeping. They had between them stretched the bonds of family to gossamer, and yet now they were proving stronger than ever.

She hated crying, and she knew that Jack

would hate it too, and squeezed her eyes dry. When she was sure that he would not hear the tears in her voice she asked, 'What about Mum? You haven't told her?'

'God, no. She'd never cope, would she?'

Their mother lived on the south coast in pleasurable ignorance of either of her offspring's lives. Beverley shook her head and smiled. 'She's tougher than you think, Jack.'

He shrugged. 'Best to leave things, I thought.'

She tried a smile and succeeded to a certain extent. 'You'll have to tell her eventually. Better now than later.'

'Maybe.'

She couldn't blame him. Their mother was a difficult woman, made near impossible by early widowhood.

But Jack had always been the favourite; much as it hurt her, it was something for which Beverley could not blame her brother, only her mother.

He grasped her hand. 'I'm telling you because I'm going to need you, Beverley. Not now, perhaps, but sooner or later. You see? Sooner or later I'm going to need you to be strong. Understand?'

She found herself weeping again, the tears this time unrestrained, her hand clenching his so tightly that it was rimmed by white flesh. She whispered, 'Shit.'

He nodded absently. 'That's exactly what I said when they told me.'

NINE

Jasper Fitzroy-Hughes had been missing for two days before Beverley got to hear about it. It was Lambert who gave the case to her, exhibiting his usual good grace and easy charm.

'Here.'

She took the file that was being proffered to her across the desk. Lambert said, 'Missing person.'

Beverley frowned. 'So why are we dealing with it? Why not give it to the truncheonheads?'

'Some more respect for the uniformed branch, please, Inspector.'

She ignored him. 'Do we know that a crime's been committed?'

'That's not the point. The individual in question has ... connections.'

It took her a moment but then she caught on. She smiled sourly. 'Oh, I see.'

Before she could articulate her cynicism, he explained, 'Jasper Fitzroy-Hughes is the son of one of the government's assistant chief medical officers.' If his words were meant to convey that here was reason enough, the tone on which they were carried exactly neutralized this impression. Lambert was doing as he had been told; just as she would have to.

'And is this priority?'

'As much as any other important case.'

'He's not the first to go missing recently, not by a long way.'

In fact there had been something of an epidemic of late. Usually the kind of people you might expect to disappear – a high percentage of homeless, two prostitutes, one paedophile – but nonetheless a slight but noticeable increase in the frequency.

'Exactly. It's starting to look bad in the Home Office returns.'

'Nothing to do with the fact that he's rich and the others were pond scum?'

'Just make sure you find him.'

It was an exceptionally unhelpful quantum of advice, one that he ornamented with a word of caution. 'The Chief Constable doesn't want any *fuss*. Handle it well and handle it quietly. He doesn't want to see the name and face of a senior government adviser all over the newspapers.'

He turned and she was left to stare at his retreating back. *What does that mean?* If she thought the jollity was over, he disappointed. At the door he turned. To her wonder the frown had actually deepened; she decided that if could only smile he would be perhaps be handsome.

Then she realized that she was being stupid.

'There are rumours.'

There were always rumours. They were a

swirl through which they moved, a hissing white noise from which any one of them could pick out whatever titbit of gossip that they wanted, whether it was true or not. It was a kind of nutrient medium for the imagination.

'Really?'

For some reason at that moment she thought suddenly of Jack. It brought with it a crushing depression.

Lambert came a little way back into the room. 'About you.'

Well, golly gosh. Dang my britches...

She closed her eyes. Jack was there but she forced herself to ignore him. 'What about me?'

She seemed frequently to be the subject of rumour – which particular senior officer was supposed to be fucking her, which particularly outrageous place they had done it in, which particular perversion they had favoured. These were the usual ones but not infrequently there were others, even more hurtful; that she was a lesbian, that she was a part-time prostitute. And all of these, as far as she could see, grew up not just because she did occasionally choose to sleep with someone, but also because more frequently she did not, because she refused the overtures that came her way with deeply depressing monotony. The egos of those she spurned, no matter how politely, would not allow them to let her pass by untainted.

Lambert's frown deepened so that she wondered whether if it went any further he would lose the gift of sight altogether, and she realized the truth behind his attitude.

You're embarrassed.

She had learned over the years not to be bothered by such a handicap and she found enjoyment in his discomfort.

He said in a gruff voice, 'They say that you and Richardson...'

'Oh.'

Relieved to be rescued from the end of the sentence, he asked, 'Is it true?'

She couldn't resist a smile as she enquired, all innocence and disingenuousness, 'Is what true, sir?'

He produced a scowl from somewhere deep inside the frown. 'Are you having a liaison?'

She kept her face straight, appeared to consider this from every position while in her mind she laughed at his drawing-room sensibilities. *Liaison? Does he get his dialogue from Emily Brontë?*

'Well, he *is* my DS.'

'You know what I mean.'

Considering that she had been accused of sleeping with every male (and some of the females) within a kilometre radius, of being taken from behind and in front and probably sideways, of having twosomes and threesomes and foursomes, of everything up to and including bestiality, she ought to have expected this. She *had* expected it, she admitted.

It still depressed her.

'No, sir.' She said this in a tone that took vehemence and enriched it with tiredness.

His stare was long and hard. As if she hadn't spoken he said, 'Richardson is a good copper.

He is also a valuable asset...'

He's black, you mean.

'When he was assigned to work with you I advised against it very strongly because I think you're a bad copper...'

'Thanks.'

'I also know your record.' She raised an eyebrow that was no more than linear suggestion on smooth powdered skin. 'I don't want him tainted.'

What am I? Fagin? She said, 'Tainted how?'

'You know what I mean.'

She didn't but she let it lie. 'Detective Sergeant Richardson and I have formed a very close, but very professional relationship, sir. We work well as a team during our hours on duty, thereafter we go our separate ways, with the exception of the occasional social drink. I think you'll find that this station has a network of gossip-mongers who work harder at spreading tittle-tattle than they do at protecting the community.'

He looked less than convinced but her uncompromising tone scored a hit. 'You deny it absolutely?'

'You fucking bet I do.'

The use of profanity in replying to a senior officer was unorthodox but it worked. After chewing for a little while on something that might have been nothing, might have been gristle, might even have been a sheep turd, he nodded. Without a further word he turned and walked out.

She shook her head; she had long ago

abandoned her attempts at establishing any kind of rapport with Chief Inspector Lambert and instead dreamed of the day when she might gain some suitable revenge on him. With Lambert around her chances of promotion were wasted to the point of mummification. She turned again to the file.

It was an insult, of course. Even if the Chief Constable – a political beast whose sole remaining ambition was a knighthood and whose whole policing policy was enlisted to forward this objective – had demanded token CID involvement in the case, it could have been handled by a sergeant. To have given it to her was yet another signal that Lambert was still intent on making her life incrementally excremental in flavour. She felt disinclined even to pick the file up, as if to do so would mean that she succumbed, that she was beaten. Eyeing it steadily she whispered to herself, 'Bastard.'

Abruptly she stood up and went to the window, staring out at the greying light above the fine Regency buildings opposite; most of these had been converted into offices for architects and accountants, or into multiple occupancies, but a few were still as originally intended, housing the families of the well-to-do. Rare pedestrians ambled to and fro two storeys below her but these she ignored; something in the sky – her career, perhaps, floating away from her, whisked by the winds of misfortune and calumny – held her attention. She hugged her arms around herself in a lover's embrace and brooded.

Behind her the door to her office opened but she was lost and didn't hear it.

Sam Richardson stood in the doorway and waited. He knew better than to disturb his superior officer when she was thinking. He closed the door quietly behind his back and waited. A full minute had passed before she came out of her reverie and turned, her face registering surprise. 'Oh, Sam.' Then, 'Yes?'

'Lambert said you would want to see me.'

She frowned. *'DCI* Lambert.'

He accepted his chastisement with the slightest of smiles. 'DCI Lambert,' he corrected himself.

She turned and went back to her desk, indicated the file that Lambert had left. 'A little task for us. Missing person. Missing very important person.'

As she knew he would, he frowned. 'A missing person? Why us?'

'Politics. It's the son of a senior civil servant.' She suddenly barked a short laugh. 'It's also, I think, a ceremonial sword.'

He didn't follow. 'I'm sorry?'

She didn't explain, merely picking up the file, handing it to him, then looking at her watch. She said, 'Make an appointment to go and see the parents tomorrow – about ten o'clock. I'm going home.'

He had an uncertain frown on his face as he left with the file.

TEN

Eisenmenger had been lately working too hard. He sat at the table in the sitting room, a laptop open in front of him, and tried to concentrate but found it impossible. He thought that this was because he was tired, but he was wrong; what he did not appreciate was that the intuition that served him so well as a pathologist was now working to undermine his whole life. He did not know that he knew that something had changed and because he had not been able to work out why he was feeling the way he was feeling, he moved through disorientation and discomfiture.

He heard the front door open and Helena come in. There was a pause while she hung up her coat before she came into the sitting room. He looked up at her and smiled and she smiled back. 'Hello, dear,' he said.

'Hello.' Her smile barely had time to flower before it withered.

'Do you want some tea?'

She did not seem to hear the question at first, had to concentrate for a moment before she said, 'Yes. Yes, please.' Even then, she did not appear to be certain.

He got up from his seat as she sat down on

the sofa. 'Good day?'

Once again, she was slow to respond. 'Yes...'

It had been a very good day, in fact. So good that she now felt crushed by the guilt of it. She had had lunch with Alan, then they had spent the afternoon in his flat.

In bed, where Alan had proved as considerate in his love-making as he was in society.

Eisenmenger busied himself in the kitchen. He called through, 'Are you all right? Not another headache?'

When this received no response, he peered around the doorway. 'What's wrong?'

She looked up at him and said, 'Come and sit down.'

He complied, a worried look on his face. Before he could vocalize this anxiety, she said quickly, 'I'm afraid it's over, John.'

'What is?'

She hesitated, stared intently at him. She felt wretched, felt that she was a bitch, felt that she had to be. 'Us,' she whispered.

The shock of this small word speared him, a stiletto between his eyes. He opened his mouth to repeat the word, then froze. There was no need to repeat it for it was a perfectly simple word that signified a perfectly simple concept. He found himself transported to a strange place, one where everything was reversed, where certainties were demolished, relationships he thought were secure were seen to be perished, where the safety and comfort of life were revealed as transitory.

He frowned but his question was plaintive.

'Why?'

'I've met someone else.' She said this in a rush, her face betraying fear; John had never been a violent man, but she had never said anything like this to him before.

'Someone else?' His voice would have been no less confused if she had said, 'Alien'. She did not reply and after a few breaths he asked in a wondering tone, 'Who?'

'His name's Alan. Alan Sheldon. He works at GCHQ.'

'A spook?'

She smiled weakly. 'Something like that.'

'A client?'

A nod.

In his eyes there was a constant look of complete bewilderment as he asked these questions; he sought information but each additional datum only worsened his condition. There was no salvation in learning more, not in this instance, yet he could not stop forming questions. Indeed, he had more questions than he knew what to do with, but all of them were pointless now. He said nothing. He dropped his head and looked down at the ground, elbows on his knees, hands clasped. Helena suddenly realized that he might be crying, reached out to him, touched his shoulder. 'John?' He looked up abruptly and there were no tears in his eyes, although his features might have been set for them. She said softly and wretchedly, 'I'm sorry.'

He nodded curtly, but then asked tiredly, 'Is there nothing more to say?'

She shook her head. She began to wish that he would show anger, for at least such a reaction would provide some justification for her calumny; but he was so accepting, she felt as she would if she were torturing a kitten. She tried to justify herself; if not to herself, then to him.

'You're a wonderful, wonderful man, John. I wouldn't have changed the last five years for anything.'

Suddenly his face betrayed something other than acquiescence to his fate; he showed something akin to bitterness. 'But...?'

'But...' She had to take a deep breath. 'But, I want to move on.'

'And I have to move out?'

'No. Not immediately, anyway.'

He was suddenly discovering anger. 'Do it in stages, you suggest? First out of the main bedroom into the spare, then out of the front door?'

She felt relief; the kitten was fighting back, trying to scratch her. 'Do you want to keep sleeping with me?'

He laughed. 'Fair point.' A pause, then, 'I won't ask if you've been using a different bed lately.'

She coloured at that. 'Maybe you'd better move out sooner rather than later.'

He stood up abruptly. 'Maybe I had.'

She already regretted her words, reached out to him. 'John...'

He had moved away a couple of metres, turned and looked down at her, 'What is it?'

'I didn't mean it. Take as long as you want.'

'If I do, will you change your mind?'

She could only shake her head. He turned away, then turned back. 'We've been through so much together. I never imagined it would end like this.'

'Neither did I.'

'What did I do wrong, Helena?'

She had no answer; there was no answer. 'Nothing.'

Eisenmenger's anger had gone, the confusion back. 'It must be something. Have I taken you for granted?'

If this were chess, this would be the move that cost him the game, that exposed the king to check. She took the weapon that he had given her and used it with calm efficiency. 'John, you could never do anything else but take me for granted. It's the way you're built.'

He thought about this, then nodded before turning away. At the doorway he paused and said to her, 'You're right, of course.' There was one final spurt of anger, though. 'It doesn't mean that you're not a bitch though, Helena.'

ELEVEN

Beverley awoke in the middle of the night, quite abruptly. She could not immediately explain her feeling of depression, her thoughts muffled by sleepiness, but then she remembered.

Jack.

The idea that her beloved Jack was dying was outrageous; over the three days since their lunch together she must have thought about it a thousand times, yet it still caused her surprise – shock even – every time it swept back down upon her, and every time she had to work at accepting it once more, at believing that it was real. A large part of her still rebelled, still hid from the possibility that her brother was actually, really, no-not-joking, going to fucking *die*.

She sighed into the darkness, enfolded by a crushing sense of loneliness at the prospect, but did not know why. It was nearly twenty years since he had left home for good and had never been back for anything more than a day. Not even when their father had died of lung cancer, coughing up blood and pus, each cough and wheezed breath seeming to inch him a little closer to agony rather than death, had he lodged with either her or their mother.

She didn't want to, but she started weeping again, more violently than when she had first heard the news, as if she felt sheltered in the darkness of her bedroom, safe to reveal herself. She felt forever lonely, if not alone. Alone with her daemons, alone with her colleagues, alone without friends. For too long, alone only with her past.

Her past was more than an impediment, more than a thing by which she was judged, it was, as far as most of those around her were concerned, her entire being. She had not only never escaped it, she had been subsumed by it; she *was* her past in the eyes of many of her colleagues. They allowed her no progression, no evolution, something that was permitted every other sentient being. Nothing she now did could ever be excused because they would not see her as a changed being.

She readily admitted her sins – to herself, if to no one else – and some of them she could even regret. She had been hasty in her decision that Jeremy Eaton-Lambert had been a killer, although his subsequent suicide had not exactly left the world a poorer place; he had not perhaps committed the double murder of his parents, but he had done enough to be brought to justice; the verdict and sentence had been his.

And yes, she had had to use a little sexual chemistry to achieve reasonable postings and purely appropriate promotions but had she been in a normal working environment – one where ability counted for more than testosterone and the right Lodge address – she was sure that she would have balked at such tactics. She was not a whore, despite Lambert's frequent assertions to the contrary, but she was a woman who had great self-belief and who looked on her beauty much as she looked on her intelligence – there to be used. Much as a man might consider using his strength to batter his way to the top, she saw no crime in using her own attributes for a similar aim; at least her way was gentler.

Beside her Richardson asked quietly, 'Are you awake?'

She smiled and said nothing for a moment. *Are you the one, Sam?*

The question was asked every night, every time that she saw him. It scared her, that question, because if the answer was no, then this time the wound would be even deeper, perhaps too deep to bear.

She waited, swallowed her tears, then said at last, 'Yes.' She heard laziness in her voice, as if the darkness had slowed time, as if something viscous flowed around them, for he, too, only spoke after several breaths had passed. 'Are you feeling as horny as I am?'

She laughed, but the sound was softly languid. In the midst of a sigh she said, 'I guess so.'

He turned towards her, his arm snaking out over her midriff. In a continuous move he came towards her, his face flowing over hers, kissing first her open lips, then her chin, then

down on her breasts. His teeth and lips caress-
ed her nipple while she cradled his head, feeling the tight curls of his hair.

She decided that she had missed this, missed
this a lot...

His hand rested on her belly but she knew
that it wouldn't stay there; she opened her legs
and his fingers obliged. She arched her back
and moaned as he brought his knees up under
his body so that he was on all fours, so that her
hands could release his head and move slowly,
strokingly down his body. As her fingertips
grasped his erect penis in the lightest of grasps,
it was his turn to stop and, his lips releasing her
breast, to gasp.

He straightened up, allowing her to bend
forward off the bed, put her hands around his
waist to take him in her mouth.

'*Shit...*'

After only a few seconds, he took her head in
his hands and gently moved it back. With a
degree of choreographed practice that resembled a ballet, she knew what he wanted, lay
back down and let him crouch astride her, his
head deeply between her legs.

Afterwards, as they lay together, her head
cradled on his arm and chest, she said, 'Lambert's heard rumours.'

'About us?'

'He wants it to stop.'

'What did you say?'

Although he couldn't see it, he heard the
smile in her voice as she pointed, 'I think I've

been fairly eloquent tonight.'

But Richardson was worried. 'No, really, what did you say to him?'

'I denied it, of course. Said it was just gossip.'

His silence was uncertain. She said, 'I would not worry, Sam. I've been here before. Lambert's just grasping for anything that he thinks he might be able to use against me. He hasn't got any proof, any real ammunition.'

She sensed – not by vision or hearing but by something more subtle – that the concept perturbed him. She waited for the inevitable inquest into what exactly she meant by that remark.

But he still said nothing. Eventually she broke the silence by asking, 'What is it?'

There was a pause. She heard all sorts of doubts and adversative conjunctions in the darkness. *Here we go...*

At last he said, 'I love you, Beverley. You're fantastic, you know that?' This ought to have cheered her but the tone told her to be cautious, told her that the words were treacherous.

A pause and she was tempted to finish his sentence for him, so certain was she where they were headed, but she held her fire.

'I don't want any trouble. I can't afford it. My career...'

She almost laughed. *Talking of careers, have you heard the one about the ever-so-promising female detective who got a reputation as a loser?* She said tiredly, 'So you love me very much, but you're terribly sorry. Is that it?' She could not keep the bitterness out of her sentences.

But Richardson surprised her. It was with surprising – and heart-warming – vehemence that he said, 'No! That's not it!'

She lifted her head. There was no light in which to see his face but she looked up at him anyway. 'What, then?' she asked in a whisper.

He said nothing for a long while longer, then there was a deep, almost dying sigh. 'I guess we'll have to be even more careful.'

He hugged her slightly.

She continued staring into the blackness for a long, long time before reaching up to kiss him. He was surprised by this; even more surprised to discover that she was crying.

As she closed her eyes to sleep she thought drowsily, *Twice in one day. I must be going soft.*

TWELVE

When Billy still hadn't returned by the next morning, his mother really began to worry. By the early evening she had become so distracted she was driven to break previously absolute taboos.

She walked slowly up the stairs and stood outside the door to Billy's room.

Billy had never threatened his mother with either word or action but he had made it quite clear that this was *his* room. The rest of the house might be in her name (and in the council's housing portfolio) but beyond the door was his domain. What occurred, what was housed, what was listened to and what was watched in there – all these were solely his business.

She had never broken this injunction.

She knocked, although the chances of invoking a response were infinitesimal, and even when there was merely the rumble of traffic to listen to she still hesitated. The move of her hand to the door handle was accompanied by a rising feeling of dread, composed perhaps partly of fear that her calumny would be discovered, partly of terror that she would uncover all sorts of secrets that were best left to fester, and perhaps partly also because she really did not want to uncover what might have happened to her son.

Nevertheless, she turned the handle and pushed the flimsy door inwards.

Despite all else that was going on in her head she tutted at the mess; screwed clothes of all varieties lay strewn around the floor, the bed was unmade, an ashtray full of cigarette butts, cans of beer (mostly opened) and a large, opened packet of condoms were on the dressing table. The pillow on the bed was greasy and looked dirty in a decidedly unpleasant way. She fought disappointment with a mantra that she knew well. *Boys will be boys.*

Absently she picked up litter from the floor, packets of crisps from the surfaces, while searching ineffectually for evidence of where

Billy might have gone. She found well-thumbed sex magazines and cheap-looking videos with titles that she didn't understand over pictures that she understood only too well, but she didn't find anything of help in her quest. She straightened the bedclothes and sat down on the sagging bed heavily. What should she do now?

Billy, she knew, had few close friends and a goodly percentage of those were in prison. He didn't have a regular job either. Not that he hadn't tried; he'd worked for nine months as a storeman in a local garden centre (and she was sure that he'd had nothing to do with the disappearance of those chainsaws), and for over a year in a local undertaker's. This last he had to give up because he had found the work too upsetting, taking off weeks on end with stress.

In fact, now that she was faced with the problem of finding him, she discovered that there were precious few places to start and the only likely one she could think of was out of her reach. She knew that Billy drank in the Three Tunnes and she wondered if someone there would have news of him, but it was two bus rides away. She did not feel that her legs would be up to it.

She made her slow, pain-filled way back down the stairs, feeling now not just dread but fear and loneliness.

THIRTEEN

The house was just to the east of Cheltenham town centre, a private road, an air of easy exclusion. Here was peace, here was contentment, here was certainty that money still bought certain privileges, even in a world such as the residents found themselves occupying, a world that had changed irrevocably and incomprehensively for most of them. It was an enclave, every bit as embattled as one in a war-torn country, every bit as under siege as Mafeking had once been.

Clarissa Fitzroy-Hughes had the face of a woman close to the edge of despair and both Beverley and Sam assumed that this was the natural result of a son gone missing. She was thin, perhaps made thinner by anxiety, and primly made up. She answered the door of the large late-Edwardian house almost as if afraid to expose herself to the outside, as if she feared that by doing so she was inviting contamination into a cloistered world. Beverley felt somehow dirty as she showed her warrant card to this small, late-middle-aged woman and asked, 'Mrs Fitzroy-Hughes? Inspector Wharton and this is Detective Sergeant Richardson.'

Like most people she didn't spend long looking at the card. 'Come in,' she said eagerly, almost pathetically. She stood aside to allow them to pass from the plant-strewn porch into the deep, dim, antique-strewn hallway. From there she directed them to the room on their right, a large sitting room with furniture that was old but not antique; it had the air of a house that had been in the family for generations. While they sat back in sagging, worn armchairs, Mrs Fitzroy-Hughes perched on the front of hers, as if afraid of being swallowed by its maw. Everything about her was clenched together – her forearms, her knees, her shoulders, even the words she used. Her phrases were condensed and hurried and, in contrast to most people's mode of speech, seemed to be emitted when she was breathing in rather than out; thus each speech ended on a rush and a rising note of something halfway between panic and command.

'As I believe Sergeant Richardson explained on the telephone, we've come about your son.'

'Yes, yes.'

'He's gone missing.'

As if this simple statement of undeniable truth came as a shock she gasped slightly, mouth falling open, and Beverley noticed that her bottom teeth were rotten. Pressing a handkerchief under her nose, dabbing at it as if it were sore, Mrs Fitzroy-Hughes nodded, her eyes wide.

'Does he live at home?'

'Not all the time. He has a small flat in the town centre.' She gave them the address. 'He spends a lot of time there, but he comes home quite frequently.'

'What does he do?'

'He's a student nurse. At St Benjamin's.'

'He didn't want to become a doctor, like his father?'

Mrs Fitzroy-Hughes donned a smile but it must have been too uncomfortable, perhaps chafing around her collar, because she soon let it drop to the carpet. 'No.'

Beverley could smell secrets but she said nothing except, 'A touch of rebellion?'

She tried the smile on again, found it no more amenable. 'Something like that.'

Beverley considered this; out of the corner of her eye she saw Sam look up at her, then back down to the notebook. She asked, 'How long has Jasper been a nurse?'

Mrs Fitzroy-Hughes said in a quiet, low voice, 'A year.'

'You last saw him when?'

'A week ago last Wednesday.'

Nine days before.

'When did you first miss him?'

'At the weekend. It was my birthday. He never misses that.'

'Does he live on his own?'

'He lives with Gary ... he's his flatmate.'

Beverley made no reaction as, she was sure, neither did Richardson. 'Gary is also a student nurse?'

'Yes.'

'Do you know his surname?'

'Allen. Gary Allen.'

'And have you talked with Mr Allen? Has he any idea where your son might be?'

'They went out to a party on Friday night. They got ... separated. He hasn't seen him since.'

'Where was the party?'

She didn't know.

'Do you have a recent photograph?'

Mrs Fitzroy-Hughes had clearly anticipated this request and she went at once to the ornamental table by the window where, next to an obscenely large cigarette lighter made of onyx, there was a cardboard folder. From this she produced a large photograph. It portrayed a young man with fair hair, faint freckles, blue eyes and slightly protuberant teeth. He did not strike Beverley as overwhelmingly attractive, but then ugly people went missing, were abused, tortured or murdered, every day; they had as much right to the benefits of modern society as the beautiful ones. 'That was taken last year, when Jasper left school.'

Beverley took it, looked at it briefly, then handed it to Richardson. She asked, 'Is Jasper an only child?'

He was.

'Can you give me the names of any close friends? From school?'

She produced three names, all male. From an address book in the hallway she found addresses which Richardson noted down while Beverley ran through in her mind the differences between what she had been told and what was the truth.

'And what about Professor Fitzroy-Hughes? Can we see him?'

They couldn't. 'He's at the Department of Health in London today and tomorrow – staying overnight.'

'But he is contactable...?'

Mrs Fitzroy-Hughes was doubtful. She gave them a number. 'That's for his PA. She may be able to help you.' When Beverley looked less than impressed, she added, 'Sorry.'

Beverley was running out of the easy questions. 'Tell me, Mrs Fitzroy-Hughes, has there been trouble at home?'

'What do you mean?' Her tone was a troubled mix of indignation and innocence.

'Rows, that kind of thing.'

Somewhat confusingly, Jasper's loving mother first shook her head then, almost at once, grimaced as if she had swallowed a bad oyster and said, 'Well ... you know. Families...'

Beverley, who was glad that she didn't personally know many families like the Fitzroy-Hughes very well at all, nodded understandingly. Gently she asked, 'How bad was it?'

Their witness was beginning to cry again but no one reacted, as if this were an embarrassment that polite people didn't talk about. Slowly Mrs Fitzroy-Hughes told them of an argument – 'It was silly ... Just a misunderstanding...' – some two weeks ago.

'What was it about?'

She seemed to find it difficult to convey this. 'My husband spoke his mind. He always speaks his mind. He told Jasper that he didn't like some of the people that Jasper was mixing with.'

'Who? Gary?'

She didn't say yes, but then she didn't say no, either. Instead they were given, 'Some of Gary's friends are a bit ... well, unorthodox.'

Beverley reflected that *unorthodox* was an interesting synonym for *homosexual*. 'How bad was this argument?'

She shrugged. 'Oh, the usual. Slamming doors, raised voices.'

'Violence?'

'Oh, no.' She sounded shocked, perhaps genuinely so.

'Was Jasper into drugs?'

Mrs Fitzroy-Hughes almost jumped up in her vehemence at that one. 'No!' This was accompanied by a vigorous shake of her head and something that for the first time approached anger.

Yet Beverley wondered if there was a firm foundation for her certainty. Blandly she said, 'I'm sorry if the question upsets you, Mrs Fitzroy-Hughes, but I have to ask. It might be relevant.'

She had calmed, albeit only slightly. 'He wasn't, I can assure you.'

Beverley smiled. 'Well, unless there's anything else you can tell us at this moment, we'll take it from here. We'll be in contact as soon as we have some news.' She stood up, Richardson following her example. Mrs Fitzroy-Hughes, however, had reverted to distraught distraction. Remaining seated and looking up at them she asked, 'Where has he gone? What's happened to him?'

Beverley switched effortlessly into reassurance mode. 'I'm sure he's all right, Mrs Fitzroy-Hughes. The vast majority of people who go missing turn up within a few days.'

'But he's already been gone for nine.'

'It's still early days.' When this produced no noticeable relief Beverley said in a slightly less clinical, more empathetic tone, 'Look, Mrs Fitzroy-Hughes, it's not as if he's a minor. I expect there's a perfectly reasonable explanation. All we're doing is making sure. Believe me, I'm one hundred per cent certain that we're wasting our time and your son will make contact sooner rather than later.'

Beverley's face was searched before there was a quick, jerked nod. Her eyes were filling again and she brought the handkerchief up to them with a dabbing motion. Richardson was amazed that it could hold any more moisture. She stood up with a sniff followed by a smile. 'I'll show you out.'

And it was outside, as they climbed back into the car and Beverley stared straight ahead and Richardson started the car, that she asked, 'Well?'

He turned the wheel hard to the right and the car moved away from the house slowly over the tarmac. 'Well what?'

'What did you think of her? Of this "missing person" case?'

He turned left on to the road; there were

several potholes that he had to avoid before reaching the gates that marked the start of the public highway. 'She dotes on him; Professor Fitzroy-Hughes, I'm not so sure about.'

She watched the houses grow less salubrious as they headed towards the town centre again. 'I'd guess that Professor Fitzroy-Hughes has a serious problem with his son. Perhaps the fact that he's in nursing, with a male flatmate that Daddy doesn't like.'

Richardson took his eyes from the road. 'Which would be worse? The fact that his son's gay or the fact that he became a nurse and not a doctor?'

She waved her right hand in suggestion that he should pay attention to the elderly female cyclist wandering shakily across the road ahead. 'I would guess that the good Professor would have indigestion over both.'

Sam was quiet for a while before pointing out, 'Of course, we might be entirely wrong about the Professor. We haven't heard his side of it.'

She said with a grin, 'You think so? I would say that we know exactly what he had to say. In fact, I'm surprised that Mrs Fitzroy-Hughes didn't once have to consult her script.'

'That's very cynical.'

'That's because I *am* very cynical, Sam. I would say that Professor Fitzroy-Hughes decides most things in that house. His wife plays number two, the little woman, good for organizing dinner parties and ticking off the gardener, but not for making the important decisions.'

The cyclist turned left and he accelerated away. 'Aren't you just stereotyping?'

She laughed. 'Of course I am. Haven't you learned, yet, Sam? People *are* stereotypes. We can't escape it, because you know what? Those who refuse to be stereotyped just seem to be eccentrics, another stereotype.'

Richardson wasn't so sure about this easy classification of humankind but he didn't argue. 'Where to?'

'I'd quite like to know why Mr Allen is apparently so unconcerned that his flatmate – for which we might reasonably substitute the term "lover" – has gone missing.'

FOURTEEN

Jean Whipple hadn't wanted to cancel Billy's regular order of cigarettes from Mr Raman but after thirty-six hours with neither sight nor sound of him, economics forced her to act. She felt as if she were betraying him by doing this, as if this were a sign that she was losing faith, that by this she would lessen the chances of his return. Mr Raman was sympathetic and tried to cheer her up with exhortations of optimism that she feared were groundless. 'You know these youngsters, Mrs Whipple. They live for the moment, for enjoyment, not for others. And who can blame them? Responsibility comes to crush us all down far too quickly; why shouldn't they try to run from it when they can?'

Which was all very fine but she knew that Billy *had* accepted responsibility for her a long time ago, when his father had died in a drunken fall off a railway bridge. Never once before had he shirked that responsibility and she knew he would not now have done so willingly.

Something was wrong.

'I expect you're right, Mr Raman,' she lied with a smile she didn't feel.

The banging on her front door came about twenty minutes after she had returned home. She was at that moment wondering if she should go back up to Billy's room to search again for whatever clues might be in there and the sound of the assault on the yellow-painted woodwork caused synchronous feelings of guilt and hope. Perhaps it was Billy, forgotten his key again. She moved as quickly as she could to the hallway and opened the door eagerly, but it wasn't Billy.

A large twenty-year-old with a scowl stood outside. She recognized him, although it took a moment for the name to come to her. Spud, or something ... He looked at her for hardly any time at all, then switched his attention to the hallway behind her. With his eyes searching the darkness he asked abruptly, 'Where is he?'

She was frightened. His whole demeanour was one of menace, a threat of violence in his face and in the clenched fists. 'Who? Where's who?'

'Billy.' He said this angrily.

As frightened as she was, the concept that her son was the object of the aggression before her caused her to move to block his searching gaze and to say, 'He's not here. Why do you want him?'

The eyes moved back to her. They were dark eyes, underscored by deep grey bags. He hadn't shaved for a while and his breath smelt on her face, especially when he leaned towards her and said nastily, 'He tried to mess with my girl. I don't like that.'

She couldn't keep querulousness from her voice as she said, 'He's not here.'

He was again searching through the little that he could see of the house interior. 'Mind if I check?'

He was actually moving to push past her as he asked this, a question that was as imperative as a command. She surprised herself and her thudding heart as she said loudly and firmly, 'Yes, I do.' Her arm came out to block him, one that he looked down at with a slightly shocked expression. 'Go away.'

His eyes flicked from her arm – as thin and breakable as spun sugar – to her face, then back to the arm. There passed several moments in which she knew that he was going to push on in, perhaps knocking her to the carpet as he did so, then they heard a vehicle pull up across the street. She looked over the intruder's shoulder and saw Mr Raman in his old blue delivery van – the one with the ghostly remains of its previous owner's name still visible on its sides as if haunting it. Mr Raman called out to her from across the traffic, 'Are you all right, Mrs Whipple?'

Her visitor looked around, then abruptly stepped back. He hurled her a venomous glance before shouting into the house, 'I'm gonna fucking get you, Billy Whipple. I'm gonna fucking get you and kill you, you hear?' With a further glance at Mr Raman, now frowning angrily at him, he spun around and stalked off.

In the event, because she was shaking so much and because she felt so weak, Mr Raman had to stay and make her a cup of tea, thus delaying his deliveries.

It was a small house on the end of a terrace of four. There was a small garden of sorts, one that sported a single rosebush and a dustbin in a sort of microcosmic representation of modern urban living. It was next to a Methodist church and opposite a community hall; posters outside tried to provoke excitement in Beverley's breast by promising her a night of prize bingo yet, unaccountably, failed in this mission. The supermarket on the nearby corner was large enough to be ugly, small enough to be useless. This was on a large crossroads in the middle of which was a cuprous statue covered in verdigris and pigeon guano; it depicted a military man on a rampant horse, presumably once someone who meant something – perhaps a victorious general, perhaps

91

even a royal – undoubtedly now someone who meant nothing. The final indignity was that a public toilet – notorious as a 'cottage' – stood beneath it and this had somehow transformed the statue into something sordid, the idea of a stallion as advert for promiscuity. Piles of garbage had appeared around the lampposts but even if they had been removed by the wave of a wizard's staff there would have remained an ineradicable air of decay.

Beverley looked around as she stepped from the car. She seemed to spend most of her working life in places like this, yet she could never accustom herself to them. She felt conspicuousness radiate around her like an eye-searing aura, as if she were Venusian and wearing a shiny silver suit.

'This is it?' she enquired of Richardson.

'Apparently.'

She gave the environs another quick once-over, as if to check that she had got it all right. 'I think the son of a senior civil servant can only be making a statement by living somewhere like this.'

There was no one in or, at least, no one responded when Richardson rang the doorbell. It wouldn't have been the first time that Beverley had stood outside a house in which there had been someone bloodied and dying, perhaps already dead.

'What now? St Benjamin's?'

She looked up at the empty bedroom windows. 'I suppose so.'

She hoped she was right to leave so quickly.

FIFTEEN

St Benjamin's was huge and it sprawled, extending tendrils throughout the locality – an ophthalmology department in one street, plastic surgery in an adjacent square, physiotherapy up a steep hill, many of the buildings so well camouflaged that even those with a map were wont to walk past their intended destination because they missed the graffitied sign. And, being huge, it required a not inconsiderable serfdom to keep it happy; underlings who beavered away in the belly of the beast, who served it as workers serve a queen. Gary Allen might have been in any one of thirty buildings, any one of two hundred rooms. Even Richardson's inspired suggestion to locate him through the Human Resources department engendered an hour of frustrating wrong turns and the belief in signs that pointed in ambiguous directions. It seemed natural, therefore, that the confusion and chaos should continue inside Human Resources, that no one should know how to locate a specific nurse, that they shouldn't even know how to locate the person who would know how to locate him. A further forty minutes of the allotted span of the universe passed away before they were reasonably sure that Gary was working on an oncology ward.

Before they left this Kafkaesque bureaucracy, Beverley risked one further enquiry. 'I wonder if you could tell me if Jasper Fitzroy-Hughes has reported in sick?'

It took fifteen minutes but eventually an answer was received. Yes, he had. On Monday afternoon.

As they walked away down the dingy corridor, Sam asked, 'What does that mean?'

Beverley didn't reply because she didn't know.

'Adrian? It's John.'

He was tired; he had not slept last night, but he was far more tired than that. He felt tired in a way that no human being ought ever to feel.

'I've been thinking over what you suggested.'

He was back in the sitting room, sitting at the table before the window. He felt like an intruder now, a guest in the home. He had endured the night in the spare bedroom, every breath taken in bringing the smell of a place that was not normally lived in, that was as personal as a hotel room, every breath taken out one of despair. He had reiterated in his head what happened that evening and, more importantly, why it happened. He had gone through the years they had spent together, examining each of the many highs and, he genuinely thought, the few lows. He tried to work out what, if anything, he could have done differently. This was what he did; he was by nature and training an analyst; he was a brilliant analyst because he brought to this an unworldly intuition.

For this problem, though, his intuition had failed. The morning found him no wiser, no happier, no more certain.

That morning he had heard Helena rise early and he had stayed in his room until she left the flat; only then had he risen like a thief, seeing the things around him with eyes that were, if not different, then newly educated.

'It's against my better judgement, Adrian, but I think I'll take you up on it.'

He listened to the reply, then, 'Tomorrow? You've cut it a bit fine, haven't you?'

He looked down on the road outside, saw a police car prowling past as Professor Quick told him that he would be doing him a big favour.

He laughed. 'OK, but you owe me one, Adrian.'

He had yet to appreciate how big a favour.

The charge nurse was so camp he couldn't have been gay.

'What do you want?' He didn't pout but there was something about his lips that suggested it was only by effort of will that he refrained. The inevitable warrant card was shown. 'Oh.' This suggested not only disappointment but also disapproval. The lips did a little dance, skirting with that ever-threatening pout. 'Is there a problem?'

The police and problems were as inseparable

in people's minds as sex and sin.

'I believe you have a nurse working here called Gary Allen.'

He had been looking at Richardson as Beverley spoke. He transferred his gaze to her. 'What about him?'

'Can we speak to him?'

'Well, you can...' He made it sound as if what was possible may not have been desirable. '...But I wouldn't at the moment.'

'Why not?'

'He's doing a manual evacuation.'

Beverley had a nasty feeling that she could guess what he was talking about, but Richardson asked anyway.

'Poor Mrs Muckle has faecal impaction. Gary's helping her out in cubicle three. I'd wait until he's finished if I were you.'

If the actual terms had not been sufficiently descriptive, the tone alone would have painted the picture; the slight pucker – a sort of signed period mark – only added to the clarity of the vision in their minds. He gestured with his head – tossed it, would have been a more accurate description – towards a room behind him. 'You can wait in my office if you like.'

It was barely more than a walk-in cupboard, its only window giving a view of the ward, its desk entirely occupying one wall. There were only two chairs, one of which Beverley occupied while Richardson leaned conspicuously against a noticeboard prominent on which was a poster advertising a forthcoming dinner-dance. Beverley murmured, 'Whatever you do, don't stop to tie your shoelaces.'

Richardson gave her a wide easy smile. 'I can't think what you mean.'

They had to wait ten minutes before a tall, rangy young man appeared in the doorway. 'You want to see me?'

'Gary Allen?'

'That's right.'

He was gently spoken with a sad look about blue-grey eyes and the last traces of acne on the cheeks. His skin was greasy. He was drying his hands on paper towel that he tossed into a wastepaper basket at Beverley's feet. Neither Beverley nor Richardson proffered their hand in welcome. She made the introductions. 'It's about Jasper,' he guessed.

'You're his flatmate.'

He nodded. Without being asked he sat down with a deep sigh. He gave the impression of concern to the point of depression.

'When did you last see him?'

'Friday night. We went to a party.'

'Whose party?'

'Chap called Steve Bright.' Richardson heard dislike in his tone but Beverley either ignored or missed it.

'What address?'

'A flat in Pittville.' He gave the address, which Richardson noted down as Beverley said, 'If he lives in Pittville, he's not short of a bob or two.'

He shrugged. 'I guess not.'

'I take it Mr Bright isn't a friend of yours.'

'I hardly know him.'

'So how come you went to his party?'

'Jasper wanted to go. Jasper likes going to parties.'

'Whereas you're a pipe and slippers man?'

He didn't like the tinge of sarcasm in her voice. 'I prefer peace and quiet occasionally.'

She glanced across at Richardson to see if he had picked up the zeitgeist; here was half of a couple, not a man talking about an acquaintance.

'Jasper knew him?'

'Met him a few weeks before, when he was out clubbing.'

She nodded, then changed direction and changed gear at the same time. 'What happened at the party?'

He looked at her, a frown on his face. His Adam's apple was prominent and dancing nervously. 'Nothing—'

'Yes, it did,' she interrupted. She said this with a degree of certainty that was not about to be contradicted. 'You said that it was the last time you saw him. You went with him and you were presumably planning to leave with him, but you didn't. So what happened to change the plan?'

He said through a sigh, 'We had a row.'

She had already guessed that. 'About Steve Bright?'

He looked up at her when she asked this, then quickly dropped his head. 'I wanted to leave but Jasper wouldn't. Bright was making eyes at him all evening; I went for a pee and when I came back I found Bright with his hands all over him in the kitchen; his hands were so tightly clamped on his backside he was practically fisting him.'

'So you had a hissy-fit?' It was the first time that she had made reference to his sexual orientation but he didn't seem bothered.

'You could call it that. I separated them – practically had to call out a man with a crowbar – and got Jasper alone. Told him what I thought of him.'

'Heatedly,' she suggested.

'Fairly.'

'Did you get violent?'

'Of course not!'

'Did Jasper?'

He paused at that. 'He pushed me out of the way ... that was all.'

She thought it sounded genuine; Gary didn't strike her as the type to put up his dukes...

But that didn't mean that he wasn't the type to take his revenge in other ways, at other times.

'Where was Mr Bright while all this was going on?'

He raised his shoulders slightly. 'He wandered off. Seemed to think it was funny.'

'What did you do then?'

'I went looking for Bright but I couldn't find him.'

'Why not?'

'It was a big party. There were a lot of people there.'

'All of them gay?'

He smiled sourly. 'No. Not all of them.'

'Did you know any of them? Any at all?'

'A few. Not many.'

'I'd like you to give the names to Sergeant Richardson, please.'

He seemed to have a problem with this. 'But...'

'You do want to find Jasper, don't you?'

He closed his mouth again and began hesitantly to recite names to Sam and, while he did this, she watched and assessed him. *Jasper's lover. Outwardly concerned ... and inwardly? Not as calm as he would like us to think – is that because of anxiety about his lover or anxiety over being discovered? Homosexual murders are notoriously nasty...*

She asked, 'So tell me, Gary, if you're so worried about what's happened to Jasper, why haven't you contacted us? Why leave it to his parents?'

For the first time he showed some signs of discomfiture. 'I assumed...'

But whatever he assumed seemed momentarily lost to him.

'You assumed what?'

He shrugged and with more confidence said, 'That he'd gone off with someone.'

'Was he prone to "go off" with people?'

'He'd been known to.'

She smiled. 'But he always came back?'

He smiled a small smile of secret pride. 'Yeah, after a day or two.' His face, however, couldn't carry it for long. 'Until now.'

She nodded, a picture of complete understanding.

'How often did you row?' She asked this abruptly, catching him by surprise.

A momentary pause for first indignation then resignation. 'Quite a lot, I guess.'

'Violently?'

It ought to have produced outrage but instead there came only a quiet as telling as a confession. Eventually he murmured, 'Sometimes.' He kept his head low.

She said nothing and continued to scrutinize him, using the silence to draw out more information, uncover another aspect, perhaps disclose the very thing that she needed to know. They heard someone laughing just outside the door, a slightly nasal, almost manufactured noise that could only have come through the upper airways of their new friend, the charge nurse, but no one reacted.

The sociological pressure to fill the silence worked its magic and eventually he said, 'I love Jasper.' And he began to weep...

Richardson concentrated on his notebook but Beverley had no such sense of discomfort. She asked softly, 'Do have any idea where he might be?'

He looked up with red-rimmed, watery eyes. She thought he looked devastated, like a little boy who had lost his mother in a crowd. She thought, *This is true love*, as he said, 'I thought it was Bright. I went to see him, confronted him, but he denied all knowledge. Said Jasper had left with someone he didn't know, someone called Ray.'

'Ray what?'

'Axenfeld.' She made him spell it for Richardson.

'Have you got an address for him?'

He shook his head miserably. 'I've asked around – people who were at the party – but no one knows him.'

She nodded slowly, her face neutral while she heard the faint sound of alarums. She continued to scrutinize him but now his misery occupied him completely and he did not mind the silence in the room.

It seemed like a good time to address the one remaining issue that was really bothering her.

'The Human Resources Department tell me that Jasper phoned in sick on Monday afternoon...'

She saw at once that he was terrified and guessed why.

'It was you, wasn't it?'

'I...' He dropped his head.

'Why would you do that, Gary?'

His head was shaking slowly but he didn't reply.

'You see how that looks, don't you, Gary? Jasper's missing and you're making sure that no one's worried. It might suggest that you had something to do with his disappearance...'

'No!' The tears were back, as was the vehemence. 'I thought he'd gone off with Axenfeld or Bright ... I thought he'd be back in a day or two ... he still might be. I didn't want him to get into trouble, so I made out that he was sick. I've done it before.'

Which was entirely feasible, but she wasn't

about to let him know that. She said nothing for perhaps twenty seconds, content to scrutinize him while he sat in front of her, head in his hands. Eventually she stood up. 'Thanks for your time, Gary.' Her tone was soft but that was just a cloak for uninterest. Gary had given her all that he could for now; he had therefore to be discarded, at least for the time being. Compassion was nowhere to be seen.

They left Gary in the office, still crying and walked through the ward. The charge nurse was exchanging persiflage with an elderly lady, perhaps Mrs Muckle, newly invigorated by Gary's attentive care. In the corridor she said to Richardson, 'So tell me what you think.'

He pulled his thoughts together. 'Well, he's obviously pretty cut up about it.'

'Do you believe him about the phone call?'

'It's possible...'

'So you think he's got nothing to do with Jasper's disappearance?'

He sensed that she was baiting a trap. 'I think we should talk to Stephen Bright first.'

She nodded. 'Without a doubt. If Gary's telling the truth, it sounds fairly odd, this story of someone whom nobody knows walking off with Jasper.'

'Do you think he's dead?'

She said at once, 'Oh, yes. The only question is who killed him.'

SIXTEEN

It was Arthur Sutton's first day back at work and his colostomy still wasn't working properly; his recovery from the cancer operation had only just been completed when he caught some sort of gastric flu and had suffered terrible diarrhoea. The colostomy had leaked as a consequence and even now its contents were still liquid and horrible, little more than slurry.

He hated the colostomy as much now as when he had first been alert enough to be aware of it on the day following his operation. It wasn't even as if he would ever see the back of it. It was as much a part of him as his fingers or his nose, an atrocious disfigurement that he could never forget. Moreover it wasn't the only carnage reaped upon him, for he could not wipe from his mind the knowledge that his arse was now ineradicably sewn up, even if this indignity was not quite as visible as the bag.

He *missed* sitting on the toilet and straining.

A part of him recognized that he was displaying monstrous ingratitude, scolded him for not living every day happy to be alive, savouring every extra hour. He had received a reprieve from cancer, one that would have killed him, they had said, within three months; even if he would not receive the final all-clear for some years, he had at least been given a stay of execution. He ought to have been exultant.

Exultancy, however, was a difficult, distant prospect on a wet and surprisingly cold summer's evening, the remaining daylight still little more than a leavening of the night's darkness. Arthur did not enjoy his job of 'security guard', a title that he knew was modern gilt applied to the age-old profession of 'nightwatchman'. He had to put on a stupid uniform made of heavy navy blue cloth that chafed around the back of his neck, and he was forced to wear a peaked cap that made him look like a traffic warden; the whole outfit smelt of stale fat and cigarette smoke, odorous relics of its previous inhabitant. He also had heavy shoes, provided by the firm, that were curiously uncomfortable, large areas of his feet apparently floating in the foetid air inside them, supported by tight pressure points that were painful when he donned the bloody things at four in the afternoon, and that became white-hot needles of agony by the time he was halfway through his shift.

His patch was the light-industrial estate just off the Swindon Road in an area known as Swindon Village. Perhaps it had once been a village but now that was a gross misnomer, a wilderness of warehouses, superstores, fast-food restaurants and industrial units bordered by vast housing estates that harboured a continuous supply of anti-social behaviour and outright crime. He spent his working night wandering around a large number of car-body-work specialists, plumbers' merchants, builders' merchants and other small businesses while on the horizon electronic superstores, DIY stores and furniture warehouses formed the most obvious sentinels of an endless vista of concrete that had obliterated the small piece of green and pleasant land that had once existed there.

It was no great surprise to discover the slightly opened door at the back of Walker and Son, Wood-turner and Carpenter. Probably twice a day he came across some sign of forced entry or mindless vandalism; not infrequently he discovered the results of a robbery, perhaps even a ram-raid. On two occasions he had interrupted the crime; the first time he had, against company orders, intervened and received for his efforts a sustained beating, six weeks off work and a severe reprimand from his boss. The second he had zealously followed standing orders, retreated over the road and phoned the police. On both occasions the thieves had escaped.

He might well, therefore, have noted it down, walked past and, at a safe distance, reported in to the office.

He didn't, though, because of the blood smeared on the door. It formed a curious, almost hypnotic pattern, one that was slightly eerie, might almost have been a picture, although a picture of what he could not say. The heavy rain of the night before had faintly splashed it but had not been able to get directly at it because of the wide overhang of the roof and because the high piles of palettes on either side had sheltered it. Arthur Sutton was not a devotee of abstract art but this particular example spoke to him.

He walked forward into the gloom between the palette towers then stood and listened, hearing nothing, not even the scurrying of rats. He switched on his torch and saw a deformed parallelogram of dusty floor through the narrow gap in the doorway; the darkness to either side and beyond was ominously black, a sheet on which his mind drew imagined monsters. Trying to keep as quiet as possible he stepped to the door, away from the gap, and knelt down.

Was it blood? Or was it paint?

Whatever it was there were drops of it on the doorsill.

He reached out with his fingers and brushed it lightly. He put his hand up before his eyes and rubbed reddened fingers and thumb. It was sticky and cold, just like paint but, when he tentatively sniffed them, he knew that it wasn't something he would ever want to see on the walls of his house.

Now was the time to turn and walk away rapidly, bypassing the office to talk directly to the police. Follow protocol, perhaps do someone some good. It was straightforward really. So why did he first hesitate, then put his hand high up on the door, avoiding the blood?

He pushed gently...

...the door didn't move.

Certainly he should have walked away then, could never have imagined a situation in which he wouldn't. Except that he didn't.

With thoughts of countless, cliché-packed horror films raining down upon him he pushed harder. The door moved slightly, then moved back. It was a soft, only slightly elastic resistance without accompanying sound; it was a silence that menaced him as it taunted him.

Perhaps it wasn't human blood. Perhaps it was a dog or something.

He pushed the door again, was disappointed but not surprised that once again there was soft-spoken opposition.

Then why was it so high up the door? Bloody big dog...

He shoved back, really hard this time and whatever it was gave way, at first with a rustle, then with the sound of something falling.

Something big.

This time the door didn't attempt to return to its starting position and he could make out the room in greater detail. A few empty metal shelving units, decaying cardboard boxes, dust; inexplicably there was a legless and bald shop dummy lying on the floor. Its right arm was stretched out to him as if it were beseeching him, as if it were the source of the blood, and it had died in the darkness of this place, alone and naked.

If only.

He was nervous now. Griping pains were gnawing at his belly, stabbing into the colostomy. He had never known anything like it before and he wondered if this were a new sensation that he would have to learn to live with. He stepped inside, his foot immediately finding broken glass that crunched oh-so-loudly inside the room, as thunderous as a gunshot inside a metal drum. He froze, not consciously but simply unable to move; God had decided that he should stand there, half inside the room, the door still hiding what was behind it. He made use of this paresis by listening, hearing nothing except the ongoing, almost echoing crack that would not die in his head.

Eventually he took a deep breath and found that he could once again move.

Surely there's nothing here ... It's not really blood ... Behind the door, it's just more boxes ... Probably filled with mouse droppings and chewed paper.

He had almost convinced himself that normality had not switched off, that he would in a moment be on his round again, calling in to report the unsecured premises, when he cleared the door and saw in the half-gloom the toppled body of Billy Whipple, the blood making a hole of blackness underneath him.

SEVENTEEN

Pittville in the early morning was, as it had always been, pleasant. Even the weather could not erase its pleasantness. Joseph Pitt's ideal town, where pleasant people lived in pleasant surroundings, pleasantly ignoring the world around them, had remained pretty much pleasantly intact, except for the fact that it was growing unpleasantly smaller. Cheltenham Spa was no longer a living and breathing spa, its waters were now a minor player, its bathing pools as dry as an old lady's skin; the Pump Room was an artefact of a bygone age, still as beautiful but now held in aspic, a place to visit for a concert, a wedding reception, a place in total contrast to the modern world that surrounded it. Even the parkland that rolled away and down from the Pump Rooms, tree-dotted and seemingly always verdant, was somehow a thing of the past, as nostalgic as it was attractive.

Bright, it transpired, lived on the ground floor of a large detached house now converted into six flats. The front garden had been turned into a cramped car park with a brick enclosure for dustbins. When she and Sam emerged from the car and looked up at the house before them, Beverley saw stately elegance; elegance, moreover, that had been carefully groomed and nurtured. The whitewash on the walls was fresh, the paintwork around the windows bright, the windows regularly cleaned.

Richardson said wryly, 'Not exactly on the breadline, I'd say.'

'I wonder what Mr Bright does.'

'Makes money, at a guess.'

'A lot of it.'

It looked like the kind of place where rising young executives, perhaps in the media, perhaps in property development, might return at night to measure just how high they had risen *that* day. They walked up to the large, brightly green and newly painted front door and Beverley said, 'You start the questioning.'

He was surprised but, she saw, pleased.

Beverley had half-expected Bright to be out, earning that week's million or cutting a deal to consign a dozen orphans to the poor house, but he answered the doorbell at once, dressed rather strikingly in a short gown of crimson silk. He was undoubtedly good-looking, perhaps thirty or thirty-five, with extremely short blond hair and dark, dark eyes above a square jaw. It was clear that he worked out, making a statement with his body; to whom he was making it wasn't entirely clear. His eyes as they appraised first Beverley and then Richardson signalled no obvious preference. *Maybe,* thought Richardson, *he doesn't distinguish.*

The only blemish that he sported was a rather corking black eye; one that looked to be

111

a day or two old, for it was starting to turn from blue to green at the periphery.

'Mr Bright?'

'Yes.'

They showed their warrant cards, which he barely bothered to read. 'What is it?'

'May we come in?'

He hesitated. 'Why?'

A lot of people were like this. It didn't necessarily mean anything. She explained patiently, 'Because we'd like to talk to you about something and we'd rather not do it in a public place.'

And still he hesitated until there came a shrug and a dismissive, 'If you must.'

The flat was neat and elegant, and the external impression of opulence continued in the lounge, which was spacious, high ceilinged and beautifully furnished. They sat around a highly polished wooden coffee table, their spectral reflections deep within the dark brown wood aping them as they talked. 'We're looking into the disappearance of Jasper Fitzroy-Hughes.'

Bright raised his eyebrows but this was clearly a response born of etiquette rather than deep concern at this news. 'Hasn't he come back yet?'

'You knew him, I understand.'

'Hardly.'

'But you invited him to a party here.'

'I invited sixty people to a party here. It doesn't mean I was "best friends" with all of them.'

'So what does "hardly" mean?'

He was leaning back in his chair, one arm over its back, one hand playing with a golden, perhaps gold, cigarette lighter. His whole attitude was one of supreme confidence. Beverley found herself speculating what he had to be quite so irritatingly confident about. He said, 'I met him out clubbing. Seemed a nice kid.' He might have been describing a stallion seen at the horseflesh sales.

Beverley suddenly interposed. 'This is an exquisite house, Mr Bright. What do you do for a living?'

'Antiques.'

She smiled. 'There's money in antiques.'

'If you know where to find it.'

'And you do?'

He didn't bother himself trying to find a verbal reply. Instead, he got up and went out into the kitchen. As he walked back through the doorway, he threw something small at her that she caught. It was an emerald brooch; old and beautiful and heavy, as in heavy with wealth.

She said as she examined it, 'It's beautiful.' It was, although she would rather have stuck a spike deep in her ear than wear it.

Bright was sitting back down. 'I bought that for twenty-five pounds. I will sell it for three thousand.' He smiled. 'Yes, I know where to find it, Inspector.'

She was about to hand it to Sam, but as she held it out, Bright abruptly stood up and grabbed it from her. He said smoothly and with a wide smile, 'Thank you, Inspector.'

The silence that followed was slightly embarrassed and into it, Beverley said, 'So which demented old lady did you defraud to obtain that, Mr Bright?'

His smile was far too strong to succumb. 'As with all of us in the antiques trade, I do house clearances. The unspoken contract is that the householder knows that he or she may be giving away something valuable, but can't be arsed to sift through it all to find it; I'm the one who *can* be bothered.'

Sam said, 'For which you get paid.'

Bright shrugged. 'Nine times out of ten, I sift and I get sweet FA. Things like this brooch are rare and precious.'

It was Sam who brought the conversation back to relevant matters. 'So you met Jasper out clubbing. Which club?'

He frowned. 'The Senate, I think.'

The Senate was a gay club. Richardson enquired, 'What happened then?'

At which Bright smiled. 'Did I bed him?' He almost laughed. 'No, I didn't. I had a few drinks with him, we exchanged numbers, then we went our separate ways.'

'Did you meet again before the party?'

'Nope. When I thought about having the party, I came across his number. Rang him up and invited him.'

Once more Beverley interrupted. 'Do you have parties often?'

For reasons not quite clear to either of them, this seemed to disconcert him. 'Not very, no,' he said after a brief but noticeable pause. She nodded, her expression one of understanding acceptance of this answer.

Once more Richardson took up the cudgels. 'We've been told he left with someone called Ray Axenfeld.'

'I think so. I certainly saw him talking to him.'

'Tell me about Mr Axenfeld.'

Abruptly Bright said, 'I'm being a poor host. Can I get you some tea or coffee?'

Richardson didn't even look across at Beverley. 'No thanks. About Mr Axenfeld.'

Bright, who had begun to rise, sat back down. 'He's a friend.'

'Where does he live?'

'Couldn't say.'

'What does he do for a living?'

'Don't know.'

Richardson was genuinely surprised. 'He's a friend but you don't know where he lives or what he does for a living?'

'You don't understand my way of life, do you, Sergeant?'

It was Beverley who said, 'Tell us, then.'

'Ray and I go clubbing together. There are no ties, no questions asked. We enjoy...' it was with a knowing smile that he elided slowly '...each other.'

If he had hoped to embarrass them, he had chosen the wrong police officers. 'But he has other friends? Who would know how we might find him?'

'I really couldn't say. I'm not trying to be difficult, Sergeant, but that's not the way it works, you see.'

Beverley sighed. 'But he appeared, as if by magic, at your party. We know that he talked to Jasper – who else did he talk to?'

'I really couldn't say. The duties of a host, you know.' But they didn't know.

'OK,' said Richardson patiently, 'presumably amongst the sixty people present at the party there were at least a few who knew the elusive Mr Axenfeld.'

'Possibly.'

Beverley leaned forward. 'I think you should find a nice clean piece of paper, Mr Bright, and a nice antique pen. Then I think you should list for us the names and, where you can, addresses of every single person present at the party.'

'What, all of them?'

'Absolutely every single one of them.'

He didn't look happy; indeed, for the first time he appeared distinctly sour. Beverley's impression was that a mask had just been lifted. 'Why?' he demanded.

'Because Jasper Fitzroy-Hughes has disappeared and his father is a very important man who wants him found.'

'Important? Who is he?'

'Senior civil servant.'

'How senior?'

It was clear that his interest had been tweaked for the first time. 'Very.'

And with the interest came something else. He said thoughtfully, 'Oh.'

'Does that make a difference?'

He shook his head. 'No. Should it?' But for

some reason they both saw that it did. He fetched the paper and a decidedly unantique pen in a much more subdued mood.

Suddenly the door to the living room opened and in came a squat, large-breasted girl of about seventeen. She was wearing a very short, very lightweight wrap-around gown and yawning. When she saw Beverley and Sam it made no difference at all. 'You didn't wake me,' she said to Bright.

He looked up from his labour. 'Business, darling. Not now.'

'But...'

'Why don't you make me some coffee, eh, sweetie?'

She hesitated, then nodded as she left the room. Bright caught the glance that Sam and Beverley exchanged, then smiled. 'I told you that you didn't understand my way of life.'

Sam said in a monotone, 'Clearly not.'

When Bright had written down perhaps forty names, not all with contact details, he slid the paper over the table's surface at Richardson.

Richardson perused the paper, the neat handwriting. 'Is that all?'

'I exaggerated. It must have been fewer than sixty.'

'And the ones without addresses or phone numbers or emails?'

He shrugged. 'Like I said, sometimes it's pretty casual.'

For the first time since they entered, Richardson glanced at Beverley. It was she who made the decision. Standing up abruptly, making it plain that she wasn't satisfied, she said, 'Thank you, Mr Bright. That'll be all for now.'

He was back to his charming, oh-so-confident self. 'Glad to be of help.'

He walked them to his front door. Before she left, Beverley said, 'By the way, Mr Bright, could I have a business card?'

His smile broadened and thinned. 'I don't use them.'

'Then what name do you trade under? You do have a shop, don't you?'

'I'm a middle man. None of the overheads of the retailer.'

'Really? So how do people contact you?'

It was obvious really. He said simply, 'They know where I am.'

He had thought that the interview was over but Beverley enjoyed disconcerting people like Bright. Before he could shut the door she asked suddenly, 'How did you get the black eye, Mr Bright?'

Taken aback he said after a moment's hesitation, 'I tried to "get to know" someone at a club. Their partner objected.'

'Did you fight back?'

He shook his head. 'I got what I deserved.'

They left him and walked back across the parking area to their car. Sam said to her across the top of the car, 'He's up to his neck in it.'

She nodded, but then asked, 'But in what, exactly?'

They drove out into the road, turning right to head for the town centre. 'Check every name on the list, then check Mr Bright. Find out everything about him, right down to his make of underpants.'

'Calvin Klein, at a guess.'

They had nearly reached the ring road before she spoke again. 'He was worried when he found out what Jasper's daddy does for a living. I wonder why?'

Then the message came through. A body had been found in a warehouse in Swindon Village.

EIGHTEEN

Whatever Eisenmenger had experienced last night, it could never be described as 'sleep'; it was somewhere between stupor and fugue, a strange distortion of melancholia, a flight of ideas, of fancies, of nightmares. Had his eyes closed? He could not say and realized that he had lain there in that hideous spare room as if in an isolation tank, deprived of normal sensory inputs, his mind occupying itself with phantasmagorical hallucination.

Yet, incredibly, Eisenmenger's mobile phone somehow managed to wake him from unconsciousness. It had reached its third warble before he found it, switched it on and clamped it to his ear. 'Eisenmenger.'

A voice he did not recognize said, 'Dr Eisenmenger? My name's DS Richardson.'

Eisenmenger looked at his watch. He found

to his incredulous shock that it was eleven o'clock. 'What is it?' He asked this although he knew exactly what it was.

Good God. So soon? I only agreed to do this a little over twelve hours ago.

'I've been told you're the on-call pathologist.'

'Yes.'

'A body's been found, sir.'

And so it starts again.

He was aware that his perceptions were distorted by tiredness and the lateness of the hour, but this did not help. He was immersed by impressions and emotions he could not control, transported back five years. It might almost be that he had awoken from an elaborate dream, that his life with Helena had been nothing more than a fantasy, that Marie – the girl he lived with before meeting Helena – might only just have killed herself. 'Where?'

'On an industrial estate in Swindon Village.'

Eisenmenger looked at his watch. He heard a fine drizzle pattering against the glass of the window.

I thought I'd left this behind.

He knew that it was illusional but he appeared to have the scent of burnt flesh in his mouth; it was human flesh, Tamsin's, the little girl who died in his arms, who made him think that he did not want to do this any more. He said, 'I can be there in forty minutes. Where do I go?'

He was given an address, noted it down, then sighed. 'OK.'

'Very good, sir.'

He got out of bed, afraid to hesitate, feeling stiff. Having dressed quickly, he called the department and told them that he would not be in until early afternoon, then opened the door and moved out into the hallway. He was almost out of the flat when he heard Helena open the door to the sitting room. He turned, thinking immediately that he should not have done. She asked, 'What's happening?'

'Sorry,' he said. 'Work.'

Why am I apologizing?

She frowned with uncertainty. 'You're doing forensic work?'

'A little sooner than expected,' he admitted.

'But I thought you said you didn't want to do it.'

'I don't.'

With which he turned and stepped out into the corridor, shutting the door behind him.

She remained standing staring at the front door for a few seconds. When she turned away and went back to her bed, her face was fixed although her eyes were wet.

'Well, well. Billy Whipple. Whipple by name, whippet by nature.'

Richardson looked up at her from his crouched position by the body. 'You know him?'

'Billy's a valued customer, a regular patron of the criminal justice system.'

'Not anymore.'

She knelt down beside Richardson, careful just as he had been not to touch anything. 'No,' she sighed. 'Not any more.'

'Stabbed,' observed Richardson, somewhat unnecessarily. Beverley didn't comment, merely nodding slowly. Billy's brilliantly repulsive yellow leather jacket was now covered to a large extent with blood and dirt; it didn't help his colour-coordination, but then it didn't make it too much worse either. 'From the blood on the outside of the door, it looks as though he came in here to hide, presumably because he was being chased.'

Still Beverley didn't speak, staring intently at Billy's pallid, lifeless face, now given to her in profile.

'Inspector?'

She responded but only slowly. When she looked across at him Richardson asked, 'Are you all right?'

She nodded. 'I know his mother. Lovely old lady; lived for him. Relied on him for everything.'

'Oh.'

She took a deep breath through her nose then she stood up, looking around the room. The only illumination was from a torch held by a uniformed constable and a large electric lamp on the floor by the body. 'Can't we get some better light in here?'

'It'll be here shortly.'

She didn't acknowledge this assurance, merely holding out her hand imperiously for the constable's torch then, when he had surrendered it to her, proceeding to examine the murky corners of Billy Whipple's last resting place. Richardson asked, 'What was his trade?'

Without turning around she said, 'Anything and everything that was pathetic and illegal. Poor Billy was a foot soldier in the ranks of the criminal fraternity, a grunt, nothing more. He started out by shoplifting sweets, CDs, computer games and cigarettes, then moved on to "twocking" before trying his hand at burglary, which was when he finally ended up inside for a while.'

'The usual career progression, then.'

'If you can call it a career, or even call it progression.' She continued to poke into dusty, dirty shadows. 'What was this place?'

'Used to be a carpenter's, but it's been empty for two years now.'

Her attention was at that moment caught by something for she paused and then reached into the pocket of her suede blouson, bringing out a pair of disposable plastic gloves that she put on. Then she stooped and reached down behind a filing cabinet, producing as she straightened up a syringe that she held carefully between forefinger and thumb. She murmured, 'Well, well.'

Richardson went across to her, producing from his pocket a thick, clear plastic evidence bag that he held open. As she dropped it in he asked, 'You think that this is drug-related?'

She made a face. 'Billy never dealt as far as I know, but who can say? If he thought he could make money and thought there was no risk, he'd have had a go at anything.'

As Richardson sealed the bag she returned to

the corpse, looking down on it as if in judgement and peeling off the plastic gloves slowly. 'My God, the poor little bastard must have been blind as well as stupid if he thought that jacket was a good idea.'

'Perhaps he was murdered for crimes against fashion.'

No one laughed.

Without another word she went outside; when Richardson followed her she was examining the blood staining the outside of the door.

'As you say, this suggests that he used this place as means of escape, presumably from whoever stabbed him. That would mean that the syringe is irrelevant.'

'Unless he'd used this place before, perhaps to cut a few deals out of the sight of prying eyes.'

'Then why stab him out here? Why not in the privacy and darkness of the warehouse?'

'An argument, perhaps.'

She chewed this a while, then decided that she didn't like it. 'Too much speculation is bad for the digestion. Until we've had a proper forensic and pathological examination we don't know anything. We don't know if it was a single stab wound or if he was in a fight. We don't know if he had drugs on him or in him, if he was robbed or just murdered for the hell of it.'

A decrepit black BMW pulled up at the kerbside about twenty metres away and from it emerged a familiar figure.

She was surprised, relieved too. 'John?'

He nodded in acknowledgement but his face did not change at all. The word 'Beverley' was uttered cautiously and his eyes looked at her, but they were imprisoned by the set of his face, held hostage by something, warned not to communicate. She frowned, aware as surely as if she were telepathic that he was in some sort of pain. She asked, 'It's been a while. How are you?'

'Fine.' The word was a down beat and, moreover, a full stop. *I don't want to go there*, it said. 'You've got a corpse, I understand.'

He was brusque, businesslike, sending out messages that the lines of communication and interaction were to be defined only by him and there would be no tolerance of transgressions. She made a point of eyeing him carefully before saying neutrally, 'He's in there. Billy Whipple, ex-petty criminal.' She gestured with her head, placing her hands firmly in her jacket pockets. 'We need to exclude a drug connection and we need to know how much of a struggle there was.'

Eisenmenger nodded, said in a business-like manner, 'I'll see what I can do.'

Richardson nudged her. A tall van had drawn up and two women and one man were stepping from it, going around to the back. 'Forensics,' said Richardson unnecessarily.

'About bloody time.'

'Traffic, I expect. They've got most of Princess Elizabeth Way dug up again. It's making chaos during the school runs and at rush hour.'

Beverley had no interest in school runs. 'Whatever. I want the entire area searched for bloodstains. I want every building checked and any occupants interviewed. Get a statement from the man who found him – what was his name?'

'Sutton.'

'Yes, him. The nightwatchman.'

'Security guard.'

She laughed. 'Oh, yeah. Silly me.' She began to walk off as, over her shoulder she called, 'And then we'll have the pleasure of attending the post-mortem.'

'So I get all the good jobs.'

She paused and turned, smiled. 'Just think how good all this will prove for your education.'

He failed to look appreciative. 'What are you going to do?'

'To tell an old woman the worst news that she can possibly be given; almost certainly to destroy her world and very certainly to shorten her life. Do you want to swap?' He shook his head. She added more gently, 'And after that, I've got some personal business, but I'll try to get back for the autopsy.'

NINETEEN

Dressed in clean fibre-free overalls and disposable theatre-style cap, Eisenmenger spent a long time just standing over the body, looking down on it, conceivably even praying over it, since he was heard to mutter occasional words and phrases, although what they were could not be determined. Richardson watched him from a safe distance, saying nothing, interested in how he approached his task. He had now had the chance to observe a clutch of pathologists at their work and he was becoming impressed by the degree of variation they displayed. Charles Sydenham performed for an audience, assuming a persona that fooled no one; he wanted all to know how intelligent he was, all to bow down before the weight of his intellect, yet consistently failed to achieve this. In contrast, Derek Browne, who presented a character that was completely genuine and, at the same time, completely repulsive, did manage to impress with his insight and professionalism; he was an ursine man who dressed shabbily, indulged publicly in some of the grosser human habits, and thought there was nothing so funny as wolf-whistling some unlucky female passer-by. There was also Lauren, a small, nervous young lady who seemed to have brains but no confidence and who looked, moreover, as if she had meant to go into poodle-grooming but ticked the wrong box on the university application form.

Eisenmenger, though, was new to him, although he had heard something of his reputation. *A maverick*, was the majority opinion, although one or two of his fellow officers used the rather less diplomatic words *Fucking weirdo*. Beverley had occasionally mentioned him, usually when Sydenham had cocked up either by omission or commission, and John Eisenmenger's name was evoked in angry questioning of the gods about why they had taken against her and why they could not have sent her a decent pathologist to work with.

Richardson's immediate impression was that Eisenmenger was closer to the *fucking weirdo* end of the spectrum than the *maverick* end. His scrutiny was so intense, he seemed to be not so much assessing the body and the scene as sucking it in, hoovering it up, excoriating it. There was a degree of concentration that approached meditation, that had something religious in its fervour. Richardson had never seen this before and, indeed, was slightly disturbed by it. Most pathologists – and most professionals involved in a murder – were either clinical and cold about it, or they were flippant, or they were somewhere between the two. This callousness was their defence because people who were affected by the crimes that they investigated were not going to survive long; Eisenmenger, though, seemed to be very deliberately immersing himself in the death of this weak and pathetic human being, perhaps even immersing himself in all death. Richardson could not imagine that such behaviour would lead to a long and healthy mental life.

Eisenmenger suddenly seemed to come back, to surface, not breathless but appearing almost disconcerted. He looked up at Richardson. 'Where's the photographer gone?'

'Awaiting your instructions.' Richardson turned to a constable, ordered him to find him.

For the next thirty minutes, Eisenmenger directed a pictorial record of the body's position and state, including all the bloodstains and smears on and around it. He was most interested in Billy's face, with photographs of every aspect taken at every angle. Throughout all this, Eisenmenger radiated an almost fanatical concentration on the task before him, something that did not even dissipate when he thanked the photographer and looked up at Richardson. 'Right, I'm done. When forensics have finished, the body can be moved to the mortuary.'

Richardson nodded but Eisenmenger had already turned and was walking away from the sordid deathbed of Billy Whipple.

TWENTY

'Hello, Jean.'

'Inspector Wharton!'

She knows.

'How are you, Jean?'

'My legs are awful, but I get by.'

Beverley watched her eyes flit between the faces of her visitors, watched also the suspicion feeding beneath the surface. She hoped desperately that Jean Whipple would meet her at least some way along the road, that she would already have considered the worst.

She must know why we're here. Of course she knows. Why also would I have a uniformed female PC with me?

'May we come in?'

She hesitated as if to refuse would keep the tragedy at bay, out of the house; although it was a tragedy that was as yet unreal because it was unrealized in her head, the shadow of it was still clearly unsettling her. Beverley stepped inside and from her position by the door Jean Whipple said, 'Go into the sitting room.'

The house was small and in reality there were few other places to go unless they climbed the stairs to the bedrooms and bathroom.

Beverley's chosen companion for this task

was Melanie Bruton, small and brown-haired and, importantly, possessed of a remarkably passive temperament. Another asset, given that the situation was one requiring at least sympathy if not empathy, was that she had somehow managed to retain her compassion for members of the public despite all that the citizenry insisted on throwing at the police. She followed Beverley into the small and crowded room, sitting on one of the dining chairs against the wall by the window; Beverley sat on the small two-seater sofa. Jean Whipple hobbled in after them, supporting herself on an aluminium frame, and asked, 'Would you like a cup of tea? I was just about to make one.'

Beverley didn't like telling an old lady that their only son had been murdered and she didn't like tea either but she said that, yes, she'd love some.

And we'll put lots of sugar in yours, Jean. You're going to need it.

'Bruton will make it, Jean,' she suggested, casting the aforementioned a look that she should jump to it. Bruton stood up and played her part. 'Oh, yes. I'll make it. You sit down and talk to Inspector Wharton.'

They might just as well have told her there and then. She complied without arguing but, as she sat down in her customary chair, her demeanour was one of complete deflation, total loss. Beverley waited until Bruton was busy in the kitchen, crockery making a discordant melody against which she began her performance. 'I'm here about Billy.' She heard

131

her voice sounding soft and sad despite strenuous efforts to resist displaying too much pity too soon.

The old woman nodded calmly. She had put her legs up on her footstool and Beverley noticed that the bandages were just beginning to show orange-brown staining where something was seeping through. There was a smell in the room, age and damp, but also something more unpleasant, something suggesting rottenness and infection.

'I thought you were.' Beverley began to believe then that her task would after all be easy, that Billy's mother really had anticipated her news and already started the long, perhaps never-ending road to acceptance, but the old woman's next words punctured that hope, left it dying, leaking its goodness into the old dusty carpet at her feet. 'He's in trouble again, then.'

Beverley heard the kettle beginning to boil, a busy wet roar, while cupboards were opened and searched in the quest for teabags and teacups. For a moment all she could think of was her own mother, how so much like Jean Whipple she was, how so much unlike too. She thought of Jack, thought that there were parallels here that she did not wish to explore.

She shook her head, her eyes on Jean Whipple, her mouth just a solemn line as she prayed that this sickening old woman would recognize the signals, that she would recognize that it was useless to continue this pretence, that ultimately the real world would break down the door and shout in her face. But Jean Whipple wasn't looking at her; looking *towards* her, but not *at* her, seeing nothing with eyes that were already as open as they ever would be. 'What is it this time? Nothing serious, I hope.'

Under other circumstances – those perhaps that didn't involve destroying someone's life – she might have entered into deep discussion concerning what, exactly, Mrs Whipple regarded as 'serious' and what, therefore, she defined as 'non-serious', or possibly 'trivial'. Presumably Billy's habit of taking cars without the owner's consent (in the current jargon, 'twocking' but basically just good old theft and criminal damage) and his later forays into the world of burglary were, in Jean Whipple's considered view, mere trifles, paltry misdemeanours indicative only of a playful, perhaps impish disposition.

'Jean...' She tried to put as much meaning into the name as she could, to make it not so much a name as a plea – *Pay attention to me.*

At last the old woman heard. Her expression, until then one of slightly cheerful politeness – as one might adopt at a party or a reunion – became suddenly still, suddenly serious, and she looked directly at Beverley; it was as though she had come out from behind a screen and Beverley had the impression that now she was seeing what had been there all along, hidden by optimism. She held the old woman's gaze as she said slowly, 'Billy's dead.'

She supposed that she could have dressed it up, prolonged the path to this terrible truth, but she saw no point; Jean Whipple would have to come to it eventually, stare at this uncaring, cruel and ultimately implacable monster and no amount of dancing around the fact, pulling her gently along would make it easier on her in the end. Jean Whipple continued to stare, her expression completely unchanged, almost as if she had become temporarily paralysed or mesmerized by Beverley's low tone and the constant rumble of traffic that underscored the gentle ticking of the clock by her side. Then she nodded, an acceptance that what she had feared but never dared articulate had come to pass.

Bruton came in then, an old wooden tray topped with Formica in her hands, carrying three cups of tea and a bowl of sugar. The china was old and cheap, reminding Beverley once again of her mother because in her memory she had used the same crockery as a child; inescapably Jack's image followed. Bruton set the tray down on the sideboard and put one of the cups down on a little table beside Jean Whipple just as the old woman asked, 'How?'

Beverley waited before replying, accepting a cup from Bruton and wondering how she would answer. When her words emerged she hated them but they were all she had. 'We think he was attacked. Probably stabbed.'

As if this piece of information was the one thing that was intolerable, that the fact of his death was bearable but the manner of his death beyond the pale, it was then that she began to cry and with the tears to collapse, to age, perhaps also to slide closer to death. Then came the crooning; not loud but all the more unsettling because of it. She began also to shake.

'I'm sorry, Jean. I really am...'

Of course she was sorry. Sorry to be there, sorry to feel as if she were somehow personally responsible, as if her words had been just as damaging as the blade that had released Billy Whipple's immortal soul from its fleshy tabernacle. Perhaps also, if she searched hard and long, truly sorry for Mrs Jean Whipple, widow and now robbed of a son.

Bruton had come to the old lady and perching on the arm of her chair had put her arm around her small, bone-filled shoulders. While Beverley watched as if a group of strolling players had come to give her a private performance of some obscure drawing-room tragedy, Bruton murmured words of solace and bade the old woman to drink her tea. When she did eventually pick up the saucer it shook so much that Beverley watched drops fly from the surface and land on Bruton's uniform.

Beverley said, 'Is there anyone we can call, Jean? Someone who can come and make sure you're all right?'

She stared at her, incomprehension again having taken her prisoner, until Bruton repeated the question. She shook her head uncertainly.

'No one at all? A neighbour, perhaps?'

She started to shake her head once more, then stopped and thought. She turned her face up to Bruton, as if she had adopted her as the main source of comfort, Beverley merely a tributary. Almost sheepishly she said, 'Mr Raman?' It was as much a query as a suggestion. The tears had inflamed her eyes, brought out the yellow flecks and engorged the cracked and broken veins.

'Where does he live? Next door?'

'He's the newsagent. He's a lovely man ... only I don't want to bother him...'

'I'm sure it won't be a bother to him, Mrs Whipple. When you've had your tea, I'll nip out and get him to come and see you as soon as he can.'

She nodded, still uncontrollably lachrymose but now the tears were unnoticed, being content to trickle away silently. She sipped her tea and then, with Bruton's help, had to put the cup down to blow her nose on a tissue that she found, crumpled and ragged, down the side of her chair.

Beverley said, 'You go along to the newsagent's, Constable. I'll stay with Mrs Whipple for now.'

Bruton nodded, gave Jean Whipple a final hug that was returned with a tremulous smile, then left. The front door had been closed barely a minute before Beverley said gently, 'I'm going to find out who did this, Jean.' The old woman had taken up her tea again, still shaky but less violently so. She stared at Beverley over the cup as Beverley continued, 'But I'm going to need your help.'

'What am I going to do now?' This was not asked but implored; she needed an answer because within her there was nothing except, possibly, paralysing terror. 'Billy looked after me; he was the best son a mother ever had.'

Whole books could have been written about the curious dichotomy between what Beverley thought of Billy Whipple and what his mother clearly did, but it would have been empty, brittle speculation. Now, Beverley could only stare at her with a single certainty – that she had just been asked a question to which she would never have the answer. She regretted sending Bruton off and with this came shame that she could not cope with this situation. She had known it would be bad – how could it not be? – but her imagination had let her down, had failed completely to envisage the sheer God-awfulness of it.

Reluctantly, almost as if driven by unseen forces, as if the goddess of pity had possessed her body and was contracting some muscles, relaxing others so that she was forced to move, to do *something*, she rose and went to this lonely, destroyed old woman and, ignoring the odour of infected, decayed ulcer flesh, she crouched down in front of her and took her hand. The skin was damp from her weeping yet still as dry as bleached vellum; the bones were like partridge bones, ready to snap if merely pressed, the veins grey, fat and sluggish.

'You've got to cope, Jean,' she whispered, 'Because you've got to help us nail the bastard who did this, because Billy didn't deserve what happened to him. I knew him, remember? He wasn't a saint, but he wasn't up for damnation; not yet, anyway.'

These words were as close as she could come to compassion, at the edge of the territory she could allow herself, verging on sentiment. She thanked God that they had some effect. The tears hadn't stopped and if anything they came more freely, but they came from a face that was more set, that had lost that vacant look of unalloyed despair. Jean Whipple nodded.

Beverley smiled encouragement. 'Good. Now, try to remember. The last time that you saw him, did Billy tell you where he was going? Was he going to meet someone?' Inevitably, the last words that she had heard her son say were that he had been going down the pub. It was a perfect, if trite, epitaph.

'Which pub?'

'The Three Tunnes. He always drinks there...' She hadn't realized that she had used the wrong tense but Beverley wasn't anywhere near pointing this out. 'It's in the Lower High Street, I think.'

Beverley grimaced. 'Oh, I know where it is,' she said quietly. Every police officer in Gloucestershire knew that particularly insalubrious den of unsober inequity. More thieves, stolen goods and nefariousness flowed through it than did lager and cider combined; whatever you wanted could be purchased there, strictly cash terms only, no receipt and no guarantee, these transactions being conducted around the back in the car park. 'Don't take this the wrong way, Jean, but was Billy into anything heavy?'

'What do you mean?'

'Like ... drugs?'

'No! Of course not! Billy was a good lad. He would never have got involved with that kind of thing. It's a nasty, dirty business.'

Strictly 'nontrivial', then.

'And has he been troubled recently?'

This made her think. She finished her tea although Beverley could see from the skin on the surface that it was now cooled to room temperature, an unpalatable concoction now made totally vile. Then she said, 'No, I don't think so...'

'Has anyone ever threatened him?'

At once she said, 'Oh, no. Not Billy. Everyone loved Billy...' But the words were no longer the sole object of her attention and they trailed off into sulky silence, sidelined by a star-bright memory that had burst upon her. 'Spud!'

If Beverley thought at all that Jean Whipple was throwing syllables at random, or that the torment of grief had led her to recite slang names for vegetables, the impulse was brief to the point of non-existence. She knew the name 'Spud', knew it very well indeed.

'Spud Carney?'

'That's him. Nasty, vicious boy. His whole family's got a reputation.' This was said as if a reputation were akin to the pox or a habit of incest.

Beverley, however, had to agree that Mr Carney was something less than the ideal citizen. He was big; big on fat, big on meterage and big on bullying. Vicious would not be an unwarranted adjective to use. She could easily imagine him delivering a fatal stab wound, but not one to one. He would mount such an attack only if the odds were heavily in his favour and the wind in the right direction; a few friends would have to be involved. His political philosophy tended towards the Mongol Hordes end of the spectrum when it came to sorting out little local difficulties. She asked, 'Did he say what it was that he had against Billy?'

'He said that Billy had tried to steal his girlfriend. He actually said that he was going to kill him.'

Beverley found all this very interesting, her hope of a quick end to the case rising. The great majority of attacks such as these were unpremeditated and due to drink or drugs or both – usually turf disputes, the turf being anything from a girlfriend to a pitch for a burger van – and almost all the rest were so poorly premeditated they were to all intents and purposes mindless. This made it easy; find the last one to have an argument with the deceased, or the one who gained the most, and there you were. Spud, therefore, replete with suitable criminal form, vicious temper and witnessed threats, might have been picked from a box of prefabricated parts labelled *The Ready-Made Perpetrator: Easy to Assemble*, with a small disclaimer underneath; *Warning – composed of small pieces on which a small child may choke.*

Bruton returned. 'Mr Raman's coming as soon as his wife returns home from work.'

Jean Whipple asked of neither of them and both of them, 'Who's going to get my pension?'

140

For the first time Beverley appreciated that she had brought to the old woman not just the loss of her only son but also the loss of her only means of support, that she was now limbless in the world.

Bruton said with a reassuring smile, 'We'll tell the social services. And your GP. Don't worry, Mrs Whipple, you won't be alone.' But all three of them knew that she would be, that she would be alone even if she were to stand in the crowd at the FA Cup Final, or to be surrounded by a billion carers, supporters, neighbours and friends. She would be alone now until she died.

Beverley, though, still had a job to do. 'I know that it's bad timing, Jean, but I need to look through Billy's things. See if there's anything there that might help me.'

She nodded at once, joining in with the spirit of the request. 'His room's first on the right up the stairs, next to the bathroom. I'd go with you, only my legs...'

'Don't worry, Jean. I'll find it.'

As she stood and left the room, Jean Whipple called after her, 'Don't make a mess. Please...'

Beverley paused. 'Of course I won't.' She smiled reassuringly.

But amongst the detritus, the pornography and the unwashed and unironed clothes, amongst the pieces of a life lived with no hope and little expectation, amongst the whole of the last estate of William Whipple, she found absolutely nothing of use.

It was a fitting epitaph.

TWENTY-ONE

'Sergeant Richardson? A word, please.'

Except it wouldn't be just one word and those words that Lambert employed wouldn't be pleasant, or easy-going, or friendly or ... well, Richardson could have inserted any one of a thousand adjectives that implied positive or companionable qualities into this list of exclusions. Richardson stood up from his desk where he had been compiling the reports that had thus far accumulated concerning the thoughts and memories of those who worked in the premises around and about the scene of Billy Whipple's exit from the corporeal realm (and which amounted to little more than nothing), and followed Lambert without a word.

When Richardson had joined the police force five years before, it had only been after much thought. He had just come out of the army, a five-year spell in which he had seen action in the Balkans and in Iraq, in which he had seen a mass grave and one of his comrades blown apart by a landmine; often in the darkness when it was quietest and when his mind had cleared of all its present-day concerns, the vision of Corporal Andy 'Knucklehead' Nuck came back to him at the moment when he ceased to be; then he saw in his memory (a false memory, the psychiatrist assured him, as if that mattered a fuck) the actual split second as the blast carried before it Knucklehead's legs, thrusting his torso upwards like an ungainly rocket destined never to reach the stars. And then he would come to from his slumberous state, so wide awake he might never have known what sleep was like, Knucklehead's dismemberment frozen at a point just too late to save him.

His time in the army had taught him about prejudice, too; he'd become something of a postgraduate student in it. All sorts. He'd seen class prejudice, gender prejudice, racial prejudice; prejudice because of age, because of body shape, because of education, because of the size of genitalia. Some showed it overtly – gloried in it, wore it as laurel wreath, a sign of belonging to a tribe – others only let it slip occasionally, in the odd remark, the slightest gesture. A small minority had subsumed it completely and, in a feat of psychological gymnastics, had managed to face in completely the opposite direction.

Lambert, he saw with perfect clarity, was one such. And even if he wasn't the swastika and knee-in-the-testicles type, he was no less pernicious for it. He believed that he was perfectly fair, perfectly adjusted, perfectly liberal in his views and the actions that flowed from those views, yet he was a racist. Not a supremacist, perhaps, but most definitely not blind to colour. Richardson's first day in the station had been marked with a peculiar interview with Lambert during which the Chief Inspector had made it plain that Sergeant Richardson was a tender shoot and Lambert was the horticulturalist who was going to nurture him. This, of itself, might have been fair enough had Lambert not then gone on to explain – obliquely, using nods and winks rather than relevant words and phrases – that the reason he was receiving such loving attention was because of his colour; Lambert the horticulturalist was tending a black orchid, unique because of its colour, but nothing else. Lambert clearly did not consider this to be wrong, although Lambert's whole demeanour told Richardson that if he had been unfortunate enough to be born a little more albino he would have been left to sink or swim according to ability, like everyone else. Richardson had remained silent whilst this self-righteous manure had flowed past him, just about hanging on despite a current strong enough to loosen his grip on taciturnity and leave him swirling about in eloquent denunciation of Lambert's hypocrisy.

'You've been assigned to work with Inspector Wharton...' He said no more but said this as if it should mean something to Richardson, but it didn't. Seemingly this was a black mark against him for Lambert breathed out noisily and went on to explain, 'She's trouble, Richardson. You'll hear all sorts of gossip about her and, for once, most of it's probably true. She's a bad copper and if it had been up to me you'd have been kept well away from her, but it wasn't up to me.' *And it bloody well should have been,* his words seemed to imply. 'So we've got to make the best of a bad job.'

Richardson watched Lambert and saw a man who was obsessed although with quite what he couldn't say. Clearly he disliked – hated, perhaps – Inspector Wharton, but Richardson sensed that it was deeper, or broader (or perhaps both deeper *and* broader) than that. Lambert seemed to see hostile intent wherever he looked, seemed to be a man besieged by enemies. He was tall and angry-looking, beginning to go not just bald but thin; a smile on Lambert seemed as unwelcome as one on the face of the Grim Reaper.

Richardson didn't think that it was particularly professional of Lambert to wade in on one of his fellow officers before Richardson had even found his desk or locker. He asked innocently, 'When you say "trouble", sir, what do you mean?'

'She's lazy, son, and I strongly suspect that she's corrupt. She's not a team player.' He paused, then leaned forward. In a lower voice he said, 'Also, she's *easy*.'

He resumed a more perpendicular posture and Richardson raised an eyebrow. He thought that he knew what Lambert meant by this bisyllabic hiss, but didn't dare request clarification, opting instead for the time-honoured, all-things-to-all-superiors knowing nod. This produced a satisfactory response when Lambert continued, 'You can't rely on her, so be warned; her junior colleagues have a habit of ending up hurt in some way.'

Richardson had raised his eyebrows at that one. 'Hurt, sir?'

'Not physically,' he was reassured. 'But they seem to become somehow *expendable*.' Keen as he was to find out more, Richardson was not given the chance for Lambert had moved on to another aspect of Inspector Wharton's behaviour. 'I'm afraid to say that she's effectively slept her way up the ranks, and I can't stand that. It makes my stomach heave, son. If you can't get anywhere by hard work and brains, you shouldn't be in the job.'

Richardson mumbled something that might have been agreement as he wondered how Lambeth squared this with his attitude to the special treatment he was meting out to Richardson. Lambeth then proffered more advice, as unwelcome as the rest. 'Be careful of her. Learn by watching what she does and then doing the opposite. That way you'll make something of yourself.'

As if this weren't bad enough, Lambeth's next conversational gambit left him slightly light-headed at its implications. Once more departing from the vertical and inclining towards the oblique, Lambeth said, 'In fact, you'd do yourself a power of good if you were to observe Inspector Wharton and remember what you've seen, if you get my meaning.'

Five minutes before and Richardson might not, but Lambeth's objectives together with his motive and means were by now uncovered to the point of obscenity. He wanted Richardson as a spy in the camp, a snitch, literally a copper's nark. At once Richardson found himself in a difficult and dangerous position. If he refused he would make an immediate enemy and a powerful one, moreover; if he acquiesced he would be doomed to the perilous, twilight world of the informer. He felt as if he were balancing on a pinnacle while having epileptic fits.

But life in the army was not so different to life in the police and he had learned the art of diplomacy when dealing with those who wielded power. He said easily, 'I have a very good memory, Chief Inspector.'

Lambert hadn't smiled at this verbal ambiguity, but he had quite noticeably eased in his attitude. A gruff nod was the closest he had come to joy unconfined.

Some weeks later, when he related this conversation to Beverley as they lay in the bath together, she had laughed harshly. 'My God! He's really desperate to get me, isn't he?'

'Doesn't it worry you? That he's so hostile?'

She had leaned forward to reach for her wine glass, causing the water to swirl around them. 'He's not the first, Sam.'

'Even so, I should watch your back.'

'And he should watch his.' She had terminated the conversation with her fingers and it had all seemed so easy.

But now he stood before Lambert once more and he was faced once more with the ramifications of duplicity and distrust.

'Where's Inspector Wharton?'

Richardson knew better than to give Lambert Gospel. 'I'm not sure, sir. Possibly she's grabbing a bite to eat in the canteen.'

'How are you getting on with her?'

'OK, sir.'

Lambert pursed his lips, staring hard at him. 'Tell me what your impressions are of her.'

Richardson was wary of that one; it smelt of trouble. 'I haven't noticed any gross dereliction of duty. As far as I've been able to tell, she's done everything by the book.'

Lambert's expression suggested that he didn't believe this and that he was therefore suspicious of Richardson. He said in a menacingly soft voice, 'I've heard rumours, Sergeant.'

Richardson knew what was coming, had been preparing for it. He replied blandly, 'About what, sir?'

'About you and her.'

Richardson knew that if he didn't lie well now, he'd do himself considerable damage. He frowned, wondering whether it would be better to attempt incomprehension or outright denial. 'That's crap, sir. Complete and utter crap.' A nicely judged pause before, 'Sorry about the language, sir.'

He studied Lambert, wondering if had made the right decision and if, having done so, his performance had passed muster; he saw that Lambert, too, seemed to be in the act of making a judgement and they were held in thrall to each other for a moment. After the world around them had breathed normally for several seconds and he and Lambert had held theirs for several hours, Richardson was informed of the jury's decision.

'Glad to hear it.'

Richardson knew better than to relax visibly. Instead, using old military tactics as he advanced on the retreating enemy with increased vigour, he said, 'It's prejudice, sir. The people who are spreading these rumours are trying to get me into trouble.'

For just a second he wondered if he had over-egged the recipe, for Lambert seemed to see something in these words that he didn't like, then he said slowly, 'Maybe you're right, Richardson.' Richardson saw that the notion grew in appeal to Lambert; it lent support to his concept that Richardson was a lesser being who therefore needed that little bit extra in the way of patronage. If Lambert had his way, Richardson would probably have been made his personal assistant.

It was with a slightly less belligerent air that he asked, 'How's the Fitzroy-Hughes case coming on?'

Richardson explained their progress to date. 'He seems to have disappeared after a party on Friday night, sir.'

Lambert had obviously been taking an interest in the case for he was right up to date with the daily reports. 'What about this friend of his – Gary Allen. Is he kosher?' 'Kosher' was a word that Lambert had taken to using a lot of late. 'I understand there might have been homosexuality involved.'

Richardson had the impression that in Lambert's world view this was not a nice thing to have involved in something. 'We haven't yet found out, sir. The Whipple killing this morning has taken priority.'

Clouds gathered with remarkable alacrity on Lambert's already unattractive features. 'It shouldn't have done,' he snapped. Richardson's moment in the sunshine hadn't lasted long.

'But surely...'

'But surely nothing, Sergeant. The despatch of some low-life like Whipple shouldn't be at the top of anyone's list of priorities; whoever did it has done us all a favour.'

Richardson found himself unable to resist putting the counter-argument. 'A murder's a murder, sir. We can't rank them...' He was not, however, to be given the time to develop his thesis before an ominous and very red light flicked on.

'Listen, Sergeant, take some advice. This is the kind of thing that I told you about. Wharton's a poor copper and this shows it. No judgement. I told her to prioritize the Fitzroy-Hughes case.'

'That was before Billy Whipple was stabbed to death. We don't even know for certain that anything suspicious has happened to Jasper Fitzroy-Hughes.'

'And the sooner we find him, the less likely it is that something will. Whipple's dead; if you do your damnedest to find him, hopefully the same fate won't befall Fitzroy-Hughes, which will make everyone happy, including me.'

Richardson was on the point of digging his grave even deeper, then caution and common sense took hold. He filled his lungs with air, then breathed slowly out and suggested, 'Well, it looks as though the Whipple case is fairly straightforward, sir. Stabbed to death following some sort of dispute. We've got a name in the frame already.'

Lambert grabbed this eagerly. 'There you are, then. Get the suspect in and wrap it up ... but don't forget the priorities.'

'No, sir.'

Lambert nodded, apparently pleased that he managed to pull Richardson back on to the path of true righteousness, away from the wilderness that Beverley Wharton and her attitudes represented. He said, 'OK, Richardson, you can go.'

Richardson left the office, feeling at once angry and amused, relieved and anxious.

TWENTY-TWO

'Hello, Mum.'

For a second it seemed that her own mother would fail to recognize her, a supremely ironic judgement on her performance as a daughter, but then Pamela Wharton's eyes widened and she said, 'Beverley?'

It was posed as a question and it seemed to

Beverley that the tone was partly wonderment, partly uncertainty. The facial expression was similarly a mix, although this one of joy and of reproof. It had been a long time since Beverley had made the journey to the south coast. 'May I come in?'

Yes, she could come in, but there was a distinct lack of enthusiasm. Now that the initial and all too fleeting pleasure had gone, her mother seemed to be left with nothing more than many months' worth of accumulated anger at apparently being abandoned by her only daughter.

Beverley's initial conversational gambit was, 'It's been a long time.'

'Fifteen months.' At least, Beverley reflected, she hadn't added in the odd days, hours and minutes. '...Give or take.' This was added with a nose that was slightly elevated, a mouth that was ever so slightly turned down at the corners, a tone that was excruciatingly forgiving.

Thanks.

Beverley's strategy to deal with this obstacle was one she had used on numerous occasions before; she chose to ignore it. 'May I sit down?'

Her mother was overweight, always had been. In later life she had been dogged by bad health – first heart failure, then emphysema, lately an underactive thyroid – and Beverley could not help but feel that she was reaping the harvest of obesity. Every meal she forewent, every time she had salad instead of chilli, all the sessions in the gym, there was at the back of her head a picture of her mother, a mantra that repeated endlessly – *I will not become like my mother.*

'Of course.'

She sat on the old sofa that she knew so well. It was a part of her history, that sofa, a constant that stood battered but unbeaten by time's corrosive passage.

A drink would be nice. Nothing too demanding … perhaps a cup of tea … I'm not asking for a complex cocktail, nothing requiring a degree in bartending.

Her mother sat opposite her, in the armchair that she had always occupied, the one that faced the television to Beverley's left. Beverley had never tried to sit in that particular chair – no more would she have dared to usurp the Queen – and she wondered if, had she tried, it would have rejected her by a biological as much as emotional mechanism.

'How are you?'

Her mother shrugged. 'Not too bad.'

'Is your breathing OK?'

'I had a chest infection last November. Had to get antibiotics.'

'But you're all right now?'

'Oh, yes.' Beverley heard the accusatory subtext as clearly as she heard the words – *What do you care?*

'Have you heard from Jack?'

'He phoned me a week ago.'

This surprised her into silence. She had assumed that he would maintain radio silence as he had intimated to her. She asked cautiously, 'Is he well?'

'He didn't say that he wasn't.'

Oh, well. Couldn't face it, eh, Jack? Bottled out at the last moment, did you?

She wanted then to tell her mother – it was why she had come, although she had not admitted as much to herself until now – but it was suddenly beyond her. An embarrassed silence followed, ended by her mother who asked cruelly, 'So, to what do I owe the pleasure?'

'What do you mean?'

Her mother snorted. 'I don't see you from one year to the next. Why have you decided to come to see me now?'

'Do I need a reason?'

It wasn't fair that the response to this was, 'Yes, you do.' What made it worse was the tired scorn in her voice; it made Beverley feel small again, small and guilty.

She swallowed. 'Look, Mum, I know I haven't come to see you as often as I should...'

'You've hardly come at all.'

'I know, I know, and I'm sorry.'

'You couldn't even be bothered to send me a present last Christmas.'

'I did. I sent you a gift token.'

'Oh, yes. I'm sure you put a lot of thought into that.'

Her contempt was finely judged. Beverley sighed, tried to suppress her rapidly increasing anger, said, 'Look, I'm here now, aren't I?'

Her mother considered this, a judicial pose. She nodded eventually but it was a meagre thing, grudgingly given. Beverley said, 'It's

154

your birthday soon. Perhaps you could give me some ideas for presents.'

This was greeted with a slightly more gracious nod, although nothing in the way of practical assistance in the task. Then, 'How are things going with your job?'

Her mother had not approved of her career choice but it had seemed to Beverley at the time that she had not approved of anything she had done.

'Not too bad.'

'No more trouble?' By which she meant no more 'demotion'.

'No, no more trouble.'

She lapsed into silence, then perhaps to relieve the embarrassed silence she asked at last, 'Would you like a cup of tea?'

'Yes, please.'

She had trouble getting up and Beverley had to help her, and felt even guiltier. *She won't be here forever.* She followed her mother out to the small kitchen that was filled with memories for her – the old dresser, the cooking knives with their cracked bone handles, the horrid tea strainer that was a souvenir from Great Yarmouth. Beverley picked this up idly as her mother filled the kettle; wondering why on earth anyone would want to remember Great Yarmouth; amnesia seemed to her to be a better option.

Her mother said, almost to the cold tap, 'He's ill, isn't he?'

'What?'

She took the kettle to the gas ring (she had

always refused to use an electric kettle, just as she refused a microwave oven and a dishwasher), said to it, 'Jack's ill, isn't he?'

'How...?'

At last she turned to Beverley. On her face was a look of worry. 'I'm not stupid, you know, Beverley. I may be old, my body might be slowly dropping to bits, but I haven't lost my marbles yet. Jack's no better than you when it comes to keeping in touch, but suddenly he rings up out of the blue. "Just a chat," he says, but I could hear something in his voice. He was making small talk but that was just to stop talking about something else. He sounded tired, too.

'And now you turn up and I stopped believing in Father Christmas and his little elves a long time ago.'

The kettle was starting to growl and Beverley had nowhere else to go. She nodded but said nothing, staring intently at her mother.

'What's wrong with him, Beverley?'

'Hepatitis.'

She frowned. 'That's the liver, isn't it?'

Nodding she said, 'An infection.'

'But he'll get over it, won't he?'

'It's progressed to cirrhosis.'

She saw shock on her mother's face. 'Oh, my Lord,' she said. Beverley saw her face turn suddenly grey, her lips blue. She began to sway and Beverley had to step forward, take her arm. 'Here, come and sit down. I'll finish the tea.'

She led her back to the sitting room, then

returned to the kitchen, where the kettle was now boiling. She had trouble finding the teapot but the tea was still where she remembered it; there was only full-fat milk in the fridge – her mother had never been one for healthy eating – which made Beverley shudder as she put it in the cups. Having sugared her mother's she poured in the tea, then took them into the living room. 'There,' she said. Sitting back down, she asked, 'Are you all right now?'

Her mother nodded but she didn't look anywhere near well. When she picked up the cup, there was a slight tremor. She sipped at it although it was quite obviously going to be too hot. The cup went back down with too much of a bang. She asked, 'Cirrhosis. That's drinking too much, isn't it?'

'Not necessarily. Bugs can cause it. That's what's happened to Jack.'

She nodded but it wasn't obvious that she was overfull of comprehension. She considered things before, 'But he'll be all right, won't he? They'll give him drugs – antibiotics – and make him better?'

'I don't know, Mum.' She didn't know; she dreaded but she didn't know.

The tea was tried again but it was proving stubbornly heat retentive. 'That's what they'll do. He'll be all right.'

Beverley picked up her cup of tea but the minute fat globules on the orange-brown surface proved an effective deterrent to consumption. Her mother was running through things, rehearsing her optimisms. 'They can cure so much these days ... I watched a programme last night about a boy who was born without a face ... the surgeons gave him one. It was amazing!'

'Was it?' Beverley found the thought of watching such a programme about as appealing as the tea.

Suddenly, 'How did he get it?'

Beverley knew what she meant but she still played dumb. 'Get what?'

'That disease. How did he get it?'

'I don't know, Mum.'

More deep considerations.

'I saw this programme' – of course she had. Her mother lived her life through the cathode-ray tube; it was a life informed by the box, circumscribed by it and effectively ruled by it – 'that said that only gays get hepatitis.'

Beverley couldn't stop herself. 'For Christ's sake, Mum. Jack's not gay!'

Her mother was obdurate. 'Then where did he get it?'

And Beverley's only answer was a confession of ignorance as she insisted stubbornly, *Jack's not gay.*

She could see clearly, though, that her mother was thinking other thoughts.

TWENTY-THREE

Another day, another death, another post-mortem. To Beverley, a veteran of such circuses, this was no different to any other; she was inured to the sights, the sounds, the smells; she heard nothing new when the pathologist talked of contusions, lacerations, penetrating wounds, displaced fractures; she had come to find the evidence that was on display of the worst of human excesses to be tedious. Eisenmenger didn't help either. He had never had a good line in banter but today he wasn't worth the price of omission; the silence became so dense, so suffocating that she even found herself yearning for a bit of Sydenham-like behaviour. Charles Sydenham might be prone to error and an arrogant bastard, but there was a certain amount of amusement to be had in watching him; he was a frustrated Barnum of the dissection room, delighting in grotesquerie; he wanted everyone there to applaud him, to best all those around him; he wanted to exhibit himself as the star performer, the only one in the room who was indispensable. Only trouble was, he was slapdash; he was so dedicated to amazing his audience, he not infrequently forgot to do the job properly. All mouth and star-spangled trousers was the good Dr Sydenham.

Richardson had asked on their way to the mortuary at Cheltenham General Hospital, 'Is he really any good?' His tone suggested that he would not be able to believe an affirmative.

'Oh, yes. He'll tell us what we need to know, and he won't miss anything.'

'He seems a bit morose.'

She had responded, 'He does seem to have something on his mind,' she agreed, and didn't add, *I'd quite like to find out what.*

Eisenmenger appeared, dressed for action and trailed by Carter, the mortuary technician. He was a small man who managed to survive without the bother of combing his hair in the morning and who had given many hours' employment to tattooists both professional and amateur over the years. Despite the appearance, Beverley knew him to be really rather an excellent mortuary technician, one of the kind who were indispensable, as opposed to the other sort, who were as expendable as toilet paper. Eisenmenger disappeared through a doorway on the far side of the dissection room leaving Carter to make such arrangements as arranging the dissection instruments, zeroing the electronic scales, giving the knives a final sharpen.

Beverley asked Richardson, 'How's it coming with Mr Bright and his party guests?'

'Dempsey and I have managed to talk to about half of the ones for which I've got details, and they've all so far checked out. It's the ones who are just names that bother me. It's going to be tricky to get any further with those.'

'Convenient, perhaps.'

'They can't all be involved with Fitzroy-Hughes' disappearance.'

'No, but I bet there's at least one, maybe two, who are. The others are just on the list to cloud the issue. You're asking everyone about Mr Axenfeld?'

'Yes, but no success yet. One or two of them think that they might have heard the name, but no one can actually tell me anything about him.'

'And Mr Bright?'

'No bad odours so far. I've run him through social security, National Criminal Records, Revenue and Customs.'

'Check with the fences – lean on them. Also check with some legit antiques dealers, see if they've ever heard of Mr Bright.'

'Right.'

As Eisenmenger re-entered the room, so too did two members of the scenes of crime team, each with a camera; into the viewing gallery came Chief Inspector Lambert.

Richardson stood up, Beverley didn't. Lambert sat beside her and said, eyes on Eisenmenger, who was dictating into a microphone that hung down above the corpse, 'Don't bother sitting back down, Sergeant.'

Richardson, who was in the process of doing just that, paused, looked for a second uncertain, then straightened up. He left the viewing gallery without a further word; Beverley didn't show any reaction at all. Eisenmenger had made Carter turn the body so that Billy Whipple's back could be examined and photographed.

'Where were you this afternoon?'

'Talking to Billy Whipple's mother, and making her day and mine simultaneously. A jolly time was had by all.'

'It took you a long time. You didn't come back to the station.'

'I didn't feel I could rush it. I don't know why, but I thought telling an old woman she's just lost the only one in the world who ever cared for her, that she was now going to go to her grave alone, sort of merited a bit of due diligence, a bit longer than a brief call and a breezy, "Oh, by the way... "'

Lambert, still refusing to look in her direction, saw Eisenmenger talking with Carter although the conversation was largely lost through the window. He said, 'You're wasting too much time on this.'

She turned to look at him, to stare at him. For a long while silent she then asked, 'Too much time on murder?'

'That's what I said.'

'Have I missed something? I know we don't make much effort on minor things like property crime, but I had sort of assumed that was so we could give the murders, rapes and assaults a decent go.'

And still he wouldn't look at her; Eisenmenger was measuring the hole in poor Billy, wiping away the blood, directing photographs both before and after his cleansing; it was interesting, but it wasn't *that* interesting. Lambert licked his lips as she stared at him and for the first time she saw that he was under strain, that he wasn't enjoying what he was doing.

He murmured eventually, 'This is nothing. A useless little man, killed for drugs by another useless little man. A minnow eaten by a carp; dog shit consumed by a fly.'

'Do you know something I don't?'

'You have another theory? There was evidence of drug-taking where he was found, wasn't there?'

'Yes, but that doesn't mean anything. If he'd been found in a bus shelter, would you assume that his killer was a bus conductor?'

'Don't be flippant, Inspector.'

'And how do you know that it was a man? You don't need a Y-chromosome to stick a knife into someone.'

'I understand that a man – Spud Carney – threatened him.'

'Almost certainly he threatened him *after* Billy died.'

'So?' This was a challenge, not a question.

'If he knew Billy was dead, why pop round to his Mum's and make silly threats?'

'A double bluff. Everyone will think he must be innocent if he threatens Billy's life when Billy's already stoking the fires of hell.'

This was so preposterous she had trouble keeping her contempt in check; when her voice came back to her it bulged dangerously with scorn. 'Such a fiendish game of bluff and double bluff doesn't sit easily with your "fly feeding on dog shit" hypothesis.'

Lambert's face became set, an expression she was quite used to witnessing usually, as now, at close quarters. 'Have you located Mr Carney yet?'

'Not yet. He's gone to ground.'

'I want him found by the end of tomorrow; I want him charged with murder and then I want you back concentrating on more important matters.'

She asked with a trace of a sneer, 'Such as the Fitzroy-Hughes case?'

He became even stiffer. Out of the corner of her eye she saw Eisenmenger beginning the first incision in Billy Whipple, his scalpel at the Adam's apple. She didn't want to watch him slit Billy open but neither did she want to stare into the less than loving eyes of DCI Lambert. He said slowly, coldly, 'If you fuck the Fitzroy-Hughes case up, Inspector Wharton, you're finished. Not even you could shag your way out of that one.'

He's definitely under stress. Just as he's putting the squeeze on me, someone higher up is putting the squeeze on him.

'How, precisely, might I fuck it up?'

'By not finding him ... by finding him too late.'

It's too late already. To Lambert she said only, 'I won't fuck it up.' She heard confidence in the words that belied her concerns.

He was silent for a moment. Billy's tongue,

never a particularly well-controlled organ, now hung rather incongruously outside the mouth to the left of the throat. He said eventually, 'That's good.'

He relaxed at last, drew back slightly, then nodded. Through a deep sigh, he murmured again, 'That's good.'

He sounded as if he were trying to reassure himself; trying and not quite succeeding.

TWENTY-FOUR

She found Richardson in the mortuary office, on the phone. He was listening to someone, not speaking; he watched her as she began opening drawers of the filing cabinet and the desk, the doors of a cupboard. She found what she was looking for on a shelf behind a copy of *Gray's Anatomy* that must have been at least forty years old.

It wasn't the best whisky but it was good enough.

Richardson said, 'OK, well, keep an eye on the house but keep looking ... try all the pubs, and try the hospital.' He put the phone down, all the while looking at her. 'It's a trifle early for me, in case you were offering.'

'It's not mine to offer,' she pointed out.

'Which begs the question of why there's a bottle of whisky hidden in the mortuary office.'

'Carter likes a tipple. It doesn't make him a bad man.'

'And what about you? I don't recall you needing liquid elevenses before now.'

'Circumstances alter cases.'

'Lambert's got to you.'

'Just a little.'

'Why? What did he say?'

'He pointed out that I had my priorities all wrong. Seems that it's obvious that Spud Carney killed Billy Whipple, so why don't I spend twenty-five hours a day looking for lost little rich boys?'

'He made much the same point to me this afternoon ... after he'd asked about certain rumours he's heard.'

She laughed sourly. 'I hope you put him right.'

'I think so.'

She nodded, whispered, 'Good,' as much to herself as Richardson.

'He might have a point, though,' ventured Richardson. 'I can't believe this is going to prove to be the crime of the century.'

'He also pointed out that the only outcome that wasn't going to burn my tail feathers was a reunion between Jasper and his loving Mummy and Daddy.'

'Maybe that's what's going to happen. You're not always right.'

How very true. The problem was that somehow she knew that this time she was spot on. Jasper Fitzroy-Hughes had managed to get himself entangled in something. She didn't know what – she didn't know how she knew – but she *knew*. Bright was involved ... she'd come across his type before, the kind of man who had power and knew, moreover, how to wield it. It wasn't the power that corrupted; more often it was that the corrupted sought power.

She said, 'Maybe.'

Richardson didn't press the point. There was silence for a moment before she asked, 'Who were you on the phone to?'

'Dempsey. I've left him trying to find Carney.'

'And?'

'His parents swear blind that he hasn't been back home since yesterday evening, but they've refused to let Dempsey in to verify that without a warrant.'

'The Carney family being the solid upright citizens they are, I'm very surprised to hear you say that.'

'I'd bet a lot of money that he's there, but we can't do much more at the present. Another possibility is his workplace. There's a lot of places to hide in a hospital.'

'A lot of places to obtain drugs, too. Make sure that Dempsey checks up that there have been no restricted drugs going missing of late.'

Richardson made a note of this. 'You think it was Carney, then?'

Did she? She wasn't sure ... or rather she was sure that whatever Lambert might want to believe, Carney wasn't going to be bright enough or subtle enough to misdirect everyone by threatening to kill Billy after the event. Carney already had sixty-seven convictions, mostly for petty theft and minor crimes against the person; he was a prime candidate to kill someone in a fight and then run away, but not one to think of complex bluff and double bluff, to play mind games with the police.

The consequence of that was that he must be innocent ... but at least she wanted to talk to him first; she wasn't about to make assumptions about his lack of culpability without gathering all the evidence and sitting down with him for a few hours of good, old-fashioned questioning. She said noncommittally, 'I don't know.'

More silence before she looked at her watch. 'Eisenmenger's going to be at least two or three hours more. There's no point in both of us hanging around here. First I'm going to have another chat with Gary.'

'You think he might be involved after all? How?'

One of the many things that Sam had yet to learn about solving crimes was that making theories came a long way behind asking questions. Her reply was heavily sarcastic.

'I think, Sam, that he might be able to help me understand either what happened, or how it happened, or – if I'm lucky – both.'

She saw anger pass across his face like a passing train in the distance. When he replied there was no trace of irritation but she didn't doubt that it was there, caged and hidden. 'Of course. I shouldn't have presumed...'

She didn't want to hear him apologize. More softly she said, 'Then, I think I'll go and try my luck with the Carney family; see if they'll be more amenable to the feminine touch. Failing that, we'll have to find a friendly magistrate.'

TWENTY-FIVE

Gary Allen was not at the hospital and so she went to the house. She was surprisingly undelighted to discover that she still had the chance to win fabulous prizes at the bingo and there was perhaps a touch more guano on the statue (although not enough to make a material difference); no one had emptied the dustbins and the gardener hadn't called. She rang the doorbell and waited. An old woman wandered by, presumably on the way to the supermarket but not in so much of a hurry that she didn't have time to slow right down and stare at Beverley with an expression that could have been the result of interest, could have been the result of psychosis. The evening was far advanced, almost ready to lose the fight with night, and it was growing cold.

Eventually the door opened and Gary peered out; he was bleary-eyed, unshaven, dressed only in a shabby black dressing gown of something that was probably meant to pass for silk but looked to her eye more like unwashed poly-ester.

His face changed when he saw who it was. 'Oh.'

She could see that he was caught between hope and dread, between the desire to ask if she had news and the terror that she might. She said at once, 'I need to ask you some more questions, Gary.'

He nodded, mouth open, stood back with the door open so that she could enter.

The interior was a striking contrast to the environs. Neat, clean and carefully furnished, there had clearly been a lot of thought put into the decoration; all the more so because she suspected that it had been done on a budget. No two pieces of furniture matched but on the whole was good; only emulsion had been used on the walls but it had been used well; there was a scent of cleanliness wherever she went.

He led her into the kitchen which was small and painted in bright primary colours. 'Coffee?'

She said that she would, then, 'Did I wake you?'

'I'm on nights.'

'Sorry.'

'No problem. I should be getting up anyway.' He began searching around in cupboards. 'I'm afraid we've only got instant.'

So was she but said bravely, 'Fine.'

As he spooned brown granules into two mugs she asked, 'Late night?'

'You could say that.'

She waited until the boiled water was going in before she asked, 'So you're not missing Jasper, then?'

The reaction was sudden and loud and fairly expressive as the kettle was slammed down on its stand and he hissed at her, 'What the hell do you mean by that?'

She saw the tears in his eyes, knew at once that he hadn't killed his boyfriend, but before she could say anything more he said angrily, 'I've spent most of my waking hours looking for Axenfeld, if you must know.'

She ought to have felt shame but there was only professional interest.

'Did you find him?'

'No.'

'Did you find anyone who knew him?'

He had turned back to the coffee, was stirring it disconsolately. 'I found people who'd heard of him, but no one who knew him.'

Which she found interesting of itself. He asked, 'Milk and sugar?'

'Nothing, thanks.'

He presented her with her mug as if she'd won it as a prize, then indicated that she should sit at the breakfast bar that projected from the wall.

'Tell me about Jasper.'

He stirred into his mug both milk and sugar then remained standing by the kettle. His description came quickly as if rehearsed. 'Jasper was pretty wild. Full of anger and full of happiness. He was either laughing fit to bust or ready to kill.'

Perhaps that's what happened; perhaps he killed someone and has gone to ground. 'And on the day that he disappeared? What was he full of then?'

His answer was simple. 'Both, as always.'

Thanks, that's really helpful. She asked, 'Would I be completely barking to suggest that maybe Jasper didn't get on with his father?'

Gary took his time taking a drink of his sweet white coffee. 'I'm probably not the best person to ask to judge.'

'I can't think of anyone better at the moment.'

It took him a moment to see the point, then said thoughtfully, 'Jasper fell out with his father about four years ago and I suppose he never really fell back in.'

'Why?'

This was greeted with scorn. 'Isn't that obvious? Do I really have to tell you?'

Well, actually, he didn't. 'You mentioned something about him having gone off before...'

He shrugged.

'Tell me about it.'

'It never meant anything.'

She suggested, 'Tell me anyway,' as she wondered what his problem was.

More coffee and perhaps with it an infusion of courage. 'He was a romantic. He'd meet someone, fall head over heels in love, then get over it. That's all.'

'And this would only last a couple of days.'

'Usually.'

'Usually? Does that mean it ever lasted longer?'

He hesitated, as if this were painful. 'Once.'

'How much longer?'

'A month.'

While she absorbed this he added, 'He was older. Jasper met him when he came in with a kidney infection.'

'Did you know where he was at the time?'

'No.' It was clearly painful for him. There weren't actually tears in his eyes and there wasn't a catch in his throat but he had become repressed, his speech clipped.

'Who was this man?'

'Hertwig. Emmanuel Hertwig.'

'Where does he live?'

'Cirencester.'

'Do you have his address?'

'He's not involved. I rang him.'

'All the same ... if you don't mind, Gary.'

He wasn't keen but he found it for her. He insisted. 'Look, believe me, Hertwig's not involved in this.'

'Just because he tells you he's not, I'm afraid I can't just take his word for it, Gary.'

He shrugged. *Have it your own way.*

She finished her coffee, aware that he had something more to say. She liked silence, she decided; it had far more power to make people speak than did a rubber cosh. He said eventually, 'Jasper's a fantasist.' This pronouncement was made as if it were the same as being an onanist or a polygamist.

'What do you mean?'

'He tells people what they want to hear.'

She didn't understand and he had to add, 'In

173

social situations.'

It was the emphasis that did the trick. 'For sex?'

He nodded. 'His usual story is one of destitution – how nobody loves him, how he's all alone, how he's just looking for love. It turns some people on. That's how he got Hertwig.'

She felt as if a whole new world was being unfurled for her perusal. 'He gets a kick out of this?'

'So did Hertwig; so did the others.'

'Others?'

'Like I said, they were only one-night stands. He always came back.'

'When he went off, did you know where he was? What he was doing?'

A sour look on his face as he nodded. 'Oh, yes. He made damned sure I knew what he was doing.' The picture that was developing before her was very different to the one that she had hitherto assumed. He insisted, 'But this time there's been nothing. That's why I know there's something wrong.'

'But you didn't contact us. You left it to his mother.'

The briefest of pauses and then once more he began to cry. It was only after a few seconds that he could speak. 'I only wanted to show that I could cope without him! I thought he was just being a bitch, trying to punish me, trying to make me look a fool in front of other people.'

He weeps well. Perhaps too well...? A thought occurred to her. 'What about S and M? Was he into that?'

His reply was immediate. Through a runny, sniffling nose he said, 'No.'

Was it too immediate? 'And you used to let him do this? Run off with other people?'

His head dropped and came back up before he said as fiercely as his tears would allow, 'I didn't *like* him doing it – I hated it – but Jasper was Jasper. Sometimes he found me...' His shoulders went up then down again quickly. 'Boring.'

It was clear that he considered this an insult beyond compare and she felt sorry for him but she felt sorry for lots of people and didn't think it fair to single just one out. He was weeping again as she said in a businesslike tone, 'Well, thanks for the information, Gary. I'll let you know if anything turns up.'

He showed her out, barely speaking as he did so, his eyes downcast.

She hoped that the conversation had done her more good than it appeared to have done him. At least she now felt that she had a better idea of Jasper Fitzroy-Hughes than hitherto, although she seriously doubted whether this new information was in any way relevant to why he had disappeared.

TWENTY-SIX

'Good morning, Mrs Carney.'

'He's not here. I told the other one. Haven't seen him since yesterday.'

It was dark and cold and Beverley wouldn't have minded not going into the grotty, run-down squalor that passed for Chez Carney. Even though the streetlight outside the house wasn't working, she could see that the lawn was a dying thing of patch and weed and there were three motorbikes and the dustbins over-flowed and stank; despite this, she thought the ambience likely to be preferable to that which she would find inside. But she was determined that inside she would go.

'Does he often not come home?'

'Sometimes.' The word was chosen carefully – as much was written on her pinched features – so as to sequester information in a place well away from Beverley's gaze.

'So where does he go?'

A shrug. 'Could be anywhere. A mate's, probably.'

'Which mate?'

'Any one of several. I gave some names to your friend.'

Mrs Carney was a curious shape. She had

clearly married young and the subsequent progeny had done her pelvic floor few favours; she had long hair that was strikingly, not to say frighteningly blonde, and a facial complexion that had not so much suffered from smoking as had itself been smoked, like a herring. She had a small head and a well-named bust that looked as if God had given one too many steps on the foot pump of life whilst constructing it. She might have been fifty-five but Beverley knew that she was thirty-nine; she knew this because Mrs Carney had a varigated criminal past that included assault, shoplifting and drug-dealing.

'Mind if I come in and look around his room? I might find a clue.'

'Yes, I do.'

'That's not very helpful, Mrs Carney.'

Mrs Carney failed to be shocked by this observation.

'You haven't asked why we want to talk to him.'

Just a flicker, but Beverley saw it, as the good Mrs Carney said, 'The other one told me.'

'No, he didn't.'

Mrs Carney clearly considered arguing this point, then decided not to risk it in view of Beverley's (entirely manufactured) confidence. Instead she said in a low voice, 'It's about Billy Whipple, isn't it?'

'What about him?'

'I heard he's dead, stabbed.'

'And why would that involve your son?'

Mrs Carney had fancied a paddle by the seaside and found that the rip tide was strong;

already she was getting into water far deeper than she thought. 'Everyone knows they had a row...'

'And you're afraid that Spud killed Billy because of it, are you?'

She rushed to contradict this assertion. 'No!'

'Then why not tell me where he is?'

'I told you, I don't know.'

Beverley could have pitied Spud's mother; it wasn't her fault that the God had inadvertently dipped into the bag marked 'shit' when it came to making her brain. It wasn't her fault that she had been born into a life without exits, without even a horizon to aim for. She could have pitied her, but didn't. She sighed, hoping that it wasn't too theatrical. 'Very well. I am now going to disturb a judge as he enjoys his well-earned repose and ask him for a warrant to search your house. In view of the threats uttered by your son, I expect to be back here in two hours when I am sure that I'll be reassured that you're not harbouring your son.'

She walked away without a further word, got in her car, then drove away; as she was aware that Mrs Carney was watching her, she didn't acknowledge DCs Sabin and Dempsey as they sat in their car some hundred metres up the street. She stopped around the corner, switched the engine off and waited.

It took thirty minutes. She grew cold in the car because she couldn't run the engine and there was a puddle of sick not far away that her eyes kept returning to despite everything she did to stop them. Then they found something to distract them as Dempsey's voice, distorted but recognizable, came from the radio. She unhooked it and said merely, 'Well done,' before starting the engine, turning the car in the road and driving about fifty metres past the street where the Carney family were blissfully domiciled. Here there was a wide back alley running between the ends of gardens in varying states of disrepair and despoliation. About a hundred metres down it she could see Dempsey kneeling on a prostrate figure while Sabin looked on. She strolled along the alley past dustbins, soot-dappled bushes and assorted lock-up garages; she couldn't see them but she knew that within very few metres there were a good many rats, not all of them human.

'Hello, Spud.' She was quite conversational in tone as she crouched down beside him. The side of Spud's head was being pressed against half a brick that protruded from the uneven, compressed soil of the alley; his nose was about half a metre from a pile of desiccated dog turd which Beverley saw no reason to remove from his view. 'Off somewhere?'

He was unable to speak properly because the heel of Dempsey's hand was over his cheek and jaw but he made a special effort and told her to do the usual. She stood back up. 'Arrest him. Suspicion.'

As she walked away, Mrs Carney appeared and began to spew forth torrential abuse aimed at Beverley and the two constables. Beverley walked on without looking back.

TWENTY-SEVEN

Carney was safely stowed in an interrogation room when Richardson phoned and said that Eisenmenger had finished the autopsy.

'Anything of interest?'

'Oh, yes.'

'What?'

'I think you should see this for yourself.'

'I'll be there in half an hour.'

The traffic was bad because there was a pile-up on the M5 and everything was being diverted through Cheltenham; as if that weren't bad enough the road that led to the mortuary was being dug up which meant that she had to take a detour past the playing fields of the boys' college and the pseudo-classical colonnade of the main hospital building.

Carter let her in and she went straight into the fridge bay where Richardson was awaiting her. He said, 'He's in the dissection room.'

She went through the double doors to find Eisenmenger sitting on a stool speaking into a handheld dictation machine, Richardson standing back and watching him. Although he saw her come in, he did not stop what he was doing and once again, she was aware that there was something wrong with John Eisenmenger.

180

She thought to herself, *Helena*.

She waited patiently until he made the decision to stop. When he did so, she said, 'What have you found?'

He launched into his report at once, without having to think about it, just another solo for a seasoned performer. 'As far as I can judge, he's been dead somewhere been thirty-six and forty-eight hours.'

She stopped him at once. 'That long?'

If it had been Sydenham, she would have been faced by a man who took offence at being thus questioned; Eisenmenger had always taken interrogation as an opportunity to reconsider his findings. In this at least he had not changed. 'Well, rigor's well and truly gone, so that would suggest a minimum of thirty-six hours, although if he had been physically exerting himself just before death, that might make rigor pass even more quickly.'

'So, it could be less than thirty-six hours?'

He frowned. 'I don't think so. There are signs of early putrefaction – some skin marbling on the upper torso and green discoloration of the anterior abdominal skin – so, judging by the relatively low night temperatures, I'd say he's been dead at least one day and two nights.'

'OK. What else?'

'He's been pretty effectively beaten up. I'd say professionally.'

She perked up at that one. 'Why?'

'As far as I can judge, just three blows to the face, but they were hard and effective, and there are bruises on both arms that could be fingerprints. He was held while someone went to work on him.'

Richardson asked, 'But you can't say with absolute certainty that it was a professional job, can you?'

Eisenmenger shrugged, readily conceding the point. 'No, I can't, but there's very little that I can ever tell you with certainty. All I do is give opinion. That's the thing about medicine, Sergeant; it's an art as much as a science, and there are few certainties.'

Beverley murmured, 'I don't imagine that Spud Carney would have confined himself to three blows.'

Richardson shrugged dubious agreement as Eisenmenger went on, 'I haven't found much else externally, apart from the wound in his upper abdomen.'

'And what about it?'

He seemed to ignore her, saying, 'For the sake of completeness, the only natural disease of significance was an appendiceal carcinoid.'

'What's that?'

'An indolent tumour. If it's not removed, it might kill you eventually, it might not.'

'Is it relevant?'

For the first time she actually saw him smile. 'No.'

She forgave him his teasing. 'So, what about the wound in his abdomen?'

'Mr Whipple was stabbed with a single-edged but curved blade that was pointed and only three centimetres long. The handle was approximately twelve centimetres in length.'

After what Eisenmenger had just said about opinion and certainty, this sounded miraculous. She had always reckoned that forensic pathology was over-hyped and that most of its exponents were overpaid – but for once this sounded like gold indeed. It was only on the television that the pathologist was able to give such detail about stab wounds; normally they wouldn't even comment as to the likely size of the blade, let alone such arcana as single-sidedness and length.

'You're sure?' This was almost reverential.

'Oh, yes.' He reached across to the bench and produced a plastic evidence bag that appeared to contain nothing but blood. 'It's clean,' he said when she hesitated to take it from her.

It was incredibly light and at first she thought that there was nothing in it; it was her fingers that proved her wrong.

A surgical scalpel blade.

She looked up at Eisenmenger. He explained, 'It was embedded in his spleen.'

Beverley had said nothing for the first ten minutes of their journey back to the station. The traffic was still heavy but she was no longer in a hurry. She had things to think about. Eventually she said, 'What do you think?'

Richardson had been waiting for this. He said at once, 'I don't think it exonerates Spud. He worked as a porter in the hospital. He could have got hold of a scalpel easily enough.' She said nothing and Richardson went on, 'We should have the warrant to search his house and his locker at work within the hour. That may tell us.'

She reflected that maybe it would but that almost certainly it wouldn't. She had a picture in her mind of a murderer and Spud Carney just wasn't the right shape. 'It hardly seems to be his likely modus operandi, Sam. A baseball bat or a broken bottle I could buy, but not something as delicate as scalpel. You'll be telling me next that he has a degree in the classics.'

'He's still got to be the number-one contender.'

She couldn't deny this, but nor could she deny her gut instinct. 'We should have enough now to be able to get a search warrant tomorrow for the Carneys' house and the hospital where he works. You can take care of that and I will go and see about buying an heirloom.'

Eisenmenger had planned to go looking for a flat to move into that evening, but the autopsy changed all that. He could not face returning directly home to Helena's – he now thought of it as Helena's exclusively – and, most unusually, spent most of the night in a bar in the centre of Cheltenham. He returned to the flat only in the early hours – not drunk, not even tired – when Helena had been long in bed. He slept hardly at all.

TWENTY-EIGHT

Mrs Carney had attempted to clean Spud's room, of course; they would have expected no less from a loving and loyal mother. She had vacuumed and dusted and emptied the pedal bin of its crumpled tissues with semen stains, and its cigarette butts and cans of lager – they found all this in the neighbours' dustbin but nobody felt inclined to undertake forensic analysis on any of it – and she had taken whatever drugs she had discovered and flushed them down the toilet. Unfortunately in her haste she had spilled some of it in the drawer of the bedside cabinet – only cannabis, Dempsey reckoned – and so their search was not entirely without result.

Their search of the hospital was at least unhandicapped by efforts at concealment. They talked to the Head Porter (his office door proclaimed that he was the Chief of Portering Services, which to Beverley was just uncontrolled language inflation) but he seemed unable – perhaps unwilling – to comment much upon Mr Carney. Spud had, it appeared, been a fairly anonymous member of the portering staff; he was occasionally late and once had gone AWOL, claiming later that his father was dying (although he recovered, only to die again some months later). He had not been unliked and he had not been particularly aggressive with his work colleagues; he had never mentioned Billy Whipple by name.

Richardson got into conversation with another porter and a slightly different picture emerged, however. Spud Carney had not been popular, at least with some of his workmates; Spud had had his friends and the rest were at best ignored, at worst subjected to low-level bullying. Richardson's informant did not accuse him of criminality, just unpleasantness.

The head porter was prevailed upon to open Spud's locker, the only physical space that it seemed likely to be worth searching.

But worth it, it was.

They found a scalpel handle and with it three scalpel blades, still wrapped.

Richardson was delighted, feeling that he had proved a point, that Beverley's caution had proved mistaken and he was a point up in the game. All he needed now was forensic evidence linking Spud with Billy's death – blood aerosols were always a good bet in this sort of situation, but the odd fibre from Billy's clothing or perhaps a few flakes of paint from inside the warehouse where Billy had died would be almost as good – and he would come out of this business aces high.

He was a happy bunny as he drove back to the station.

TWENTY-NINE

'It's absolutely beautiful, isn't it?'

The voice was cultured and assured; Beverley heard within it the song of a predator about to feed. She turned and watched the smile from which the words had come collapse. 'Oh.'

'Hello, Theodore. How's business?'

It was impressive how quickly the charm vanished leaving not a single whit behind. 'Inspector. What do you want?'

She frowned, shook her head. 'Not very welcoming, Theodore. I might be here to buy something.'

'You're not, though'

She smiled sweetly. 'No.'

'So what do you want?'

A couple came and stood outside on the pavement, peering in at the window, pointing at things and talking to each other. They were middle-aged and dressed smartly – typical Cheltenham visitors and perfect fodder for the dark-adapted carnivore that was Theodore Noonan. Beverley watched him eye them hungrily, as if he hadn't fed for days. 'How is the antiques trade?'

He winced. 'Business, please. Plumbers trade; I do business.'

'So do dogs,' she pointed out, which didn't help his pain.

He gave up trying to be hoity-toity. 'Well, whatever...'

The couple were taken with a big brass dinner gong and Theodore couldn't resist glancing at them as if they were his children playing by the side of a busy road.

'So, are you fully occupied? Lots of custom?'

'Oh, you know. Some good days, some bad.'

He wore a cravat and a pocket watch; he did so not because he liked wearing such things but because he was in costume. He played the part of the gentleman antiques dealer and his stage was dressed accordingly. Aged landscapes on the walls, regency furniture scattered about serving as surfaces on which items of jewellery, porcelain, silver, gold and pewter lay scattered, or as bookcases for incunabula. A suit of armour, a regimental drum, a pikestaff and a display of early twentieth-century toys and teddy bears. It was all here and all set the scene for the tales with which Theodore bedazzled his customers.

'Is this a good day?'

'Oh, no.' He eyed her balefully. 'It's bad. Very bad.'

She failed to spot the hint. 'Really? Summer in Cheltenham and you say you're not doing well?'

He said nothing. The couple clearly couldn't make up their minds; or rather she wanted it and he didn't.

She picked up a tatty rag doll that had been

flopping in a child-sized wicker chair under what appeared to be a shrunken head. She sniffed the doll, smelled something she didn't like. 'Is that real?' she asked, indicating the head.

'Alas, no. Carved ivory from the late nineteenth century; valuable but not as much as the real thing would have been.'

'Where did you get it?'

He made a show of excavating for the memory – breath held, eyes raised, mouth open, brow furrowed – before saying, 'I'm sorry...'

The couple were coming to a conclusion and appeared to be on the point of entering.

'Surely there can't be a trade in stolen ivory shrunken heads?' she asked. Theodore winced but then the door opened and he could only hiss imploringly, 'Please!'

She watched them enter uncertainly. It was quite a large shop – bigger than it looked from the outside, on a side street off the upper High Street near the hospital. It was quite dark – not without reason – and cluttered; people entering it had to tread warily lest a careless movement cost them several hundred pounds. Once again, there was method in Theodore's habit of putting the fragile and breakable items near the doorway. Beverley said in a low tone, 'Tell me about Stephen Bright.'

'But I have customers...'

'And you have a criminal record for possession of stolen goods.'

'Oh, really! That was a single offence, fifteen years ago,' he pointed out.

'Nevertheless, it doesn't look good on the

CV, Theodore. Shall I tell that nice, law-abiding couple about it? Do you think that they'll be impressed?'

The people in question had negotiated the china assault course and were looking in their direction. Theodore called out gaily, 'I'll be with you in a minute!'

The husband – or perhaps it was the lover, Beverley wondered – nodded and smiled. Theodore turned back to Beverley. 'I'm not your informant, you know, Inspector.'

'Yes you are,' she contradicted simply. If he thought to argue, her meaningful glance at his potential customers produced taciturnity. A brief interval ensued during which he rebuilt his pride and she waited.

'Stephen Bright?' he said at last.

'Correct.'

'I don't think I know the name.'

'Lives in Pittville. Calls himself an antiques dealer. Medium height but works out; bit of a muscle man. Fancies himself something rotten. Either homosexual or bi.'

He snorted. *That* hardly helps, not in this business.' More thought; it appeared to be deep but Beverley suspected that this was deceptive like a pond. Eventually, 'No, nothing comes to mind.'

She said sadly, 'Oh, dear.'

'I'm sorry...'

'You will be, Theodore.'

The couple were back at the gong. She called out to them, 'Excuse me!'

They turned in time to see Theodore, hands

up in attempted supplication while the redhead who had called out was looking at them. 'Yes?'

'I think there's something you should know.'

The husband's – lover's? – expression became curious. 'Yes?'

But before illumination came, Theodore said to her in an urgent undertone, 'I know him. He's *unofficial*.' From which she deduced that he abided by whichever laws he chose to. 'Lots of money, though.'

Beverley turned to him. 'How much?'

'Megabucks. The word is, he's an agent for someone else.'

'Does he know what he's doing?'

He shrugged. 'Pretty much.'

'Does he bother about provenance?'

He didn't speak, only shook his head. By the shop window they were becoming restive. 'How does he pay?'

Theodore sighed at that one; this was too close to personal. She had to raise her eyebrows to get a response. 'Cheque.'

'Show me one.'

He glanced at his quarry, then back at her. 'Please!'

'Show me one,' she repeated, the tone identical.

'Not now!'

'Tonight, then.'

'I haven't got any. They're all cashed.'

She smiled sadly ... and that was enough. Theodore didn't even wait for her to take breath into her lungs to call across the shop. 'All right, tonight.'

She hesitated, then nodded. 'Good. I'll be back at five thirty.'

Moving back through the shop she stopped at the door and said to the couple, 'That man saved my life. He donated his bone marrow when I was just four years old and saved me from leukaemia. I can never repay him. I thought you ought to know that.'

THIRTY

As Sam seated himself in the coffee room and opened the caramel fudge bar he was only dimly aware of the group of uniformed constables sitting around the table behind him. He could not have said how many there were and he had not recognized any of them; they were background, nothing more.

Sam liked caramel fudge bars and he looked forward to his daily indulgence; one caramel fudge bar and one cup of white coffee, no sugar. The coffee in the restaurant was a lot better than the stuff he used to have to endure in the army, too. As he ate he thought about their current investigations, about how different were the victims, about how death and disaster came to all classes, all creeds...

There was no specific comment that brought his attention back to the present and to the small part of the present that was the table of officers behind him. It was more the tones that told him that they were talking about him. He began to listen.

'...I don't mind being told not to abuse them or kick the shit out of them, but I do want a level playing field...'

'...You won't get one, not with this fucking government...'

'...I heard he's fucking Wharton...'

'There's a surprise. Who isn't she fucking?'

'You, for a start.'

'Up yours.'

Laughter.

Sam closed his eyes. This kind of thing had been a constant in his life since forever. Sometimes he thought that it had improved, sometimes he knew that it was, if anything, worse. Suppressed, it only grew, became more vicious. In the army it had been, if anything, better. They called him 'coon' and they made jokes about his 'donger' and his hypothetical love of bananas, but they had been his mates, his muckers, the ones in whose hands he placed his life, the ones who relied on him to safeguard theirs.

He stood up. Not violently, not demonstratively, just as a man who had finished his break might, one who was now ready to return to duty.

He smiled at the little group of enlightened social analysts as he passed.

Eisenmenger did not take the first flat he was shown that lunchtime, but he didn't exhibit his customary care and diligence. It was a furnished, one-bedroom flat in Fairview on a short-term let; not a bad place and at least convenient for both the hospital and the town centre. He would leave work early to collect his belongings and be gone from Helena's life in less than five hours.

The shop was already shut up by the time Beverley came back at just before five thirty and she thought, peering into the even deeper than usual gloom of the interior, that Theodore had decided to run away rather than stick to the agreement. She was considering her options – all of which involved extreme suffering for the antiques dealer – when he turned the corner into the road, carrying with him a bag of groceries. He looked unhappy, unhappier when he saw Beverley awaiting him.

She called, 'I thought you'd run for cover.'

'Only food.'

'You might have missed out on business.'

'I doubt it. No one else has even looked in the window since that couple earlier.'

He was unlocking the door to the shop, the bag between his feet. She asked, 'Did they buy the gong?'

'Yes ... and a rather nice Edwardian brooch.'

'Not a wasted day, then.'

The lock proved a tricky, recalcitrant thing requiring two hands and judicious rattling of door and key. When it yielded it did so with much protest. He turned to her, 'They were most peculiar, actually. Kept on about how wonderful I was, and how they admired me.'

'Really?'

He looked at her quizzically but she kept her face straight and he was left uncertain as to what was going on. He led her through the shop, weaving through it with assurance born of experience; she followed in a more sedate manner. At the back was a door, also locked but giving in with more ease, leading through to a small office. There was a tremendous mess here, as if he had spent years piling magazines and dusty brown files – all bulging with receipts, letters, cuttings – to the ceiling and then decided to push them all over.

The desk was small and beautiful, made of walnut; ninety per cent of what Theodore sold out of the shop might have been either fake or dubiously acquired or both but he knew the good stuff when he saw it. Behind it was a nineteen-thirties-style office chair that was on casters but that had been snared and immobilized by paper.

He reached across and plucked a cheque off the blotter on the green leather surface of the desk. 'There.'

It was for six thousand pounds and it was drawn on the number three business account of a company called Vermilion Ltd. There were two signatures, one of which was unintelligible, the other of which could be just made out as Stephen Bright.

'Who's this?' She meant the second signature.

'Not the foggiest.'

'Vermilion? Who are they?'

He didn't know.

'What was he paying for?'

'A bureau. Rosewood and in perfect condition.'

'Genuine?'

She upset him with this. 'Of course,' he said haughtily.

'Stolen?'

He didn't even hear that one.

'And you deliver it where?'

'I don't. He picks up.'

She looked at the cheque. 'How much has he bought off you?'

'That's the third thing in two months.'

'What else?'

'A Scottish landscape and a chandelier, but I now he's been hoovering up stuff from far and wide.'

She said eventually, 'OK.'

Which he was pleased to hear; he was considerably less pleased at what he saw.

She folded the cheque and put it in her inside breast pocket.

'Hey, that's mine!'

'Evidence, Theodore.'

'But I need that. My cash flow...'

'You'll get it back in due course.'

'You don't understand. The margins in this business are very tight. I operate with little room for manoeuvre and any shortfall like that is going to cause me considerable problems.'

'Sell another Mona Lisa.'

He winced. 'That's below the belt.'

This was met with a shrug.

He tried one last gambit. 'If I don't cash it, he'll get suspicious.'

Which made her stop to think.

'OK,' she said after a short while. 'I'll take a copy for now, then retrieve the original from the bank later. Have you got a copier?'

He moved several boxes of postcards exposing a small desktop copier. It took five minutes for the thing to warm up, scan the cheque, then produce a copy that was less than optimal but adequate.

She folded the copy and put it into her handbag. 'You owe me for this, Theodore. I could have insisted on taking that cheque.'

He smiled weakly but said nothing. When he had shown her out and locked the door behind her (after a brief struggle) he muttered to the suit of armour, 'Bitch.'

THIRTY-ONE

It was something of a shock to Beverley to discover the identity of Spud Carney's legal representative. She had not thought to ask Richardson and so when Helena's cold gaze met hers as she walked into the interview room, she had trouble controlling her expression. Helena, of course, had prior knowledge that this moment would come and was therefore prepared, this preparation taking the form of features perfectly set in formal but frozen hostility, a permafrost chilling the room almost to zero. She was, as usual, well made up, but this could not completely hide the signs of stress beneath; the redness in the eyes, the sense of tautness around the mouth.

Well, well. The other player in the game.

Seeing these things allowed Beverley to recover her poise. She came into the room, nodded to Helena and sat down next to Richardson opposite Spud Carney.

When seen close up, Spud Carney had a certain animal quality that Beverley found slightly intimidating. As a rule and under the right circumstances she found animal charm within the male members of the human species attractive, but in Spud's case she made an exception, possibly because the animal he most closely resembled was a pit-bull terrier and one, moreover, with toothache. He had a rounded head that had been shaved to reveal on the crown an interesting tattoo of a couple engaging in a possibly illegal sexual act. He had small piggy eyes and a mouth that was accentuated by a jutting chin; his complexion was poor as was his personal hygiene. This concoction of English manliness was completed by a row of ear studs on either side. She was surprised to notice that he didn't have tattoos on his knuckles but surmised that was because they'd been scraped off.

'So, tell me, Spud, why did you do it? Was it drugs?'

She knew that it wasn't. Spud used drugs but didn't sell them and Billy hadn't had the brains to deal in penny chews let alone drugs of abuse; his toxicology results had all been negative and none of the drug-related detritus at the scene of death had had his fingerprints.

'I don't know what you're talking about.' He was confident; not cocky but confident. It made Beverley nervous although she showed nothing either to him or to Helena, who was assiduously making notes.

'Why did you kill Billy Whipple?'

'I didn't.'

'You threatened him. Said that you were going to kill him.'

'I didn't kill him.'

'Charlene said that she thought you meant it. So did a lot of other people in the pub.'

Richardson didn't move and she couldn't see his face but she sensed his reaction – disapproval. As far as he knew, neither Charlene nor anyone else in the pub had said any such thing. Beverley, though, wasn't interested in minutiae, not when she had her attention fixed on a far bigger prize.

She saw anger in Spud and suspected that Charlene was going to have a little chastisement if he got out of this mess. She was saddened by the knowledge that this would probably not come as a great surprise to Charlene and would not, therefore, prompt her to re-evaluate their relationship. He muttered, 'I just said that. He got me angry.'

'Why?'

He shifted in his seat, looked at the twin-deck tape recorder that was turning steadily to their side. 'He was chatting up Charlene.'

'Off limits, is she?'

'She's my bird.'

Dempsey had done a good job talking to a lot of the regulars at the Three Tunnes and a great deal of the background story about Charlene and Spud had come out. 'I thought you'd had a bust-up. Maybe Billy thought so, too.'

'Just 'cos we had a row doesn't mean she's up for grabs.'

He made it sound as if Charlene were a commodity to be swapped and, Beverley thought ruefully, maybe she was. 'He trod on your toes and you didn't like it.'

'He got me riled up,' he admitted.

'How much were you riled up?'

'What do you mean?'

'Were you just slightly miffed or really cross?'

'I got angry.'

'Really cross, then.'

He looked uncertain and glanced across at his solicitor who was doodling on a pad of paper; she had drawn a rocket, which Beverley found most intriguing. He said slowly, 'Yeah.'

'You and Billy have a history, don't you?' He frowned, clearly not understanding what she meant, so she explained, 'Three years ago, Billy was admitted to hospital with severe facial, chest and abdominal bruising following an incident outside your local, the Three Tunnes. Several passers-by identified you as his assailant; they said you kicked him and punched him on the ground.'

He had his head low as he said, 'They were wrong. It wasn't me.'

'There was talk then of a dispute about a girlfriend, I recall.'

'It wasn't me.'

Helena interjected, 'My client wasn't charged with anything.'

'Only because Billy suddenly couldn't remember whose size-ten Doc Martens it had been treading all over his head and private parts.'

Helena shrugged. To Spud, Beverley asked, 'How cross were you then?'

He said nothing.

'Fairly cross, I'd say.' Still nothing. 'And then he went and did it again. Cheeky sod never learned, did he? Always trying to poach your girl, trying to have a quick one whilst your back was turned.'

He reacted. 'He never did that.'

She raised a thin, almost unidimensional eyebrow. 'No? Are you sure, Spud? Are you completely positive Billy never got inside the knickers of Charlene?'

He was becoming angry and she appreciated how easily incensed he became. 'Shut fucking up.'

It wasn't exactly the Queen's English and maybe that was why she ignored him. 'You're not, are you?' This was a goad, as powerful as a cattle prod.

'That's crap!'

'That's not what some people are saying,

Spud. There's a widespread rumour that Billy was quite chummy with Charlene, maybe that he was playing insert the salami with your girl-friend as the hiding place. What do you say to that?'

Once more she sensed moral outrage from Richardson and she made a note to remember to educate him into the ways of the real world. Maybe she wasn't being totally truthful, but that wasn't the point; it was how Spud reacted that mattered.

He was becoming pale, his hands were clenched and his lips were drawn back in a near-feral expression; an anthropologist would have had a whale of a time with Spud. Through teeth that were clenched and even at his tender age stained yellow by nicotine, he hissed, 'Shut up, you hear? Charlene's mine ... she wouldn't...'

'Yes, she would. In fact she did, and you killed Billy Whipple because of it.'

Suddenly he stood up and shouted at the top of his voice, 'I DIDN'T KILL HIM!' He banged the table with his fist. Helena reached out a hand and said calmly, 'Sit back down, Mr Carney.' He did as suggested, looking angry still. To Beverley Helena said, 'I really must protest if all you're going to do is to try to goad my client into losing his temper. Deliberately trying to intimidate him will not sound very good should this come to court, Inspector.'

'I'm just trying to establish the truth.'

'Badgering Mr Carney until he quite reasonably becomes stressed isn't going to get you very far in that.'

Beverley smiled at her. She said curiously, 'You lose your temper quite easily, don't you, Spud?'

He glowered at her but refused to reply.

Her foot tapped Richardson on the ankle who said at once, 'We found a scalpel handle and three blades in your locker at the hospital, Spud.'

Spud swung his glower round to Richardson but declined to enter into discourse on the topic.

'Why do you want scalpel blades?'

He hesitated before saying, 'They come in useful sometimes.'

'What for?'

'Cutting things.'

It was Beverley who said, 'Cutting drugs or people?'

Now he positively glared at Beverley. 'Neither.'

'What do you cut, then?'

Whether it was his imagination or his memory that failed at that point was up for later debate; whichever it was he said nothing.

Richardson pointed out, 'We know what Billy was stabbed with.'

Poor Spud was not quick to join up the dots. He asked sarcastically, 'So what?'

Beverley supplied his answer. 'A surgical scalpel. It's identical to the one in your locker.'

Realization dawned and there was a comical expression of horror; it was so theatrical a drama student trying it would have been instantly expelled.

'It can't be!'

Beverley didn't even bother to react, she just watched him, a professional assessing a performance.

Is that genuine?

She didn't want it to be. She wanted to solve a case, move on, and perhaps there would once have been a time when she would have done just that; she hoped that those days were gone, though. Now she was listening to her instincts not to her desires.

'It wasn't me ... It wasn't...'

He had turned to Helena who hesitated for a moment; Beverley saw it and felt a glow of pleasure. Helena said to her, 'Have you identified the precise scalpel that killed Mr Whipple?'

'Not yet.'

'So this is circumstantial in the extreme. My client works in the hospital – it is not out of the question that he might have such things in his locker...'

'That he might have stolen them, you mean.'

Helena shrugged. 'That is for you to prove; it is also for you to prove that my client had something to do with the death of Billy Whipple, an accusation that he denies absolutely. Are you planning to arrest and interrogate every surgeon in the hospital?'

'If witnesses tell me that one or more of them threatened to take Billy Whipple's life, then yes.'

They stared at each other and even Spud sensed that here was more than the ritualistic posturing of police and solicitor. Richardson waited, aware that the atmosphere in the room was about as relaxing as that found in a boxing ring; no one was more surprised than him, however, when Beverley stood up quite suddenly and walked from the room; he stared after her over the heads of Carney and Helena, noted the look of satisfaction on her face. Then he hurriedly terminated the interview and followed his superior out of the room.

THIRTY-TWO

He found her in her office, closed the door gently. She looked as if she'd just had bad news.

'What's wrong?'

'He didn't do it.'

He sat down, and not just because he was astonished by her attitude; he had never seen her like this before. 'Why do you say that?'

'Because I know.'

He had heard answers like that before, but only from suspects. He said nothing, contented himself with looking at her. He found her intensely attractive, despite the age difference. *You're practically a toy-boy.* It was a thought he'd had before now; he found it strangely intoxicating, part of her attraction. The icing on the cake was that she might have been ten years older than he was but the beauty was not solely in his eyes. He still saw other men look at her and want her, still felt the pleasure in that. She leaned back in the chair, looking up at the ceiling. The decorators had been in six months ago; they'd been in but it wasn't absolutely certain that they'd done anything in the way of painting. The ceiling had been smeared with something but that only drew attention to how dirty the old emulsion had become. She murmured eventually, 'I think we should let him go.'

'Are you serious?'

'He didn't do it.'

'Why?'

A moment passed. 'He was genuine.'

'You can't be sure of that.'

The head came forward. 'Yes,' she said as she looked at him. 'I can.'

'He was acting...'

'His left testicle's got more processing power than his brain. He could no more act convincingly than he could give birth to twins.'

He took a deep breath. 'And the evidence? Are we going to ignore that?'

'We haven't got any.'

He wondered if she were all right; perhaps it was the time of the month. 'Yes, we have. The argument, the scalpel, his form...'

'None of it means a thing, Sam. They had an argument the day before – they were always having arguments. Billy was a chancer and Spud's a thug.'

'He beat the shit out of him once, and that

was over a girlfriend.'

'Exactly. He didn't stab him. Most importantly, he didn't stab him with a scalpel.'

'He probably didn't work at the hospital then.'

She stared at him trying to articulate what she felt; she failed and, with a soft sigh, she stood up abruptly and asked, 'What was in Billy's pockets?'

He had to fetch the evidence bag from the filing cabinet by his desk. He emptied it on to her desk and she examined it minutely.

'Is this for his house?' She held up a grubby Yale key.

'Yep.'

There wasn't much else to look at. She discovered a pen, held it up and frowned. 'Where did he get this?'

'It's only a pen.'

'G.G.S. What does that mean?'

'He probably nicked it.'

'But where from?'

Richardson didn't know and couldn't see why he should care. 'A golf club?' She stared at him questioningly and he explained, 'Something Golfing Society?'

She said merely, 'Check it out.'

He had to force exasperation back into its hole. 'If we let Spud go, he'll scarper. Are you really so certain that he's innocent? Do you want to risk losing him for good?'

He could see that this perspective worried her. 'I just don't think it was him.'

'We don't have to rush into it. We've got time

to let him stew before we decide. Forensics on
the stuff we found in his locker and his clothes
will be back tomorrow. If that comes up
positive, we've got him.'

She considered this, then, 'OK.'

He stood up to return to the interrogation
room to make arrangements to get Spud safely
tucked up in bed.

She said softly, 'Check up on G.G.S.,
though.'

He looked back and nodded. *Thanks.*

THIRTY-THREE

It was past midnight and the supermarket was
almost completely empty, giving an eerie
atmosphere as if something horrible had happened to the population of the world, perhaps
zombification, perhaps mass kidnapping by
aliens. Some buildings, she reflected, were not
meant to be empty; they were defined by the
people within them. Airport terminals, schools,
supermarkets were such places and those who
found themselves inside them when empty
were unsettled, hearing ghosts and echoes in
the unaccustomed silence. It didn't help that
she was tired and, if she were being honest with
herself, depressed.

Who would be bothered if Spud Carney were
sent down for the murder of Billy Whipple?

Spud, obviously; and, she was fairly confident, Mr and Mrs Carney (although Spud's father was actually in prison on the Isle of Wight, serving fifteen years for armed robbery). But who else? Not Lambert, that was sure; Lambert wanted this grotty little crime solved as quickly as possible so that proper attention could be paid to more important problems. Lambert's was not an uncommon attitude amongst the police and she could see the sense of it; most of the work of the police was generated by people like Billy Whipple and Spud Carney and so if one of them died and another could be put inside for it, there was a double benefit to be gained.

She picked up some apples, rejected the bananas, preyed heavily on the peaches, then moved on to the tomatoes.

Sam was convinced that Carney was guilty, too. There would be no dissenters, no saintly do-gooders to fight her, to whisper against her. She would be safe and she would be the hero; it wouldn't make Lambert suddenly love her and it wouldn't make her chief constable, but it would help her long, slow rehabilitation.

Such a shame, then, that she didn't want to do it.

She hated cheese of any kind but Sam loved it, almost lived on it. Cheddar, the stronger the better. She picked something that described itself as 'extra mature' – why, she wondered, did people not grow 'mature' and 'extra mature'; why did they have to grow 'old'?

If forensic examination of the scalpel handle

or Spud's clothes showed evidence of Billy's blood, she would happily commit him for trial; she would read out the charge herself, savour every syllable, watch as he made his puerile, unconvincing protestations.

Yet, just as she knew that God had made her legs precisely the right length to reach the ground, and just as she was absolutely positive that all estate agents had small dicks, so she knew that it wouldn't. There would be no forensic corroboration of Spud's guilt.

And she would not...

Someone bumped into her. She turned around, looked to see who it was.

She found herself looking into John Eisenmenger's eyes.

Lambert, who seemed to walk the corridors of the station as if he had died a few centuries ago having committed some ghastly, inexcusable crime, caught up with Richardson just as he was leaving for the night.

'Sergeant?'

Richardson turned, suppressed a sigh and waited while Lambert came on towards him down the corridor.

'Inspector Wharton not around?'

As it was one in the morning Lambert should not have been surprised at her absence but his tone suggested that he was close to uncovering gross dereliction of duty. Richardson said mildly, 'She left about an hour ago, sir.'

'Did she?' He frowned. 'Are you off home?'

Why the fuck shouldn't I be? I've been here for

seventeen hours.

'That's right, sir.'

Which wasn't a lie. They both knew that what Lambert had really asked was, *Are you off to sleep with that slut?*

Lambert pursed his lips. Before he could say anything more, Richardson said, 'You're here late, sir.'

Suddenly Lambert became strangely vague. 'Oh, you know,' he said before pausing as his mouth formed a grimace and his head shook slightly as if he were clearing it. He added, 'Work, you know. It never lets up.'

'Yes, sir.'

There followed a pause until Lambert said, 'You've arrested Carney, then.'

'That's right.'

'You'll be charging him tomorrow, I expect.'

Richardson wasn't about to be too committal on that point. 'We'll get the forensic reports back tomorrow.'

Lambert nodded. 'And the Fitzroy-Hughes case?'

A bit of a problem; it was something else on which he didn't want to be too committal. 'No breakthrough yet, I'm afraid.'

Lambert, it now turned out, was keen on commitment on this particular case. 'No? Why not?'

'Well...'

Lambert had spotted a high horse and, with breathtaking speed, he had saddled it, donned his jodhpurs and put his left foot in the stirrup. 'Look, Sergeant. I don't seem to be getting through to people here. The Whipple killing is nothing. He was pond-life and whoever murdered him was just a predator. Nobody gets excited when a frog kills a fly, do they?'

'No.'

'So clear up the loose ends, then move on to more important things. Do I have to make things any plainer?'

Since Richardson wasn't in any way visually handicapped, he didn't. 'No, sir.'

Lambert had actually assumed a trace of a snarl. 'Good.' He retreated slightly but it was only a tactical withdrawal because he quickly came back with, 'And make sure that Inspector Wharton understands that. Billy Whipple's dead – Jasper Fitzroy-Hughes might not be. We look after the living.'

'Yes, sir.'

Lambert at last relaxed. 'Good.' He nodded at Richardson. 'You've done well on the Whipple case, but it's the Fitzroy-Hughes case that matters. Even if Inspector Wharton doesn't realize that, I want you to.'

He walked away, leaving Richardson to shake his head slowly as he looked at his retreating back.

'You're looking good.'

Beverley had always found lying easy and many years of practice had honed her art, but she had trouble making that one sound anywhere near convincing. Eisenmenger not only did not look good, he barely looked alive. His face was drained – of blood, of emotion, of

212

vitality – and in the absence of these, it was almost as if his flesh was decaying; there was the look of the cadaver about him.

The cafeteria in Tesco's supermarket was hushed as if they were in a place of worship, somewhere to come to abase themselves in front of the false gods such as mammon, perhaps. There was a certain degree of eerie irony that the only other customer wore a dog collar; he sat hunched over some preposterously named caffeine concoction and could easily have been praying to it. Their only host was a bored-looking girl who read a gossip magazine as she sat behind the till and chewed with a degree of dedication that she probably never applied to anything else.

He said lifelessly, 'So are you.'

He was clearly very tired. They drank black coffee but she doubted that it would do much for him; his face suggested that he was beyond tired. She had taken pity on him as soon as she had seen him and although he had at first demurred, she had insisted that they should sit and talk, despite the lateness of the hour.

'A little odd to bump into you here, John.'

He shrugged. 'I could say the same about you.'

But I'm a single woman; you're in a partnership, aren't you, John?

She had never been afraid of asking awkward questions. 'How's Helena?'

That produced something a little more animated than the previous lifelessness. 'She's fine.'

'Run out of sugar, did she?'

The vicar, whom it appeared had been falling asleep, suddenly jerked and raised his head; it was only a temporary respite from his malaise, however. The girl behind the till climbed off her stool, and wandered out the back, perhaps to plug herself into the grid and get recharged, probably because the chewing had depleted her batteries. 'What do you mean?'

'And, of course, life isn't worth living with hair that's washed but unconditioned.'

He stared into her eyes; she hoped that what he saw in hers was a bloody sight less alarming than what she was looking at. He lowered his head to sip his coffee while she waited for him to respond. When he didn't she said, 'We've been through a lot together over the years, don't you think?'

He frowned. 'I suppose so, yes.'

She said nothing for a moment as she sampled her own coffee. Then, 'In fact, come to think of it, I've saved your life on one or two occasions and Helena owes me a few favours.'

He was wary. 'What are you getting at?'

She explained succinctly, 'I think you owe me the truth, John.'

Once more he declined to comment. It must still have been scalding hot but he drained the cup and said, 'Thanks for the coffee. Got to get back.'

He stood up but she took no notice. She said quietly, 'I saw Helena today.'

He stopped. 'Did you?'

She looked up at him. 'Representing an

odious little yobbo. She did rather well for him.'

This backhanded compliment unsettled him. 'She's a good solicitor,' he said after a pause, but she caught something impersonal in his tone, as if it were a description of someone seen through a glass, someone at a distance.

Beverley nodded. 'I've always known that. It's as a fully paid-up member of the human race I think she needs a bit of revision.'

Once he would have reacted to that, but this time there was nothing; no response at all. He merely twitched his lips, a movement that seemed to express exhaustion more than anything else, then abruptly left her. She watched him to the door, all the while thinking, *I wonder where you're going, John.* His two bags were full of groceries and she hadn't missed that they included the basics of life – tea, coffee, milk, orange juice, bread – as well as a few luxuries; if he was going back to snuggle up to Helena, then Beverley Wharton was top of the shortlist to become the next Metropolitan Police Commissioner. She knew that he was on his own, for whatever reason, and this was not just a matter of idle curiosity. She had always been attracted by John Eisenmenger, although why she could not say; he was not particularly tall, nor particularly handsome, and he clearly had a problem expressing his emotions. Set against that, he wasn't ugly either, and he radiated a feeling of confidence and safety that appealed to her.

Not that she was free at the moment to

indulge in a casual liaison, not with Sam on the scene. Not that she would have said that she loved him (she had never said that about any lover) but she certainly had a fondness for him. In truth she had a lot of this commodity for him. She had no intention of squandering it. She stood up, the coffee now too cold for her taste. The vicar was asleep again; she noted as she passed that he had a silver cross clutched in his hand: perhaps he knew something that she didn't about the neighbourhood.

THIRTY-FOUR

Richardson failed to shake Mrs Carney, who maintained with the kind of dogged determination that had seen East Enders through the Blitz that her son had been home during the time span that John Eisenmenger reckoned had been the likely period in which Billy Whipple had died. He therefore moved on to Spud's known haunts – most of them pubs, but a fair sprinkling of bookmakers, amusement arcades and kebab shops – only to discover that Mrs Carney had done a good job in spreading the word and thereby ensured that no unfortunate discrepancies occurred and no one, try as they might, could recall seeing Spud anywhere in the neighbourhood during the time in question.

All that changed, though, when he returned to the station.

Dempsey found him at once. 'Somebody left a message.'

'Who for?'

'Didn't say.'

'Who left it?'

'Anonymous.'

'I see. Male or female?'

'Male.'

'What did he say?'

Dempsey handed him the transcript. It was brief. *Mrs Carney enjoys bingo.*

Richardson looked at him, eyebrows raised. 'Is that it?'

'That's it.'

'What does it mean?'

Dempsey had ears that stuck out and that moved whenever his physiognomy changed; as he made a face indicating his ignorance they moved up and back in a form of synchronized ballet. 'She's in debt?' he hazarded.

Which was why he was forty years old and still a constable.

Richardson took the note to his desk.

Was it code, perhaps? It certainly had the un-attached, almost surreal quality that coded messages – at least in the books that he had read – possessed. In structure it resembled things like, *The birds fly south for the winter*, or *Beware of the one-legged man, his mother has a glass eye*. This idea had an attraction but the question that followed was difficult to answer. If it was a coded message, it implied that someone at the station knew the code, yet the message hadn't been for any specific person. How would the sender know that their contact would get it?

If it wasn't code, then presumably it was to be taken at face value. Spud's mother liked bingo ... and why not? Lots of middle-aged women did; it was a well-established custom. Some women went night after night...

Then he twigged.

Beverley was back at her desk and examining the photocopy of the cheque when Richardson found her.

'There you are.'

It was clear he was excited. 'Here I am,' she agreed mildly.

'I've got news.'

Which she had guessed. 'Tell me.'

'Spud's alibi is blown apart. His mother was at bingo during the time she said that she was at home with him, during Eisenmenger's window for Billy's death.'

She was hardly surprised at this news; the thought that Spud and his mother spent cosy nights together, perhaps knitting socks, perhaps doing the cryptic crossword in *The Times*, was always going to be as indigestible as a lump of coal. 'You're sure?'

'I spoke with the manager of the bingo hall. She actually won that night. Only a hundred pounds but she proceeded to get drunk; threw up over the barman. He remembers all right.'

She found herself in a dichotomy; it had been obvious that Spud's alibi was no more truthful

218

than a lawyer's promise, but that didn't help her believe that he was the murderer. Spud, she was certain, was quite capable of homicide; it was just that she did not believe that he was capable of this one. Whatever ... they would have to question him again. He would have to be made to confess to whatever he had been up to. She looked at her watch. 'OK, contact his solicitor. We'll talk to him again in an hour.'

He left and with him went the enthusiasm; the lacuna was filled by questions which, by the time he had returned, had sprouted into a thicket. 'How did you find out about this, Sam? You must have covered an awful lot of ground.'

'I didn't have to. We had a tip-off.'

'Really? Who from?'

'An anonymous male rang us this morning.'

... Her face fell. 'Oh.'

He didn't understand. 'What's the problem?'

There was so much to say, so much for him to learn. She said only, 'I don't like playing the puppet.'

THIRTY-FIVE

It was with an uneasy alliance of satisfaction and dismay that Beverley read the reports from the forensics laboratory. Their examination of everything taken from Spud's home and work proved negative; there was no trace of any of

Billy Whipple's DNA, no trace of anything untoward, with the exception of evidence of cannabis found both in his room and in his locker at work.

'What now?'

She wanted to let him go, now confirmed in her conviction that he was, in this instance at least, innocent, but she also wanted to know exactly what he had been up to that night.

'Try again, Spud.'

Spud looked confused, adrift, and his solicitor looked just as bored as always, and Beverley thought that she could easily go mad if she had to sit through too many more interviews in which the suspect looked perplexed and their solicitor wanted to be anywhere else but there. 'There's been a mistake,' he offered. It wasn't a good offer – a cruel person might have said that it was pathetic – but she could see that she wasn't going to get better.

'Only on your part.'

'No...'

'Spud, we know your mother wasn't at home with you. Unfortunately she decided to make a spectacle of herself at the bingo and no one's going to forget that night in a hurry, so we know that you and she didn't share a jug of cocoa and play cribbage together. Which leads me to ask, what did you do after Billy ran out of the pub?'

'I went home.' He spoke slowly as if aware that every word might be booby-trapped, might explode and injure him. He even glanced to his right, where Helena was sitting; she did not return the compliment, preferring to stare at his interrogators.

Beverley's dilemma now was whether to jump on him at once, at the start of the lies, or later, when he'd woven a shaky fabrication. 'I want to get this absolutely straight in my mind, Spud. You got a bit riled up in the pub, didn't you? Billy had made a move on Charlene and that was verboten...' He didn't know what 'verboten' meant but he followed her gist and nodded. '...So having chased him halfway up the Lower High Street, threatening him with death, you took a deep breath, then went home alone.'

'That's right.'

'What about Charlene?'

'What about her?'

'You just left her, did you?'

'She'd gone by the time I got back.'

I don't blame her. 'So you went to look for her ... I expect you wanted to talk to her.' He shrugged. 'Did you look for her?'

He was uncertain and she could see another choice, another lie, slowly forming inside his thick-walled cranial vault. 'I looked for her a bit,' he offered at last. As tasty morsels went, it was a stinker.

'A bit?'

'Yeah, a bit.'

'Where?'

It was too easy really. Every time he was called upon to perform creative thinking, the circuits overloaded; if the top of his head had been transparent she'd have seen wires burning out, sparks fluttering randomly. Eventually, 'Her place.'

'No, you didn't,' she said simply. This contradiction didn't even surprise him. He accepted it, merely casting his gaze downwards as she said, 'Charlene tells me that she went home as soon as you came into the pub – seemed to think you might be angry with her – can't think why, but anyway ... She tells me that you didn't come after her. She says she hasn't seen you since.'

Silence.

Beverley added, 'So where did you go?'

More silence before, 'Like I said, I went home.'

Give up, Spud. Don't waste my time... All right, so you went home. What did you do there?'

He was suspicious. 'What do you mean?'

'You went home, but then what? Did you shampoo the dog, do a jigsaw, masturbate?'

From the frown she guessed that he was having trouble with the concept of 'doing' anything; Spud's whole life had been dedicated to avoidance of such a concept. 'I watched the telly.'

'So what did you watch?'

Not a difficult question, she might have supposed – a slow full toss rather than a late-breaking bouncer that threatens the head – but Spud judged otherwise. He paused for thought. Rather endearingly, when he concentrated, his mouth hung open and his tongue protruded slightly; half a lifetime ago Beverley had had a cat that used to do that, and that cat was stupid too.

'Come on, Spud. It's not that tricky a question. What was on the telly?'

She could see that he was working up to another whopper, steadying the nerves, trying to produce something safe but believable. 'The news.'

She nodded encouragingly. 'Good ... What was the main story?'

Oh, dear ... If Spud had been anything more than only nominally human she could have been prosecuted for cruelty. No animal charity would have allowed her to inflict the kind of anguish that he went through before whispering with a shrug, 'Something political.'

Which wasn't a bad answer when measured for cunning. She didn't bother to pursue the subject. 'What else?'

Brains, almost literally, were racked. Helena seemed to have become caught up in this human tragedy, this drama of Everyman, and was now actually looking at her client as if willing him to try a bit harder. He tried again. 'The football!' This came out almost triumphantly.

Beverley didn't know – could not have been more pleased to be ignorant on the point – whether or not there had been football on, but that was hardly the point. 'Which match? Who was playing?'

Whole species died out in mass extinctions as they awaited the answer. 'Man United,' he proffered eventually.

'Who were they playing?' She almost winced as she asked this, expecting another period of geologic time to pass, but Spud surprised her.

'Madrid.'

Since football to Beverley was little more than an illustration of how puerile the human race could be, she about to continue probing Spud's story when Dempsey, until now silent beside her, said, 'No, it was Liverpool.'

Spud did his best. 'That's right,' he agreed eagerly. 'Man U v. Liverpool.'

But Dempsey had to disappoint him. 'No. It was Liverpool who were playing Madrid. I watched it.'

Beverley couldn't help but smile as she turned her attention back to Spud. 'Oh, dear...' she murmured. Spud began to speak but she hadn't finished. 'Look, Spud, can we forget this? I know you weren't at home that night, so don't bother trying to convince me otherwise.'

Silence was her reward, after five seconds of which she added confidentially, 'I don't happen to think that you murdered Billy Whipple, you know.'

Spud was, perhaps understandably, surprised to hear this; surprised but suspicious. He continued to say nothing.

She went on. 'Problem is, it looks bad for you. You threatened to kill him and he was murdered with a scalpel, just like the one in your locker at work. The worst thing of all is that your alibi's crap.' He was watching her; she judged that what passed for reasoning was firing a few neurons behind the eyes. She said,

'Give me a good alibi, Spud. Give me the truth, and maybe I'll believe you.'

It was a slow process, but he decided eventually to tell her. 'I did a deal.'

Helena said at once, 'I think that I should advise my client...'

Beverley didn't even look at her. 'You should advise your client that I'm not interested in his drug habits at this precise moment. You should advise him that if he wants to get off a murder charge, he should give me a few more details about this deal.'

Spud had stopped talking, mouth open as if his vocal apparatus had seized up, but at least Helena wasn't arguing the point. Beverley prompted, 'What was the deal for?'

'Stuff. I'd arranged to meet in the station car park.'

'What stuff?'

He wanted not to say but even he realized that he had gone too far for taciturnity. 'Shit.'

'Heroin?'

A nod. Dempsey said in a monotone to the tape deck, 'The suspect has nodded.'

'Who were you meeting?'

He said nothing so she had to remind him, 'I need to know, otherwise it's not an alibi.'

And still nothing. His head remained bowed. She sighed and was about to get hard with him when he suddenly mumbled sadly, 'Dean Treacher.' He sounded so devastated he might have been betraying the Resistance to the Nazis.

She felt almost sorry for him. 'What time did

225

you get to the car park?'

''Bout half-seven. He was late, though. Didn't show till nearly eight.'

'Then what?'

'We did the deal.'

When he seemed disinclined to continue she prompted him with, 'I need more, Spud. You didn't stay in the car park all night, did you?'

He shook his head. 'I went to the Lido.'

She knew that he hadn't gone there for a swim.

'Why there?'

'To shoot up.'

'You were alone?' A nod, which was described for the tape deck by Dempsey. 'It was still open at that time, wasn't it?'

'Yeah.'

'So you what...?'

'I got in at the back, near the hospital – there's a hole in the fence. I waited behind the storage huts until it shut. Then I shot up.'

'Do you often go there?'

A shrug.

'Who saw you there?'

He actually laughed. 'You don't do it in front of an audience.'

'So no one saw you?'

He took a long time to say it. 'No.'

'And when did you leave?'

Another shrug. 'Christ knows. It was dark ... maybe midnight.'

Which, of course, was no alibi at all.

Back in her office, Beverley sat staring at the

surface of her desk; there was a confluence of scratches there that her mind could not stop reconfiguring into an old man's face. Richardson and Dempsey sat in front of her and waited.

'What do you think?'

'Isn't it obvious?' Dempsey's question was noticeably tinged with incredulity. 'He did it.'

Richardson said nothing; he was looking at Beverley closely, though.

She asked Dempsey, 'Why do you say that?'

'You said it yourself. He threatened Billy, he possessed a scalpel and he's got no alibi.'

She considered this before asking Richardson, 'And you?'

She knew that Richardson was considerably smarter than Dempsey, as was proved when instead of jumping in with gay abandon he said cautiously, 'It certainly looks to be a strong case...'

She expressed surprise, though. 'Does it? In what way? Because Spud threatened to kill him? I bet he does that to someone five times a day. Because a scalpel was used, perhaps?'

She asked this of Dempsey who, being a man of telescoped rather than telescopic intellect, responded with, 'Yes.'

'I don't think so. I think a scalpel's a pathetic weapon. I think someone like Spud would have gone for a carving knife, or a hunting knife. Something made out of machismo.'

'Perhaps it was all he had.'

She didn't even pretend to hear that. 'We've got no forensics linking him or the scalpel handle to the crime.'

'That doesn't mean anything. Perhaps he had more than one handle. He could easily have disposed of the clothing, too...'

It was as if she weren't listening as she said thoughtfully, 'And as for the alibi, I believe him.'

Dempsey almost jumped in his surprise. 'You what? You can't!'

Once more, a peculiarly selective deafness settled upon his superior. 'It's so pathetic, it has to be true. Also he's incriminating himself as well as one of his mates...' She asked Sam, 'Are we looking for Treacher?'

'Someone's going around to his place now.'

She nodded. 'Of course he'll deny it...'

Dempsey jumped in. 'Exactly, so that makes Spud's story useless as an alibi...'

'So why give it as one?'

The look on Dempsey's face suggested that he thought Beverley was being stupid. His ears had been in their elevated position for much of the conversation and they showed no sign of descending as he explained, 'For the same reason he first said he was at home.'

She shook her head. 'This alibi grasses up one of his mates. He wouldn't do that lightly, certainly not if it were just another lie.'

'But he's desperate not to get done for the murder; he'd say anything.'

But Beverley had gone back to the face on her desk and was impassive for long seconds before suddenly saying to it, 'Let him go.'

Even Richardson was caught by surprise by

that one.

'I'm sorry?' he asked.

Looking up she said with a perfectly straight face, 'Let him go. He didn't do it.'

Dempsey's response to this was a somewhat loud, 'You're bloody joking!' Which was odd, because nobody, least of all Dempsey, was laughing.

She would have been perfectly within her rights to bollock him within a centimetre of his miserable life. Instead she said, 'No, I'm not. Let him go on bail.'

When Dempsey had left (still unable to believe what he was being asked to do and ears still correspondingly high), Richardson asked her, 'Is this wise?'

She sighed. 'Wise? No. Right? Almost certainly.'

He didn't look at all convinced.

THIRTY-SIX

Eisenmenger looked around the sitting room with eyes that did not see the furniture or the emulsioned walls or the threadbare, dirtied carpet; his eyes only saw what was not there – the comfort, the thought, the feeling of homeliness that he had been used to living with, that he thought he had left behind years before when he stopped being a student. The sofa on which he was sitting had not been comfortable, he guessed, when it had been new, and that had been a good many summers – a good many backsides – ago. Now it was feeling its age and, presumably in retaliation, making him feel his own. He was drinking a glass of Merlot; it was not bad Merlot, but it was from a glass that was milky with dishwashing and that was cheap; it shouldn't have done, but these facts spoiled the taste of the wine. He could not stop himself thinking that the wine would have tasted so much better had he been at home and had Helena not ended their relationship. It partly intrigued him, partly annoyed him that the taste of something so nice should be so subjective.

It was his third glass that night and he had the feeling that it would not be the last; nor would it be the last time that week; it wasn't the first either. The units were racking up and he didn't care because he was a human being and he could not forever live his life thinking about his future, especially not when the present was something he could not see beyond.

He still could not quite understand what had happened to his life; the words were in his mind (after all, they boiled down to just a sentence – *Helena has met another man and would rather be with him*) but the legion of inferences and corollaries of this were still roiling around within his subconscious, refusing to land, refusing to let him grasp them and assimilate their significance. One thing, though, was starting to become plain; that he could not live the rest of his life like this. His present circumstances had to prove temporary, lest he himself prove less than permanent.

He spent the rest of the evening drinking and thinking such thoughts. He was never quite sure exactly when Beverley Wharton began to enter them.

Helena met Alan that night and although she was pleased to be with him, she did not sparkle. Afterwards, they went back to her flat and made love in the night, but she could not enjoy it. John Eisenmenger had gone, but his shade remained.

THIRTY-SEVEN

Lambert didn't have anything going for him at all. Nothing at all. He wasn't, Beverley had long ago decided, in any way attractive to look at, for a start. Not that she had ever found less than perfect physical beauty a complete bar to more intimate relations; most of the men with whom she had slept during her life had been made of something less than physical perfection, some of them perhaps even physically unappealing (when she came to in-depth analysis of their virtues). Yet as she had lain beneath them – while they sweated and panted and (on occasion) with each breath shared a little of that last cheese and onion sandwich that they had bolted in their haste – she had been able to draw some compensation from identifying somewhere within them just a tiny spot of sex appeal. Maybe not there in bucketloads, but enough to give a sugar coating, to remind her that she was with another sexual creature, something that had humanity and emotion and reacted accordingly.

Lambert, though, had not the slightest scintilla of any such thing. He was asexual, vegetable, unbending; cataleptic with disapproval of Beverley and all that she represented, he had become so immersed in outrage that he had completely failed to notice that he had drowned in it and was now a lifeless corpse. She could no more imagine Lambert copulating than she could speak Swahili.

From the moment they had first met they had disliked each other intensely, and through the years from familiarity had grown not so much contempt, more hatred; it had been proof beyond all doubt that there was not only a God but that He was a vengeful God that they had been forced to work together for so long.

As she stood in his office now, she looked not at him as he fulminated but at the wall behind him, finding it a more restful, more attractive thing. It was plain but not ugly; it did not assault her senses, did not radiate hatred. In the long run, it might prove boring, but for the time being she could see its advantages.

'Well?'

She switched effortlessly back to Lambert; she didn't need to search her short-term memory to determine the context of this interrogative. Spud. 'I don't think he did it.'

'I do. Understand?'

She was about to argue but then she was overwhelmed by resignation. It would do her no good to debate the issue anyway; why waste time and energy?

'It was just as well I found out about his impending release and stopped it.'

She was genuinely shocked by this news. She asked almost involuntarily, 'You did what?' Synchronously she thought, *Dempsey.*

'I stopped it. Mr Carney remains in custody. I'm taking over the case.' She thought, *Are you, indeed?* Lambert was continuing. 'You've wasted too much time on it already. I told you, I want you to concentrate on the Fitzroy-Hughes disappearance.'

OK, Constable Dempsey. I never forgive, and I never forget.

She ought to have been outraged that her position was to be undermined, that she was being called incompetent ... but she didn't think that she was. There was something fundamentally wrong with the case against Spud – it was constructed from the wrong materials and shaped badly – but if Lambert thought otherwise, it was better for her that she had nothing to do with it anymore. She even wondered if Lambert might fall flat on his sour, disapproving face. A delicious thought: it would be vengeance that was not only cold but on silver service.

And, without doubt, *that* was the best way to serve the stuff.

She allowed a look of anger to show because he knew he would like that, then said stiffly, 'If you say so.'

'I do.'

She enjoyed the satisfaction she saw in his eyes and suppressed a smile. *We'll see.*

He nodded curtly, clearly pleased that she had been cowed, that was she was submitting to his authority. 'So how far have you got with the Fitzroy-Hughes case?'

'I think he's dead, sir.' It would have been more welcome if she vomited down the front of his trousers and she knew it.

'Rubbish! Why?'

'Because he's got no reason to run. He's not a runaway, no matter how you look at it.'

'That doesn't mean he's dead.'

'It does if he just vanishes without saying a word, without leaving a note, without talking any clothes or valuables or even much money.'

His expression suggested he wanted to argue but all he said was, 'He was last seen at this party, is that right?'

She nodded. 'Hosted by Stephen Bright. We're trying to locate and talk to everyone present to determine where he went after that.'

'How far have you got?'

In truth she didn't know exactly. 'Just over half of them. The problem is that there was no formal guest list and Bright claims not to have been too bothered about entertaining uninvited guests.'

'Have you any reason to suspect Bright?'

'I'm not sure ... nothing concrete but...'

'Let me save you some time. Bright's clean.'

Now this was a surprise. 'May I ask how you know that?' She forgot the 'sir', but she abhorred hypocrisy and tried to avoid it whenever possible.

'It doesn't matter.'

She frowned. 'Friends in high places, is it?' she guessed.

Lambert smiled. 'As a matter of fact, no. Not everyone's corrupt in the police, Inspector.'

Ouch. Golly gosh, that hurt. She murmured, 'I'm glad to hear it.'

Lambert stared at her for so long that he seemed to have entered some form of trance; was it conceivable that Lambert was some sort of Buddhist? Had he learned how to meditate, perhaps? Was he seeking a level of enlightenment known only to a lucky, devoted few?

And then he came to and said coldly, 'If you must know, two months ago, he was caught up in the investigation of a hanging. His background was looked into then ... nothing was found. It would be a waste of time to cover old ground.'

'"Caught up in"? What does that mean?'

'He was having some sort of relationship with the deceased.'

'And?' It didn't sound much to her. There must have been something else to prompt a police investigation; hangings were three a penny unless somebody got suspicious.

He didn't like being interrogated. 'I don't know. Ask Starry – he looked into it.'

She smiled because she was a polite girl and she was grateful. 'OK, I will.'

She stood up, waited a second for dismissal, but received none, then walked out without a further word.

Eugenie Lyon had come to a decision at last. She had tried to square her findings with some rational explanation – with an explanation of any kind, in fact – and she had failed completely. It was not a situation that her training had prepared her for and she did not think that it was a situation that *any* training would prepare her for. She had decided, therefore, to swallow her pride, swallow any vestige of dignity, and ask for help. She had also decided that the least painful person to consult would be John Eisenmenger.

THIRTY-EIGHT

'Jack?'

His eyes were open but she knew that he was seeing nothing. In the half-light of the High Dependency Unit his greyness camouflaged him against the bed sheet. His lips were not only an asphyxial blue, they were retracted, thinned to mere marks on his face; an artist's impression of a man dying. The room was hot; hot and horrible. It was a place to work in, not a place to be ill in or possibly to die in. Why couldn't they even try to disguise the inhumanity of the place, the clinical unconcern with which they punctured and measured and incised and excised and assessed? Everything was functional, nothing was emotional; the environment sucked out the humanity of the patient, left them nothing more than another component in the medical machine.

He had bled catastrophically, almost exsanguinated. It had been sudden, one moment well, the next fountaining bright-red blood over his tongue; no pain, just haemorrhage. It had been in the morning, a time of bright sunlight and optimism that the day was going to be a good one. The ambulance crew had been able to do little to stop the blood, their only possible course being to pour water back into him while they rushed him into casualty; as he lay there now he had tubes from bags that hung above him running into both wrists and his left ankle.

As soon as they could they put a camera down inside him, not bothering with anaesthesia or sedation; they had found *varices*. She hadn't known what *varices* were, had therefore asked; *veins*, they had said. *Veins at the entrance to the stomach.* She had wondered why they didn't call them *veins* then, but being the good relative she had said nothing. They had tried to stop them bleeding by injecting them with something that squeezed them down, had had partial success. He had been given proper replacement blood and here he lay now, half-unconscious.

He's in borderline renal failure, they had said, *but he's young ... that's good.*

Was it? she wondered. Was it good to be so close to death so far from old age?

Behind him a machine beeped, a dark yellow line, chasing after itself, performing regular gyrations. It was an icon of medical extremity, a cliché of someone dying, and as such she was offended by it. Too many cardboard dramas on television, too much fake blood and fake acting, had turned this into a caricature, had devalued it, made it trite.

Except the underlying reality was far from trite. Part of her life was in danger of dying in that bed in front of her. She and Jack had never been in each other's lives to any great extent – after puberty they had each had their own agendas to follow and to a great extent their lives had separated. But they had never grown so far apart as to become strangers; their lives had run on parallel but close lines, close enough to see what the other was doing, far enough to feel free from interference. This detached connection had grown stronger with maturity; she might not have seen him from one year to the next but those occasions had been worth waiting for. If he had not been her brother, she sometimes thought that he might have been the only one she could ever have contemplated marrying. She was touched that he had chosen to live close by at this time of crisis in his life.

Something whispered to her to ring her mother. It would be the proper thing to do, but she couldn't bring herself to. She would panic, would insist on coming, despite the impracticality of the distance. And when she couldn't she would worry, be unable to sleep. She would keep pestering. Beverley would be bothered continuously, the hospital also. No, better to say nothing at present.

After all, Jack was going to recover. Her mother need never be bothered.

After an hour she left. He had not changed, certainly not come to, and she was inexplicably grateful for this. He needed rest, she reckoned; there would be time for consciousness later.

Better to lie there.

Just not too long.

At least, Eugenie reflected, Eisenmenger had not been either exasperated at her stupidity, or annoyed by her inexperience, or derisive of her apparent incompetence. He had listened to what she had had to say and then just sat there for a long time – so long, in fact, that she had begun to wonder if he were actually thinking about something else entirely. He seemed to be so distracted – had seemed fairly lost and forlorn when she had entered his office – after she had finished that she came close to prompting him to respond. He did not, she decided, look exactly untidy, but there was something about him that looked no longer as dapper, no longer as alert, as he had when he had first started the locum in the department. She understood that he had recently started on the on-call rota for forensic pathology, though; she put this slight dissipation in his appearance and manner down to a few late nights spent at crime scenes and in the mortuary.

After a long few minutes, Eisenmenger said slowly but with reassuring deliberation, 'Well, it seems to me that there are three possible explanations, Eugenie.' She said nothing and waited. 'The first,' he continued, 'is that one of the kidneys is not a human kidney. It could, for instance, be a sheep's kidney. In that conflagration, I doubt that the rescue people would have noticed an extra animal body at the scene.'

She nodded; it seemed plausible.

'The second is that is that the motorcyclist really did have three kidneys—'

'I've checked,' she interrupted. 'There is no known recorded case of an individual with three, perfectly formed kidneys. There are cases where people had two normal kidneys together with an embryological remnant, but in each of those instances it was barely recognizable as a kidney proper.'

He nodded but said, 'Don't discount the possibility completely. Just because it's never happened before doesn't mean it *can't* happen.'

She was well aware of the medical aphorism, *Never say never in medicine.* 'And the third?'

'Is the simplest. That he was a courier, carrying a donated kidney somewhere.'

She was taken aback by the simplicity of this idea, taken aback too by her stupidity in not thinking of it herself. Of course, that was the most likely...

Eisenmenger suggested, 'Why don't you arrange with Bristol to do some DNA analysis on the three kidneys to see if one of them is non-human or if they are all human and genetically identical? I'll have a nose around the life and times of the motorcyclist. See if anyone knows what he was carrying and where he was coming from.'

THIRTY-NINE

Stephen Bright gave the boy a kiss but found the taste of him stale, no longer as succulent, somehow almost repellent. It was always thus, and he wondered idly why it was so. He was realist enough to know that it was a kind of promiscuousness – and arrogant to be proud of this – but it was not a *deliberate* thing; the boys were disposable and he supposed that this was because he was not fundamentally a gay man. He enjoyed other men, but he did not think that he could ever love them; they were merely sex toys and he had quickly bored of his toys as a child. The girls were different, though. No matter how young they were, no matter how unsuitable, how stupid or how expensive they were, there was usually the question some-where in the back of his head concerning whether this would be the one that became more than a two-day or two-week vacation, more than sex, more than seduction-exertion-relaxation-separation.

There would be problems, of course. His life was not conventional – far from it – and he was habituated to secrecy. He did what he did and had to explain it to no one other than with vague talk of 'antiques' and 'business interests'; he rather suspected that he would have to construct a complex web of deceit (at least in the first instance) were he ever to allow a sexual partner to become any other kind of partner. He lived in hope, though; it was low rather than high hope – and so he did not let it rule him – but he rather enjoyed being teased by such things...

He closed the front door and was about to head for the shower – sex made him feel deliciously dirty, but there was a time and a place for dirt, no matter how delicious – when he thought to make himself some more coffee. He liked coffee, could drink huge quantities of it, especially in the mornings and especially after he was again alone, again in charge, once again the centre of his world. He smiled; he had long ago decided that he would not allow himself the decadence of false modesty – why should he not consider himself the most important thing in his life? He loaded the filter machine, and whilst waiting for the water to pass through it, he busied himself checking his emails.

He had two email accounts, both for business but for two very different businesses. One was for antiques and, his speciality, incunabula; a profitable but fundamentally boring business. The other was ... different, and even more profitable; it was infinitely more exciting, too. He liked the idea that he was indulging in something if not unique, then so unusual as to be all but. He thought of himself as a small part of humanity's always astonishing ability to invent, improvise and progress. He was at the forefront of modern thinking, too, for his second business was the ultimate in recycling.

The illegality of it only made it all the sweeter.

Most of the email traffic from the antiques business was routine – the most exciting was an offer of a small but (he was assured) authentic early Brueghel – and, in context, so were the majority of the emails concerning his second business venture. One though, piqued his interest; he had been waiting for it some weeks, had made sure that he was fully prepared. It was a very important commission, worth a great deal of money, and one that was likely to lead to a whole new and very lucrative market. Get this right, and he knew that he was going to be wealthy, verging on the fabulously wealthy.

He replied to the email in the affirmative, that everything was ready and that the merchandise would be en route in the next seventy-two hours; he would let the buyer know then when to expect receipt. He then turned off the computer, and went to his bedroom, past the unmade bed, thence into his walk-in wardrobe at the end of which was a small floor-mounted safe. From this he took a pile of about twenty A5 white envelopes, each with a name.

He selected the one with *Helena Flemming* written on it and could not help but smile. He had never met her, although he knew more about her than almost anyone else on earth. He knew most of her medical history and much of her social history. He knew her habits and he knew her preferences.

Crucially, too, he knew her weaknesses.

The phone call from the hospital had come when she was at work and she had left without speaking to anyone. When she got back to the flat there was, as she expected, a message from Sam asking what was going on. His voice held concern but she wondered if there was something else there – irritation, she thought. How did she feel about that? She couldn't tell whether to be pleased that someone cared enough to be irked or concerned that he was perhaps beginning to be proprietorial.

There was another message.

Hi, Beverley. It's John. Can you ring me when you have a chance? I need to see you.

He'd left a mobile number. She put it into her own mobile, allowed her thumb to hover the green 'call' button, then let it relax, a smile on her glossed lips. Was this work or pleasure, she wondered. Which would she enjoy more?

Why was she unaccountably so suddenly delighted?

She found a bottle of white wine in the fridge

and opened it. It was still light but the sun was low and the light sluggish and old. She went to her favourite spot to think, to the bay window at the back of the house. From here, because the house was built on the edge of the Birdlip escarpment, she could look out along her garden as it dropped away gently, and see beyond Gloucester and Cheltenham, spread out in the evening light. She enjoyed the feeling of elevation and also the feeling of separation; when she was here, she was out of the arena, in another place, able to be someone else for a short while.

She ought to ring Sam, explain her sudden disappearance from the station; it would be a simple thing to do, one that he perhaps deserved, but she wasn't going to. Her annoyance that he should assume some sort of rights over her was too strong to ignore; they had made no definite date for the evening, so what she did was irrelevant to him. It was her business and her business alone if she chose to fly to Paris, or go cave-diving, or to see an old acquaintance for whatever reason...

She looked at the wine as she held the glass up in front of her, a beam of intense but dying sunlight in its straw-coloured body; it was good, she decided, but not good enough to hold her in the flat all evening.

She dialled the number that John had left. He answered at once, as if he had been waiting.

Perhaps he had.

'Hello, Beverley. Thanks for getting back so quickly.'

'You said you wanted to see me.'

'Yes. Something interesting has come up. I'd like to discuss it with you.'

Was she disappointed that it sounded more like business than pleasure? She decided that she could live with it. 'Why don't we do it over a drink?'

There was no hesitation where once there would have been. 'Fine. Where?'

'Somewhere out in the country. Along the river. The Red Lion at Wainlodes.'

'I know it. Would you like me to pick you up? I can be there in an hour, if you like.'

She would like.

The River Severn's passage through Gloucestershire is stately and, except at certain times of the year, slow. It is on average perhaps fifty metres wide and its banks are for the most part gently sloping and wooded, thus allowing numerous riverside pubs to exist in the county. The Red Lion was a secluded inn near Tirley, right at the river's edge and thus regularly flooded; when it wasn't, it was a delightful, restful place, soaked in an atmosphere of rural isolation.

When Eisenmenger had arrived, she had been outside, waiting on the pavement. She had climbed into his car and he had driven off at once, barely looking at her, mumbling only a soft, almost hesitant, 'Hi.' She had surmised from this that if his ties to Helena were somehow strained, they were yet to be entirely severed. Nothing much was said until they had parked the car at the pub, about half an hour later. Because the weather was hot and the sun still relatively high the pub was crowded but they found a table outside by the river and sat down with their drinks. She sipped her white wine while he watched her. 'I expect you're wondering why I wanted to see you,' he said.

By both nature and training, Beverley had never liked dancing around gorillas that lurked in the corners of a room; she had a pathological dislike of treading in their dung. Accordingly, she asked, 'You want my help, I assume?'

He nodded. He was staring at her and in his eyes he could see fear; for a moment she was puzzled, then she guessed where it stemmed from. He was terrified that she was going to ask about Helena.

He had every right to be.

'Of course I will, John. I've never let you down before, have I?'

'No,' he admitted.

Before he could relax, though, she said, 'But I think we need to be straight with each other if we're going to work together again. That's only fair, don't you think?'

She could be very cruel, almost psychopathic in the way that she manipulated people when she sat before them in the interrogation room, but even she had difficulty as she gazed on the look in his eyes as she said this. It seemed to be a long time before he nodded and whispered, 'Of course.'

She didn't hesitate. 'Have you and Helena split up?'

More silence; a wasp buzzed around then shot off towards a child's ice cream to their right. She was suddenly aware that his body shape was subtly changing, tensions being released, others being taken up; his face, too, seemed to be hanging on to its shape only by an effort of will. His whisper this time was even lower. 'Yes.'

Even as she felt a thrill shoot through her – elation, vindication, exultation – her heart melted at the news because of what it was so clearly doing to him. To say that she had never taken to Helena barely scratched the surface; even before Helena had decided that Beverley was somehow responsible for the destruction of her family, on the few occasions that they had run across each other professionally, Beverley had thought her uptight to the point of shrivelled, as cold as liquid nitrogen, as humourless as genocide. Afterwards, her opinion of Helena had taken a bit of a nose-dive.

Yet John Eisenmenger had fallen for her, and Helena for him. Beverley did not bother to wonder at the whys and wherefores of this – shit happened all the time, after all – but she had somehow decided that she did not like it, that she would like to see it end. Now that she had her wish, though, she for the first time appreciated that her joy might not be universally shared.

She wanted to reach out to him but instinct told her not to; she said gently, 'I'm sorry, John.' He wasn't crying, but it was a fight, she could see, and she suddenly regretted asking him, saw that she had been cruel and single-minded.

As usual.

A fish leapt from the slowly flowing river. It was behind his back, not that he would have bothered about it if he had seen it. The splash was loud enough to hear and a child's voice said, 'Look at that, Mummy...'

There was no chill in the air, despite the fact that the day was drawing to a close and this almost unnatural warmth, together with the humidity from the river, leant an almost surreal, turgid sense of dreaminess, one in which the midges moved in slow motion over the water and the thick luxuriant foliage of the trees on the opposite bank seemed to be undulating as the air currents rose and fell.

With an effort, he said, 'So there it is.'

'Do you think it's permanent?' She tried not to sound too nosey, hoped that she was conveying compassion; it was a tricky thing to do, she knew from experience.

His answer was surprisingly harsh. 'I haven't decided yet.'

She fought back a small smile; he had backbone, then. She quite liked that. It was time, though, to move on from the subject. 'You were going to ask for my help.'

He took a drink, becoming steadier, more like the old John Eisenmenger. 'Yes. A curiosity, almost certainly nothing more.' She didn't rush to judgement. He had introduced her to problems with casual remarks such as that before, and in many of them, there had lain a core of evil.

'OK. Tell me about this "curiosity".'

He did so; it was simply put and in ten minutes he had finished and had handed over the information that the coroner's office had sent to Eugenie Lyon. Whilst she read it, he looked at her expectantly.

On 19th June this year Mr Peter Alan Dingwall, aged thirty-seven, a motorcyclist, was travelling south from Cheltenham towards Cirencester on the A417 when he was in collision with an Austin Maxi, registration number L333 HSP, just south of Birdlip. The motorcycle careered on to the opposite carriageway where it fell under the wheels on an oncoming heavy goods vehicle. There was a subsequent fire. Mr Dingwall was the only fatality.

Mr Dingwall's general practitioner states that he was a rare visitor to the surgery; his last visit was nine months ago when he attended because of persistent indigestion. He was given a prescription for Protium and has not attended since.

A coroner's post-mortem is requested to establish the cause of death.

She said, 'But it could easily be an animal's kidney.'

'It could,' he replied, but said it slowly. 'Except that why aren't there two? Why aren't there any other organs at all? The coroner's report doesn't mention sheep or any other large animal – and we're talking at least a large

250

dog or a sheep – on the road; and this is the A417, don't forget. It's a dual-carriageway, not a country lane.'

'And you don't think that the dead man might have been some form of genetic mutation?'

'Extremely unlikely to the point of vanishingly rare, but the DNA analysis will confirm it in a few days.'

'Leaving the possibility that he was transporting the kidney.'

'For donation, you mean?' He smiled, his personal problems banished to the back of his mind. 'I've checked the hospitals – no donation was made that night anywhere in either Gloucestershire, Herefordshire or Worcestershire.'

'What did the Mr Dingwall do for a living?'

'The information we've been given doesn't say.'

She found herself forced to point out the obvious. 'Maybe it *is* an animal kidney, John, and maybe he was carrying it; maybe it was for his tea.'

He had to admit that he hadn't thought of that; she saw a rare moment of uncertainty, the kind of thing that she and others experienced several times every day. 'OK, that's possible,' he conceded.

'In which case, no case to answer.'

He frowned thoughtfully. 'I suppose not.'

She smiled at him. 'Your sixth sense isn't always right, John. I think it's let you down this time.'

He managed a return smile. 'Probably.'

FORTY

As she let herself in there was another message awaiting her. She played it because she feared it might be from the hospital, but it was Sam again. He still sounded discomforted, somewhat snotty with her, clearly ever so slightly paranoid that she had not been in contact.

Sod you, Sam.

She phoned the hospital; Jack was 'stable'. She didn't want stability, she wanted improvement, but she made herself sound grateful and went into the bathroom for a shower before bed, reflecting how much she had enjoyed the evening; enjoyed it so much that maybe she wouldn't mind taking it further.

Maybe.

She climbed into bed, put out the light at once.

FORTY-ONE

She knew the next day was going to be shitty and, inevitably, it was; the only positive was that when she phoned the hospital they told her that Jack was conscious, though groggy. She asked them to tell Jack that she would be in to see him that evening.

Which left the shitty part. The fallout from being taken off the Whipple murder was bad enough but it became immediately obvious that Sam was not happy. When she walked past his desk on the way to her office he kept his head down and pretended to be scribbling something on a pad of paper; she wondered what – his top-ten totty list perhaps.

Suddenly he seemed too young for her, too far from maturity.

Grow up, Sam.

She had barely sat down before the phone rang and she could find no surprise at all that it was Superintendent Braxton inviting her to come to his office; 'inviting' as in 'demanding'. When she left her office, Sam had vacated his desk. She passed Dempsey in the corridor who couldn't meet her gaze, thus confirming her suspicions that it was he who had gone running to Lambert. The walk up to the third floor was long, giving her enough time to recall the conversation of the night before; oh to be in Braxton's position, hand out the crap to other people.

She knocked on the door and was rewarded with an immediate, barked, 'Come in.'

Braxton was standing behind his desk, a bad sign.

She and Braxton had always got on reasonably well. He had never tried to abuse his position, never so much as suggested that he considered her anything other than a colleague, never intimated that he thought her a bitch or a tart or a thing of contempt. He was a gentleman; he swore but only in moderation, he sometimes went out for a drink after work but never drank too much, he opened the door for women. He was tall, balding and hawk-nosed but not hideous; he was widowed with two daughters, both at university, both studying modern languages.

There had been more than one occasion when Beverley had suspected that God was playing a trick, that Braxton should have been a headmaster, or perhaps a psychiatrist, and there was some beer-swilling, lecherous semi-hooligan who was trying desperately to figure out Class 3B's timetable or to treat a sufferer of obsessive-compulsive neurosis, probably by smacking his head against a wall.

But even gentlemen could be incandescent with fury.

Except that Braxton showed this in ways other than a loud voice.

'Sit down, Inspector.' He didn't smile – a bad sign.

She complied, although she didn't want to; it placed her at a psycho-sociological disadvantage.

He said nothing, merely looking at her and not, she guessed, because he had suddenly discovered pulchritude as a metaphysical concept. She was forced to speak.

'I take it you want to talk to me about the Whipple killing, sir.'

'Chief Inspector Lambert has complained about your conduct.'

She assumed the poker face that she had taken to wearing for decades now. It came in useful whether she was at work or, on the odd occasion, when she had found herself lying under some Godhelpus senior police officer who thought that he was some sort of love machine.

Chief Inspector Lambert can sit on a spike...

'Has he, sir?'

'He practically accuses you of dereliction of duty. Says that you were going to let the chief suspect go, despite overwhelming evidence.'

'Despite what *he* calls overwhelming evidence. I call it holier than the Pope's underpants.'

If he found the quip amusing, it failed to cause any ripples on the surface.

'He is your superior officer, Inspector.'

'That doesn't make him infallible, sir.'

She saw his eyes close as if he were suddenly tired to exhaustion. 'I know you and Lambert don't always agree, Inspector, but I had hoped that the pair of you would have let professional concerns supersede your divergence of views.'

Shouldn't we have Lambert in for this tête-à-tête? I mean, it takes two to tangle.

'I don't think Carney did it, sir.'

'Chief Inspector Lambert does.'

But Chief Inspector Lambert's a shit copper. 'May I ask your opinion, sir?'

To judge from the look on his face, poor old Braxton – the lower ranks called him 'Giblet', which was supposedly frowned upon by people such as Beverley – discovered this question to be a teensy-weensy bit indigestible. 'Well...'

She saw the weakness, went through it without touching the sides. 'I know I've got a reputation, sir, but surely you've seen enough to judge that I'm not too bad a police officer, sir.'

A smile twitched across his face like summer lightning. He turned away and went to a shelf full of box files, contenting himself with staring at them for a second or two. Then he turned abruptly, almost as if they had whispered to him some advice, and said, 'But I have seen enough to believe you're a good one, Inspector?'

'I honestly and truly believe that Carney didn't kill Billy Whipple.'

'Then who did?'

It was an odd question; it implied that there could only be proof of innocence unless someone else had been found guilty.

'Does that matter?'

'Chief Inspector Lambert assures me that

Carney had motive, means and opportunity.'

The Holy Trinity of police investigation, and just as open to heretical disputation. 'I thought we'd moved on from that mantra.'

He suddenly became angry. 'The Chief Inspector has ten years' more experience than you have.'

'I know, sir.' She tried to sound reasonable because she liked Braxton and he had in the past been courteous and pleasant to her. 'But that doesn't change my opinion of the evidence. I can't escape from the view that Spud didn't do it.'

She saw that he was slightly mollified by this and she hurried to consolidate this small piece of progress. 'I'm not saying that Carney didn't do it, I'm just saying that I don't believe it yet, not on the evidence so far found. Chief Inspector Lambert is clearly a little more convinced of the evidence than I am; it's only a question of degree.'

Braxton listened to what she said, then sighed and sat down – good sign, she thought – lips pursed, clearly looking at things from a new perspective. She had not just pressed the right buttons, she had performed a complex calculation and created out of bleakness quite a pleasant-looking vista. He said after a short pause, 'Very well, Inspector. I accept your explanation.' If she thought she was home free and completely unscathed, he hurried to disillusion her. 'But next time you're to behave more professionally, understand? I don't want to hear again that you've let your problems with Chief Inspector Lambert interfere with the smooth running of an investigation.'

'No, sir.'

He nodded curtly, a period mark at the ending of the telling off, a sign that they were to move on.

'What about the Fitzroy-Hughes business?'

Oh, please. Not you, too.

'No breakthrough yet.'

'The Chief Inspector also had some views on the conduct of that case, as well.'

'Did he, sir?'

Braxton looked almost sad, as if he had expected better of his children, as if this squabbling really was very juvenile. He said, 'Yes, he did.'

'Well, now I'm off the Whipple case, I'll be able to devote more energy to it.'

He nodded slowly. 'You do that,' he advised.

She assumed that the interview was at an end and therefore she stood up but before she had moved away he said almost in an undertone, 'Chief Inspector Lambert said one more thing, too.'

She paused, wondering what this next toxic trinket would be.

'He implied that your relationship with Sergeant Richardson was something more than professional.'

Of course.

She frowned. 'Sir?'

Braxton was smiling. 'I told him that just because the gossips in the station say something, it doesn't necessarily mean that it's true.'

He dropped his head and she was left examining his pate and wondering why it was so shiny; did he polish it? 'Thank you, sir.'

No response. She walked to the door but just before she opened it he said, apparently to the blotter, 'Break it off, Beverley.'

FORTY-TWO

On her return to her office, she got out from her desk drawer the photocopy of Theodore's cheque and looked at it again, wondering what it meant, if it meant anything at all. Her door was open and after a moment Sam came in. He said nothing and neither did she; her eyes flicked up but returned almost at once to the sheet of paper, leaving him to stand in front of the desk. His feet were slightly apart, his hands behind his back, a military stance that he adopted naturally.

When she spoke it was with easy authority. 'I want you to find out everything you can about Vermilion Ltd.'

'Who are they?'

'They fund Stephen Bright's antiques operation.'

'What are you going to do?'

Which was actually none of his business. 'I'm going to speak with Inspector Starry.'

'Why?'

She kept her temper well leashed; she still liked him, after all. 'Because he's going about saying Stephen Bright is a wonderful man who saves kittens from drowning and I don't believe it.'

Sam remained there, standing as if militarily at ease, his presence well and truly in the centre of where her attention ought to be. She asked, 'Something wrong, Sam?'

To which he reacted with immediate diffidence, saying after something of an inaudible stutter, 'Lambert's charged Spud with Billy Whipple's murder.'

'Good. I hope they're both very happy.'

After which he actually made a move to go but then, as if his feet were adherent to the dirty, stained carpet of her office, he ended up remaining in exactly the same position.

Knowing exactly what all this was about, Beverley looked up at him. 'Problem, Sam?'

'I rang last night.'

'I know you did. Twice.'

'You didn't ring back.'

'No.'

'May I ask why?'

She thought, *No, you may not,* but what she said was more conciliatory. 'It matters to you, I see.'

'Yes, it does.'

He really is smitten.

She could have lied, she could have told him the whole, complete and unadulterated truth or she had have done what she did.

'You don't own me, Sam.'

'No, I know, but...'

'So what's the problem?'

He couldn't say, of course, as she'd guessed, but this shyness proved so painful to behold that, to her own incredulity, she found herself softening. 'Sam, my brother's been taken ill. I went to visit him last night in hospital.'

'Oh.'

He was now even more discomfited which in turn produced even greater guilt in her. But why? He began to apologize, as if he knew what he was doing and was determined to make her suffer. She had to cut him short. 'Please, Sam, it's all right. No problem. I understand.' During which, she counted three lies for the price of one.

'I was worried, you see...'

For which read *paranoid*.

But at least he was contrite. She said quickly, 'I was just with Braxton.'

'Yes?'

'I think we'll have to cool things for a while.'

The paranoia descended again, as she saw from the frown. 'What do you mean?'

'He gave me a direct warning, Sam. He knows and he wants it to stop.'

'Yeah, but...'

'He was serious, Sam.' Which stopped him trying to protest but which did nothing to increase his quotient of happiness. She offered, 'Just for the time being.'

He nodded; not enthusiastically, more what the discerning might have described as 'hesi-tantly'. 'OK.'

'Good.'

A pause before she said, 'I'm sorry.'

This time a nod but at least this was closely pursued by, 'I'll check out Vermilion.'

She smiled at him. 'Good.'

He said, 'I looked into Gary Allen.'

'And?'

'Nothing incriminating. No record to speak of.'

'What about this chap Hertwig?'

'I'm off to see him now. Do you want to come?'

She shook her head, could see no point in travelling all the way to Cirencester for a negative; Starry's views on Stephen Bright she found far more enticing.

He left then. Left her feeling an immiscible mix of relief and remorse.

FORTY-THREE

Inspector Reginald Starry was close to retirement and, in the opinion of his colleagues, had been all his life. He had been born old and would die old; oldness had claimed him for its own, groomed him, nurtured him, pruned him even. He did not have a spark of life, more a pilot light of it. He wasn't a bad copper, though; just not inspirational. You didn't go to Reg Starry for the pep talk before the big

match; he was more of a post-match com-
mentator, who always had the answer but a bit
too late and was always moaning about how
badly it had gone.

She found him in his office, drinking tea. He
drank a lot of tea, did Reg; he made it in his
office in a small china teapot with loose-leaf
tea. Refused tea made with teabags and
exhibited something akin to apoplexy if he
discovered he had been given tea made in the
mug.

'Do you want a cup?' he asked affably. In
his office the atmosphere was comfortable,
serene, almost somnolent; he might have been
at home, pondering whether to have a potter
around the dahlias.

'No, thanks.' She sat down, then asked,
'Mind if I sit?'

He didn't, of course. He had been doing the
crossword although not apparently with great
success since only five down had been filled in;
she wondered where he found the time and
whether she would find any if she looked there.

'What can I do for you, Beverley?'

'I'm told you know something about Stephen
Bright.'

'Do I?'

His frown accentuated the liver spots on his
forehead. *Faded* was the word that seemed to
sum him up best. She did not think, however,
that he had faded from anything brilliant.

'Antiques dealer who lives in Pittville. Bit of
a playboy, I should judge. He was mixed up in
a hanging.'

He made the connection. 'Oh, yes. Curious case.'

She was immediately interested. 'In what way?'

'A middle-aged woman hanging herself. Not the normal epidemiological profile. Unusual to see a petticoat hanging there from the rafters.'

'What was her name?'

He stood up, went to a filing cabinet; whilst he was searching through it he asked, 'What's your interest in Bright?'

'He's name cropped up in a missing person's case.'

He found the file, turned and opened it. 'Here we are – Violet Esterly.' He came back to the desk, put it down in front of him. 'She was a lab technician at the General. Found hanging in her garage at 4 Crimea Close, Maisemore; her husband had gone out with the dog. Two teenage sons. The garage was locked, accessible from the house but that was secure too.'

'Note?'

'As usual, no.'

'If the house was secure and she was known to be depressed, why were you involved?'

'I wouldn't have been, except that the husband made a fuss. Apparently he came across his wife's mobile-phone bill, found a lot of calls to Mr Bright. Said that he must have had something to do with his wife's death because of a mobile-phone message.'

'What did the message say?'

'Something about being sorry if she ended the affair.'

Which sounded odd to the point of impossibility to Beverley; the Stephen Bright she had met was a love 'em and leave 'em merchant. He wouldn't be too bothered about ending an affair, probably had six on the go at once, each of a different sexual orientation.

'Is that it? She wanted out of a love affair? A vague text message?'

Starry became defensive. 'I didn't think much of it either, but the poor sod of a husband went bonkers; he made a fuss to the coroner, who in turn got us involved. When I told him that I thought there was nothing in it, he threatened to report me, to write to the papers, all sorts. No matter what I said to him, he wouldn't listen. It was obvious to me that it was a suicide – everything pointed to that. There was a family history, for a start, and her husband said that she'd been a bit down of late. They'd had money troubles – defaulted on the mortgage a couple of times. There was nothing sinister at all; the only slightly odd thing was the money, and that's easily explicable. I think it's entirely possible that Bright threatened to blab about it to her husband unless she carried on the affair. She was stuck. This was the only way out.'

'What money was this?'

'Bright was paying her money, but so what? Bright's well off; there's no reason why he wouldn't give his mistress the odd few quid now and again.'

'Can I see the file?'

She sensed reluctance but he complied and

turned the file around. It was cachectic, almost a précis of an investigation.

'And what was Mr Bright's story?'

Starry smiled. 'He wouldn't admit it at first, but then he came clean. He was having an affair with her, all right.'

To outward scrutiny Beverley was reading the file but in reality she was trying to discover why she didn't like this story. 'How old was Mrs Esterly?'

'Fifty-three.'

'Attractive?'

He hesitated. 'Isn't that in the eye of the beholder?'

'You've presumably beheld a photograph of her. Did you think that she was attractive?'

He said gravely, 'I wouldn't have said so, no. But that doesn't mean that Stephen Bright didn't fancy her.'

From what Beverley had seen of him, she doubted very much that fifty-three-year-old laboratory technicians were Stephen Bright's cup of Darjeeling. 'And you were absolutely satisfied that this was suicide?'

He became affronted. 'Of course. The pathologist was quite happy.'

Which, as far as she was concerned, meant bugger all. 'Thanks.' She stood up.

'Satisfied?'

She paused, turned, smiled. 'In a way.'

FORTY-FOUR

Violet Esterly had lived with her husband, Brian, in a house that was modern, fairly well kept, but small. It was in Maisemore, just to the north of Gloucester, a pleasant enough place with only one problem; because it was close to the Severn and relatively low-lying, it had an amphibian existence, spending as much time in the water as out. Beverley found herself in a small close, all the houses similar, all of them compact; each was accompanied by a garage but only number four's was open. It was empty; perhaps, she thought, it would never be used again.

She wondered if there would be anyone in but the ring of the doorbell produced a response after two minutes. 'Mr Esterly?'

A nod. She couldn't miss the sense of loss that hung around him.

She showed her warrant card. 'May I come in? I'd like to talk to you.'

'What about?'

'Just a quick chat about your wife.'

He didn't understand, but he was intrigued and he let her in without much hesitation. The first thing she noticed was that the house was cold, despite the sunshine; the second thing was that it was untidy. It had an air of recent neglect, a house previously ordered now gradually decaying into dishevelment. Computer games were piled unsteadily by the console under the television in the corner; the sofa was half hidden by newspapers and magazines, some open; three empty beer cans were on the coffee table; a pizza carton had been squashed and forcibly inserted into an unwilling and undersized wastepaper bin.

'I was just going through things ... trying to work out what's what.' As he came out with this curiously uninformative statement he gestured at the dining-room table that was visible through an arch in the room beyond. It was hidden by a kaleidoscopic array of papers, notebooks, chequebooks and scraps of paper. He added, 'She didn't have a will.'

He moved some papers and she sat on the sofa and he slumped down with something that was the mewling offspring of a sigh and groan into a straight-backed chair that had previously been the last resting-place of a crisp packet. 'Bit of a mess,' he commented in apologetic tones. He gave forth the air not just of sadness but of exhaustion.

She didn't say anything except, 'It must be very tough for you. I don't want to take up much of your time.'

'It's all right, I've got plenty of that. Compassionate leave. They've given me a couple of months off.' He sounded proud, as if most men wouldn't have received such largesse from them, whoever 'they' were. 'Actually, it's nice to talk to someone. People tend to avoid you, don't want to get involved.' He was balding, with small eyes and a mouth that she judged would always have been sad. 'What can I do for you?'

'This might be painful for you...' Actually she knew bloody well it was going to be painful – as in excruciating – but she had a job to do and no tears to shed. 'It's about someone whose name cropped up in connection with your wife.'

'Bright?' He asked this suddenly, almost eagerly.

'That's right. Stephen Bright...'

He was off, now. Animation coming from emotion coming from ... what?

'I knew that there was something going on. She'd been so odd recently. Secretive ... Tired, too.' She was about to ask another question when he continued, 'It was so easy for her, you see. She used to do on-call at the lab. I wouldn't know if she was at the lab or not, would I? I had no reason to check up on her. They might even have done it there, at the hospital ... the on-call technician has a room to sleep in.'

She could see that he had obsessed about it.

'Could I ask how you learned about the affair?'

There was a dislocation and she was momentarily uncertain of what had happened, and then she realized; her use of the word 'affair'. He stood up abruptly. 'I'm neglecting my duties as host,' he said. 'Tea? Coffee?'

She didn't want anything to drink but she did want to have an excuse to linger as long as possible. 'Black coffee, please.'

'Sugar?'

'No, thanks.'

He smiled. 'I should have guessed. Someone as slim as you wouldn't take sugar.'

He left her with that and went to the kitchen. She looked around the room for family photographs, found none. Perhaps there was more to this marriage than he would like her to believe. He returned to the room with two thick porcelain mugs on a wooden tray; he handed one to Beverley. On the side were the words, *SEX ADDICT.* When he saw her looking at it he said quickly, 'I'm sorry! I didn't mean...'

She smiled reassurance at him. 'No offence.' The irony didn't escape her, though.

He sipped his milky coffee and then said, 'You were asking how I found out about it.'

'If you wouldn't mind.'

'It was only after she'd done it...' He stopped abruptly, looked up at her then quickly down again. 'Hung herself. I was going through correspondence, the stuff that had just piled up ... the first thing I noticed was that someone was paying her money. I thought that was a bit odd but I didn't pursue it and, anyway, I'd come across her mobile-phone bill, found that she was calling this number a lot. I didn't recognize it.'

'What did you do?'

'I rang it.'

'And?'

'I got an answerphone. Steve Bright wasn't in, but I could leave a message.'

'Did you?'

'No.'

'And what did you do then?'

'I tried to talk to him several times, but with no success. Then I found that text on her mobile.'

'What did that say?'

He put his coffee mug down on the floor beside his chair; he was so keen to do what he wanted to do that the coffee slopped everywhere. He scurried out of the room and for the first time she sipped her coffee and then discovered the reason why he didn't care if the coffee went on to the carpet. He returned with a mobile phone. 'Here.' He thrust it at her having pressed the buttons to bring up a text. 'That was the last text she received.'

Think very carefully. If you end it now, I'm afraid I'll have to tell everyone our secret.

'What did you make of that?'

'It's obvious, isn't it? She wanted to end the affair and he didn't. He threatened her ... forced her into a corner. The only thing she had left was...' he paused awkwardly, '...to take her own life.'

Well, that was one interpretation, she thought. 'Tell me about this money.'

'It was in her bank statements. We've each got a personal account so I wouldn't normally know what she's got in there. She'd been receiving large amounts of money at regular intervals. Usually a thousand quid.'

'How? Cheque?'

'Cash.'

'How often?'

'About every six weeks.'

Blackmail. This word was so loud in her head she barely heard what he said next. 'Pardon?'

'She'd just bought herself a new car. I wondered at the time how she was able to afford it ... now I know.'

'So you told Inspector Starry.'

'No, I told the coroner's office. They were taking statements, that kind of thing. I told them what I'd found; said it needed looking into. When I told them about the money, they referred it to the police straightaway.'

She could see it, but she didn't like it.

'Do you know for how long the affair had been going on?'

He shrugged. 'Months, I guess.'

'Had she done anything like it before?'

'Never.' The certainty in his voice might have had solid foundation, might have covered quicksand.

'Have you any idea how she might have met Mr Bright?'

This question surprised him, apparently one he had never before considered. 'No,' he decided after a moment. 'No, I don't.'

She thought about what she had learned as she sipped the coffee and tried not to wince at its flavour. She found herself wondering if he was more hurt by Bright's largesse than by the cuckolding as she held up the mobile phone. 'Has anyone checked this over?'

'I've looked through the inbox and the numbers called. There's nothing else I could see; some of it was gibberish, though.'

One man's gibberish...

'No forensic examination's been done, though? Nobody took it away?'

'No.'

'May I? I'll give you a receipt for it.'

He looked momentarily unsure, as if to do this would be give away a part of his memory for her. Then, 'Sure. Why not?'

'Thanks.'

She scribbled out an official receipt. 'One more thing. Do you have a recent photograph of your wife?'

'Um ... yes, I think so.' He stood up, looking around the room as if for clues. Clearly, reflected Beverley, a close and loving couple. He said, 'Hang on a minute,' then left the room, returning a few moments later with a photo album. 'These were taken last year at some sort of social do at the laboratory.' A few seconds' rapid leafing through the album and he finally found his wife in a group of three in a bowling alley. She was quite large, had short-cut dark hair and features that were slightly masculine.

'Thank you,' said Beverley, handing the album back to him.

'Do you want to keep it?'

'That won't be necessary.' Now he seemed disappointed, as if an image of his wife were one thing he really would have liked to have disposed of. She said politely, 'Thank you for your time.'

'Not at all, not at all.' He was suddenly animated. 'It's been nice ... break in the routine. You know, makes a change.'

'Of course.'

He led the way to the front door. She expected him to open it but although his hand went to the latch, it hesitated there.

'I mean it ... I've really enjoyed it.'

She nodded but didn't really know what he was getting at.

'I'm lonely, you see...'

'I understand.'

'I don't suppose—?'

She caught on just before he said the words and interrupted as quickly as she could, 'I'm sorry, Mr Esterly, but I'm late already. I really must be going.'

He said at once, 'Of course, of course...'

He opened the door. 'Goodbye, then.'

The tone wasn't hurt or offended, just resigned. She walked quickly back to the car. She kept her eyes straight ahead as she drove away, aware that he was looking at her and it was only when she was on the road back towards Gloucester that she shook her head. She didn't know whether to be amused or alarmed or shocked.

FORTY-FIVE

Jack was pale and far from his normal self but at least he was alive and at least he was no longer comatose. As he sat in the chair by his bed blood dripped into his left forearm and, just for good measure, clear fluid – perhaps saline, perhaps tap water, perhaps vodka – dripped into his right.

'You look like a puppet.'

'A rag doll would be more like it. I feel as though my bones have been dissolved.'

She bent down and kissed him, then sat on the bed.

'I can't stay long.'

He smiled. 'Getting fed up already? I understand.'

'Now...'

He held up a hand causing the bag of clear fluid to swing briefly and stiffly. 'Only joking, sis.'

She nodded and smiled. 'You're looking a lot better.'

'I should hope so. I understand that last time you came I was close to death.'

She put her head from one side to the other slowly. 'I've seen you better, but I reckon you were no worse than the time you drank half a bottle of Uncle Rufus's Calvados.'

He grinned. 'I'm not sure which was worse – the hangover or his dressing down.'

Their mutual laughter lightened the mood and for the next twenty minutes the talk was of shared memories that neither had revisited for a long time.

The only slightly discordant tone was struck just before she came to leave him, when she asked something that had been bothering her for some days.

'Why did you come, Jack?'

'Sorry?'

'Why did you come here, to Gloucestershire? You've got no ties to the place.'

'You're here,' he pointed out but she knew from his tone that this was not the reason.

'And?'

He was evasive. 'Do I need another reason?'

'No...'

'Well, then.'

And he would say no more; much as she wanted to press the point, she didn't; possibly fearing that he would get angry, but possibly because she was afraid of what the answer might prove to be.

There were no preliminaries – no 'Hi's' or 'How are yous' or introductions – merely the words, 'All three kidneys are human and two are from one individual, the third is from another.'

'You're certain?'

'One hundred per cent.'

She thought, *So he's right yet again.* To Eisenmenger, she said, 'We need to meet. Do you want to come here or shall I come to you?'

He looked around at his flat. 'I'll come to you.'

She looked at her watch. 'Make it a couple of hours. I have some phoning to do.'

She knew the coroner's officers vaguely. A pleasant trio of retired policemen, they were tasked with gathering information about deaths, working on behalf of the coroner in order to determine whether there should be further investigation, usually in the form of an autopsy. If the death was not suspicious (if no other party had been implicated) and for a variety of legally defined reasons the death could not be certificated, then they asked a local pathologist to perform an autopsy; if, following that, the death was thought to be unnatural, an inquest would be convened and it would fall to the coroner's office to make further investigation to determine the precise circumstances of the death.

They worked strict office hours and so she had to call Neil Dawson, the chief coroner's officer, at home. That her call was not well received was obvious from the impatient, somewhat peremptory answers her questions provoked.

'Tell me about Peter Alan Dingwall.'

'The motorcyclist? What about him?'

'Have you had a chance to look into the death yet?'

Beverley heard him becoming defensive at

once. 'We've taken some statements, but it's only been a few days. The pathologist's report hasn't even reached us yet.'

'Who was he?' She realized at once that she would be taken literally and added at once, 'What did he do? What was he doing when he died? Where was he going?'

'I'm afraid I can't remember.'

'Then perhaps you'd better get to the office and look through the papers. I'll ring you there.'

'But it's late.'

'And this is potentially a murder, Mr Dawson ... Shall we say half an hour?'

'But...'

She cut the connection.

FORTY-SIX

She was aware that Dawson hadn't been a bright star in the constabulary firmament, more a brown dwarf, although to be fair to him it seemed that some of his predecessors had been more akin to dark matter. When she phoned the coroner's office Dawson sounded disgruntled to the point of being completely without gruntles.

'Have you managed to find the case papers?'

'Yes.'

'If you could give me the facts, then...?'

A sigh then in a monotone of exasperated boredom he began, 'Mr Dingwall, aged thirty-seven, was a motorcycle courier. He ran his own small company. He was born in Torquay but moved to Gloucestershire thirteen years before. A variety of jobs – minicab driver, delivery-van driver, milkman – before he set up a small courier business two years ago.'

'Was he working on the night that he died?'

He heard him turning pages. 'Yes, he was.'

'Who for?'

'He had picked up a package from an address in Cheltenham and was on his way with it to an address in Cirencester.'

'What was in the package?'

There was a pause as he looked through the paperwork. 'Here we are,' he said, 'It was an antique silver snuffbox.'

She suddenly felt oddly cold.

Afraid that she already knew the answer, she asked, 'Who was the sender?'

'Stephen Bright.'

There must be a hundred people with that name in Gloucestershire...

But no way is this a coincidence.

'What address was the package picked up from?'

The answer, when it came, was even more startling.

'A firm of funeral directors – Gorlin, Goltz and Son. An address in Swindon Village.'

'You're sure?'

'Yes...'

'Not a private address in Pittville?'

279

'No. It's quite plain.'

She paused, then said distractedly, 'Thank you.'

He was about to ask if that was all she needed from him when the phone went dead.

She was still deeply puzzled when the buzzer sounded and she admitted John Eisenmenger to the building; a few moments later he sounded the bell and she opened the door. He said at once, 'What's wrong?'

She found that she couldn't speak properly, in fact could only shake her head and whisper, 'Don't ask.'

She led him into the sitting room and sat him down. Without asking, she fetched two wine glasses and a bottle of red wine from which they were filled. He said, 'If it's inconvenient, I'll come back another time.'

'No,' she said at once. 'It's very convenient.'

He didn't look convinced but waited. She swallowed some wine and then recounted what she had found out from Neil Dawson.

'So he *was* a courier,' he said to himself.

'But carrying a snuffbox, apparently. And, to make it all even more peculiar, he picked it up from a funeral directors.'

'Deceased's property?' he guessed.

'Maybe. I'll see if I can get to see his paperwork tomorrow but I doubt that it's going to have the word "kidney" crossed out and "snuffbox" inserted.'

'And no snuffbox was found at the scene?'

She shook her head. 'If it was ever there, I doubt that it would have come through the conflagration too well.'

He was silent for a while, rubbing the rim of the wine glass against his upper lip, looking at everything and nothing. She watched him, finding herself admiring the way that he could lose himself in such abstraction so totally; he gave the impression of communing with something, of a preternatural omniscience that was almost spiritual, almost alarming. He suddenly took a breath in. 'Tell me more about Mr Bright.'

She had indicated that she was interested in Stephen Bright for other reasons and now she filled him in. When she had finished, Eisenmenger was again intensely thoughtful. 'Stephen Bright's a common name; it could easily be coincidence.'

'I agree, accept that it's not at all a common name amongst antique dealers in the fair county of Gloucestershire; there are no others, in fact.'

'And he might be connected with the disappearance of this young man?'

'And also with the apparent suicide of a middle-aged woman in Maisemore.'

More silence, then he murmured, 'Mr Bright has an eclectic CV.'

'He's involved, John. What he's involved in, I don't know; but definitely involved in something, and it's something illegal.'

'Copper's instinct?' he asked, eyebrows raised and a faint smile on his lips.

'That, and experience. I've met people like him before; they radiate disdain, wallow in their perceived power over others.'

'Difficult to catch, though, I would think.'

'Almost impossible, usually. I mean, look at Bright. Two people connected with him have died and one has disappeared who is almost certainly dead, yet despite what I think, he's completely clean; I know he had something to do with at least two of them, but I'm nowhere near proving it.'

'There's potentially another death he's connected with,' Eisenmenger pointed out quietly.

'Which one's that?'

'The owner of the kidney.'

It was later – much later – and Eisenmenger asked, 'So what do we do about all this?'

Unusually, Beverley had allowed herself to become as drunk as the man she was drinking with. She found her mind clouded and had to think for a moment. 'We have a human kidney that is unaccounted for. Under the Human Tissue Act, that is by definition an offence.'

'So the forces of law and order can swing into action, then? You'll be reporting this?'

That was what she ought to have done; that was what she would have done ... under different circumstances. She said vaguely, 'Of course.'

He missed the significance of her tone, drank yet more wine. She had put on some Ravel and the sinuous rhythms were insinuatingly mesmeric. She was thinking about precisely what she would do.

One thing was for sure. She would not be

282

telling Lambert.

Like Eisenmenger, she drank some more wine and Ravel played on.

FORTY-SEVEN

Helena had enjoyed the meal although Alan had thought the service rather shoddy; being Alan, he had not made a fuss and someone not knowing him might not have appreciated that he was less than enamoured of things, but Helena had spotted the signs – the slight shortness of the responses (although never less than polite), the minimal restriction in body language, the near indefinable sense that he was not enraged but saddened by this turn of events.

It was this supreme economy that she found more and more was the thing she found most attractive about him. He seemed so perfectly self-contained, so wonderfully serene within himself; it was a serenity that was strikingly different from John Eisenmenger's, and this was a revelation of wonder to her. She had always assumed that serenity was a uniform entity, the same no matter where it was found, but now she knew different. Eisenmenger's serenity had been contained, outwardly smooth and perfect, yet hiding huge inner tensions, like the huge forces contained with a single drop of glass. Alan's, though, seemed to be a calmness that was present through to his core; it permeated him, was present in every cell. He really seemed to have learned to come to terms with himself and with the world.

She found herself relaxing in his company in a way that she had never known before. Her life had known so many traumas, so much pain, that she had always assumed that respite was a thing gone from her, that she would never again reach safe harbour. Yet she had. It sounded in her head like romantic slush, but she could not help thinking that when she was with Alan, she had reached a place that she had been searching out for a long time. She did not regret her time with John Eisenmenger – far from it, for he had undoubtedly helped her on her journey from the depths of her depression following the deaths of her parents and the suicide of her stepbrother – but she realized now that they had gone as far as they could go together.

She only hoped that John realized that as well.

On the way to her flat in the taxi, they murmured to each other in the low voices that people who are recently in love use while the taxi driver looked straight ahead and pretended to listen only to the radio and the messages coming through from his control. The taxi driver was asked to wait whilst Alan took Helena up to her flat – he had an early morning meeting and wanted to do yet more preparation for it – and then told to take Alan to his own house in Bishops Cleeve.

After Alan had left her, Helena tried to cope with the feeling of disappointment by busying herself with percolating some coffee and running a bath.

The doorbell rang.

Completely without evidence, she assumed that it was Alan, returning for some reason, perhaps something stupidly romantic, perhaps something prosaic like he had mislaid his keys. She went at once to the door and opened it without checking who it was.

FORTY-EIGHT

'Sam?'

He was walking past the open door of her office; she didn't need to see the look on his face to know that he was an unhappy token black sergeant; even as he turned, his body language was drenched in something that struck her as very close to angry disappointment. His face was impassive but impassive in a cold, furious way. 'Inspector?'

How many ways to say a word? At least a thousand, and every one of them either a different weapon or a different caress. She had lived too long to pay too much attention to the moods of those she worked with, even if she had shared a bed with them. 'Can I have a word?'

He came in; there was something of the adolescent called into the head teacher's study about all this, she reflected. There was a silence – it was not *a* silence, it was just *silence* – as he stood before her. She indicated that he should sit down but, when he did so, it was stiffly. She did not have to think too deeply to work out what was wrong with him, but such personal considerations were irrelevant to her. One lesson that she had learned early was to separate life in her bed and life in her workplace; she would have probably hung herself by now if she hadn't.

'I want you to look into a company for me. It's a firm of funeral directors called Gorlin, Goltz and Son. They're located in Swindon Village.'

He noted it down but then spoiled it all by asking, 'Why?'

She considered her response to this. Had it come from a sergeant who was not clearly a severely wound-up and borderline-insubordinate sergeant, she might have supplied at least a token reason for wanting the information. As it was, she asked simply, 'Why not?'

'I was merely wondering if this has any relevance to our ongoing investigations,' he said, but said it, as far as she was concerned, all wrong. There was a degree of stiffness about him that reminded her of a young Chief Inspector Lambert.

'I don't know, Sam. If I had to justify every occasion I wanted some information that might or might not be relevant, I'd suffocate under the paperwork.'

'I'm very busy at the moment.'

'Aren't we all?'

'Is this relevant to the Fitzroy-Hughes case?'

She did well, she thought, because she didn't erupt at this. 'No.'

'The Chief Inspector wants us to concentrate on that case, doesn't he?'

'The Chief Inspector wants us to use our initiative, I hope. Why don't we do that?'

She looked down at her papers but all her attention was on Sam; she did not need eyes to know that he wasn't happy. She let things ride for a few seconds before raising her gaze to him and asking tiredly, 'What is it, Sam?'

'Where were you last night?'

'I meant to ring you, I'm sorry.'

'Is it your brother? Were you at the hospital?'

She thought that she could just have said yes, lying by omission rather than commission and feeling the better for it, unaware that he would have been seen through this deception. As it was she decided that she had a point to prove.

'For a brief while.'

'You weren't at home. I rang several times.'

She flipped. 'Look, Sergeant. Just accept that I wasn't at home, OK. Where I was and what I was doing and who I may or may not have been doing it with is my business and only my business. Got that?'

She saw the anger creep into his face, petrify it into a mask. 'I see.'

'So can we move on, please? Perhaps try and behave like professionals?'

She could have been wrong, but she suspected that every muscle in his face contracted at that. His reply was stiff. 'Yes, Inspector.'

She would almost certainly have said something at his attitude but the phone rang. 'Yes?'

'Inspector Wharton?'

Cultured voice, one of authority.

'Yes.'

'I am the father of Jasper Fitzroy-Hughes. I am told that you are in charge of the investigation of my son's disappearance.'

Had Sam not been scrutinizing her, she might have sighed at this. 'That's right.'

'May I ask what progress you've made?'

A question to which there was but a single answer. 'As far as we can judge, the last time your son was seen was at a party...'

'Held by Stephen Bright. I know that.'

Do you indeed? She explained patiently, 'I'm in the process of checking out everyone who was at that party ... especially someone called Axenfeld who was, we believe, the...'

'The person he left with. I know that, too.'

He might have been a senior civil servant and grand high panjandrum of some government department, but she was starting to feel the need to express some irritation. What didn't he know? 'He's proving particularly hard to trace...' She paused, half expecting him to update her on that one, too, but there was only silence. 'We're also looking into Mr Bright's background, just to make sure...'

'I understand that Mr Bright has been previously investigated, though.'

She snapped; she shouldn't have done, but she did. 'Look, Professor. I really don't see the point of this phone call. You seem to know more about this investigation than I do.'

'I do, don't I? Aren't you ashamed of that?'

She was shocked. 'I beg your pardon?'

'It seems to me that you're out of your depth, Inspector. You've no more idea of what's happened to my son than I have.'

'I probably care more, though...'

Beyond any doubt at all, the brief silence was describable only as 'stunned'. It became very clear very quickly that senior government advisers did not expect to be talked to in such a manner. She heard the air sucked into his lungs and when the response came it wasn't so much spoken as hurled. 'How ... dare you!' The voice became pinched and sibilant, emitted through a mouth, larynx and throat that were contracted.

'I'm sorry...'

He was uninterested in her apologies. 'It seems to me that you are unfit to be in charge of this investigation since you are clearly no nearer to finding my son than when you visited my wife some days ago.'

'I don't believe that Stephen Bright is as squeaky clean as previously thought.' She said this almost out of desperation, atonement for her rudeness.

'What makes you say that?'

And there the folly of her rash admission became apparent. What, in totality, was her evidence against Stephen Bright? She didn't like him, but she had come to accept that, no matter what her wishes, the world was full of such people and she couldn't get rid of them all. Then there was some sort of unexplained relationship with a dead lab technician; unlikely and overwhelmingly tacky as it appeared to be, it in no way constituted a criminal offence. And lastly the name of Stephen Bright had come up in a completely unrelated investigation, again without obvious criminal intention. By no stretch of the judicial mind were any of these a hanging offence, at least not under the present government administration.

Not yet, anyway.

'There are indications...'

'I think you're prevaricating, Inspector. You have nothing, do you?'

'I wouldn't say that.'

'If I don't have notice of some progress within the next twenty-four hours, I shall be speaking to your superiors.'

As if he hadn't already been speaking to them; one of them, anyway. *Lambert,* she guessed. But what could she say?

'I assure you, Professor Fitzroy-Hughes, I am making every effort to locate you son...'

But he had already cut the connection. She looked at Sam. 'Daddy wants results.'

He said nothing in reply, content merely to shrug as if to say, *Your problem, not mine.*

Eisenmenger was signing a cremation certificate in the office of the mortuary at Cheltenham General Hospital when the phone rang.

Normally he would have left it to be answered by one of the mortuary technicians, but he knew that all three of them were busy cleaning the dissection room down after a morning filled by five autopsies, and so thought to be helpful by picking it up.

'Mortuary. Yes?'

The voice that replied was broad Gloucestershire. 'It's Wrights here. Will Mrs Cartwright be ready to pick up this afternoon?'

He didn't know – why should he? 'I'll get someone to help you.'

The phone was put down but then immediately picked up again. 'Sorry to bother you,' said Eisenmenger, because he was always polite, 'but have you heard of the firm Gorlin, Goltz and Son?'

He heard at once.

FORTY-NINE

There was perfect silence between them as Sam drove them to the premises of Gorlin, Goltz and Son, Funeral Directors and Monumental Masons. Beverley's first thought as she stood outside and surveyed the walls with their barbed-wire crown around the yard was that it seemed unnecessarily secure; surely they didn't have *that* much of value inside?

They had parked in the small visitors' parking area and went through the front door into a small reception area in the corner of which was a middle-aged woman behind a desk. She looked up at once. She had close-set eyes, hair hennaed almost to death, red-framed glasses and a dark suit that was just a little bit too small. There was a closed door behind her.

'Can I help you?'

'I'd like to speak to the manager, please.'

'Mr Taussig is busy. Can I ask why you wish to see him? Is it about funeral arrangements?'

'No. We're from the police.'

The close-set eyes widened behind the spectacularly awful optical apparatus that adorned her face. 'Oh...'

'If Mr Taussig could take a break from his business, I'd be very grateful.'

'I'll see. He may be with a client.'

From which it wasn't clear if she meant someone living or the dead. She picked up the phone and dialled an extension number, asking whoever responded where the aforementioned Mr Taussig was. 'I've got a couple of police people out here wanting to speak to him.'

She listened, then, 'All right, then.' The phone safely back in its home, she told them, 'He'll be out directly.'

Sam, who had been looking at a print of Turner's *The Fighting Temeraire*, turned and asked, 'Busy?'

She shrugged. 'Not particularly.'

'Big place, though.'

292

'Is it?'

'What goes on back there?' He indicated the door.

'There's a chapel and there are the offices, and then there are the rooms where they do what they do.'

This last tautologous contribution to their understanding was uttered in a faintly disgusted tone, as if she didn't want to think about 'what they did'.

'I take it you don't get involved with that side of things.'

The shake of her head was vigorous enough to count almost as a rigor. 'Goodness, no!'

Before she could add to her indignation at this concept, the door under discussion opened to admit a man of above-average height with broad shoulders and mopped brown hair. He was sporting a broad smile that Beverley at once knew was no more than a tool. He wore gold-rimmed glasses that were, in contrast to the receptionist's, beautifully understated, a wonderful example of the principle that less is more. 'Good morning. My name's Lletz. I'm the assistant manager. Mr Taussig is occupied at the moment.'

Beverley made the introductions, then, 'Can we have a private chat with you?'

'Of course. This way.'

He led them through a short corridor that ended in a small office at the back of the building; on the way they passed on their left a larger general office. The door was open and Beverley saw that the window on the opposite wall was boarded. Another corridor led away to the right; all the doors off that one were closed.

The office was neat but boring. Shelves of box files along two walls, a single set of filing cabinets, a cactus on the windowsill; there was no hint of humanity, not even when Mr Lletz sat at his desk, seeming slightly too large for his accommodation.

He bade them sit and there were two chairs for the purpose but the room was so small that their knees touched. Mr Lletz leaned forward interestedly, making no reference to the cramped accommodation. 'I must say, this is very exciting. We don't usually get the police calling on us. We come across them, of course, during the course of our work, but a personal visit is most unusual.' He had an accent.

Something to the east, Beverley decided.

'We're here because the name of this business has cropped up during the course of an investigation.'

'Really? In what way?'

Sam produced the pen, protected by a thick plastic evidence bag. 'Do you recognize this, sir?'

Lletz took it, peered at it. Sam said tiredly, 'Don't take it out of the bag, please, sir.'

It was handed back. 'It's one of ours.' He said this matter-of-factly.

'May I ask who has those pens?'

'Everyone. Anyone.'

'Are there a lot of these pens in circulation?'

'Oh, yes. We use them in the office, of course, but we also hand them out to suppliers and

clients. They're a very useful form of advertising.'

'Roughly how many of these have you had
made?'

'Golly, I couldn't say. Hundreds, thousands,
probably.'

Not what she wanted to hear.

He enquired, 'Is that all?'

Which was odd. She could see that Sam
caught it, too, because he looked across at her.
She said, 'I suppose so.'

She stood, as did Lletz; he had just straightened up, unbent his knees, head coming up
when she asked, 'What does the name Billy
Whipple mean to you, sir?'

He stopped and she caught something in the
way that he momentarily froze that told her he
knew that name very well indeed. She could
not have put into words how she came by that
knowledge, but it was as certain as the eventual
end of the world that he was going to hide
something when he said, 'Whipple? Nothing, I
think ... no, nothing.'

'Are you sure? He had this pen in his pocket.'
She was speaking in the past but he didn't
comment on or react to this and so there was
thus another piece of evidence counting
against him.

'As I said, anyone could get hold of one.'

'Billy Whipple wasn't the kind of person to
got hold of one.' She left it at that, left him with
the problem of filling the gap.

'Oh...' He frowned but whether it was in an
attempt to recall information or to fabricate it

she could only guess. Then he brightened. 'Oh, yes. I remember now.'

She waited, suspecting that what he had remembered was a lie. That was good; she liked lies. They almost invariably told her more than the truth.

'He applied for a job here. Some weeks ago.'

'What kind of a job?'

'Assistant funeral director. Not a very intellectually demanding job.'

'Do I take it he wasn't successful?'

A shake of the head. 'He wasn't really suitable.'

'Have you filled the vacancy?'

'Alas, no.'

She paused, her face suggesting that she was entirely satisfied, before asking, 'Could I see the paperwork?'

'Paperwork?'

'Billy Whipple's application. You must have some sort of formal procedure for the purposes of Customs and Revenue, National Insurance, that kind of thing.'

She rather enjoyed the look of discomfiture on his face. 'Well, I don't know...'

'You can't have destroyed it already, surely.'

The flusterment increased. 'I'll have to go and look. Everyone's out, you see ... at interments.'

He squeezed past them and went into the general office muttering. Beverley looked at Sam with her eyebrows raised and a smirk on her face. They heard muttering with undertones of filing-cabinet drawers being opened and shut. This went on for several minutes, then there was silence. He returned after perhaps three minutes, an open file in his hand. He thrust it at Beverley. 'Here we are.'

Surprised, she took it. A scrawled letter in terrible writing asking for an application form; awful grammar, a signature that was little more than a mark. There was also said application form, equally untidy, equally unimpressive.

'How many applicants were there?'

'Only the one.'

'Not a good response.'

Lletz shrugged. 'This is an area of high employment.'

'High crime also, unfortunately.'

He wasn't interested and merely asked, 'Satisfied?'

She handed the file back. 'Totally.'

It was clear that he assumed that the interview was over, but Beverley seemed in no hurry to leave. She said, 'Your job must be fascinating.'

Lletz was surprised by this conversational gambit. He said uncertainly, 'Well, yes, it is.'

'Do you know, I've never seen the inner workings of an undertakers'.'

'Funeral director,' he corrected. 'We prefer that to "undertaker".'

'I'm so sorry ... funeral director.'

'It's not that exciting, really.'

She hastened to contradict him. 'But it is! Embalming, for instance. How do you do that?'

She was aware that Sam was as perplexed as

Lletz, although not showing it. Lletz said hesitantly, 'Well...'

'Could I see?'

'Oh, I don't think so.'

'Not a body, of course. Just where and how you do it. The equipment you use.'

He didn't want to, but she knew he would; he didn't want to appear suspicious in any way at all.

'Very well. If you'll follow me.'

He led them back down the corridor, then opposite the general office they turned left. This corridor led them past a door on their left and then one on the right; at this last he stopped and, when it was opened, he revealed an air-conditioned room in which were two white porcelain slabs. Beside each was a device that looked like an upright vacuum cleaner. A thick clear plastic tube led from each of these to a stainless-steel spike that was long and thick. There was a door in the far left wall of the room.

'Here we are,' he said. He went to the machine, picked up the metal spike. 'The embalming fluid's put in here...' – he indicated the vacuum cleaner – '...and we make cuts in the right side of the neck, one through the jugular vein, the other through the carotid. We introduce this needle into the carotid, and put a drain tube into the jugular. This machine pumps embalming fluid in which then pushes the blood out of the body via the drain tube.'

'How much fluid does one body need?'

'It depends on the body. About fifteen litres

298

on average.'

'Don't you ever get blockages?'

'Quite often. We have to make an incision somewhere else if we do. We do that anyway to embalm the cavities.'

'Which means what?'

'We introduce embalming fluid into the abdominal and thoracic cavities.'

'You mean you stab that thing into the corpse?'

He winced at her phraseology. 'We make a small cut and introduce it.'

Beverley seemed fascinated, Sam merely bored. She asked, 'And what's in embalming fluid?'

'Formaldehyde – that's a preservative – is the main ingredient. There's usually a pink dye to enhance natural colour.'

'Gosh! I didn't realize! It's fascinating, Mr Lletz.'

He bowed his head deprecatingly.

Her next question had an innocent, almost overwhelmed air. 'So is that it? All you need to do to bury a body?'

'Oh, not at all. There are so many things we do; there are the cosmetic enhancements, and the precise coffin requirements, for a start. And then we have to ensure that the body remains clean.'

She didn't have the courage to ask what he was talking about.

He led them out but as they walked back past the general office she indicated the boarded window and asked casually, 'What happened to the window?'

Lletz said at once, 'A stone. Thrown by a child.'

'Not a break-in, then.'

Lletz found this amusing. 'Who would want to break into an undertakers'?'

She noted immediately his use of the word 'undertakers' but refrained from comment.

Sam murmured, 'A burglar might,' to which Lletz said, 'Well, not in this case.'

Beverley said no more and walked on. The front office was still the sole demesne of the secretary. Beverley asked, 'You're owned by a company called PFC, aren't you?'

'That's right.'

'And they're owned in turn by Vermilion.'

'Are they?'

'Don't you know?'

Lletz smiled. 'I'm only a humble assistant manager. I don't really know much about the intricacies of who owns what.'

'Perhaps Mr Taussig does.'

'Perhaps.'

Beverley nodded as if she understood perfectly.

FIFTY

Eisenmenger didn't exactly have a list of people he never wanted to hear from, although the names were there in his subconscious, floating and orbiting each other like stars in a nebula of glowing hideousness. It consisted of the usual suspects (Hitler, Vlad the Impaler, Ted Bundy, the Partridge family) – as well as some more personal ones that he had encountered during his life, amongst which (newly added and shining especially brightly) was Mr Alan Sheldon.

Imagine then, his surprise when he answered an unknown number on his mobile that evening.

'Dr John Eisenmenger?'

'Yes.' The voice was cultured and authoritative, he thought. Not police, but possibly a solicitor or barrister.

'My name's Alan Sheldon.'

Eisenmenger was not given to outrageous demonstrations of surprise but he almost broke his own rules of behaviour upon hearing this particular utterance. It took a conscious and not inconsiderable effort for him to stop any noise from coming out his mouth, or his voice to sound calm before he replied, 'And what can

I do for you?'

Without a pause – a pause that Eisenmenger would have found helpful – Sheldon said, 'I appreciate that you probably don't want to hear from me, but I hope that you'll forgive me when you hear what I have to say.'

Deep, deep, and yet deeper breaths...'And that is?'

The first sign that this was anything other than some sort of taunting social call came at this, because there was a definite count of three before he said, 'Helena has gone missing.'

Eisenmenger found it difficult to know how to react. He wrestled with several reactions – such as, *And...?* followed by, *Then go to the police* ... ending with, *Perhaps she's come to her senses ...* – but voiced none of them. He had thought hard long, hard and many times about Mr Alan Sheldon and not much of this had been positive, but he had known from the first that this man was not stupid, was anything other than hysterical or prone to exaggeration; in fact his impression of the man, shorn of the inevitable prejudice, was that of an agonizingly, distressingly decent and normal man. It hurt him to admit it, but he could do nothing else.

'I assume,' he said in a voice that he was impressed sounded calm and businesslike, 'that you're completely sure of your facts, Mr Sheldon?'

Of course he was. He had checked with her office and found that she had not reported in and had missed several appointments; when they had tried to contact her home number and her mobile, like him they had received no reply. He had called round to discover that her milk had not been taken in and her flat was deserted; her neighbours had known nothing. 'I know she would have told me if she weren't going to be around. I became concerned when she failed to meet for lunch today.'

He had a way of talking – actually, a way of imposing himself – that Eisenmenger found at once excruciating and awe-inspiring; *I know*, he was saying. *I have no need of this alien thing called doubt.*

'Have you contacted the police?'

'They weren't interested.' He sounded faintly incredulous and from this Eisenmenger found hope; this man might consider himself a master of his universe, but in this he found himself in a very different and very strange universe, one in which he was most definitely not the master.

Eisenmenger did not bother to explain the mores of the British police, how responsible adults not known to be at risk were given the freedom to disappear for quite long periods of time before it was considered worthy of constabulary attention. He asked instead, 'Do you have any particular reason to believe that she might in danger, Mr Sheldon?'

'No. None whatsoever.'

Eisenmenger had to think very hard about this. He was finding it very difficult to reach an objective decision because of all the emotion he was battling, the emotion that was telling him to put the phone down at once – either with or without some explosive fricatives – and get on with what remained of his life; yet he knew Helena – was fairly confident that he knew her deep and complex character far better than this suave, self-confident, Johnny-cum-lately – and this was worrying. Helena did *not* just disappear, not unless there was something wrong. What it was, he could not think, but he knew (and had known as soon as Sheldon had told him) that this was not trivial.

He sighed. 'OK, Mr Sheldon. We had better meet.'

FIFTY-ONE

Beverley and Sam were on the dual-carriageway back to Cheltenham before she spoke. 'He's lying.'

'It all looked convincing to me.'

'He knocked those papers up as a cover. He was good, I'll allow him that, but it was a nicely acted charade, nothing more.'

'What about the note from Billy?'

'Forging a note from a semi-literate like Billy hardly takes much skill; it's not quite as daunting as replicating the Sistine Chapel in your living room.'

'If you thought it was a forgery, why didn't you take it for comparison?'

'Because I don't want him to know that I think he's lying.'

'Why not?'

'Because when you're hunting something you don't go blundering in shouting your head off.'

He didn't say anything but she knew that he was unhappy. *Poor Sam ... unhappy about everything at the moment.* She went on, 'And then there's that bollocks about the broken window.'

'You didn't believe him?'

'Of course I didn't believe him. Do I look as if I've got dung for brains?' She didn't wait for his considered opinion on that. 'No, that was where Billy Whipple broke in.'

'How can you say that?'

'Because it makes sense.'

'Does it? Not to me.'

She didn't really care whether Sam followed her reasoning or not. Ignoring his less than enthusiastic endorsement of her deductive skills, she went on, 'I think that Billy Whipple broke in there on the night he died. It's between the Three Tunnes and his house, don't forget.'

'You can't know any of this for sure.'

'So why did Lletz lie about the window? There's a thick hedge not a metre away from that window; there's no way on earth it could have been broken by a kid throwing a stone. If, though, we postulate that it was Billy Whipple doing what Billy Whipple did, it explains a few things; for instance, how else did he get hold of that pen?'

'He could have got it anywhere. You heard what Lletz said about how many they give out.'

'He could have, but he didn't,' she said stubbornly. 'He got it at Gorlin's when he broke in.'

Sam knew better than to continue the argument but her next words were too outrageous to allow him silence.

'And that was where he was stabbed.'

'You what?' He looked across at her, which was not altogether wise as he very nearly went into the back of the car in front, which was braking at the roundabout.

'He was stabbed at the undertakers'.' Her tone was matter-of-fact, almost puzzled that he wasn't following her.

'How can you say that?'

'It's more believable than Spud sticking a scalpel in him.'

'Why would an undertaker have a scalpel?'

'Sam, weren't you listening? How else do you think they make their incisions to embalm the bodies? They don't go down to the super-market and buy a packet of razorblades. They use scalpels.'

'We don't know that for certain.'

'You heard him. When they embalm a body, they first make small incisions to get at the blood vessels. What do you think they use? A kitchen knife or a piece of broken glass?'

She could see that he still wasn't convinced but at least he didn't argue. He took the right-hand lane and then turned into the road that led past the station. He said at last, 'Shouldn't we tell Chief Inspector Lambert? He's taken over the Whipple case.'

She'd been half-expecting this. 'Lambert's a happy bunny – why spoil that? He's charged Spud with the murder so anything we say is

306

only going to make trouble; anyway, he'll dismiss it as irrelevant.'

'But surely, out of courtesy to the Chief Inspector...'

She didn't show any reaction to this remark but internally things were different. Sam was suddenly talking about courtesy to Lambert, doggedly using his full title. She sensed a change in the wind, cooler air blowing in, a hint of rain.

'I don't quite follow, Sam. Do you think Billy was stabbed at the undertakers' or don't you?'

'I think there's little evidence to support your theory; there's none at all unless we can get a forensic team in there.'

'As I'm proposing a theory you don't believe, I don't see why you're so keen to convey it to Lambert.'

He didn't look happy but he had no convincing answer to that. They continued their journey in silence but she was well aware of the air of discontent that filled the car.

FIFTY-TWO

Back in her office, when she was sitting behind her desk but Sam was refusing to do anything except stand at ease and stare straight ahead, she asked, 'What about the party guests?'

'I've got as far as I can … nothing.'

'Nothing at all?' She didn't think that it sounded incredulous but Sam heard otherwise.

'That's what I said.'

'No description of Axenfeld?'

'That's not what I said. In fact, by the end I had fourteen descriptions of him.'

'Ah.'

It was a recurring problem – ask a witness for a description and if you're lucky you'll get one; ask two and you'll almost certainly get two. It was an arithmetical progression that rested on the universal law of human unreliability.

'Some of them coincide in one or two particulars, though.' He said this sarcastically.

'What about Hertwig?'

'A sad little gay man, all pink and lace. In a bit of a twitter that he should be considered a suspect.'

Perhaps in a bit of a twitter for another reason, Sam.

She said, 'You don't think he's involved?'

'No.'

He said this as if this were her last chance, that by excluding Hertwig he had exhausted her last chance at success in the case.

She watched Sam leave the room, wondering what he was going to do and knowing at the same time exactly what he was going to do. She waited only a short while before calling Dempsey into her office. Dempsey, she hoped, could be relied on to be discreet.

'I've got a couple of jobs for you.'

'I'm a bit busy at the present: the Chief

308

Inspector's asked me to help out with the case against Carney, taking statements and suchlike.'

The Chief Inspector can go and...

'These are high priority.'

'Yes, but...'

'Look, Dempsey. Taking corroborative statements is the work they give to the donkeys, isn't it?'

Dempsey, who had often been compared with mammals of the asinine kind, didn't like to agree too readily with this rather blunt assessment of the task he had been given, but equally did not wish to argue with a superior officer. He said, 'Well, I suppose it's...'

'Right. Whereas I'm asking you to help me with an ongoing investigation.'

'What about Sergeant Richardson?'

'He's got his hands full looking into another aspect of the case.'

Dempsey was at heart a decent and helpful copper. He had a strong presentiment that all was not what it seemed but he nodded nonetheless. 'OK.'

'Good. I want you to see what you can dig up on Gorlin, Goltz and Son, a firm of funeral directors in Swindon Village; especially the manager, a man by the name of Taussig, and the assistant manager, Lletz. Also I want everything you can find on a woman called Violet Esterly. You've got a head start on that one because Starry's already taken a preliminary investigation and the coroner's office will have taken some statements as well.'

'Coroner?'

'She hanged herself a couple of weeks ago.'

Dempsey noted the names down assiduously. When she added, 'And don't tell Lambert what you're doing,' he looked up suddenly, a questioning and faintly alarmed look back on his heavy-set features. She added, 'For now.'

If this last was supposed to calm him, it appeared to fail.

'But...'

She suddenly appeared in his face. 'Please, Dempsey,' she pleaded. 'Don't be a silly boy.'

She stayed until six but Sam did not reappear; she had wanted to talk to him, apologize. Guilt was an affliction she still felt even if she did not opt to show it.

Oh, well ... Give him time.

But when she was walking from her office down to the car she changed that decision because she saw Sam emerging from Lambert's office. He spotted her and paused briefly but almost at once his eyes left her and he walked quickly away. She watched his broad shoulders, remembered how she had once thought them exquisite; now they were slightly absurd, those of a man who was shallow, who thought too much of himself.

She continued out of the building.

FIFTY-THREE

Eisenmenger's meeting with Sheldon was difficult, as he had known it would be; the two of them sat in a small tea room in Montpelier and had the kind of polite conversation that only two very civilized and very antagonistic men can have, a combative one with Sheldon taking up defensive position behind a cup of Darjeeling, Eisenmenger behind a large Americano. At the end of it, though, Eisenmenger knew for certain that Helena's disappearance was significant; he had not softened his opinion of Sheldon – there was nothing of 'grudging respect', or 'reluctant admiration' within him as he walked away having pledged to do what he could to help – but he had at least satisfied himself that Sheldon was prone to hysterical misinterpretation of normal happenstance. His resentment still burned – was possibly even more incandescent – but as much as Helena had hurt him and he wanted to hurt her back, this was different, this was a different game, and one in which he was on her side.

How, though, to help?

He had nowhere else to turn, except to Beverley.

FIFTY-FOUR

'What the hell are you doing?'

Jack said simply, 'Packing.' He didn't stop or even turn round as he spoke. His movements were slow and there was a distinct tremor about them, as if Beverley were looking at an old man; the impression was heightened by his sallow, faintly yellowed expression and apparent stiffness.

'But you can't! You're too ill.'

He didn't bother with a reply. She went to him, put her hand on his forearm, felt how cold and greasy the skin was to the touch. He looked up at her. 'I'm getting better.'

'Have they said you can go?'

'No, but...'

'There you are, then. You must stay here.'

He shook his head. 'It's doing me no good in here.'

'Of course it is. What happens if you bleed again?'

A shrug, a smile. 'I can't spend the rest of my life in this room. I could walk out of here next week and begin to throw up blood as soon as I got home.'

'Even so, it must be in your best interests to stay in a little while longer...'

He looked at her – she had the impression he was looking *into* her – and then let out a long breath, relaxed and sat – almost flopped – back down in the chair by the bed. He suggested, 'Shut the door, then come and sit down.'

She did as he asked, but reluctantly, slightly puzzled by the conspiratorial turn.

'You remember how I said that there was no cure, not even a transplant?'

She nodded.

'Well, maybe I was premature.'

'A cure? Someone's offering you a cure?'

But it wasn't that easy. He smiled at her enthusiasm, said, 'Let's just say an extension. A few more years than I'm likely to get as things stand.'

'Who?'

'That's the point. It's not for public consumption. The docs here know nothing about it.'

She didn't understand. 'So where is it?'

He shook his head. 'As a matter of fact it'll be abroad.'

But she still couldn't follow what he was implying. 'You mean it's experimental, this treatment?'

After the briefest of hesitations he said, 'Yeah.' Then more confidently, 'Yeah, something like that.'

'Where abroad?'

'Central Europe.'

She found herself elated yet simultaneously disturbed. She sensed evasion, perhaps misdirection; she wanted to believe that here was the best news she'd had in a long time yet she smelled something rotten about it.

'What is it? A drug?'

'Something like that.'

'Is it safe?'

He smiled. 'Does that matter to me? My whole existence is suddenly unsafe.'

'But has it been tested?'

'That's where I come in. I'm the guinea pig.'

She didn't like the sound of that but before she could voice her concerns he said, 'Look, sis, until I heard about this, there was no hope at all, only a time limit. Now at least there's something I can cling to. Don't deprive me of that.'

'I'm not trying to, Jack. I'm just trying to make sure you don't do anything stupid.'

'What, me? Do something stupid?' he enquired in mock astonishment. It was a good act, but she knew that she was being pushed away. This must have come across on her face because he leaned towards her and took her hands in his. 'This is no big deal. If it works, then I've gained the world; if it doesn't, I'm no worse off.'

Once more she sensed that she was not being told everything and that what she was being told was not entirely as it seemed.

'Why the rush?'

'Because they're ready for me. I had a telephone call this morning.'

'Who from?'

'The clinic.'

'They're going ahead even though you're still

so weak? Is that wise?'

He was becoming angry and she could see that it was because he was lying; she had seen such a reaction many times before. 'Look, the sooner I start, the better. Surely you can see that, Beverley? I don't want to hang around here for no good reason when I could be somewhere getting some effective treatment.'

Yes, she could see that, but she was still certain that all was not as it seemed.

'How did you hear about this treatment?'

She had been in too many interrogations to miss the barely perceptible switches in tone and substance as the lies kicked in. He said, 'I was told about it.'

She didn't want to be in the position of believing that her brother was lying, that he was a suspect in something, and when she asked, 'Who?' she tried to make it sound as if she were merely interested.

'One of the nurses. She said that her father had had similar treatment.'

There was something about his tone that made her wonder if he were lying. She knew that he was lying but didn't know whether it was all a lie, mostly a lie or merely barely a lie; she suddenly decided that she didn't want to know. She just wanted reassurance and, accordingly, she asked him gently, 'Are you certain you want to go like this? Shouldn't you go into the treatment a little more deeply? Take your time about it?'

'No,' he said vehemently. 'I've been given a deadline. They want me there within twenty-four hours, or it's no deal.'

'Deal?'

He looked flustered. 'I meant...'

'Are you paying for this, Jack?'

The way his head dropped told her.

'Oh, for Christ's sake, Jack. Don't be an idiot. You're being taken for a ride.'

'No, I'm not.'

'Of course you are! What's this place called? Where exactly is it?'

His anger flared suddenly. 'Look, sis. Keep out of this, OK? This is my life, my decision. I believe that this might be my last chance. I'm not going to hang around here waiting to bleed to death, thinking all the while that this might have saved me.'

'But what if it's just a con?'

He shrugged. 'Easy. I'll die poor.'

Which was reasonable, at least.

A thought occurred to her. 'Does this have something to do with why you moved here?'

His smile was full and reassuring and consumed the whole of his face as he said, 'Not at all! I wanted to be close to my sis, that's all.'

He held out his hands to her and she took them at once. 'Let me make an idiot of myself, eh? You can always say that you told me so.'

She began to cry and they held each other in a tight embrace for a long moment. Then he whispered into her ear, 'Trust me.'

She knew him, knew that he was going to do it, whatever she said. After a moment's pause she nodded. 'OK,' she said. 'If you think that it's worth it.'

He said then something that she didn't understand.

'I only hope God will forgive me.'

But then in came a doctor and the ward sister for one final attempt at persuading him to stay, and she had no chance to ask him what he had meant.

After this last time that she ever saw him she walked out of the ward her head holding many questions but one piece of certainty that was louder than everything else. He had lied when he had told her why he had come to Gloucestershire.

FIFTY-FIVE

After his conversation with Sam, Lambert wasted no time. He went immediately to see Superintendent Braxton, who had been on the point of leaving; Lambert's appearance in his office was, in consequence, not well received.

'I thought you ought to hear about this immediately, sir.'

'Did you?'

'Sergeant Richardson has just been to see me.'

'And?' His tone was wary.

'He told me what Inspector Wharton's been doing.'

Braxton had swum through office politics for

a good number of years and had survived only by metaphorically holding his nose; that the stench had not clung to him was a miracle. He viewed Lambert's presence before him now as a man on a life raft might view an elephant determinedly swimming towards him – a danger to shipping.

Tiredly he enquired, 'And what has she been doing?'

'Undermining my investigation and my authority.'

Braxton had guessed as much. His request for elucidation was uttered with eyes closed and something of trepidation in the words. As expected, the elephant was trying to clamber aboard and the raft was rocking dangerously.

Lambert repeated what Sam had told him while Braxton listened; the Superintendent's entire demeanour was one of a man who would rather have been doing anything other than what he was doing at that moment. At the finale, Braxton was silent for a moment.

'I see.'

'She's trouble, George. Her whole career has been built on backstabbing and sexual favours and as if that wasn't bad enough, she's not even a good copper.'

Braxton murmured forlornly, 'She's never shown me any sexual favours.' It wasn't certain whether he meant Lambert to hear this.

'You probably didn't ask.'

They had known each other a good number of years; Braxton didn't particularly like Lambert, although he had never expressed this sentiment aloud, and he didn't have a particularly high regard for his detective abilities. He considered that Lambert had no imagination, a vital ingredient in the work of criminal investigation.

Perhaps Inspector Wharton had too much, though...

'What's your opinion of her theory about the undertakers?'

'It's cock and bull. A complete flight of fancy. I think she's dreamed it up to undermine my case against Carney.'

'I'm not sure that's a reasonable assumption.'

'Why else hasn't she told me about this? I had to hear about it from Richardson, and she told him specifically to say nothing to me.'

'Yes...' Braxton wasn't sure that he was very impressed by the part played by Sergeant Richardson in this business. Then, 'But, of course, you've hardly made yourself particularly amenable to her, have you?'

'What do you mean?'

'I can see that she might have expected you to give a very poor reception to her theory.'

'That's because it's rubbish.'

'Frank, there's more to command than authority.'

'What does that mean?'

'I know your opinion of Beverley Wharton is less than zero, but have you ever considered a different approach?'

'What does that mean?'

'Maybe you should try to educate her rather than condemn her.'

Had Braxton suggested that he should strip naked, bend over backwards and play the National Anthem using only sphincter control and a lot of baked beans, Lambert would not have betrayed greater surprise. 'You must be joking. She's beyond "education".'

'No one's that far beyond redemption. Beverley is fundamentally a good enough police officer. She's had some notable successes in her career.'

'And she's been involved in some spectacular cock-ups, too. Perhaps even been responsible for them.'

'You know as well as I do that she was exonerated of any intentional harm...'

'Would you want her backing you up if it came to laying your life on the line?'

Since, at the age of fifty, Braxton's idea of laying his life on the line was going shopping, he didn't consider this hypothetical scenario to be of much relevance. 'That was a long time ago, Frank. She was inexperienced...'

'Or vindictive.'

'That's not fair...'

'And look at the way she's handled this Fitzroy-Hughes thing.'

'What about it?'

'She's hardly made any progress at all. All she's done is go off on yet another tangent about someone she's taken a dislike to.'

'Stephen Bright.'

'That's right. We know that he's clean. Starry looked at him in connection with another case.'

'You know how difficult a missing-person

case can be, Frank. They're entirely different to killings.'

'She's looking in the wrong place again. It's a pattern of behaviour that shows consistently poor judgement. She was never particularly good, and now she's lost it completely.'

Braxton was a cautious man and at the end of the day he was tired; he was not about to rush to condemnation on the say-so of Chief Inspector Lambert who would, had he been given the chance by a benevolent deity, have expunged Beverley Wharton from history.

'I'll talk to her...'

'I think...'

'I don't, Frank.'

Lambert, who had thought that he was on the point of winning a great victory, saw suddenly that such prizes are not so easily won. A brief thought of further argument was born but breathed only once and that with a dying gurgle.

'Oh.'

'You've given me your opinion. Let me, your commanding officer, decide what I want to do about it.'

Lambert didn't like it and didn't want to hide that fact but he knew better than to speak further. He stood stiffly. 'Very well.'

Braxton smiled at him tiredly. 'Thanks for telling me your concerns, Frank.'

Despite his keenness to leave the office he stayed a little while longer, his mood deeply pensive. Just that afternoon he had received a call from the Divisional Commander asking his opinion of Beverley Wharton. Nothing overt had been said during the course of this conversation but Braxton had the distinct impression that there was some interest amongst the top echelons in Ms Wharton.

But he could not say whether it was a benign or malignant interest.

FIFTY-SIX

The call of the answerphone greeted her and she thought tiredly that here was evolution in action; a new species had been created, complete with its own mating call and she, the householder, was required to engage with it. The offspring would most probably be sterile but one in a million, perhaps a billion, would produce something of value, something that mattered.

Four messages, and she could easily guess that they were all from the same person. *Sam.* He was becoming a little too clingy, a little too obsessive. Sam had not understood the rules of the game, it appeared; he assumed that the relationship was something that it was not.

She deleted all the messages without listening to any.

What now, though?

It occurred to her then with horrible, sickening shock, that she was bored, that sexual intercourse was to her nothing more than relief from lassitude and ennui.

Was her life so empty? Had she nothing but copulation to occupy her?

She fiercely denied the affirmatives even as she feared that she was lying when she did so

'Fuck you, Sam.'

There was her career, as well, though.

Except that it had stalled some years ago...

Was everyone against her? Did Sam really have to dive straight into Lambert's bed just because he was pissed off with her?

Every man she had ever trusted had betrayed her in one way or another; only those she had kept at bay, far from the heart of her, had not hurt her...

Yet...

She poured herself a deep gin, made herself feel a little better by adding some tonic (but not a lot), flopped on to the grey leather of the sofa. She didn't want to give up on men, not completely, not yet anyway.

She accepted deep down that she needed the bastards.

She just didn't need most of them ... didn't need any of the ones she'd met so far.

When the phone rang she was actually falling asleep.

'Yes?'

'Inspector Wharton? It's Theodore Noonan.'

Of course it was. The cultured tones – those of an upper-class con man – were unmistakable. She wondered why he was calling as he usually treated her like a nasty dose of leprosy, not so much passing by on the other side of the road as turning around and running away as fast as possible. 'Why are you calling, Theo?'

'I was in Swindon today, at an auction.' She said nothing, assuming that this was a preliminary to something an ounce more interesting. He went on, 'I found myself in conversation with some contacts in the trade that I hadn't seen for a long time.' *Contacts in the trade.* She suspected that this phrase was the mother of all euphemisms for 'criminal fences'. 'Stephen Bright's name came up.'

At last she discovered interest in what he was saying. She sat up. 'What about him?'

'It's not his real name.'

Her attitude had suddenly transformed completely and was now so sodden with interest it was dripping on the floor at her feet. 'And what's his real name?'

'Treves. Michel Treves.' He spelt the surname for her.

The name meant nothing to her. She asked, 'Anything you can tell me other than a name, Theodore?'

There was a cultured pause. 'He is said to have had a varied CV,' he said arcanely, making it perfectly clear that he was not referring to academic achievement.

'Go on.'

'I am told that there were very few areas in which he did not take an active interest ... including people-smuggling and, reputedly, murder.'

'Then why don't I know about him?'

'Because up until a few years ago he was based in Eastern Europe. He had associates over here, but kept very much out the way, in the shadows.'

'Where in Eastern Europe?'

'Czechoslovakia as was.'

'How long ago was this?'

'He settled back in this country about six years ago. Calling himself Stephen Bright, of course.'

'What nationality is he?'

Theodore's voice held a smile. 'Who knows?'

'So why did he suddenly decide to pop up here under a different name?'

But Theodore claimed not to know, although Beverley could not tell if he were lying; she admired Theodore for his ability to fabricate with perfect facility. He assured her that there was nothing more he could tell her and she had to accept this. She was about to end the conversation when he suddenly said, 'You will remember this, I hope, Beverley.'

She knew at once what he meant; this had followed the standard path of a conversation with an informer. He wanted something in return. 'Not much to remember, Theodore.'

'Oh, Beverley.' He sounded genuinely hurt. 'Surely we have been friends too long for you to be so cruel.'

Theodore amused her, she could not deny, and consequently she could not suppress the smile that curved her lips. '*If* this proves worthy of the air and electricity you've used in telling me, Theodore, I might bear it in mind in future dealings.'

And Theodore said with perfect confidence, 'This is the genuine article, Beverley. My contacts are totally reliable.'

'We'll see.'

She was about to put down the phone when he said quickly, 'Oh, and one other thing, Beverley.'

'Yes?'

'Stephen Bright has *friends*. Some of them in a blue uniform.'

'In the police? How come?'

Theodore sighed condescendingly. 'How does one usually acquire useful friends, Beverley? Bribery is a tried and trusted method, I am told.'

As she put the phone down, she reflected that she had heard him use words and a similar tone a hundred times before whilst rooking some poor saps in his shop.

And then the phone rang again, and this time it was Eisenmenger.

FIFTY-SEVEN

Beverley could not own to enthusiasm. She seemed to find herself rescuing Helena Flemming more than was fair in a universe that was supposedly imbued with natural justice. Why her? She didn't like Helena, and Helena (she had it on the most excellent of authority) most decidedly did not like her. True, she was committed to the crap in the oath of allegiance, but surely it was someone else's turn? Why couldn't Lambeth have the job of saving the human equivalent of Aunt Bessie's frozen roast potatoes for once?

'And there is no one who has any obvious motive? None of her clients?'

'Sheldon says that he has checked with her PA through all active and recent files, and there's no one obvious. I have no reason to doubt his assiduity.'

Beverley wondered, but had already decided that she did not really care. 'We tend not to take too much interest in missing persons after a day, John, for some very good reasons. Most of them aren't missing, for a start.'

'Most of them aren't middle-class professionals with no motive to disappear and who vanish without any warning,' Eisenmenger pointed out.

'I'm up to my eyes in it, John. I could do without this.'

'You're up to your eyes in missing persons ... and now we've got another one.'

But she was fairly well immunized against sophistry. 'We *may* have ... Given time, this may all become something more than your speculation, but not yet, John.'

Eisenmenger shook his head. 'Helena wouldn't just vanish, Beverley. You know that as well as I do.'

Beverley found herself less than impressed.

'John, she's dumped one man, what makes you think she hasn't done so again?'

One of her rules was that she did not do regret, although she was tempted to break this as soon as she heard her words. She looked at his face, aware that his complete lack of reaction was in itself a reaction, and one that told her how much she had hurt him. He said in a voice that was completely calm, completely without sign of emotion, 'Not this time, Beverley. This is not her style.'

Which she recognized had some truth in it.

Her reluctance, though, was not entirely born of antagonism for Helena; she really did have a lot on her plate ... She was about to refuse, to tell him to come back in twenty-four hours and then she *might* be able to help him, but common sense kicked in; she needed friends and Eisenmenger, she knew, was a useful companion to have. Sam was drifting from her, the enemies were gathering at the gates; she could not afford to antagonize him.

She made a show of reluctance. 'OK, John, as it's you, I'll see what I can do.' She allowed him a wash of gratitude before, with consummate timing, she added, 'But I may need something from you...'

FIFTY-EIGHT

In the middle of the night Beverley awoke without the comfort of waking and *knew*.

She was alone, back in her own bed; the alarm clock impassively and anencephalically broadcasting to everyone, anyone and almost no one that it was four-fifteen in the morning. She breathed deeply, the reality of her sudden knowledge swirling all her other thoughts into mud. She knew what she knew but had to work out what it meant, where the context was.

In the morning she was in early. She had barely slept in the past four hours but she wasn't tired, not yet. Plenty of time for that.

Much thinking to do.

By the time Dempsey arrived she was even more certain that she had seen the beginnings of what was going on. She didn't wait for him to come in to her, found him at his desk just putting his lips to a mug of coffee.

'I've got another job for you.'

Dempsey wasn't good in the morning; he never got to be superb but he generally worked his way up to not too bad by the middle of the afternoon. Before noon, though, he was definitely below par. 'Have you?' Of all the words that could have been used to describe his tone, 'enthusiastic' would never be among them.

'Michel Treves. He was based in Czechoslovakia until about five years ago. Not sure of the nationality. I want to know everything about him and I want to know it by three o'clock this afternoon.'

Dempsey looked about ready to shit himself; given that detection was generally regarded as involving brains, she rather doubted that he was equipped for life in CID. Tentatively – knowing full well, she suspected, that the question would not be well met – he asked, 'How do I do that?'

Beverley might once have launched her entire arsenal at such a question; Dempsey had been in CID for two years now, yet had learned little. It was not, she appreciated, fully his fault because he had the brains of a cowpat, and there was only so much you could learn on the continuing professional development courses provided by the Home Office; most of the important stuff was learned by trying to catch the crap that was thrown at you on the job, and then remember it.

And Dempsey had Teflon gloves.

'Start with Interpol, then try immigration.'

He ingested this and then did a spot of digestion, although it turned into indigestion. 'What about the Fitzroy-Hughes case?'

'This is priority.'

Dempsey could recognize inevitability when he saw it. He nodded, his eyes on the mug of coffee that he had been forced to put back down when she approached him. He had the air of a cow being herded towards the abattoir.

'OK.'

She walked away. Dempsey sipped his coffee and tried to draw what comfort he could from its flavourlessness.

She approached Sam without any qualms, refusing to feel shame.

'What have you got on Vermilion?'

'I'm waiting for a mate to call me back from Serious Fraud.'

'Phone him. I want all there is to know by eleven.'

His mouth opened in protest but he shut it again quickly; she was already walking away from his desk.

FIFTY-NINE

Helena came to a semblance of consciousness, but only a faint one. The sounds that met her ears were distant and distorted, curiously reverberant; the light that came to her eyes was bright and without much meaning; she was aware of movement, but was aware too of it not being right, of it being movement into dis-orientation.

She closed her eyes just as her brain managed to make out words in the sounds that came to her ears.

She's waking up...
Let her. No matter...
I don't like it when they wake up...
Taussig, you are so squeamish. Awake or asleep, it
makes no difference. Not to them. Not now...

SIXTY

Beverley could raise little surprise when the call came to attend Superintendent Braxton's office; her only thought was, *So soon again?*

This time Braxton was sitting behind his desk and staring directly at her as she entered. The atmosphere was not good but he was at heart a polite, well-brought-up old stick who invited her to sit before beginning the bollocking.

'I had DCI Lambert in here last night.'

'Sir?'

'He kept me late; rather irritated me.'

'Oh, dear.'

A spasm of anger crossed his face. 'He made some very worrying allegations against you, Beverley. Very worrying indeed. I wouldn't be too flippant if I were you.'

'No, sir.'

Satisfied that she had achieved the required level of contrition he continued in his previous vein. 'How *are* you progressing in the Fitzroy-Hughes case?'

She took a deep breath.

'The last sighting we have of him was at a party given by Stephen Bright...'

'But I understand that Stephen Bright has no criminal record.'

'No, but—'

'So what have you got against him?'

She could have told him what she suspected, what she had been told by Theodore, what seemed to be crystallizing in the air around the disappearance of Jasper Fitzroy-Hughes, her certainty that he was dead, but she failed to find the will to do so. She was enough of a realist to know that when she told him that all she really had was a few oddities and a gut feel he would be profoundly unimpressed.

'Nothing concrete,' she admitted.

'Oh, dear.' He seemed disappointed, almost saddened. 'Oh, dear.' A sigh before, 'What else?'

'We've excluded the boyfriend as far as we can. There was a question about a man called Hertwig but he appears to be clean.'

'And the party guests?'

'We talked to as many as we can...'

'Nothing?' This, tiredly.

She shook her head.

He sighed but at least it was in sympathy. She went on, 'It's possible that he left with a man called Axenfeld but no one seems to be sure about this, except Bright.'

'And that's it?'

She nodded.

A second's silence that only heightened the impression that he was in mourning, then, 'I'll give you another day. I can't do more than that.'

'That's not long, sir.'

He sighed. 'I know it's not. But I have to agree with DCI Lambert – you don't seem to have got to grips with this one. I can't afford any more time to be wasted.'

She wanted to argue but knew that it would be a futile reaction. Braxton was not only considerate and courteous, he was constitutionally obdurate. 'Yes, sir.'

There fell between them an awkward silence and she wondered what it portended.

Eventually Braxton said hesitantly, 'I had a phone call yesterday ... about you.'

'Sir?'

A nod. 'Someone seems to be taking an interest in you, Beverley.'

She could guess what had prompted that. 'Do they, sir?'

This time a smile. 'I wonder why...?'

With her face perfectly straight, her tone perfectly level, she said, 'I really couldn't begin to say...'

The conversation drooped as Braxton seemed to be unable to pursue the subject. He murmured eventually, 'Well ... mysterious ways, eh?'

Since there seemed to be little more to be said she stood up half expecting him to say something further but although his eyes were on her he remained silent, the only communication being a slightly sad smile. She wondered what that meant.

* ⋆ *

At noon her mother rang her. It was unprecedented that she rang her at work and it caused her immediately to worry.

'Beverley?'

'Mum? What's wrong?'

'I've been trying to contact you.'

Had she? Her mother's voice cut across Beverley's puzzlement. 'I left a message last night at your flat. Didn't you get it?'

Shit! She reflected morosely that it didn't do to delete messages blindly. Since she was being nagged about not responding to messages, it seemed unlikely that there had been a catastrophe, though.

'I'm sorry, I haven't had a chance to listen to my messages yet.' It was a lie, albeit more beige than white.

'I wish you'd let me have your mobile number...'

This was an old bone, one well and truly chewed through. Beverley ignored it. 'What's the matter, Mum?'

'Isn't it obvious? Jack. Jack rang me. Said he'd been in hospital.'

'I know...'

'I know you know, but you didn't tell me.'

'I didn't want to worry you, Mum.'

'Don't you think I'm worried now?'

'There was no point, Mum. You couldn't have come up in time. It all happened so quickly.'

'I deserved to be at least told.'

She was right, of course; Beverley had known

335

it all along. 'I know and I'm sorry, but...'

'That's typical of you, Beverley. You've always tried to exclude me. What have I done to deserve it?'

Beverley found herself mentally tallying up everything that her mother had done to her when she was young – the emotional black-mail, the constant drizzle of disapproval no matter what she did, the faint, almost invisible and always somehow damning praise – but conserved a tactful silence.

After a couple of seconds of silence her mother asked, 'He will be all right, won't he? He said he was fine, but I know Jack...'

The tone was fearful and Beverley was re-minded that her mother was no fool whatever her idiosyncrasies.

'I'm sure he will be, Mum.'

'Will you make him come and see me again? Soon?'

He clearly hadn't told her that he was flying out of the country. She hesitated, unsure of how much to say.

'Please, Beverley?'

And Beverley, despite all her grievances, heard her voice break as she said, 'Of course I will. Of course I will.'

Sam knocked on her office door at five to two. When he came in, his face might have been impassive, might have been disgruntled. He stood in front of her desk and said, 'Vermilion is a wholly-owned subsidiary of a company called XT Investments.' The day was sunny, becoming hot, but the ambient temperature between the two of them was failing to respond.

'And what does Vermilion actually do?'

'What *doesn't* it do would be an easier question to answer. It seems to be mainly some form of specialized international transport firm – things that need special handling, refrigerated goods, precious livestock, that kind of thing; anything that needs more than a couple of beefy men and a white van.'

'So they would be equipped to carry valuable antiques?'

He shrugged, not really caring. 'Presumably.'

'What do you mean by "refrigerated goods"?'

'Medical supplies. Vaccines, that kind of thing.'

She considered. Some of it made sense; some of it, though, made nonsense. Why would they own an undertakers'? 'Who controls XT Investments?'

'I can't get to that. It's not a UK company.'

'Where is it based?'

'The Czech Republic.'

She suddenly felt weirdly excited; so much so that it took her a moment to find her voice. 'Have you managed to find any names associated with this company?'

'Not yet.'

She could guess one, though – Michel Treves. 'Keep digging, OK? And tell Dempsey what you've found; he's investigating something for me that involves the Czech Republic, and maybe there's a link.'

She assumed that this would be the end of the exchange, but Sam remained in status quo.

'Yes?'

'May I ask what's going on?'

'Haven't we been through this before?'

She watched his face become hard, angry. For a moment he seemed to be searching for the right words to use, then he found them. 'I think you've got a death wish.'

She raised her eyebrows. 'And I think that makes two of us.'

'This is a waste of time, Beverley. We've been tasked with finding Jasper Fitzroy-Hughes, not farting around looking into companies that buy antiques. Stephen Bright's clean ... that's been proven.'

She saw then that she had a choice. She could tell him to sit down, to put aside his feelings of betrayal, and to listen to what she had to say, to try to convince him that he might not be able to see it, but that what they were doing was very relevant indeed; or she could continue to shut him out because she no longer trusted him, because she feared that he would run straight back to Lambert's loving embrace and sob into his lap.

She chose wrong.

'Thank you for your views, Sergeant. I'll take them into account when it comes to your annual appraisal. Now run along.'

She held his stare, dared him to argue or talk back. He yielded first as she knew he would, turning smartly – almost on the spot in good military style – and marching out.

Which left her with no one professional to confide in.

Not that that had ever particularly bothered her before. She was used to working things out for herself, not ceding anything to anyone.

It was just that this problem was a corker. She knew that she was on to something huge, something of far greater significance than the disappearance of a rich man's son or the death of low-life.

What, though?

Vermilion funded Stephen Bright who had bought a lot of antiques; he had once been called Michel Treves who had been based in Czechoslovakia and so was a company called XT Investments that owned Vermilion.

She was a naive and sentimental girl but even she strongly suspected that there was only one reasonable explanation; William of Occam himself would have been straight in there, wielding his razor and slashing away all the other convoluted explanations she might have attempted to construct.

There was no escape from it.

Bright was using antiques to launder money.

Which answer only spawned an even bigger and uglier question; what was he doing to generate the money he needed to launder? And generating enough money to manufacture a watertight back-story so that routine police probing would not reveal that he was an imposter, which could not be done cheaply. Whilst she was about it, nor could bribing the police, at least not bribery that was worth doing; Theodore's clear implication had been that Stephen Bright had been indulging in worthwhile bribery, that of senior officers, people who could do things for you or, more pertinently, avoid doing things.

To add to all this, Stephen Bright was implicated in the life and suicide of a middle-aged, rather frumpy laboratory technician and the disappearance of a homosexual young man from a rich family. How did that all factor in?

She knew – she *knew* – that they were somehow connected, yet what could possibly link those curiously immiscible occurrences?

Yet if that were the case, why was she not being warned off investigating too keenly the disappearance of Jasper Fitzroy-Hughes? Why was it that the Whipple killing was forbidden fruit?

Vermilion also owned an undertakers' where, she was sure, Billy Whipple had been stabbed on the night that he died. She could therefore see why Michel might not want her becoming too keen to exonerate Spud and thereby rouse a dog that was not so much sleeping as comatose.

Which suggested that maybe Gorlin, Goltz and Son were something more than funeral directors because whatever people thought about undertakers (when they thought about them at all) theirs was not generally considered a violent creed. Therefore when Billy broke in he either stole something or saw something. She thought it far more likely that it was the latter because his body had had nothing (except the pen) that might be considered in any way incriminating for the funeral-director-ship and she was convinced that he had been stabbed well away from where he died, had run there to hide while bleeding to death.

What was there to see in an undertakers'?

What might an undertaker do that would interest Stephen Bright, ostensible antiques dealer and apparently once calling himself Michel Treves?

There was no answer to any of these. They seemed as insoluble as the problems of dandruff and world peace.

SIXTY-ONE

A knock on the door. Dempsey had a troubled look on his face which beat the usual vacant puzzlement.

'What have you got for me?'

'You know you asked me find out about Michel Treves?'

'What of it?'

'That would be Michel Pierre Treves?'

'Possibly. What about him?'

'I did as you told me, contacted Interpol. I also did searches in the usual UK databases – CRO, Customs and Revenue, DSS, Immigration – nothing in any of them, though.'

She hadn't expected there to be. She'd have been surprised by even a parking ticket. 'And?'

'And half an hour later, I got a call.'

'Who from?'

Dempsey looked positively pained; perhaps it was a particularly vicious curry from the night before but she fancied it was likely as a result of the phone call. 'Someone calling himself Chief Superintendent Hicks.'

'Hicks?'

He nodded.

'What did he say?'

'He asked if I was making enquiries into Michel Treves.'

'To which you presumably said yes.'

Dempsey nodded. 'He then asked why.'

'Ah.' She could see where this was going. 'So you gave him my name,' she guessed.

Dempsey nodded.

'What did he say to that?'

'Nothing.'

That, she had to admit, was a surprise. 'Nothing?'

'He just thanked me politely, then hung up.'

She stared at him, trying to compute the significance of this new development, afraid that she could do it all too easily. Hicks was one of Bright's insurance policies; a hefty bribe to a senior policeman – perhaps close to retirement, possibly embittered that he had failed to achieved that final promotion to boost his pension – with little to do, except perhaps to wake up when somebody started asking questions about Michel Treves, find out who was doing it and why. Bright, it seemed, had set up his own little burglar alarm, one that would be triggered by the over-curious or over-zealous. And she had blundered into it.

And she had been wondering where Michel had been getting his information from and now perhaps she had her answer. Hicks might have been pumping Braxton or, more likely, Lambert for information on her activities, then passing it back to Bright.

For some reason, that thought was distinctly perturbing.

'Do you want me to carry on?'

She shook her head. She hadn't expected to discover anything anyway, had only done it because she was always thorough, never one to leave any alleyway unexplored. 'No, don't bother.'

Dempsey was about to leave, happy that he hadn't been shat upon – although Beverley, in contrast, had the uneasy feeling that the shit had only just begun – but then she remembered her promise. 'But there is something else you can do for me, Dempsey.'

He paused, looking worried. 'What?' he enquired, somewhat rudely.

She told him about the possibility that Helena Flemming was missing. 'Discreet enquiries with the neighbours, her fellow-workers, that kind of thing, OK?'

'But...'

'Yes,' she said tiredly. 'I know that she's only been gone a short while, but do it anyway, OK?'

Dempsey left her office, clearly puzzled about the request but too versed in her ways to question it too much.

SIXTY-TWO

She remained in her office for some time after that, her head still buzzing with speculation and formulation, these two laced with something that was closely akin to dread. She *knew* that she was on to something and something huge, and if anything positive could be taken from Dempsey's peculiar conversation with Chief Superintendent Hicks it was that she was close and that Bright was at the very heart of it, if she could only sort it all out before she drowned in cack. She looked around the room but Sam was nowhere to be seen.

Where the hell was he now?

At which point he entered the room and he looked across at her, and although his expression was unreadable she sensed that something significant had happened.

And then, behind him, Lambert came in and the look on *his* face was painfully obvious.

Triumph.

What now?

Lambert appeared at the far door to the general office and called to her in her office through the open door, 'Could you come with me, Inspector Wharton?'

Dempsey, sitting at his desk, looked up at that, and even he was able to pick up the metaphysical overtones that had suddenly sounded around him. Beverley complied but languidly. When she reached Lambert she asked, 'Where are we going to go, Frank?'

She had hoped to antagonize him but she received only a smile. 'Superintendent Braxton has some news for you.'

He turned and walked out, forcing her to follow while she wrestled with dreadful premonitions.

They were premonitions that were only worsened by the presence of a newcomer when she entered Braxton's office. Lambert had taken up position to her right while the Superintendent stood in a corner by the window; it was the newcomer who was the leader in this drama, who had occupied prime real estate behind Braxton's desk.

She knew at once who it was, where he was from. Complaints Investigation Bureau. She had had plenty of time in her past to study his type, met enough of them to spot the mould from which they were made. People of his ilk all looked, sounded and smelled the same. They all *acted* the same; they inhabited the role and enjoyed doing so. They found peculiar pleasures in being the custodians of the custodians; in being better than the angels.

She shut the door, came to stand about a metre in front of the desk; no one moved. Braxton and Lambert seemed to have taken up their marks and were afraid to do anything until told to do so and the man behind the desk didn't change his stance for a tediously long time until, from a place that was clearly deep, dark and cold, he said, 'We have received a letter of complaint against you, alleging that you attempted to extort money out of a gentleman by the name of Stephen Bright.'

'What?' She had expected something bad but not this, not a piece of fantastic fiction; an accusation of public indecency would have been preferable to this.

'You attempted—'

'That's crap!' Braxton winced at her language; Lambert merely looked even more sour and disapproving than usual; this newcomer into her life – whoever he was – didn't react all. She continued, 'I haven't done any such thing! I've been trying to nail the bastard ... and been criticized for my pains.'

She looked significantly to Lambert, who snorted.

Braxton took a deep breath in his corner but failed also to ride out of his stable. The stranger – average height, full dark hair and sporting a sneer that she suspected might have long ago become permanent – said, 'In particular, he claims that you demanded a sum of five hundred pounds in order to drop your investigation into his business.'

'And you believe this?'

Braxton took on an embarrassed look.

Before anyone could say anything more, she swung around to the stranger. 'Would you mind introducing yourself? If I'm to lose my job or perhaps even my liberty, I'd quite like to know who's playing the executioner.'

He wasn't unhandsome; perhaps a trifle old but once he would have been a catch. He said, 'Superintendent Hawkins.'

Which wasn't nearly as interesting as she had hoped. At this point Lambert clearly decided that he wanted to join in the sport. 'We believe the bank statements.'

Hawkins picked up two sheets of paper, both photocopies, both bank statements. One had her name and account number at the top, the other had Bright's name. On the day before, she had received a credit of five hundred pounds; five hundred pounds had gone from Bright's three days before. She hadn't deposited the money, couldn't explain it...

...Except with the words, *a set up.*

My God, Bright was good. He had been plotting this even before she had triggered his burglar alarm.

'When did Mr Bright make this complaint?'

'Late last night. A full statement was made and supporting evidence was produced at that time.'

Oh, well done, Bright. Well done, indeed.

She went on the offensive; she had nothing else that she could do.

'Is that it?'

Hawkins asked in response, 'Isn't it enough?'

'No,' she said forcefully. 'It's not.'

Before her accusers could wade in with the Dobermanns and the stun guns Braxton came

347

forth with his more amenable pooches and a fly-swat. 'The audit trail is clear; the money that left his account is the money that was put into yours.'

She couldn't believe that she was in the presence of such imbecility.

'Do you really think that I'd be dumb enough to accept a cheque as a bribe? Do I look as if I've got sauerkraut between my ears?'

Hawkins didn't say either aye or nay to that one but he did comment, 'You gave him a cover story. You sold him an emerald brooch.'

She felt herself falling into lunacy. 'I what?'

Hawkins had it in an evidence bag. Of course it was the one that she had handled in Bright's flat. She was completely unsurprised when he said, 'Your fingerprints are on it.'

'Anyone else's?'

'Only Stephen Bright's, as one would expect.'

She had been in similar places before – places where from every direction disaster approached with a maniacal expression on its face – and she had only one answer left, to voice her suspicions in front of as many as people as she could; if she were wrong, it would make no difference and, if she were right, she might just save herself.

'This is nothing but a frame-up because I am close to what he's up to. I think that he might be involved in the disappearance of Jasper Fitzroy-Hughes and also in the murder of Billy Whipple.'

Hawkins looked around at Braxton and Lambert; it was the latter, of course, who spoke. 'This is pure fiction. Billy Whipple was murdered by a loser called Spud Carney in an argument about a girl, but Inspector Wharton insists on peddling this crap and undermining my case.'

Hawkins turned back to her. 'Well?'

But, of course, she didn't have anything to back this up really. Just certainty.

She sighed. 'Can I get this straight? I extorted money from Bright in order to have me cease my investigations into him. In order to cover up the fact I'm engaged in an illegal act, I give him a stolen brooch?'

'That's correct.'

'If Mr Bright's so squeaky clean, why didn't he just tell me to do my worst?'

'Is that an admission?'

She took a deep breath but managed to hold back the avalanche of abuse she felt exploding within her. What was the point? Instead she asked, 'So where did I allegedly get hold of this brooch?'

Braxton explained apologetically, as if it was his entire fault. 'It was stolen in a burglary last month. One in Leckhampton.'

She almost laughed. 'So I fence stolen goods as well!'

Braxton nodded in sympathy. 'I don't believe it either...'

Lambert, however, was all too keen to believe; he seemed to treat credence in her guilt as a religion. 'It's not for us to judge,' he opined piously. 'We'll leave that up to the proper authorities.'

By which he meant Hawkins and the rest of the Goon Squad, the police's own investigators.

She tried to ignore what he was saying, how he was goading her. To Braxton she said, 'But I didn't stop investigating Bright, did I? If he'd paid me the money, why didn't I move on to some other poor sap?'

Braxton sighed, giving Lambert the chance to heap on a bit more scorn. 'Because you wanted more, didn't you? You decided he was good for a couple of thousand, but that was your mistake, because he decided that enough was enough.'

'For fuck's sake!' She turned to Braxton. 'You can't believe this!'

Braxton gave her a twisted, sorrowful smile. 'It doesn't matter what I believe. It's out of my hands.' His eyes turned to Hawkins who said coldly to her, 'As of this moment, you must consider yourself suspended until further notice.'

She asked of no one in particular, 'What's Bright afraid of? What is it that he is afraid of having exposed?'

SIXTY-THREE

Sam sat at his desk, unable to work, unable even to think about working.

Shit!

Until a few days before he had looked on Beverley Wharton as something of a swashbuckler, someone who had a bit of flair, a bit of bravado, but who was basically working for the same thing as everyone else in the department. The events of recent days, however, had forced on him a radically new perspective; suddenly Beverley Wharton was revealed as dangerous and corrupt. Corrupt, moreover, in both her professional and her personal lives.

Everything that had previously seemed so odd became obvious now that he had been given this new viewpoint. Her ceaseless pursuit of Stephen Bright in spite of all the evidence pointing to his innocence of any crime at all had been part of her scheme to blacken his name; that way, she couldn't lose. If he paid up, she would have let it all drop and no one would have been any the wiser because everyone thought he was an upright citizen; if he refused to pay, she would frame him and enhance her own reputation by pointing out how she had said all along that he was crooked.

Lambert had been right about her. He might be racist but he was at least not tainted goods.

And if she had done this to Bright, what about all the other things he had heard about her, that she had always so vehemently denied – the rumours of corruption, of using her looks to gain advancement, of her part in the death of Jeremy Eaton-Lambert. How much of the truth had he heard that morning as her tears had flowed? Just how culpable had she been?

He began to wonder just where he might find his friends in future.

SIXTY-FOUR

Beverley went home but she knew that she wasn't going to stay there and sulk; she was too angry for that, too eager to make them see how wrong they were; wrong about her, wrong about Bright, wrong about Billy Whipple's death. Somehow, and she didn't have the foggiest notion precisely how, the deaths of Billy Whipple and the disappearance of Jasper Fitzroy-Hughes were connected, and by even more obscure means the case also encompassed Gorlin, Goltz and Son and Vermilion.

At first she was too incandescent to think rationally but she forced herself into calm, taking a shower, breathing the hot-water vapour deeply and slowly, allowing the water to run down her while she stood perfectly still in its spray, concentrating on the faint coruscation of her skin. Then, dressed only in a black cotton gown, she went to the window at the back of the house and stood there looking out while thinking deeply, a large glass of white wine in her hand.

And, calmer, she found herself in admiration of what Bright had done to her; right from the start, he had had the forethought to lay a subtle trap. It had been so subtle that she had not been aware of it until this evening; the brooch so carelessly tossed to her and then, she now appreciated, artfully retrieved before Sam could put his fingerprints on it. She had, she now realized with some chagrin, woefully underestimated Bright, but she would not do so again. She might admire his skills, but she also wanted to have vengeance upon him; she owed him and she would repay him.

Some time and some several glasses of wine later – and thus perhaps slightly maudlin – she picked up the phone and punched in a number she knew off by heart.

'Sam? If you're there, please answer.'

But if Sam was at home he either couldn't or wouldn't hear.

'It's not true, Sam. None of it. I don't care if Lambert thinks I eat babies but I do care what you think, Sam. I'm sorry for what I did and I understand what you feel about me as a person, but you've got to believe me when I say that I didn't try to frame Bright. Bright's up to his neck in something and it's linked with

Gorlin's the undertaker...'

She stopped, aware that she was talking to herself as much as to anyone else. It was probable that Sam would just delete the message as soon as he recognized her voice. As she put the phone down she became suddenly aware of solitude. Solitude was the price she paid for her existence; it plagued her, a recurrent contagion, a scrofulous infestation that she could never vanquish, that only ever lay dormant, ready to strike again.

Without Sam there was no one who would take her side, fight for her, pick away at the deceptions to uncover the truths. Lambert would look no further than his satisfaction at her predicament; Braxton would be sorry but perhaps not surprised; Dempsey would scratch his head and get on with something else. Only Sam might have had the instincts to wonder, if only he had had the will.

She had only herself to blame that he didn't.

The phone rang. She gasped, irrationally convinced that this was Sam calling her back, but it was not; it was Dempsey, sounding hesitant, apologetic and afraid for his life. 'Sorry to disturb you at home, Inspector.'

She said patiently, 'Tell me, Dempsey.'

SIXTY-FIVE

It was getting dark.

The dark was where badness lived. When she was young her father had told her tales of bogeymen, of things that lived in cupboards and under the bed; he had been scolded by her mother but both Beverley and Jack had loved these stories, even as they were terrified by them and they had always made him tell them more.

She felt now that perhaps those tales were coming alive. Whatever was going on was nasty. People were being killed and she had an awful feeling that the reason was monstrous.

But she had no proof.

Not yet anyway.

No one was going to get it for her. No cavalry, no knights, no heroes.

Her life had always been lacking in heroes.

You'll have to do it yourself, girl.

She'd been accused of corruption and if that were proved she would at the best be asked to resign, at the worst end up on trial.

A bit of breaking and entering would hardly be noticed.

Which was when Eisenmenger rang her.

SIXTY-SIX

She told him to wait until midnight, not for romantic reasons but purely because of the very practical consideration that before then there would be a trickle of drinkers wandering home from the pubs, taking the shortcut through the trading estate. It wasn't easy, though; she assumed that this was how troops waiting for battle felt and she certainly remembered similar feelings waiting for certain police operations to start. Nervous, almost hysterical, she tried to read, tried to watch a DVD, tried to listen to the radio; nothing helped, nothing distracted her. In the event all she did was wait.

Sam did not phone.

It was drizzling and Eisenmenger was not by nature a man of action. The prospect of what lay ahead, even if it went to plan, was making him feel sick; the horrors of what would happen if it went wrong – and he was fairly sure it would – were so terrible that their very existence made him feel slightly faint. He would have treated Beverley's request for help with a contemptuous laugh, except that he owed her. Time and time again she had come to his aid, or to Helena's, and although she had not said it explicitly, implicitly had been the message that it was time to pay her back a little.

Eisenmenger's heart had never before ruled his head – something of a handicap in his love life, he knew – but this was a first. Now it pounded, thumped, thundered in his head so forcefully that with every pulse he felt a tremor pass through his whole body; now his heart seemed to be this monstrous steam hammer barely contained within his chest, twitching and straining to come loose and wreak havoc in his body. He found himself in such a state of anxiety that he experienced something that he had before only ever read about – dislocation, the feeling of disembodiment so that he was an observer inside his own head. As he stood with Beverley outside Gorlin, Goltz and Son, he found himself wondering, *Why am I here?* He knew the answer, even as he kept asking this question time and time again.

In the dark the building looked even less like a funeral directors, even more sinister. Strip the sign from it and undertaking would be the last profession a passer-by might suppose was its purpose, given its gaunt appearance. She had seen defence laboratories and drug depositories with less imposing walls with a less vicious-looking crown of barbed wire and broken glass. The gates were solid enough to withstand the most determined of ram-raiders, even ones that came in Sherman tanks and used stolen howitzers. Maybe, Eisenmenger heard himself think with sour amusement, Gorlin, Goltz and Son dealt with livelier dead than usual, ones that were liable to break out

357

when no one was looking.

Or maybe they just didn't want people breaking in after midnight.

The corporeal Eisenmenger said quietly, 'It's not like any other undertakers I've ever seen.'

Beverley agreed tiredly and with more than a trace of irony, 'They are certainly security conscious.' She thought then, *Billy Whipple had got in, though; it couldn't be that hard, surely.*

She was no cat burglar, scaling walls and slipping unseen and without physical trace into the most impregnable of buildings, and Eisenmenger, she was fairly sure, would be no better; they would have to emulate Billy and use brute force, very much breaking before entering. They walked once around the building, looking carefully at every window and around the front door. They spotted two things – firstly that all were shut, secondly that there were two burglar-alarm boxes attached to the wall. Ninety per cent of the psychology of an alarm was to deter would-be thieves and therefore many such boxes were dummies, not even connected to a system. Beverley guessed that Lletz and Taussig and their friends would not want the racket of an alarm to draw attention to the activities within, but that didn't mean that it might not be a silent one; if it was, she had grave doubts that it was connected to an official security centre.

More likely to someone near who had a shotgun by his side.

They would have to risk it, though. They had to know what they were up to.

SIXTY-SEVEN

As it happened Sam spent the night with a rather attractive constable, newly transferred into CID, by the name of Maureen. He had noticed her glancing at him from time and time and it so happened that he bumped into her on his way from the station to the car park and she asked if it was true about Inspector Wharton. He hadn't wanted to talk about it but then discovered that that was exactly what he wanted to do, and he had suggested that they should discuss it over a drink; they had gone first to the social club then on to a late film.

At its end, he had decided that he had not really enjoyed the evening, partly because she had an annoying habit of sniffing after every sentence and partly because he could not get Beverley out of his head. Still feeling deeply wounded by Beverley's callous disregard of what he had thought was a true bond between them, he kept asking himself what he had done to deserve such treatment and how he had managed to get her so wrong. Even as he realized that he was becoming obsessed with her, he kept reiterating these questions to himself, but with every repetition finding less satisfaction. Now he returned to his flat in Leckhampton deeply depressed; Maureen had hinted that she would not be averse to the evening continuing but he had somehow failed to spot these signals and she had therefore been disappointed in her desires.

He noticed that a message had been left on his answerphone and dutifully played it.

Sam? If you're there...

He switched the machine off at once.

SIXTY-EIGHT

The boarding over the empty window frame gave eventually but she was aware of how much noise they made as they forced it free. They weren't bothered about someone outside hearing them, but the thought that there might be someone inside – maybe a lot more than one – listening to their subtle entrance filled them with the heebie-jeebies. It hardly seemed worthwhile trying to keep to silent running after that but they did so anyway.

It was dark but she was at least familiar from her earlier visit with the layout of the office in which they found themselves. She moved quickly between the desks in the darkness with Eisenmenger following, very much the junior partner. She found herself wondering how far Billy had got before he was discovered. It was silent and completely tranquil and ought to have been deserted but she was fearful that it was anything but, that the quiet was manufactured, a pretence. She didn't even have the reassurance of supposing that they were merely in an empty office; for all she knew there were dead bodies out the back, ones that didn't care whether it was day or night, light or dark, whether they were alone or with company. She didn't dare to switch on the light but had brought a torch.

Eisenmenger heard himself ask, 'Do you want to look through those?' He was indicating the filing cabinets.

Beverley shook her head without saying anything. It would almost certainly be futile, and they didn't have the time for random searches through files and paperwork, especially in what was obviously a general office. The files in Lletz's office might conceivably have offered more appetizing pickings but on a cost–benefit analysis she opted against even that. She wanted to see some of the rooms at the back, what they contained.

She gestured that they should move out into the corridor, then towards the room where Lletz had demonstrated the art of embalming; it wasn't this room but the one opposite that interested her. She tried the door but it was locked; when she tried the one to the embalming room, it opened. She wondered what was hidden in the locked room.

From behind her, Eisenmenger watched as Beverley moved onwards down the corridor towards two more doors, one on the right, one on the left. The first, on the same side as the embalming room, proved to be open and behind it were lockers.

He thought, *A changing room. Why not? Embalming must be fairly messy work...*

The other door, though, was also locked.

He looked on as Beverley glanced back along the corridor seeing that both the locked doors were on the same side. Then she turned again; the corridor ended in a yet another door. When she tried the handle, it too would not open.

From his detached vantage point, Eisenmenger thought, *Some doors are open, others not. Some doors therefore hide things, others don't.*

Beverley's only dilemma was which one to open first.

She chose the nearest, the one at the end of the corridor.

She had brought with her a souvenir of an old case, a short, lightweight jemmy made of carbon fibre, hinged in the centre; when it was folded it was easily carried in an inside pocket of a jacket. She put this in the narrow gap between the door and the frame, then levered it gently. It took three attempts before the lock gave, the noise shattering any calm she had managed to fool herself into feeling.

At this noise, Eisenmenger thought, *Oh, shit...*

SIXTY-NINE

They entered darkness but the cone of light from the torch revealed the details of a workshop, the smell of wood dust and glue taking her immediately back to her schooldays. Coffins of different builds and races leaned lazily against the wall to their right, to their left there were sheets of chipboard and plywood; in the centre of the room a hybrid of the two, an embryo sarcophagus. Beyond were double doors that Beverley guessed led out into the yard. When she tried them these too were locked but she guessed that the hearses would be on the other side.

Their footsteps were loud and hard because, Eisenmenger saw, the floor was concrete. He noticed how cold it was, saw the refracted light of the torch in the vapour of their breaths. He was aware of himself thinking, *Why is it so cold?* The evening was cool but in here it was far beyond that.

Beverley turned around, scanning the silence of the room with the torch in the light of which they saw a workbench and racks of tools whisk past. She tried not to think about gremlins, corpses and cadavers. There was an identical door next to the one by which they had entered; it would lead into one of the locked rooms. Somehow it seemed more inviting to force entry through this door than the one in the corridor.

The jemmy came into play again.

This door proved somewhat harder to force but after a few minutes of concentrated effort it succumbed. The noise was just as loud but she felt it to be less intrusive. The light revealed a bed.

They moved into the room; there was nothing but a bed. There were no windows to the room, a further door opposite, and it might have been merely some sort of overnight rest room except for one strange anomaly. Beside the bed was a drip stand.

Eisenmenger heard himself wonder, 'What does that mean?'

He watched Beverley go to the other door.

Pushing the door open revealed a small room, perhaps three metres by four. Cupboards along the wall, more cupboards beneath. There was a smell about this room, one that was familiar.

He saw her walk in, the torch light moving slowly along the cupboards, past a closed door and then a second one opposite, until she came to a dust cover; the shape beneath was about a metre and a half high and slightly less than a metre in depth and width. Eisenmenger sensed that this was important although he couldn't say why, certainly not what it was.

From his detached position Eisenmenger looked on as she put the torch down on the adjacent cupboard so that at least some of its light shone on the shape, then she pulled the cover upwards.

And the odour in the atmosphere suddenly had for him a name.

Beneath the dust cover there was an anaesthetic machine. He had breathed in that odour a hundred times before.

It was a smell that Beverley had smelt only a day or two before when she had visited Jack. The unmistakable and inimitable scent of hospitals.

She felt dizzy with too many emotions to fit inside her, that fought with each other causing her breathlessness; elation that she had discovered something, that her suspicions had not been erroneous, that Gorlin, Goltz and Son was not just another provincial undertaker; her ignorance of what this could all be about fed her dread, produced something that was close to paranoia when she considered the myriad possibilities, most of them macabre; fear of discovery; desire to see more, to see what was in the third room, the one beyond...

She looked at Eisenmenger.

Eisenmenger looked back at her. He did not do or say anything more than stare at her. He did not understand anything, and could feel fear within himself.

Steadying her nerves by deep breathing and wishing that she had something more effective, more pharmaceutical to call upon, she moved to the door on the right.

This door wasn't locked. She pushed down

on the handle, exposing the darkness beyond.

This one was locked but she hadn't come this far to wimp out now. The jemmy hardly had to sweat.

Pitch black. The torch beam seemed pitiful, picking out small details, like looking at fleas on an elephant's hide with a magnifying glass and trying to figure out how many teeth it had.

Yet she already knew the precise dentition of this beast. As the light moved around she saw everything she had expected to see – more cupboards, stainless-steel trays, a suction machine in a corner similar to the one Lletz had shown them in the embalming room, something that she guessed was an autoclave...

And in the centre of the room...

An operating table.

SEVENTY

Eisenmenger stared at it for perhaps ten seconds, shocked back into some sort of sense of reality. It might have been ten geological periods as he tried to assimilate this awful truth, as the implications seeped into him, sprouting incredulity and revulsion in equal volume.

It wasn't a replica, it was real. Operations were done on it. Not embalming, not minor

surgery, not veterinary medicine ... major operations on real people.

What the hell?

There was something hideous about all this,
something that was so far from normal experience that he felt as if she were trampling into
surrealism. This was a fucking undertakers',
wasn't it? What in all that was holy would they
want with all this crap?

Beverley looked around again, seeing once
more what she had seen the first time. It was
still an operating theatre.

But operating on whom ... and for what
reason?

Suddenly it was claustrophobic beyond en-
durance and she turned and went at once and
without heed back into the anaesthetic room,
thence to the work room, leaving Eisenmenger
to look around. By the time she had climbed
back out into the night air she felt ready to
scream. She had to take deep breaths, and then
more deep breaths, fighting panic and nausea
and dread and disbelief. For the first time she
appreciated just how similar an operating
theatre was to a torture chamber.

She had to tell someone about this, tell them
that she had been right. The only person she
could think of was Sam. As she was getting out
her mobile, Eisenmenger joined her.

He said in a voice of wonder, 'I checked it
over pretty thoroughly. It's fully equipped and
state of the art.'

She looked up at him, took a moment to find
words. 'But why?' She knew that it would not

be good, that it would be very far from good; she also knew that a small part of her was close to guessing what it was all about. Eisenmenger, though, knew exactly what it was all about.

'Isn't it obvious?'

She had the phone to her ear, had yet to hear the first ring, when two figures holding small pistol-shaped objects emerged around the corner of the building. She heard the first ring as she looked up and, as did Eisenmenger, spotted them; neither had any time to react before the pistols were pointed at them and fired.

They both knew agonizing, twitching pain before nothingness.

Sam's phone rang just once as he was in the shower. He heard it through the wet white noise of the water spray, paused briefly in his ablution then, hearing nothing more, continued.

He thought nothing more of it.

SEVENTY-ONE

Eisenmenger came to first and, he saw, Beverley shortly after. They were seated in office chairs. They were comfortable chairs and Eisenmenger might have enjoyed sitting in his, except that both his wrists were handcuffed to

368

it, one to each arm, as was Beverley, and except that they were in the general office of Gorlin, Goltz and Son, the broken window (now once again boarded) behind them. There was a pain behind his eyes and between his ears that was booming and sludging, that peaked and troughed, the heights of the crescendo almost beyond belief. And he ached. Jesus, how he ached. If he'd been trampled underneath a rugby maul, he couldn't have felt worse.

He looked across at Beverley, saw that she, too, was experiencing similar things. The room was no longer dark; too bright in fact. Every light in the room was on; all of the ceiling lights and all of the desk lamps. It was thus easy to see that he was wearing a pale blue towelling dressing gown under which he could feel that he was naked; Beverley was wearing a similar one.

Beverley's first question was, *Who undressed us?*

Her second was why there was a bloodstain on the arm of the gown and why there was a pain in her arm. It was the dull pain that she remembered from vaccination and the time that she had been in hospital and they had taken blood.

The memory of the operating theatre came back, a sudden illumination of shock. This was all horribly connected somehow.

The door opened and Stephen Bright came in. He was smiling, might have been just popping into the office for a chat, perhaps on his way somewhere. He sat down without speech on a chair just inside the room. He looked first at Beverley, then at Eisenmenger, his face possibly impassive, possibly faintly amused, but saying nothing. It was quiet and cool in there, almost serene. No external noises to disturb their pocket of tranquillity. No one said anything, perhaps a competition.

If it was, he won, of course. Eisenmenger asked eventually, 'What time is it?'

He looked at his watch. 'About ten o'clock in the morning. A pleasant Sunday; lots of people off to church, some of them cleaning the car, that kind of thing.'

Sunday morning. They wouldn't be missed for a long time...

Not losing the smile he said after a pause, 'I'm sorry about incapacitating you.'

Eisenmenger was about to ask for some clarification, but Beverley, her mouth desiccated, and feeling as if mummified tissues were moving against each other, said, 'Tasers?'

Bright nodded. 'They are so effective.'

Eisenmenger said sourly, 'And painful.'

Bright turned to him and said, 'Sorry.' He might almost have meant it.

Beverley finally managed to swallow, achieving small relief in her throat. 'I'm sure you are.'

'I couldn't let you contact anyone else,' he explained. 'We had been watching you for some time on CCTV, and when you produced the mobile phone, we thought it prudent to act.'

Eisenmenger asked, 'How do you know we won't be missed anyway?'

He was a picture of confidence. 'I don't,' he said simply. 'Which is why we must hurry.' With which he ignored Eisenmenger and came to sit in a chair in front of Beverley. 'May I ask what you know?'

'Who undressed me?'

She found herself wondering if she had made a joke. Certainly he seemed to be tickled by something. She waited patiently, having little other option, given the circumstances.

He said eventually, 'Don't worry, my dear. Dr Taussig was very gentle.'

'*Dr* Taussig?'

But of course it all fitted, given what she had seen just down the corridor. She looked across at Eisenmenger, who nodded at her slowly, his face impassive.

Bright asked again, 'Now, would you mind telling me what you know?'

She might have felt like shit warmed up and her mouth might have been little better than a camel's rectum, but she at least had the pleasure of being able to say, 'We know you're a murderer.'

'Do you?'

'Of Billy Whipple.'

He sighed. 'Of course you do, but what else?'

'What else matters?'

'Good point,' he decided after a moment's consideration.

Once again the room was allowed to be silent. He sat in his chair, quite relaxed, apparently without cares. She held out again for as long as she could before asking, 'So what are

371

you up to in this house of delights?'

His eyebrows rose slowly and elegantly, arching as they did so. 'Don't you know?' he asked mockingly.

'I know you're going to kill us.'

He made a play of being shocked. 'Am I?' But then he spoiled it by adding, 'I suppose I might.' He suddenly seemed taken by the idea, repeating, 'I suppose I might.'

Wanker.

He leaned forward. 'Why not tell me what you know and then we'll see?'

She was under no illusion that his immediate itinerary had their demise figuring very prominently, but she was completely lost. What in any God's name was going on?

'Billy Whipple was stabbed here.'

A slow nod. 'But do you know why?'

She said reluctantly, 'He saw what you were doing.'

'He saw enough,' he admitted. 'Mr Whipple was not, I think, a clever man but we could not take that chance.'

Her wrists hurt, chafed by the handcuffs; her fingers were numb, all the muscles of her arms were sore. All in all (and this was instinctive and not carefully considered) she didn't want to have a clever-clever conversation with the man who was quite clearly interested only in dispensing with her company in a permanent sort of a fashion. More silence, into which Eisenmenger said quietly, 'But he never got to see the operating theatre, did he?'

He most definitely perked up at this. Turning

again to Eisenmenger, he said, 'No, he didn't, did he? You did, though. What did you make of it?'

'It makes most NHS operating theatres look Stone Age.'

He frowned, but was clearly pleased with Eisenmenger's praise. 'But why? Have you worked out why?'

It was not a question born of fear, but of excitement, Beverley realized. She saw a man living on adrenalin, who might indulge in extreme sports, perhaps.

Or extreme crime.

Eisenmenger seemed tired but she knew him well enough to find fear in that. He said simply, 'Organ harvesting.'

SEVENTY-TWO

He said it so matter-of-factly, with such an ordinary, conversational tone, that Beverley didn't at first appreciate what he had said. Only after a delay of a moment or two did she grasp the significance of his words, and with this came immediate, brilliant illumination.

Of course...

Her realization was wondrous, appreciative. It was so simple, so easy. There were not enough organs in the world and therefore a market existed; find a cheap and easy supply of organs and you had a cheap and easy supply of money. Where better, moreover, to find organs, than an undertakers'?

If Bright was surprised at Eisenmenger's words, he hid it well under a show of appreciation; he didn't quite clap his hands together, but his reaction was all but. 'You're right! Your reputation is well earned, Dr Eisenmenger.'

Beverley picked up on the fact that he knew all about John Eisenmenger, heard again the sound of one of Bright's alarm wires sounding. She said, 'Who buys them, Bright?'

He considered by looking at the tiles of the false ceiling. 'Oh, whoever's rich enough. The Russians are probably our biggest market, but the richer Indians and Chinese do us well, too.'

'How much?'

He enjoyed the questions. 'A cornea is five hundred euro, a kidney is two thousand, and a liver is ten thousand; a heart is ten thousand, heart and lungs are fifteen thousand.'

She was surprised, shocked, at how lucrative it was. 'They pay that much?'

'The price varies, of course; depending on blood type et cetera.'

Eisenmenger observed sarcastically, 'You actually blood-type? I didn't think hyenas like you bothered about such niceties. *Caveat emptor*, and all that.'

Bright professed mock outrage. 'This is a first-class service, Dr Eisenmenger. All organs are blood-typed; if the client chooses to pay our premium price, they will receive a tissue-typed organ.'

Beverley didn't follow much of this and stayed silent. Eisenmenger said, 'Your unique selling point?' He bowed his head but said nothing and Eisenmenger continued, 'All the organs removed under aseptic conditions, too. You've spared no expense, have you?'

At which Beverley asked, 'Is it really necessary to go to such lengths if you're just taking the organs from cadavers?'

At which Bright turned his attention once more full upon her, this time his attitude was both astonished and delighted.

Astonished that she should be so naive, yet delighted at the same time that she did not understand.

'But, my dear Inspector,' he said with a huge, amused grin, 'we don't use the *cadavers...*'

SEVENTY-THREE

The taser had not been more of a shock to her; nor, she saw, was it to Eisenmenger. Even the great Eisenmenger, it appeared, had not appreciated the scale of this enterprise. 'You are taking the organs from living people?' she asked quietly; deliberately so, for she was afraid that her shock would show weakness to this man.

Bright reminded her simply, 'We run a *pre-*

mium service, Inspector. Our clients do not want to buy from a second-hand shop, a grave-yard; they pay for optimum biology, the organs of those who are healthy, whose hearts are still beating when they donate.'

Eisenmenger asked sourly, 'Donate? Doesn't that imply a desire?'

Bright had no time for semantics. 'I am not about to try to justify what I do in terms of legality or morality, Doctor. It cannot be so justified; it is illegal to the point of inhumanity; it is immoral to the point of godlessness. It is, however, profitable and that is what matters.'

Beverley was about to argue – her humanity instructed her sternly to argue – but Eisen-menger interrupted. 'Do you mind if I get a few things straight about this?' He sounded interested, curious, somewhat awed, as if he had oodles of admiration for this monstrous human who sat before them, as if they were not stripped naked but for towelling gowns, and imprisoned and about to die.

Bright turned to him, but he had become at once wary. 'Of course,' he agreed cordially but with noticeable caution.

'You don't use the cadavers as a source of organs? The undertakers' is just a cover?'

Bright nodded. 'The beauty of an under-takers' is that it is a business that quite legiti-mately disposes of bodies and, as I am sure that you are both well aware, disposing of bodies is a very difficult thing to do. We, however, take them in and then transport them to the crema-torium, no questions asked.'

Eisenmenger guessed, 'Two bodies in one coffin?'

Bright smiled and nodded again. 'No one but the undertaker knows how heavy a coffin is. Take out the padding, cut up the second body and pack it around the legitimate corpse, and no one ever realizes.'

Beverley asked, 'Not even in the crematorium?'

Bright shook his head. 'The fires of the crematorium are very efficient. Apart from fillings and joint replacements, nothing is left intact.'

Eisenmenger considered this. 'Very clever.'

Which Bright accepted with grave pleasure. 'Thank you.'

Beverley had no interest in the niceties of body disposal. She had yet to make the final connection, although she could feel in the back of her head that it was there to be made. She asked, 'Where? Where do you get the organs?'

But Bright had no desire to rush to explanation. Instead, he said, 'As you say, Billy made the mistake of forcing entry. He was apprehended but struggled ... managed to get away but only after he had been wounded.' A deep sigh that might have been heartfelt. 'We looked for him, but he crawled away into that warehouse and so we missed him.'

As if he would have helped poor Billy...

She looked at Eisenmenger, who was searching Bright's face intently; his eyes flicked to her eyes and she saw in them that he, too, was wondering why Bright was teasing them. She thought, *There's more to this. Much more.*

She asked again, 'Where do you get the organs?'

Eisenmenger said quietly, 'From those who will not be missed.'

Bright looked across at him and smiled. 'Where else? The homeless, the dispossessed, the under-generation that governments so generously and so inevitably produce.'

She said almost to herself, 'The younger the better.'

Bright nodded, happy that they were all of one mind. 'Most certainly.'

The missing persons, she guessed. All young and all unlikely to be missed; except...

'Jasper Fitzroy-Hughes?' she said. 'What about him? Did you take him too?'

Bright bowed his head. 'Yes,' he said. 'He was a mistake. *Mea culpa.* I was in a hurry for a liver of his blood type and did not do all the checks I should have done. It was an error that should not have been made and will not be made again – but it wasn't, of itself, a disaster. Jasper has merely disappeared; no body will be found, no one will ever connect me or Gorlin's with the affair. Whipple's interference was a different matter altogether because there was a body and bodies have to be explained. I wasn't bothered about what you did in the Fitzroy-Hughes case, but I knew that Whipple would prove to be trouble; your appearance here justifies my fear.'

Eisenmenger asked, 'How many have you killed, Bright?'

To which Bright opened his mouth as if to reply, then abruptly snapped it shut, as if he had changed his mind. 'Is it of importance?' he replied eventually. 'The first death matters, the rest do not.'

Beverley had heard much callousness in her career, but never of this quality, this purity; here was an examplar. 'And does one get into this business? There are no degrees offered in it, are there?'

'Dr Taussig came to me in the Czech Republic and presented me just such a proposal. He asked me for the capital investment – a not inconsiderable sum – and at first I was, I admit, sceptical. It was only after a little research that I discovered there is already a not insignificant trade in human organs; private clinics in the USA represent the more legitimate end, but there are also many, many cowboys around. Mostly in the Far East, they effectively take people's money and offer them very little quality. Poor tissue-matching – possibly none at all – and organs that have not been properly preserved...'

He spoke as if he were describing builders who had bodged the kitchen extension. She wanted to speak, to tell him to stop this macabre fantasy, but she was fascinated to hear what he had to say, to see how deep into depravity he had descended. She felt as she had once done when watching some gory horror film, fascinated yet repelled by it.

'You see the business opportunity?' This was apparently a rhetorical question for they were saved the discomfort of nodding and saying that, yes, they could see how clever he had been. 'A market in which there is such a huge disparity between demand and supply is what any entrepreneur dreams of.'

Eisenmenger had the horrible impression that anything – anything at all – he said would be taken as encouragement.

Not that Bright appeared to need it. He went on to emphasize how much money there was to be made from organ transplantation, how with the worldwide shortage of organs for transplantation there was a premium to be paid on any organ, no matter where it came from.

'He had it all worked out. How an under-takers' establishment would be the perfect cover, how we needed a cover company to provide specialized, refrigerated transportation.'

Vermilion.

'I found Lletz. He had just been released from a Slovak prison but looked surprisingly well on the experience. He had originally train-ed as a nurse, but an unfortunate acquain-tanceship with analgesics led to his dismissal. He had then sought work at a funeral-director-ship, where he had learned the arts of embalm-ing. He might still be in more orthodox work had he not had an argument with his drug dealer, one that resulted in his imprisonment. By the time I met him and put my proposition to him, he was just in the mood to help me out.'

'Who buys them?'

That seemed to amuse him. 'All sorts,' he

said gravely. 'You'd be surprised. In two short years we have accumulated a database of nearly seven thousand people who are interested in our service. Of course we have to vet them very, very carefully indeed; they have to persuade us that not only are they genuine but that they are dedicated.'

'By which you mean desperate.'

He acknowledged the correction. 'They are usually sick and the sick are often ... motivated.'

He was so euphemistic he would have found a nice way to describe genocide.

'Aren't you worried about the word getting out?'

'As I said, we vet potential customers very diligently. Once the transaction has been completed, they are by definition too involved to back out.'

'Not even if it goes wrong, presumably.'

He smiled but said nothing. It was as much to postpone what Eisenmenger imagined would be inevitable that he asked, 'So you remove them here...?'

'And they're flown wherever they're needed.'

'Courtesy of Vermilion?'

He bowed his head. 'As you say, all courtesy of Vermilion. They are appropriately refrigerated and hidden amongst vaccine supplies. The beauty of having a legitimate business cover.'

The awfulness of what they'd learned, of how they'd been told, left them without the ability to speak. Then, apparently tired of explanations, Bright said then, 'You two have a choice now.' Neither of them could get overexcited at the prospect. He continued, 'You're very lucky, you know.'

She asked sarcastically, 'Really?'

'Few people have a chance like this.'

She knew exactly what he was talking about. Eisenmenger, too, had guessed. 'We're going to help save others, even as we die?' he asked with heavy sarcasm.

'And make me more money,' said Bright cheerfully. 'A lot more, I hope.'

He stood up. 'It's been a good few days,' he said, as if they would be pleased for him. 'Of course, there might be no matches for you, but there is always the budget market.'

Eisenmenger didn't want to ask, but asked anyway. 'What's that?'

'There are certain buyers who will purchase without proper provenance.'

It took Eisenmenger a moment to grasp what he meant. 'You'll sell the organs to unmatched recipients?' he asked incredulously.

Bright was nothing but nonchalance as he corrected this misapprehension. 'I sell them to intermediaries. What they do with them is their business.'

Beverley could only whisper, 'Of course.'

Bright then said cheerfully, as if it was all going to be all right really, 'But with a database of some many potential clients – and one that is growing daily – I am sure we will be able to get at least a partial match for one of you.'

Beverley looked across at Eisenmenger and

she could see from the look on his face that he, too, had the same thought.

Well, whoopi-doo.

SEVENTY-FOUR

Lletz had joined them, gun in hand, looking distressingly eager; Eisenmenger doubted that they were heading for a round of bridge or hamburgers in front of the television. Bright said, 'You'd better come with us.'

He unlocked the handcuffs and Beverley thought about taking the opportunity to try to get away but at once he grasped her head, pulling tight and hard so that her chin came up and she gasped as this new pain was added to the inventory. His other hand brought her left hand around her back and upwards, stopping just short of the point where she would have gasped again. Lletz dealt out similar treatment to Eisenmenger. As he hauled her away, Bright said into her ear, 'I would remind you that you're naked under the bathrobe, Beverley.'

They were walked forward, out of the office, along the corridor, into the anaesthetic room. It was now occupied. On a trolley was a young girl, painfully thin. Her hair was scarlet with henna, there were studs through her ears, her nose and the centre of her lower lip. She was asleep and in this state Beverley thought that she looked worryingly old, almost haggard. She wore a ghost of prettiness now degraded. There were nicotine stains on fingers with dirty nails that were covered in chipped burgundy nail polish. Everything about her was in tune but the melody was mournful.

Taussig was there, sitting and reading a magazine as if he had just come to visit, perhaps eat the grapes. Bright said, 'This is Denise. She's twenty-two years old, a mother of three.' He spoke in a voice that wasn't in any way hushed. 'She's a prostitute.'

'What have you done to her?'

'She's sedated. Peacefully asleep. Probably in a far cleaner bed here than she's ever enjoyed before.' Beverley heard Eisenmenger issue a low sigh, one of horror. Bright continued, 'As I said, Jasper Fitzroy-Hughes was a mistake; if we had known that he had such influential connections we would never have used him.'

Used him?

'We won't make that mistake again. Denise here is completely without anyone; she won't be missed, except, perhaps by her pimp.'

Beverley breathed, 'Jesus Christ...'

He failed to react, preferring instead to turn to the girl in the bed. 'Someone like Denise is potentially worth forty thousand euro. A sum that is only liable to increase as surgical techniques for transplanting other organs become more advanced.'

'But you're killing them!' She couldn't keep the agony from her voice.

He looked at her; his expression didn't

change at all as he said, 'I know.'

'That's murder, Bright.'

And still it didn't change. 'I know,' he repeated.

She looked at Lletz, who smiled at her but didn't speak; Taussig returned her stare without expression. She felt as if she were a stranger in a very strange land. Eisenmenger had his head bowed.

When Bright spoke next it was didactic; he might have been explaining the trickier bits of String Theory. 'The world is running dry, Beverley. Recycling isn't the whole answer but it's part of it.'

'Recycling? You call this recycling?'

'Denise here serves no useful purpose to anyone but her pimp and her clients, and even to them she is eminently expendable. Even as she earns money from prostitution she claims a variety of state benefits to which she is not entitled. Her removal can only benefit society.'

When Beverley spoke she found that she could do little more than whisper. 'What about her children?'

He was surprised, seemed to have overlooked them. 'Yes, well, the state will look after them.'

'So not much of a gain, then.'

She took some pleasure in seeing annoyance bloom, no matter how transiently, across his face. 'Except that I will have stopped her producing any more to suckle at society's everflowing stream.'

'Oh, for God's sake! Spare me the sickening sophistry. You murder people, harvest their organs, make a lot of money. Don't try to make yourself feel good by inventing some cobblers about the greater good.'

A moment of stunned silence was followed by a laugh that she was astonished to hear was genuinely delighted. 'You're quite correct. Well done, Beverley. Forget the social concerns. I'm a businessman, I exist to make money. This way I make a lot of it. That's all that needs to be said.'

Lletz and Taussig also joined in with the jollity.

She wanted to spoil it. 'Don't forget that you're evil, heartless bastards, Bright. I think that should be stated quite clearly.'

But the laughter didn't stop. If anything it increased. She looked from Bright to Lletz to Taussig, then back again; she was missing a joke, clearly, and still they laughed.

What's so funny?

Bright said, 'You will be aware that we have taken a blood sample from each of you.'

Eisenmenger said, 'For typing.'

Bright nodded. 'I have high hopes of at least a partial match for you, Beverley.'

'Oh, yes? Some Russian gangster, perhaps? An African dictator?'

But Bright did not seem interested. He appeared to change the subject. 'I've heard your brother hasn't been well.' She knew that there was meaning in this – how could there not be? – but she did not recognize its nature. She therefore said nothing. He added, 'Dying, they say.'

How does he know about Jack? The question resounded loudly in her head, but she thought she had the answer. After all, Bright had connections and by these he had presumably found out all that he needed to know. She was starting to appreciate that Bright always prepared and prepared well. She refused to bow to her curiosity. 'As are you, Bright. As are we all.'

His consideration of this was deep before he offered, 'You're quite right, Beverley. We're all only a footfall away from death. Your brother, however...'

He let the sentence linger, fade rather than end.

Eisenmenger realized what he was implying first. 'You're joking,' he whispered. Which was when Beverley caught on, the realization as cold and sharp as a six-inch nail. She didn't dare move, her head full of fear. *Surely not ... surely Jack can't be contemplating...?*

I have high hopes of at least a partial match...

She had wondered why Jack had moved to Gloucestershire ... had sensed an ulterior motive...

But surely not this? Surely he had not been so desperate as to come to Bright for a bespoke organ?

Bright was watching her, examining her face; he might have been watching an interesting sport, perhaps a couple making love. He said softly and mockingly after a viciously long pause, 'Don't worry, Beverley. Your brother is far too poor for this service...'

Was this another lie? She wanted to believe

him, but almost everything he had told her thus far had been deception...

He found her uncertainty pleasurable, was quite happy to prolong it. He said abruptly to Taussig, 'Tell us about Denise.'

The doctor hesitated, unsure what was going on. When his eyes flicked between Eisenmenger and Beverley, Bright said, 'Our guests would like to know and there is no reason why they shouldn't.'

Taussig remained somewhat uncertain despite the assurances but complied. From the file he read, 'Female, aged twenty-two years and four months. Blood group A, rhesus positive.' He looked up. 'Do you want the tissue-typing details?'

To Beverley, Bright said, 'You see what a Rolls-Royce service we offer? We tissue-type to as much detail as the finest institutions in the world.'

She had to ask. 'How can you do that?'

'We use private laboratories abroad. A globalized economy has certain advantages in a business such as this.'

Suddenly Eisenmenger asked, 'How do you get your "donors"?'

Bright said carelessly, 'We have contacts in haematology laboratories throughout the region. They feed us the details of various potential candidates, people who have just had surgery. Occasionally we get a commission for someone with a rare type and they search the hospital databases for us...'

Of course. Poor old Mrs Esterly...

'Why did Violet Esterly kill herself?'

He stared at her for a brief second, then returned to affable psychopath mode. 'She was weak, poor Violet.'

'Is that it? She was weak?'

'The pressure got too much for her. I had not realized just how much of a financial hole she was in.'

Eisenmenger snorted but said nothing; Beverley said simply, 'You're a cunt, Bright. A gold-plated cunt.'

Bright was too far gone in his psychosis to react to that. He carried on his explanation as if she had not spoken. 'We have strict criteria for our subjects – age between twenty and forty, no known infectious disease, no known auto-immune conditions – and if those are met we then do some social research. We want those who will not be missed, essentially.

'If after those checks we think we have a likely candidate, the technician is then asked to provide us with a blood sample – they are routinely kept for some time – and it is on that the detailed tissue-typing is undertaken.'

'You've got it all worked out.'

He missed the sarcasm, probably through choice. 'Go on, Dr Taussig.'

'In this patient's case we have identified three potential recipients, for both kidneys, and for the heart and lungs.'

The smile on Bright's face was not a thing of beauty; it had a visceral, writhing quality that precluded anyone falling in love with it. 'You see? Denise is now worth forty thousand pounds – far more than when she was an un-regarded creature wallowing in the lower strata of a society long past its best.'

'And you're going to cash her in?'

He didn't even have the shame to hesitate. 'If you wish.'

Taussig asked, 'Shall we proceed?'

Bright nodded. 'Absolutely. We must; we have more cases to process.'

They both thought that they knew what he meant by that.

And then an awful thought occurred to her, one that made her feel far worse than even the foregoing litany of horror. She looked at Bright and he caught her emotion. For a moment he was puzzled but he was a very smart, intuitive man, and it wasn't very long at all before he realized what was going through her head. A cruel smile broke out on his face.

Taussig asked, 'Shall I start?'

Bright waved him on without speaking and Taussig left the room. To Beverley he said, 'You should be happy. Her death will be benefiting another.'

'It'll benefit you, as well. Perhaps sixty thou-sand pounds.'

He paused. 'Do you know, you're absolutely right. How lucky she is to benefit perhaps four people with a single action.'

At least he didn't have the gall to smile as he said this; there might even have been a hint of sadness in his voice.

Taussig said, 'I have to get on with this case and the next.'

Bright replied, 'Of course, of course, Doctor. I mustn't keep you. We will take these two away and leave you in peace.'

And so they were bundled out of the anaesthetic room.

SEVENTY-FIVE

Sam had looked at his mobile phone, seen that the aborted call was from Beverley. He had decided that he did not need to return the call.

SEVENTY-SIX

They split them up, putting Eisenmenger in a room just off the anaesthetic room; the farther half was hidden from him, screened off. He was securely handcuffed to the radiator and left alone.

Beverley was taken to the embalming room, handcuffed to the table in the centre. Bright suddenly became very chatty as he shut the embalming instruments into a cupboard. It had no lock but it but it was well out of her reach.

'Any last requests?'

'You could drop dead.'

'That's your job.' He looked at his watch. 'It'll take Taussig a couple of hours to get round to you.'

'I can't wait.'

A smile seeped slowly across his face. 'I could help you pass the time.'

And she suddenly felt very vulnerable. 'I'm sure you could.'

She was sitting on the floor, one hand free, the other held up by the handcuffs, which were attached to a metal bar that ran around the edge of the table. She pulled her legs together and as far under her as she could manage. He saw the move and laughed.

'Modesty becomes you.'

'Fuck off.'

The room was quiet; they might have been alone in the building. He nodded slowly as if considering the idea for a moment, then came forward. He crouched down in front of her. 'Fuck off?' he asked. 'Well, now you come to mention it, fucking is something that has been on my mind of late...' He didn't touch her – she would have scratched his eyes out with her free hand if he had – but the look on his face was just as disturbing.

The door opened and Lletz came in. His face didn't alter as he said, 'Phone call. A client.'

For a moment Beverley saw anger – an anger so intense it might have illuminated the room – but it passed with a sigh. He stood up, suddenly again all smiles. 'There's plenty of time,' he promised her with sigh.

He was walking away when she said, 'If I disappear, there'll be hell to pay. People will come looking for me; they'll be all over this place.'

'And they'll find nothing. You will be sharing a coffin with Mr George Warbourg, ready for cremation tomorrow afternoon; by two-thirty, you'll be ash.'

'And the operating theatre?'

'We'll temporarily shut up shop. You and the good doctor are the last for now; after your operation, the table goes, the lighting's taken down, the cupboards are emptied and everything is taken away. Gorlin, Goltz and Son regains some store rooms and nobody knows anything was ever any different. We steal away and set up shop somewhere else.'

'They know I've come here.'

He shrugged. 'They know that you're corrupt, that you've tried to blackmail me. I don't suppose they'll really waste too much time worrying about what's happened to you. Everyone will suppose that you couldn't face the scandal.'

'Don't be too sure of that.'

If she was having any success in denting his confidence, he concealed it superbly. He walked to the door where Lletz was waiting and said before he left, 'Why don't you let me worry about the future? You haven't got one.'

SEVENTY-SEVEN

There was no clock in the room and Bright had taken her watch. She sat there, shifting her position occasionally to decrease the discomfort. She began to grow cold and, despite the erosive fear of what was coming, slightly sleepy. She gave up trying to work herself free fairly quickly and there was nothing within her grasp that she could use by way of a weapon. She stood up occasionally to relieve the pins and needles in her handcuffed arm.

She wondered what the time was. At least an hour passed and she wondered what was keeping Bright; perhaps he was getting grief from his client and she found herself hoping that it was serious grief. She began to wish that she had made it up to Sam, not for any sentimental reason but because of the purely pragmatic consideration that he might have paid attention to her abbreviated call, that he might have come looking for her.

She and Eisenmenger were on their own, though.

That's what you like, isn't it? You're a loner. You've always been proud of that.

She shook her head violently as if by so doing she could silence these thoughts; she really did not want to spend the little that remained of the rest of her life listening to such mockery.

There had to be something she could do...

The door was unlocked and Bright came back in. The smile was still there but there was something about his demeanour that had changed.

'Hello.'

She realized at once that he was drunk.

She realized, too, what he was going to do.

She stood up as quickly as she could. He shut the door, locked it once more, was leaning against it looking at her.

He said, 'Taussig's almost finished, it'll soon be your turn.'

'Is there nothing I can say? Nothing I can do?'

The smile became a grin, became a leer.

'Ordinarily...'

She saw at once what he was implying, would have to have been insensate, perhaps even de-cerebrate, to have missed it, and her immediate reaction was to shout, 'No way!'

...Yet did she have a choice? Perhaps she could use the situation to her advantage.

'What do you mean?'

She didn't want to appear too bright, too keen.

He was so excited he seemed to have lost a bit of control over his facial muscles because that grin became if anything wider and he seemed to be a knowing smile with a horny bastard tacked on behind it. 'If you didn't fight, if you were to go with the flow, well ... who knows?'

'You'd let me go?'

She was painfully aware that she might be sounding too naive, too theatrical, but Bright had clearly been spending the last hour or so extremely profitably in the company of quite a lot of alcohol. He was no longer interested in judging the finer points of human behaviour.

He pushed himself forward off the door. 'I could save your life. Keep you locked up until we'd cleaned up and gone.'

'Will you?' *Enthusiastic, but not too much. A smidgeon of pleading to finish it off.*

He really couldn't budge that grin; if she'd buried an axe in the back of his head he'd have hit the floor still smiling like a village idiot. 'I don't know. Why should I?'

Hesitation. That's the thing to do now. 'Well...' *Move into slow realization.* 'Well...' *Smile apologetically.* 'I don't know.'

He came and stood about a metre from her. He was leaning on the table while his eyes fulfilled their roving brief with gusto. 'I do.'

Do some incomprehension. She widened her eyes, parted her lips...

He said, 'If I'm going to let you go, I want something in return.'

She was getting a bit fed up with pretending to be stupid and innocent but thankfully he was fed up with prevaricating. 'I want to fuck you.'

She felt a tiny spark of relief that he had at last got around to it.

'Will you let me go if you do?'

'If you're good.'

By which she was perfectly well aware that he meant anything but good.

Look as if you're making a difficult decision. She closed her eyes before saying reluctantly, 'OK.'

He was on to her without any hesitation, hands around the back of her neck, pulling her head forward to plant his mouth over hers; there was a stink of stale booze but that was the good part since underlying it there was the stink of halitosis.

His hands moved down inside the gown. She wanted to scream, wanted to tell him that she would really rather die than put up with this, but she endured it. He forced her gown open while he carried on kissing her. She felt his hands squeezing her breasts, pummelling them; most of the men she had slept with had seemed to be under the impression that mammary glands were a sort of stress-relieving device to be compressed and squashed until she begged for submission, and Bright was seemingly of a like mind.

She at last freed her mouth from his.

'Look, we can't do it like this. Let me go.'

He was taking a few deep breaths and his hands had stopped doing their Canadian Air Force exercises.

'Stephen? Let me go.'

He looked at her with narrowed eyes, hands relaxing, falling away. 'How can I trust you?'

I need innocence. How the hell do I do that? 'What can I do?' He looked unconvinced so she gave up on innocence and leapt on to

397

ground that she knew much better. 'Anyway, it's very limiting.'

It didn't take too long for him to grasp the advantages. It took him a few minutes to find the key in his jacket pocket and it took him even longer to appose it with the lock of the handcuffs. Her relief when it clicked open was far greater than she could allow him to see.

For just a moment they stood and faced each other while she rubbed the skin of her wrist.

I've got the chance now; how do I exploit it?

She wondered whether to run, push him to the ground and go for the cupboard. She could probably just about get one of the trocars...

Moving so abruptly that she saw nothing he drew back his right hand in a fist and punched her hard on the side of the jaw. Her head was whipped back and to the right, her whole body falling away, but he followed this up with a left upper cut that was perfectly coordinated to catch her head. She was falling to the floor before this new pain was starting.

And it didn't stop then.

She managed to land on her hands and knees, the universe a cavorting, whirling, singing sickness of agony, but then he kicked, first in the stomach, then in the head. Before she could even draw breath he had grabbed her hair and her head was back, her neck exposed, and this pain was so great that she gasped despite the argument of her muscles and bones.

He said, 'You must really think I'm stupid.'

She couldn't speak; she wanted to, she wanted to tell him that actually she did, but she was too occupied with gasping and generally experiencing unpleasantness. In point of fact, it turned out that he wasn't particularly interested in her point of view. From a geographical position unnecessarily close to her right ear she heard, 'Thought you'd get away, did you? Thought I was too drunk to figure out what you were planning?'

'Please...'

Which only made him pull harder. She squealed and, of course, he enjoyed that.

'Please.'

He paused, but only for a moment, and then his voice returned. Its proximity was now so great that his breath was tickling her ear. 'You promised me.'

When she could speak she asked, 'But you'll let me go?'

She felt him move away slightly. His answer was a brief pause before he hit her across the back of the head with something that was hard enough to cause the world to darken for a second. She collapsed back to the floor, tried to rise but as she did so he grabbed her shoulders and turned her so that she sprawled on her back. Then dropped on to her, knees either side, the sudden weight completely winding her.

Then he began to strike her face with his fists, first the right and then left, again and again...

SEVENTY-EIGHT

Eisenmenger soon gave up trying to free himself. He was no escapologist and no macho man; much as he wanted to be able to wrench himself free or reach out with his toes to grab an unregarded spatula with which to twist round and pick the handcuff lock, he knew that he might as well wish to find a teleportation device in a box by his side. He therefore waited, as patient as he could make himself, trying to ignore the fact that he was starting to find his bladder rather full.

He waited an hour, hearing very little except the odd thump of footsteps in a corridor somewhere in the building and, once, the faint sound of a motorcycle roaring away; he closed his eyes as he heard this, hoped desperately that it was coincidental, that it did not signify another hideous murder. And then the door from the anaesthetic room opened and Lletz came in.

He looked at the impassive face and was rewarded with a glance, nothing more, much as a beggar in the plaza might receive. Lletz went directly past him, passing behind the screens. Eisenmenger heard faint, anonymous noises – soft rustling, gentle clanking – that he could not place.

And then a heard a faint sigh...

Someone had been behind there ... He suddenly placed the noises he had heard as the sounds of bedclothes being moved, of a drip line hitting the sides of a trolley. But there was more.

The sigh had been oddly familiar, yet such was the completely alien situation he found himself in, he could not place it, all hooks with which to recall it to memory were gone from him. In any case, how could it be familiar?

Presumably this was the next victim, the next donor destined to make his or her final unselfish contribution to the life of one or more other human beings; of course, only those who could afford it, though. He wondered which waif, which failure (or failure at least as Bright judged them) this would be; or perhaps it would be one of his 'specials', those with the rare blood types who were so valuable that Bright risked the attention that their disappearance might bring. Then the screens were parted noisily and then there was a pause before Lletz reappeared, backing out and pulling a trolley. His arms obscured the face of the poor sod who was about to die in the holy cause of profit for Bright. Only as he passed Eisenmenger did he see who was on the trolley.

The horror fell – no, avalanched – upon him as he realized why the sigh had been so familiar.

He practically screamed, 'Helena!'

SEVENTY-NINE

Beverley came back to consciousness as he was about to enter her. Her legs had been separated, his knees planted to stop her closing them; her head was encased by torment, her face was throbbing and anguished. When she opened her eyes almost nothing happened because of swelling; her lips were bruised and cracked, her cheek apparently made of a rubber mat.

He looked stupid; something at the back of her head had always thought that naked men about to penetrate her had looked fairly dumb but the sight of a man whose only concession to intimacy was to drop his kecks failed to hit any buttons whatsoever.

He wasn't even that big.

Her first instinct was to fight but his weight was upon her wrists and all she would have been able to do was to wriggle her pelvis. Better to endure it.

She had to lie there and let him do what he had to do.

All she had were slits to look through but that was enough. There was a look of grim pleasure on his face, a smirk that suggested he considered himself a victor; his breath was once more in her face, the sickly sweetness of halitosis was overpowering. She turned her head, tried not to think about what was happening to her, about this atrocity that was being perpetrated on her.

They were by the cupboard, her left hand was only a few centimetres from the door although she could do nothing about it because his weight pinned her down.

She would have to wait, endure.

She squeezed her eyes as tightly shut as she could, enjoying the pain because feeling that was better than feeling his prick within her, the rolling and rocking, better than listening to his short, staccato breathing and occasional soft grunts, better than imagining exactly what was happening.

He came as all men seemed to do, that curious mix of relief and triumph and disappointment, then dropped down upon her, his full weight dead and crushing; this shift lightened the force on her wrists and she moved them both, the left one to get as close to the cupboard door as possible, the right to distract him. She needn't have bothered, he didn't notice anything.

Her fingers found purchase on the bottom of the door but she waited; she could do nothing while he was still on top of her.

Seconds passed but counted in her heartbeat it seemed like days. He rose, still pinning here down.

'Enjoy that, did you?'

Why are they always so desperate to know if I've

enjoyed it?

She wanted to be cool, to be detached, to show that he hadn't done anything to hurt her, but such restraint was beyond her. What he had done had ripped her open, exposed her vulnerability, destroyed her belief in her own inviolability and safety, crushed her without thought or compassion.

'You fucking cunt!' It hurt her to speak and she heard the words slurred because her lips were so large and bloody and numbed.

And of course he liked her reaction. The grin broadened. 'Want some more?'

No, please. Not that.

But all she could say was, 'Fuck off.'

For a long, long moment he looked down at her, the look on his face one of consideration, a sign of an internal debate.

Then, 'No.' Abruptly he straightened up, releasing her arms, so that he knelt between her legs. She dropped her fingers from the cupboard door lest he guess what she was doing.

'You're not that good. I've had a lot better.' The grin changed into a leer. 'Still, you're looking pretty now. A few cosmetic changes have really improved you.'

I'm going to get you, you bastard.

He pulled his trousers up, zipped and fastened them.

Then he began to stand.

She lay there, limp and unresponsive, hoping that he would assume that she was broken.

I won't have long. Do I remember exactly where the trocar is? Will I be able to detach it from the

404

tubing?

'Come on, Inspector. Lletz will be waiting to prep you for surgery.' He kicked her on the bared skin of her left hip so hard that it left a deep gash. She squealed, partly because of the pain and partly because she thought he would like that, at the same time twitching herself closer to the cupboard. The fingers of her left hand found the bottom of the door.

From somewhere in the building a cry arose. It was indistinct but undoubtedly agonized, a man's voice. Bright looked up at it, his attention gone from her.

Now...

She twisted around and rose through the agony to her knees, at the same time opening the cupboard door. Everything hurt, not least her vulva, but she didn't care any more; if she survived she promised that she would listen to the complaints of her body, but for now she had better things to do.

The embalming machine was there, the trocar attached. She grabbed it, started pulling at it to free it from the plastic tubing.

She heard Bright turn, mutter, 'What the hell?'

The fucking thing wouldn't come.

He was upon her within a second, grabbing her shoulders to turn her. She brought her elbow up hard and fast into his neck and chin. He grunted, loosening his grip just a little. In the background, the anguished cries continued as a sort of demonic Greek chorus to their struggle.

Just enough to allow her to turn slightly, wrenching at the trocar, trying to free it. It remained attached to the piping but there was now some play...

Except that Bright's grip was back around her. He trod on her bare foot as they struggled. He began to overpower her, forcing her backwards against the opened door of the cupboard...

...Which gave her a little more play on the piping attached to the trocar.

'Don't be stupid, girlie.'

The halitosis came upon her once more. He had her now pinned against the right-hand door of the cupboard, hands on her upper arms so that although she still held the trocar she couldn't use it.

'Drop it.'

When she didn't, so he said again, 'Drop it.'

If she had thought that perhaps there was stalemate, she was proved painfully mistaken as he suddenly head-butted her, bringing his forehead down hard and fast on the bridge of her nose. The whole of her face seemed to explode, her head slammed back against the wood of the cupboard and what happened next was complete instinct, totally without conscious input.

Her knee slammed up hard between his legs and despite everything – the agony in her face, the gash on her hip from which blood flowed freely down her leg, the horrible feeling in her pelvis – she *felt* his balls squashed, obliterated as she did so.

And, boy, did it feel good.

That made him release her.

His hands dropped and he moved backward – well, staggered, actually.

And he'd lost the grin; things were looking up.

They looked up even more when she grabbed the trocar with both hands, wrenched it forward pulling the embalming machine out of the cupboard and on to its side, and stepped forward.

He had bent almost double, which suited her perfectly.

For the first time that day she meant it when she smiled.

He looked up at her as she crouched slightly, the trocar pointing to the ceiling. He saw what was coming which made it all the better as far as she was concerned. In the second that followed he had time to open his mouth, nothing more. The smile was beginning to cause her no end of pain because of the swelling but it was something she wanted to do and, hell, she was going to do it anyway. Then she forced the trocar upwards into his abdomen as hard as she could.

Its appearance through his back was welcome indeed.

EIGHTY

Lletz came in and although his expression had not changed, his demeanour suggested that he was not best pleased with Eisenmenger. Without a word, nor indeed ceremony, he grabbed a handful of square gauze swabs and grabbed Eisenmenger's hair, pulling it sharply so that his head tilted painfully back and his mouth opened; within a second it was full of gauze. Then Lletz walked out as swiftly as he had entered.

She refused to collapse although almost every nerve in her body was telling her to do so. Bright had gurgled a bit as he went down and there was bubbly blood at the corner of his mouth so she guessed that she'd hit the jackpot and gone through the diaphragm into his lungs, maybe even his heart. She crouched down to feel into his pockets, aware that she was picking through the belongings of a man as he died, unable to stop the disgust and revulsion because it felt as if she were robbing the dead still warm. She found first the key to the door and then his mobile phone. She straightened up and stepped over him; with a swirl giddiness came upon her and she might have fallen down, had to steady herself for a moment.

Recovered, she moved past him as she might have moved past a beggar. She was no longer interested in anything except getting out of there. The phone was a smartphone, expensive and slim. She flipped it open then dialled Sam's number at the station. Nothing. No signal.

Fucking fantastic.

She went to the wall beneath the barred window, limping very slightly because of her hip.

Still nothing.

She turned her back to the room, almost making love to the window.

Here there was a signal. Only two bars, but it was something.

She dialled Sam again.

Dempsey's ponderous voice answered. 'Hello?'

Oh, hoo-bloody-rah.

'DC Dempsey here. Can I help?'

That'll be the day.

She said, 'It's Inspector Wharton here. I need to talk to Sergeant Richardson.'

Despite everything the titles forced their way in. She noticed that his voice changed, became more austere, as he said, 'I'm afraid I don't know where he is, Inspector. He must be out.'

She cut the connection. The smell of disapproval had come from the phone like body odour. Next she tried Sam's mobile number; her experience of mobile phones was that they were either switched off or out of range or ignored and accordingly she didn't have much hope...

'Sam Richardson.'

She heard the doors slamming somewhere in the building, guessed that Bright had been missed, but didn't dare turn around lest she lose the signal.

'Sam! It's Beverley.'

'Beverley? What's going on? Where are you?'

'I'm at the undertakers'...'

Footsteps walking rapidly, approaching the room. She stopped, the handle was rattled, then the door was thumped, finally kicked. 'Mr Bright? Mr Bright? Are you in there?'

More rattling.

Should have used the key straight away. You might have been out of here by now.

'Dr Taussig needs to talk to you urgently. There's a problem with one of the donations...'

She heard Sam's voice coming faintly from the receiver although it was held away from her ear. 'Beverley? Beverley?'

A pause.

'Mr Bright?' This time the voice – it sounded to her like Lletz – was more worried. Again the door was kicked.

Then silence.

She knew that she didn't have long.

'Sam, I'm at the undertakers, Gorlin's. I'm trapped. Get some help over here.' This in a low tone.

More running outside, this time noticeably more urgent. Then the door was hit again but this time hard, as if a shoulder had been put against it. This was repeated but the door showed no sign of giving.

Yet.

It's only a question of time before they break in.

A small distance from her ear, she heard, 'What's going on, Beverley?'

Two more thumps in rapid succession and then nothing.

If they know that help's coming they'll run ... probably after they've killed me.

Whispering urgently to Sam, 'Get here quick! And no bells and whistles.' She snapped the phone shut. She had two options. Try to get out of the window, or play dumb and hope that they lingered long enough before removing her organs.

Actually, now she came to consider matters from every side and in every light, she only had a single option because the window was barred.

Shit.

She wanted to hurry but her body had other ideas. There were copious amounts of her blood on the floor where it had flowed from the wound on her leg, her pelvis felt as if someone had inserted a food-mixer and turned it on, and her head still seemed to have been infected with a liquefying fungus that was growing and growing behind her eyes with relentless cruelty. She limped over to Bright's body.

EIGHTY-ONE

Sam had been returning from Bright's apartment. No one had been home and it had already occurred to him to go back to the undertakers'. When Beverley abruptly cut the connection he was left shouting uselessly into the phone before the implications of what she had said exploded in his head.

No bells and whistles.

At first it had seemed to him to be just an expression, although an odd one, but then a bit of his brain at the back of his head began to shout at him rudely and he realized what she had meant.

Take things easy. Don't advertise your arrival.

The extrapolation from that led him to an inevitable conclusion.

She was in extreme danger.

He accelerated away (causing a middle-aged priest to swerve into a post box and say some very ungodly things) whilst phoning Cheltenham police station.

Bright's phone was infernally complicated. She knew that she had to delete her call to Sam and to the police station in case they checked it...

The next blow to the door came so suddenly

412

and so loudly she almost dropped the phone. The whole wall seemed to shake and certainly the door reverberated and not surprisingly she looked up. With billows of plaster dust cracks had begun to appear around the door frame. The second blow came rapidly and, although she was not now startled, her eyes flicked shut momentarily. This time a dent appeared in the wood of the door.

He was using a sledgehammer.

Returning to the phone she went through what seemed to be fifty sequences of menu options before she discovered the call log. She deleted the last two numbers called, then thrust it back in Bright's pocket together with the key to the room

The third blow thundered into the room and the door succumbed, splinters of wood flew across the floor and the head of the sledge-hammer peeped through only to be withdrawn immediately. She moved as quickly as she could across the room, taking care to keep out of sight of those outside, to crawl into the far corner, hunching herself up into a foetal ball. Her path was marked by drops and smears of blood and she could only hope that they would not wonder just what she had been up to.

Hope too that Sam would not be too long.

Lambert received the news that there was an officer requiring assistance as he returned from the restaurant in the company of Braxton.

Braxton asked, 'Where?'

The female constable had the answer ready.

413

'Swindon Village, sir.'

'What address?'

'It's an undertaker's. Gorlin's.'

Braxton's eyebrows jumped upwards in perfect synchrony; Lambert's did likewise but were upstaged by the rest of his physiognomy, which performed various contortions, and by his vocal apparatus, which produced a curiously strangled, 'What?'

The constable, fearing that she had somehow transgressed, repeated the name, this second time somewhat more timidly than before.

'Who sent the message in?'

'Sergeant Richardson.'

Lambert asked simultaneously of Braxton and the Lord Almighty, 'What's going on?'

Only Braxton responded. 'I don't know, but you can't ignore it.'

'This has something to do with Wharton.'

Braxton pointed out calmly, 'We can sort it all out later. For the time being, I suggest you get over there and find out what it's all about.'

The constable said tentatively, 'Sir?'

'What is it?'

'The message said to approach with caution.'

Eisenmenger felt himself drowning in horror, wrenching repeatedly at the cuffs so that his wrist was rubbed clean of skin, was now in places stripped of flesh, so that the tendons were partially exposed, engulfed in oozing blood that had run down his forearm, soaking his shirt sleeve. He screamed into the gauze ineffectually, had tried to work the sodden mass out of his mouth but it had been rammed so tightly in that he could not. He had cried so much that his face felt almost as though it had been beaten.

Eventually, perhaps after fifteen minutes, perhaps after an hour, he stopped screaming and crying and trying to pull the radiator away from the wall.

He was spent.

EIGHTY-TWO

Lletz had been wielding the axe and it was he who entered first, a machine-pistol in his left hand. His eyes were caught first by Bright's body, which now presented a striking feast for the visually weary, what with the liberal volume of blood both around and upon it, and the trocar protruding at a rakish angle from the upper part of his abdomen. Taussig, entering behind him, gasped.

'Oh, no!'

They were both dressed in scrubs, both with disposable caps on, masks around their necks.

Lletz moved towards Beverley, his expression darkening. He strode over to her, stood in front, legs slightly apart; Taussig was crouched down over Bright checking, rather unnecessarily, for signs of life.

Beverley kept her eyes and face down but she

was vividly aware of the pistol; it hung down by his side but fitted his hand with seemingly perfect precision. She was vividly aware too that it would probably cut her in half within a second if he chose to use it.

'You've been busy.'

She looked up, let him have the full pleasure of seeing her battered face. 'He raped me.'

If this was regarded as a mitigating circumstance he didn't say. He asked suspiciously, 'Why didn't you try to get out?'

'I didn't have time.'

Taussig had come over and joined Lletz in standing before her forming a two-man makeshift tribunal. He said, 'It's possible. Bright hasn't been dead long. He's still warm.'

As Lletz stared intently at Beverley, Taussig asked plaintively, 'What do we do now?'

Lletz said at once and with commanding authority, 'We get out. Sterilize the area and go. We were never here.'

Taussig looked uncertain, lost, terrified almost and Beverley might have been sore, bleeding and nearly concussed, but she recognized that here was a second in command unsuited to the position, while the third in command was eyeing the throne. He considered, then said slowly, 'Yes, yes...'

Taussig then looked back at Bright; it was as he did that Beverley saw his eyes take in the chaotic trails of blood that led to the window and back to the body. She saw him wonder.

She was sorely tempted to say something, to tell them that some cavalry was on its way, that they'd better get as far away from there as fast and as soon as possible...

But she dared not. Lletz kept twitching the pistol as if he'd quite like to use it, just for the fun of the thing; if they decided to run, it wouldn't delay them at all to put a line of rather messy perforations in her abdomen before they left.

Taussig said thoughtfully, 'If she managed to get a message to someone...'

Lletz was sanguine. 'How could she? We have her mobile.'

His colleague, though, was nothing if not smart.

'Bright had one.'

Lletz looked sharply down at her; the pistol came up and pointed directly at the bridge of her nose; she knew then that Lletz might be a nurse but he knew how to use a gun. To Taussig he said, 'Go and get it.'

Taussig walked back to the body, avoiding the blood on the floor as if he, a surgeon, didn't like to see the stuff. His demeanour as he crouched over the body and felt in the pockets was one of nauseated distress. He stood up with the phone, flipped it open, spent some minutes pressing buttons, his face nothing but frown.

'Well?'

'It's very complicated...'

'Bring it here.'

Lletz swapped the pistol for the phone and seeing the way that Taussig handled the gun, Beverley half considered making a break for it, but then sense returned. Even if her legs obeyed her with sufficient alacrity, at most she'd only be able to get as far as the corridor; after that there was nowhere else to go.

At last Lletz found the call log.

'She didn't,' he announced. Then to Taussig he said, 'You've finished the last scheduled case?'

Taussig nodded.

'We don't have the time to process these two. Put her with the other one. We'll put them both to sleep, then clear things up.'

'Why don't we shoot her now?' It was a somewhat surprising question from the meek and mild Dr Taussig and one, she judged groggily, born of fear.

'Why use a gun and make more of a mess? You can kill them both with anaesthetics when we're ready.'

Taussig looked at her, a long look of deep consideration. It went on for an inordinately long time before he nodded. Lletz took the gun back. 'Stand up.'

As she struggled to comply with this order she was well aware that Taussig was still thinking, still wondering.

She got on to her knees and began to rise when, with a loud groan, she collapsed on her side. It distracted Taussig as Lletz, who had seemingly forgotten what nurses were supposed to do, kicked her hard.

'Don't be silly.' He sounded bored.

She got up again; slowly, but hopeful that she had been successful. At least Taussig was no longer looking at the patterns of blood on the floor.

'That's better.' Lletz held out his free hand in an open-palmed gesture. 'Ladies first.'

Her limp became worse, her stiffness almost incapacitating, so that their progress to the door was slow.

Come on, Sam.

As she reached the corridor, Lletz, now the clear commander, said to Taussig, 'Have you finished the last case?'

Taussig nodded. 'Just. She's still on the table.'

'We'll take care of these two first, then clear that one up. We have a busy night ahead of us, Taussig. I want to be gone by daybreak.' To Beverley he said, 'Please get up and do as I tell you.'

She saw no possible chance to disobey and stood up painfully. A small wave of the gun caused her to move to the door where she turned right, making slow and painful progress along the corridor. She was commanded to pause at one of the doors, by the receipt of a sharp and painful prod in the back.

'In here.'

EIGHTY-THREE

Sam arrived forty seconds before two uniformed constables, neither of whom he knew well. He had parked about a hundred metres away and had been scouting around the large building, trying to work out how to proceed. They pulled up behind his car and got out, radioing in as they did so. He ran across to them.

'Is an armed unit on its way?'

'Just behind us.'

He nodded. 'Stay here. I'll be back in a moment.'

Without waiting for a response he sprinted back to the building, skirting around it and ducking down. At least because it was Sunday the estate was relatively deserted. As he disappeared around the back he was aware of a second car arriving.

Eisenmenger, traumatized almost into a catatonia, looked up as the door opened and Beverley came in. He saw her eyes were dull, her face battered, her movements stiff and sore; she saw the blood on his wrist and forearm, the look on his face, recognized that it was one of lost despair. She whispered, 'John?' but he didn't respond. She was manhandled by Lletz, forced to squat down by a radiator directly opposite Eisenmenger, then handcuffed to it as he was.

They were left alone for a moment.

Eisenmenger would not have been able to speak, even had his mouth not been stuffed with gauze. The feeling of dislocation had returned, exponentially increased; he was now not just separated from events, he was locked out of them, not just a spectator but one who was watching from a great distance.

Beverley said, 'Jesus, John, what's happened to you?' She knew that she would not get an answer, asking this only rhetorically. There was no reaction, not even a change in his stricken expression.

Lletz and Taussig returned. They knelt down in front of Beverley and Lletz put the gun to her head and told Taussig, 'If you wouldn't mind, Doctor.' Taussig filled two syringes from two small glass vials off which he had snapped the tops, laid these on the ground beside him. Next he took something from his pocket; she couldn't see what it was, except that it was small and long. Then he grabbed her right wrist, forcing her arm straight. He held up for her delectation the thing that he had taken from the cupboard.

'This is a butterfly cannula. I'm going to put it in a vein in the back of your hand.' It had bright green plastic wings on either side of a needle attached to a long clear plastic tube. 'If you make my job difficult, I will ask my colleague to shoot a hole in your foot.'

And she believed him.

Beside her Eisenmenger began to show signs of animation.

EIGHTY-FOUR

Eisenmenger knew that he had lost Helena at one level, although he could not grasp it on so many more. He saw what they were doing to Beverley, knew what it meant. Panic began to flood through him again and he became more and more agitated.

Taussig squeezed Beverley's wrist, slapped the back of her hand, then within fifteen seconds had inserted the needle into a vein. He strapped the cannula down with tape before picking up one of the syringes. Holding this between his second and third fingers he unscrewed from the end of the plastic tubing a green cap, then plugged the syringe into the now opened end. She felt the cold liquid run into the vein as he squeezed the plunger.

I really would appreciate you to get a move on, Sam...

Taussig had picked up the second syringe.

Beverley felt peculiar. Still conscious but aware that something was wrong. She was aware that Eisenmenger was jerking at his handcuffs, making muffled squeals. She moved her head to the side...

Except that she didn't.

She tried again, this time with more force, but still nothing.

She twitched her fingers, or at least she told them to twitch, there was nothing.

She was aware that she hadn't blinked for a long while, that her eyes were becoming dry...

With the closest that she had ever felt to all-out terror she realized that Lletz had paralysed her and she could no longer breathe.

For the second time in two hours, Eisenmenger had to sit, powerless, whilst he was forced to watch people die; people he loved. He felt himself breaking down as he did the day that Maria had burned herself to death in front of his eyes.

EIGHTY-FIVE

There was a sound, faint but unmistakably the noise of wood splintering. Taussig jerked his head up, the second syringe in his hand, not yet plugged into the cannula. He looked at Lletz whose expression of determined authority cracked very slightly.

'Shouldn't we just go? If someone's broken in...'

'If someone's broken in, I'll kill them. Now you take care of Eisenmenger while I see what's going on outside.'

He left the room.

Shit!

Sam had hoped to get through the broken window silently. Part of his head told him that he was getting rusty, that ten years ago he would have got through it quickly and neatly and without any sign to the enemy that he was amongst them.

Had they heard?

An irrelevant question, really.

Training, drilled – almost beaten – into him, resurfaced. He needed a diversion.

Taussig wasn't happy. Beverley watched him stand up, although her eyes no longer moved at her command so that she found herself looking only at his lower half. Even this was enough to tell her that he was a worried man.

She was becoming drowsy, colours were draining from her vision. *Oh, my God. Please, no ... I swear I'll pray. I'll become a saint, a nun ...* She began to lose the thread of her thoughts, feeling vertiginous swoops in what she saw, how she sensed.

She was dying, she knew, could only hope that she would die quickly. Yet she was a long way from that point yet. Becoming increasingly distorted, her feelings were still there – the hardness of the floor on which she sat, the wall against which she lay, the dryness of her mouth.

It was just that she couldn't move. Nothing. No muscles at all.

Eisenmenger watched everything, as he might in a dream. He saw Beverley slowly asphyxiating; he was beyond horror.

He watched Taussig close his eyes, take a deep breath, and then approach him, feeling in his pocket for something.

EIGHTY-SIX

By the time Lambert arrived there were already four marked police cars as well as Richardson's; a small crowd of interested but otherwise unemployed spectators only added to what was effectively pandemonium. No one, though, was going anywhere near Gorlin's.

To say that he was in far from the best of moods would not have adequately described his feelings. Whatever was going on would not be good; the question was whether it would prove bad for him or disastrous for Richardson and, he guessed, for Wharton.

A discreetly marked van – inconspicuous unless you recognized it – drew up; no squeal of tyres, no fanfare, just a dark van, but the gentlemen who got out of the back wore body armour.

Half to himself, half to the assembled company, Lambert said impatiently, 'Oh, for God's sake.' Then he called out, 'Who's been in charge here?'

One of the two constables who had arrived first spoke. 'Sergeant Richardson. He said that he would be back in a moment.'

'And how long ago was that?'

This threw him and so his colleague had to answer. 'Five minutes, sir.'

Lambert made a noise that was suspiciously close a harrumph. 'Right.'

Which was when his mobile phone went off. He thought about ignoring it but looked anyway to see who it was.

Curiosity congealed into bewilderment.

It was Richardson, and it was not a call but a message.

Ring me back.

Beverley briefly lost consciousness. The world was almost perpetually monochrome now and becoming blurred. She saw Taussig approaching Eisenmenger, but did not – could not – care.

Sam had gone at once into Taussig's office. He watched from behind the door as Lletz, a vicious-looking gun held horizontally, came into the corridor just outside his station.

And then his phone had gone off.

EIGHTY-SEVEN

Taussig had broken the top off the vial and drawn the clear, slightly viscous fluid into a small plastic syringe; Eisenmenger watched and marvelled that it took so little...

Lletz jerked round. His face broke into a smile.

Taussig jumped visibly as the faint sound of a mobile phone made its way into the silence of the room. The syringe had been only a few centimetres above the Eisenmenger's elbow. He hesitated as he listened.

Beverley was dying. The world was more grey than light, sounds merely surging noises without meaning.

Lletz didn't hesitate. He stepped at once into the office and loosed off every bullet in the magazine, spraying them around the room. It was over in five seconds.

Then he saw the mobile phone sitting on the desk by the forced window.

He turned just as Sam came up behind him and swung a heavy and large replica of a tombstone at his head.

Taussig nervously returned his attention to Eisenmenger. He grasped the back of Eisenmenger's elbow, paused briefly with the syringe above the skin, then plunged it in, apparently no longer caring about such medical niceties as sterilization of the skin and finding a vein. Eisenmenger felt the cold bolus of solution dissipating in his system for just a moment.

Beverley was barely alive now. From where she was the sound of gunfire was nothing but a distant distraction, the sounds of war on a different continent, something that happened on the television in a room beyond.

The burst of gunfire was quite audible to Lambert and the others outside. The phone still clamped to the side of his head he turned to the leader of the armed unit; they were already fanning out to left and right. He instructed everyone else to fall back behind cover and to get all civilians out of the area at once.

Still no one answered his phone call.

EIGHTY-EIGHT

At the intrusion of gunfire, Taussig abruptly withdrew the syringe, then looked around the room, swift, birdlike movements that were searching for danger; saw and heard nothing. He waited for a moment, then went to the door. He called tentatively, 'Lletz?'

No reply.

'Lletz?' This time louder.

Still nothing.

He turned back to Beverley and Eisenmenger, unsure what to do.

And then Sam put his arm around his neck and Taussig felt the barrel of a gun held to his right temple. He froze.

Sam pushed him into the room, looked rapidly around. 'Is there anyone else here?' This was breathed into his ear.

He shook his head. Sam could smell the terror on him, heard the truth in his trembling.

Sam pushed him towards Beverley. 'Is she alive?'

He nodded. 'Just.'

'Wake her up.'

'I ... I can't.'

The grip around his neck tightened and the pressure of the circle of metal at his temple increased. 'Don't fuck around with me. Wake her up.'

'She's paralysed. Lletz told me to do it.' He said this as if he had thought it was a bad idea all along.

'Then unparalyse her.'

'I don't know if I can. I don't have the drugs.'

Sam pushed the gun into the side of his head even harder. 'Then make sure she stays alive while I get an ambulance. And I promise you that if she dies, so do you. She's more than a colleague to me, understand?'

Taussig nodded and Sam released him. As Sam dialled for an ambulance on the mobile he had retrieved from the office, Taussig began artificial respiration on Beverley. The next call was to Lambert.

Eisenmenger felt weak, his legs something that belonged not to him but to an invertebrate, yet he insisted on going into the operating theatre, no matter how much Lambert and Sam tried to stop him. Afterwards, he knew that he had had to see it, but the sight destroyed him utterly.

EIGHTY-NINE

Helena's funeral was a big affair, a very middle-class thing. Well attended, the perfect end to an established, civilized, Western life. Eisenmenger was forced to go by his love for her, but sat at the back, letting Alan Sheldon accept the shared grief of all around him. Many tears were shed to add to those already gone through evaporation, but Eisenmenger's, although relatively unregarded, were the purest. The weather was bright and clear, only a hint of summer's death somewhere to be sensed.

Jack's funeral was quiet and attended by perhaps only twenty. The breezes were chillier now, the mornings damper and the evenings far, far earlier as autumn came to dominate, as browns and greys seeped into the greens and yellows. A quarter of those present were Jack's old girlfriends, over a half his friends from school and college; the only relatives were Beverley and her mother and a cousin, Clive, whom Beverley barely knew. He seemed a pleasant chap, though, she thought.

Beverley did her best to comfort her mother although she sensed the ever-present barrier between them to be as impregnable as ever, perhaps even strengthened by the loss of the favourite child. It was made no easier by her own guilt, by her recognition of her own short-comings.

Jack's miracle cure – an unsanctioned re-search project by a Hungarian professor of medicine involving some sort of immune therapy – had had uncontrollable side effects that left him almost moribund. When he had returned to the UK he had looked worse than when he had left; worse even than he had before. She herself had looked none too beauti-ful, since she had a stitched wound in her abdomen, a face that looked as if the House-hold Cavalry had practised changing the guard on it and a wound in her thigh. She had en-dured a four-week stay in hospital, but even after that she suffered headaches and crushing malaise and anorexia that had afflicted her for two months beyond that. Her mother had asked – had asked repeatedly – what had hap-pened but she had refused to elaborate. She had turned then to Jack but, although Beverley had given him a fuller version of events, he had only offered her comfort as he professed ignor-ance. Beverley had been grateful for that reticence.

And then he had died.

Another haemorrhage, this one even greater,

this one occurring too far from hospital.

After the funeral, they were due to go back to her mother's for sandwiches and sherry or wine but as they were walking side by side she saw Sam waiting in his car away to their right. When he saw her looking, he got out of the car, but she turned away pointedly and said to her mother, 'Are you all right, Mum?'

Her mother had not replied and she could not blame her; stupid questions did not merit an answer, not ever and certainly not now. Tragedies could either heal or irrevocably divide a family: there was little doubt which this one had done.